'*When We Fell Apart* is a marvellous [...] and suspenseful, a reminder that the greatest mysteries are those of being and belonging. Soon Wiley is a young writer to watch'
Jess Walter

'A lyrical exposition on what it's like to be biracial, with one foot firmly planted in two distinct worlds, never completely fitting in, but capable of seeing what others do not. A lonely, heartbreaking, spellbinding story of love, self-discovery, and belonging'
Jamie Ford

'Propulsive and deeply felt, Soon Wiley's phenomenal debut *When We Fell Apart* takes on the friction between family bonds, cultural expectations, and personal desires in a way that feels both urgent and intensely real ... truly unforgettable'
Abi Daré

'Melancholic, atmospheric, and consistently surprising. Like *Norwegian Wood*, there is a minor key running through this love story played out on the frenetic and lonely streets of Seoul. *When We Fell Apart* is a transportive and poignant debut'
Susie Yang

'*When We Fell Apart* explores the tender and chaotic intersections of culture, community, and the search for self. Rich with philosophical nuance, heart-stopping and exquisitely plotted, this is a novel to get lost in'
Patricia Engel

'This gorgeous debut ... explores youth, sexuality, and the freedom to choose your own destiny in a world that keeps insisting on who you should be and how you should love'
Julia Phillips

'A masterful plot that seems to move in two directions at the same time, towards the inexorable, stunning ending – unforgettable'
Alexander Chee

'In this gorgeous, poignant meditation on identity, love, and desire, Soon Wiley illuminates the liminal state of being biracial, of belonging but not, of desperately wanting the world to let you be as you are'
Angie Kim

'*When We Fell Apart* dazzles like neon on a rainy night. In lush, perfectly-tuned prose, Soon Wiley leads readers around dark corners and into the heart of a kaleidoscopic city . . . a magical debut'
Amy Gentry

'I loved this novel! An absorbing mystery and poignant love story, *When We Fell Apart* is profoundly moving, beautifully written, and utterly compelling'
Susan Elliot Wright

'A captivating journey through the bright lights and dark byways of modern Seoul, exploring what it means – and what it costs – to be ourselves and live freely'
Jack Wang

'Wiley's debut novel is poignant and powerful and will leave readers questioning who is and isn't awarded the freedom to be their truest self'
Shondaland

'Wiley has masterfully woven a story where his two protagonists come from very different experiences and places, yet share the struggle to carve out their own identities. Set in modern-day Seoul, it's also a love letter to Korea itself, but one that doesn't pull any punches'
The Asian American Podcast

'Wiley tells parallel stories in alternating, brief chapters – Min's and Yu-jin's, one a roller-coaster of suspense and suspicion, the other a gradual awakening'
USA Today

'Emotional and gripping'
Hello

'Propulsive'
Good Housekeeping

'Wiley's tale is a knockout, its assured narrative ebbing and flowing with grace while painting a haunting and anguished portrait of youth in all its quiet desperation'
Booklist

when we fell apart

Soon Wiley

SIMON &
SCHUSTER

London · New York · Sydney · Toronto · New Delhi

First published in USA by Dutton, an imprint of Penguin Random House LLC, 2022
First published in Great Britain by Simon & Schuster UK Ltd, 2022
This paperback edition first published 2023

1 3 5 7 9 10 8 6 4 2

Simon & Schuster UK Ltd
1st Floor
222 Gray's Inn Road
London WC1X 8HB

Simon & Schuster Australia, Sydney
Simon & Schuster India, New Delhi

www.simonandschuster.co.uk
www.simonandschuster.com.au
www.simonandschuster.co.in

A CIP catalogue record for this book is available from the British Library

Paperback ISBN: 978-1-3985-0176-8
eBook ISBN: 978-1-3985-0175-1
Audio ISBN: 978-1-3985-1325-9

Printed and Bound in the UK using 100% Renewable
Electricity at CPI Group (UK) Ltd

MIX
Paper | Supporting
responsible forestry
FSC® C171272

for my parents

I, a stranger and afraid
In a world I never made.

A. E. Housman

֍

She stands upon her toes and turns and turns.

Elizabeth Bishop

when we fell apart

ONE

MIN

Anything you might desire

Everyone heard it, the pop. Min knew what to do, gasping for air on the cleat-pocked grass, a semicircle of concerned teammates forming around him. Stretching the afflicted arm over his head, he slowly rotated his hand, fingertips cold, heat knifing into his lungs, and reached for the opposite shoulder, exhaling only when he felt relief, ball meeting socket again. Min couldn't help but smile. The looks on their faces.

Even the Australians had stopped playing, gawking at his dangling arm. Of all the expats who played rugby every Saturday, they were the toughest, always willing to play through a broken nose or a bruised quad, as long as it meant showing up the Brits or the Kiwis.

Min could have told them about the other times he'd dislocated his shoulder—basketball, football, a poor attempt at surfing—but he didn't. Better to leave some mystery, he thought. He'd grown used to injuries, bodily betrayal. Quick but slight, he'd taken his share of physical damage, especially in high school, where he'd insisted on playing football despite his parents' objections. He was never exceptional. Being exceptional wasn't the appeal. It was the physicality he enjoyed, the feeling of narrowly ducking a crushing hit over the middle, juking out of bounds, safe from hulking defenders intent on his destruction. More often than not, he was leveled, crushed, left blinking away stars. But there was something appealing about that, too. A part of Min liked being hit, showing he could take the pain.

From an early age Min had been drawn to competitive sports, craving their zero-sum nature, in which a distinct winner and loser emerged. He found security in having only two possible outcomes. There was no gray, no in-between. There'd been no opportunity for recreational football in Seoul, only soccer and rugby. Naturally he'd chosen rugby, prizing physicality and the risk of violence above anything else. His teammates regarded him with cautious kindness, miffed by his name and appearance. Of the expats on his team, Min was the only American, except he didn't look American, according to one of his Irish teammates, whose comments quickly garnered nods of agreement. Min only smiled. He was used to remarks like that. No matter where he went, people couldn't put their finger on him, puzzling over his ambiguous origins.

Tolerance was what Min practiced whenever he spent time with expats. It was the trade-off for getting to play rugby, getting hit. They were a lost bunch anyway, the expats. ESL teachers, ex-military, burnout backpackers, forty-year-old nothings with penchants for Asian women, these were the types of foreign men in Korea. Min considered himself different from them, somehow special, here for a reason. Biracial, Los Angeles–bred Samsung consultants were the exception in Seoul, something Min took pride in. He was here because of ancestry, because he'd never seen the country

2

whose language he spoke, because he'd never felt wholly American, because in the snuggest kernel of his heart, he hoped to find some sense of belonging.

Arm in a makeshift sling, face badged with mud, Min was forced to watch the game's conclusion from the sideline. Afterwards, there were handshakes all around, the field chewed to a camouflage pulp, bad weather threatening on the horizon. Min zipped up his duffel bag with his good hand, hoping to beat the rain. One of the newer members of the team approached him, an amiable-looking guy named Mark.

"How's the shoulder?"

"It's felt better," Min said, wary of getting sucked into a conversation.

"We're going out for drinks. Figured you'd wanna come. Take the edge off."

Mark was new; it wasn't his fault. After rugby there were usually drinks at one of the tacky Western-style bars ubiquitous to Seoul, where teammates drank Guinness and listened to acoustic Oasis covers. Min avoided those places at all costs, and after he'd declined the first few invitations, the offer was never extended again.

"Sorry," Min said, wondering why he felt guilty. Perhaps it was Mark's politeness, the way his Canadian accent swallowed vowels. "Can't make it. I've gotta be at the office early tomorrow."

"But it's the weekend," Mark called after him.

A block away from the metro the sky opened and raindrops plummeted from the high-rise-cluttered sky. Umbrellas bloomed upwards as Min weaved his way through the lurching crowd. A jet stream of humid June air funneled down the street, slanting the rain and blurring neon signs and LED billboards scrolling ribbons with the latest

3

financial news. Every storefront and city block called out in electric blues and pinks, offering up karaoke, libations, and fortune-telling.

This was what had mesmerized Min upon his arrival in Seoul a year and a half ago: the sheer magnitude of it all, the way it loomed over you, dwarfed you, obliterated the senses while simultaneously offering everything and anything you might desire. In awe, Min had watched cobblers toiling in their street stalls, boys fanning coals in the back alleys of restaurants, businesswomen checking their makeup by the glow of their phones. With its mirrored skyscrapers and pulsing chaos, the city itself had seemed to whisper in his ear: you're home. In recent months, though, these revelatory flashes had grown less frequent, and Min had begun to doubt his reasons for coming to Korea. Still, there were sights he'd yet to see, parts of the city he'd put off visiting that he hoped might yield that fleeting feeling.

By the time he was underground, Min was soaked. Warmth radiated from his shoulder blade as he wrung out the bottom of his T-shirt and waited for the train. Why hadn't he told Mark the truth? He could have easily said he'd made plans with Yu-jin, that they'd set aside their Sunday for each other. It was simpler this way, Min thought. He wanted to keep her separate, away from the usual strategizing and maneuvering that would ensue if the expats discovered he was dating a Korean woman. There'd be endless questions about Yu-jin: How'd they meet, did she have cute friends, was she a prude like all the other girls in Korea? A white lie had been better, Min decided as a train approached, the plastic barrier between the platform and the track humming to life. He'd extricated himself without having to wear the mask of civility for too long. Still, it hadn't saved him from getting wet.

TWO

YU-JIN

Leaving it all behind

Focused, driven, ambitious, obsessed: I was all those things in high school. None of this set me apart from my classmates. It didn't make me special. We knew what was at stake. Our eyes were on the prize, unflinching: gaining admittance to a university in Seoul. For those with even loftier goals, SKY (Seoul National University, Korea University, or Yonsei University) was the ultimate—admittance to any one of the three instantaneously setting you on a course for financial, social, and marital success. College wasn't just the next logical step. It was the foundation upon which your entire adult life was built. It was everything. Slip up on a test at school, mess around during night classes at *hagwon*, or, worst of all, bomb the College Scholastic Ability Test—there went your future, all your hopes and dreams gone in an instant, every future self you'd ever imagined, vanished.

I had plans of my own. Or, I should say, my family had made plans for me: Ewha Womans University. It was my mother's alma mater, one of Seoul's most prestigious schools, and an all-girls one at that, something my father particularly approved of.

But more than the promise of Ewha's rigorous education, more than its vaunted postgraduation connections, more than the alluring prospect of escaping my parents' house, more than anything, I wanted to be in Seoul, in the center of it all. As long as I was there, somewhere in that city, I knew everything would work itself out.

I didn't hate growing up in Gyeryong. It's not like it was dangerous; there was no crime or drugs. That might have at least made it a little interesting. Of course there were good schools, clean parks, a nice shopping mall, but even at an early age, I had the sneaking suspicion that the tiny city I inhabited was boring, prefabricated. Like most of the kids I went to school with, my family had moved to Gyeryong because of the military. It seemed like everyone's father, including my own, worked at the army, navy, or air force headquarters based around the city.

Boxcar administrative buildings, dull government workers in identical gray suits, military officials with matching buzz cuts—this was all I ever saw. Even the housewives wore the same dresses and blouses, never deviating from their neutral tones of beige, black, and pale blue. Uniformity engulfed the city, smoothed its rough patches, varnished it to a perfect sheen. With every restaurant serving the same three dishes, the movie theater only showing two movies at a time, and the *norebangs* updating their music catalogues once a year, I had little trouble focusing on my studies. Unimpeachable grades and a top score on the CSAT were the two goals that saved me from boredom.

I yearned for a place with grit and edge, a place with a pulse, something boiling beneath the surface. And I was almost there. I could feel it in my aching fingertips as I scribbled class notes. I could taste it in the cheap curry *donkatsu* I scarfed down between day and night classes. In three weeks, I'd take the exam and be set on my track, hurtling toward that magnificent megacity, overflowing with chaos and life. It was all I ever talked about with my friends: Seoul. Home to ambitious students, aspiring artists, high fashion models, and brilliant CEOs, it was everything we didn't have, everything we craved. I'd been to Seoul twice with my parents. We'd toured the palaces and seen the sights. I remember being astounded by the sea of pedestrians emerging from the metro, the cacophony of blaring horns during rush hour. There was an energy, a marvelous desperation to the way these people lived their lives. From then on, I knew I had to come back. And as I sat in the dingy classroom of my *hagwon*, going over one multiple-choice question after another, it took all my self-restraint and focus to sit and study. I was so close. So close to getting out, leaving it all behind.

Sometimes my friends would talk about visiting each other once we were all in college. In this scenario we'd all gotten into our top choices in Seoul. It was an indulgence, this fantasy. Except it wasn't a fantasy for me; it was a nightmare. I wanted a clean slate, an impossibility with my high school friends around. I wanted the chance to reinvent myself, start anew. Secretly, I hoped we'd never see each other again after graduation day. I was embarrassed by our dialects, our taste in music and clothes. Everything about us screamed rural and backwards; everyone would know we didn't belong. For months, standing before the bathroom mirror, I'd practiced my Seoul dialect, merging my vowels, committing each unique intonation to memory. Still, I contributed to their stories, played the game. I said how exciting it would all be, visiting dorms and meeting roommates. But each night, kneeling beside my bed, hands clenched, I prayed none of them would get into Ewha. I prayed none of them would set foot in Seoul.

The fall had been a sprint to the finish, the placement exam looming like a dark, treacherous thunderhead. I charged forward, into the fray, fearlessly. Some fell by the wayside—depression, eating disorders, mystery illnesses—but not me. My eye was on the prize. A high score in November would guarantee my acceptance in January. Some of my classmates opted to take the test after graduation, so they'd have more time to study; others took their chances with the *Susi* process, avoiding the CSAT entirely, pinning their hopes instead on transcripts, recommendation letters, and extracurricular activities. I wasn't one of those students. I didn't need extra time to study. I didn't need to take the easy way up.

The day before the examination my father took me out for ice cream. I couldn't remember the last time we'd done something together, just the two of us. He was always working, gone before the sun rose, sometimes not making it home at all, opting to sleep in the dorms at army headquarters. Like a ghost, he came and went, his presence only detectable from the half-empty bowl of fried rice on the kitchen counter, his smudged fingerprints on the doorknob from the morning newspaper.

It was a typical November day: gray, cold with a bite. We sat in the window of a cute diner-style parlor, eating offensively large chocolate sundaes. It was my father's favorite place in Gyeryong. He said it reminded him of America—the good parts of it anyway—drive-ins, milkshakes, roller-girls.

I couldn't help but smile and be happy. Despite my age, he still delighted in theatrical gestures of appreciation and celebration. It was his way: an enormous inflatable bouncy castle for my elementary school graduation party, a platinum bracelet for my sixteenth birthday, a new Mercedes for my mother's fortieth. He cared a great deal about appearances, was proud he could give those gifts.

He sat across from me, jaw square, dark brown eyes betraying nothing. My mother always joked that he should play poker for a living. "With that face," she'd say, "we'd be rich by now."

But my father never gambled. "For degenerates and fools," he'd said once, when we'd passed some elderly men comparing lottery tickets on the street. "There's no such thing as luck. You remember that. There's only hard work. Everything that comes to you is meant for you. You deserve everything—good or bad."

My mother was right. Nothing surprised him. When he did lose his temper, it was a quiet fury, churning beneath the surface until it ruptured. As a child I'd learned to read the silence, the subtle creases on his brow. Still, I wasn't always successful, incurring his wrath if my grades dipped or I talked back.

That didn't happen anymore, not since I'd understood what my parents expected of me.

"I can't tell you how proud I am," he said that day in the diner, taking my hand in his. "You know that, right? Me and your mother. We see the hard work you've been putting in. It's all going to pay off."

His phone vibrated on the table. He eyed it wearily. I was surprised when he ignored the call, smiling instead. As Chief of Strategic Planning—a title I'd memorized because I was proud—he was never without his phone. He was forever ducking out, holding hushed conversations in the bedroom. But this phone call could wait. In that moment I could feel it: paid attention to, loved. This is a special day, an important day, for both of us, he was saying.

"You're going to get a world-class education," he said, tapping away on the tabletop.

"You never went to university in Seoul."

"It was different back then," my father said, gesturing to some invisible truth. "And I climbed my way up through the military. Women can't do that. That's why you must attend a top university. I was lucky your mother was willing to look beyond my poor education."

"I already know the story, Dad," I said, cutting him off before he could repeat how he'd convinced my mother to go on a date with him. They'd met during one of his mandatory physicals for his compulsory military service, exactly twenty-one months in the marines. My mother had recently graduated from Ewha's soon-to-be-prestigious nursing program. After my father made numerous visits to the infirmary due to self-induced illnesses, she finally agreed to a date.

"I came down with anything I could think of," my father always said. "And you had to be really ill, otherwise they wouldn't let you go to the sick bay. One time I ate a bunch of spoiled meat. That laid me up for a few days. Another time I took a cold shower and walked around with wet hair in the dead of winter. I was feverish for a week!"

My mother would only smile and shake her head during the retelling of these stories, but I knew she enjoyed them. She would roll her eyes and protest. But she never left the room.

I always had trouble imagining my father doing such foolish things. I'd only known him as the serious type, always plotting our family's path forward, always mindful of our social and economic standing in our community.

"I wouldn't have stood a chance without my military uniform. By the time your mother found out how broke I was, it was too late," he used to say.

"Don't listen to your father. I think he did some irreparable damage to his brain when he was making himself sick all those times," my mother would tease.

I knew there was some truth to their banter. My father's family had lost everything during the war. Their land and property in Seoul taken, given, misplaced, and mislabeled while changing hands between the Americans and the Korean People's Army until there was nothing left. My mother's family had fared better in Busan, a point of difference I imagined caused tension between them, although I never saw evidence of it.

Moments like this reminded me that my parents had existed before me. They had lived a full and expansive life together. What kind of life that had been, I had trouble seeing. They rarely spoke of the past.

"So how are we feeling about the test?" my father said, digging into his sundae.

"I'm ready. Ready as ever."

"That's my girl. And who knows. Maybe we'll be joining you."

I tried to hide my shock. "What do you mean?"

"Don't look so happy. What? You think your father wants to work in Gyeryong forever? I've put in my time. Word is I'm in line for a promotion. Something in the government. Something in Seoul."

I tried not to panic. Everything would change if my parents moved to Seoul. With them living in the city there'd be no excuse not to live at home. It would be the practical thing to do, as my father always said.

I struggled to see a way out while I ate my ice cream, numbing myself, smiling, nodding, keeping up appearances. Maybe it wouldn't be so bad, I thought. Lots of kids did it. In fact, most did. Living in a dorm or an apartment with friends was the exception. But I'd gotten the idea in my head. It had been my fire, my fuel—that possibility: freedom.

My father watched me quietly, eyes crinkled at the edges. "Let me guess. You aren't too happy about this development."

I weighed my words. "I'm happy. I guess I just thought this would be my chance to get out of the house."

"Your independence is important to you."

Fear seized me, as I felt my moment to persuade him slipping away. "I'm grateful for everything, Dad. I just want to—"

"You've earned it, Yu-jin," he said. "Your mother and I couldn't have dreamed of a more perfect daughter. I want you to have some freedom. I can't think of anyone more deserving."

He understood then. He knew how much this meant to me. Leaning back, he studied me, a glitter in his eye. "I thought you might like living in the dormitories at first. You can spend summers at home, and if you're able to find roommates and a place off campus, you could move your third year, with financial help from us, of course. How does that sound for an agreement?"

I was stunned, ecstatic. "An agreement?"

"Yes," he said. "Our agreement."

I was so elated I only heard fragments of what he said next, but the parameters of the deal were simple. I was to major in Political

Science and International Relations. My grades would never dip below an A-minus, and upon graduating, I'd pursue a career based upon his professional recommendation, most likely something in public service or law. If I did all this, I could live just about anywhere I pleased.

The only thing my father said regarding boys was to be careful. "You have so much promise. In the future you'll have time for romantic relationships, but for now be selfish, Yu-jin. Make the most of these four years. Give everything to your studies. Don't curb your potential and ambitions for someone else. That's the worst thing a young person can do."

That was our pact, the spoken and unspoken rules. I didn't think twice before agreeing.

·╫·

On exam day, the world stopped. Planes were grounded; the stock market opened late; the entire country bowed in reverent silence to their troops of high schoolers marching off to do battle with the CSAT.

I woke before my alarm, alert and ready. For the past few months I'd practiced getting up early, ensuring I wasn't groggy or tired when I sat for the test. I ate my usual breakfast of kimchi and rice. My mother had prepared it before she'd left for the Buddhist temple. She'd stay there all morning, praying for my success. My father was having a Danish with his coffee. It smelled heavenly. He offered me some, but I shook my head. I couldn't risk upsetting my stomach.

We left the house early, giving ourselves plenty of time. My father drove without the faintest hint of anxiety through the empty streets.

In the testing center parking lot he held me close, his clean-shaven cheek smooth against my ear. "You're prepared," he said. "I know you'll make us proud."

Walking to the entrance in the chilled November air, I could feel the nervous energy emanating from the hundreds of family members who'd come to cheer us on. In the bathroom before the exam, I sat on the toilet concentrating on extracting every ounce of liquid from my bladder. Someone in the stall next to me was vomiting. I closed my eyes. I couldn't afford to be distracted. All the hours I'd put in, the all-nighters, the cram sessions, every weekend for the past three years—it had all led to this. Vomit, tears, group anxiety—it was below me, behind me.

I aced the test.

My father and mother asked how I could be so certain, and I simply said that I knew.

A month later, when the results were sent out, I saw what I'd known all along. With my test score in hand, I felt an overwhelming sense of calm. The life I'd been destined for played out before me. I saw myself sitting in university classes with brilliant women, walking down Seoul's crowded streets, living in my very own dorm room, free to come and go anytime I pleased. A deep and comforting satisfaction settled on me. My mother wept; my father could only smile and smile. Everything they'd done for me had been for this moment, and now that it was here it felt as if we'd passed into some profoundly unknowable phase of our lives together.

I called my two closest friends, Hye-jung and Hae-sook, who squealed and yelped when I shared the news. Neither had Ewha as a top choice, so I could feel happy for them. I knew they'd done well. No one would pick up the phone otherwise. Taking advantage of my parents' good mood, I asked if I could go celebrate. They said yes, of course. What could they say? I'd all but guaranteed myself a spot at Ewha. Suddenly I didn't dread seeing friends and talking about the future. Once I made it to Seoul, I'd forget all about them. They'd cease to exist.

THREE

MIN

What was the nature of your relationship?

Min looked out his rain-streaked office window, the city's contours stretched and blurred. His thoughts were on his date with Yu-jin yesterday, their walk around Seoul, headphones on, splicer swinging, music murmuring through them as they stopped at a café, mingled with the tourists at Gyeongbokgung, watched the city move. The day had been everything he'd wanted.

"I don't understand," he finally said, unwilling to face the man sitting in his office.

The detective shifted in his seat, leather creaking. He explained again in even tones that something had happened. There'd been an incident. Yu-jin was dead.

Forehead against the windowpane, Min was consumed by his last moments with Yu-jin, kissing goodbye, subway doors closing between them at Chungmuro station, long jet-black hair twirling as she turned to wave goodbye from the platform. His train car lurching forward.

Yu-jin dead? It couldn't be true. There'd been a mistake, a mix-up, Min thought, waiting for someone else to enter his office, maybe the superior of this man. He'd gotten the wrong building, the wrong guy. The wrong Yu-jin. His Yu-jin was perfectly fine. At this very moment, Min knew she was sitting in a classroom at the university, three pencils freshly sharpened to spears of lead (her good-luck charm), her fingers sliding between the pages of her test booklet, breaking the adhesive seal. The last government final she'd ever take, something they'd planned on celebrating that very night. But no one else came through his office door. The detective stared just beyond him, letting the information sink in, like a surgeon waiting for their patient to go under.

Light-headed, vision blurring, Min sat down behind his desk and focused on the stranger before him. "I'm sorry, who are you again?"

"Detective Park. I've been assigned to Yu-jin's case."

"Kim Yu-jin. You're sure you've got the right person? I was with her just yesterday." Min hated the futility of his own question. How many Americans worked at Samsung in Seoul? How many of those Americans had girlfriends named Yu-jin? It's my Yu-jin, he thought. They had the right guy. But how? It was impossible.

She'd messaged him last night after their date: Thanks for today. I'm glad you got me the splicer. Is there anything better than walking around a city, knowing someone is hearing exactly what you're hearing? Seeing exactly what you're seeing?

Had they heard the same things, seen the same things?

"Kim Yu-jin. Twenty-one. Student at Ewha. Majoring in International Relations and Political Science. Black hair. Brown eyes. Five seven . . ." The detective went on, but Min wasn't listening.

He was thinking about the way she'd looked at him from the train platform, longingly. Or had it been something else? Had it been regret in her eyes, fear? The thought that he'd missed something—a hint, a plea—terrified him.

Detective Park leaned forward on the seat of his chair. His voice was soft, like warm, soapy water. "We're still trying to find out what exactly happened, but she died in her apartment last night." His eyes were bloodshot, jaundiced from cigarette smoke and *soju*. He paused, if only to give the illusion that he found what he was about to say difficult. Min believed he'd said the words he was about to say a hundred times. "I can't say definitively, but it looks like she took her own life," he said. "I'm sorry."

No. No. Min could only shake his head. "She wouldn't do something like that. I was with her less than twenty-four hours ago. I'll call her right now."

As if to protect him from further pain and humiliation, Detective Park rested his hand on the office phone. "Just a few questions, please."

Min slumped back in his chair. This isn't happening, he repeated to himself. It's a bad dream, only a dream.

Detective Park opened his notebook and clicked his pen. "How did you meet, and what was the nature of your relationship?"

They'd met in the hallway of a high-end *norebang* somewhere in Hongdae, their respective groups belting along to K-pop and American '80s ballads in soundproofed booths. They'd smiled sheepishly, embarrassed by their cohorts' tastes in music. Min's room had been particularly nauseating, his boss demanding all the Samsung administrative assistants sing at least one Journey song, whether they could read English or not.

"I can't take responsibility for them," Min had said to her.

Yu-jin looked at her group of friends through the glass door, crooning into microphones, dancing under colored lights. "We're not exactly classing it up ourselves," she said, cinching her hair into a ponytail. Even slumped against the wall, she was tall, her eyes almost level with his.

She had studied the hallway, taking in the gold-yellow wallpaper and glossy black floor tiles. "We could just leave," she offered. "You and me."

"Like an escape?"

"Exactly," she said, reaching a hand across the narrow space between them, the thin walls throbbing. "I'm Yu-jin."

And they did leave; they absconded, just like that, left their friends and coworkers without so much as a goodbye. It was Yu-jin's forwardness, the abrupt nature of her declarations, that drew Min to her. With her, it had felt easy, natural.

They found a quiet bar around the corner, the clientele mostly taxi drivers and civil servants who studied the couple with wary curiosity. Eyes followed Yu-jin everywhere she went. She seemed aware of the attention, swiveling her hips in her dark jeans.

Min remembered how Yu-jin liked to say blue jeans were America's greatest export. Everyone thought it was democracy, but that was a lie. Blue jeans, she'd insisted.

His thoughts were interrupted. "And the nature. The nature of your relationship?" Detective Park said.

"The nature?"

Min despised the sound of his voice, hysterical and weak. What was the nature of our relationship? he wondered. Why hadn't he ever asked that question? It hadn't needed answering, he realized.

"I understand you're distraught right now, Mr. Ford, and I'll tell you what I can about the case, but right now I need you to answer these questions. I know they may seem trivial. But they might give us some answers. You want answers, don't you?"

Answers—yes, Min wanted answers, but to what, about something Yu-jin would never do, something she was incapable of? This wasn't who she was. She'd never have willingly harmed herself. Min felt hollow, a piece of him snatched away. This was a new pain, a far greater pain than any injury he'd sustained playing sports—the perforated eardrum, the dislocated shoulder, the shattered clavicle, all understandable, logical, cause and effect. But the source of this pain and disbelief was unknowable, unquantifiable. A blank. A void. All he could think was: I could have saved her.

"Can you think of anyone who might have wanted to harm Yu-jin? Anyone who might benefit from her death?"

"I thought you said she took her own life."

"That's what I suspect, but I need to eliminate all other possibilities."

Min wished he had a suspect, an individual whose name, once uttered, would explain everything. But there was no such person. "No. No one."

"Any disagreements or arguments with anyone leading up to last night?"

Min could only shake his head

"How was her relationship with her family? Were you close with them?"

"No," Min heard himself say.

"So you never met her father," Park said. He glanced at Min sympathetically. "It's not personal. Korean parents don't take well to boyfriends—too much of a distraction, particularly during university."

A politician—that was all she'd said about her father, as casually as if she were recollecting yesterday's weather. It had seemed unimportant. But perhaps it wasn't. Her parents had never known about them. It was Yu-jin's decision. Her father had warned her about a serious boyfriend hindering her studies. Min suspected his being American didn't help things. "It will cause less trouble," she'd said. And he'd agreed. It wasn't his place to say otherwise. Her parents had dreamed of their daughter gaining admission to Ewha University their entire lives, and now that she was there, they'd given her some independence. She'd wanted to keep it that way. He didn't blame her, but now he had questions. He traced over moments between them, decisions they'd made. Had she been trying to protect him from something? Had she known this was coming? With Yu-jin gone, trivial choices, random events, suddenly began to take on some sense of meaning: a sideways glance, the shadow of a frown.

Why had she even spoken to him that first night? What had she seen?

"What's it like," she'd said over their third round of beers, "always being stared at?"

"What do you mean?"

"Oh, come on." She rolled her eyes. "You're like the ideal guy here. Korean, but only half. American, but not too American, unless you've got some tattoos under there. Americans love their tattoos: barbed wire, bald eagles, and flames—lots of flames, anything flaming really, it seems like. And that nose. I bet that nose turns heads."

Yu-jin's comments should have bothered Min, as such attentions had since his arrival in Korea—when schoolchildren had stopped to take pictures of him, astounded by his height, when waitresses and bartenders asked for his plastic surgeon's name, mesmerized by his jawline, his eyelids, his nose, always his nose—but they didn't. Maybe it was Yu-jin's awareness of her own body, the obvious pleasure she took in looking the way she did. There was no hiding of her physical beauty, no shame in the value she took from her appearance.

Min rubbed the bridge of his nose. Only at night, when shadows stretched across his face, did he find the acceptance he'd hoped for upon arriving in Seoul, when he could pass for Korean. "I don't know. I probably feel the same way you do, getting stared at. It's nice at first, but after a while it starts making you feel strange. Like you don't belong."

"Trying to get pity for your good looks? What, you'd rather be ugly and invisible? Because that's what you'd be here in Seoul, invisible. No one sees you or wants to see you. Appearances matter here. You might as well embrace it. Plus, you don't really belong here. I mean, it isn't America. It's not your home."

She could be like that—blunt, even harsh—but Min found it refreshing. Still, he'd yearned to explain the ever-present fear that he belonged nowhere, forever suspended in a liminal state. But Yu-jin wouldn't have understood. How could she have? She was so sure of herself.

Detective Park cleared his throat. "How long were you together?"

"Around ten months."

"Ten months," he echoed to himself, scratching away in his notepad. "And it was"—he paused, seeming reluctant—"romantic in nature? Your relationship, that is."

"Are you asking if we were sleeping together?"

Park gave a quick nod, fidgeting in his seat.

Min recalled that first night. How had they come to stand in that same hallway, just feet apart? It had been her doing after all, hadn't it? She'd initiated everything. "Yes," he said. "We were sleeping together."

After drinks she'd asked him for money to pay for a cab back to her apartment, and he'd obliged, happy he could do something for her. He stood with her on the sidewalk in the three A.M. glow, dance clubs breathing their last gasps, bars trickling drunken patrons.

"I'd like to see you another time," Yu-jin said. "What do you say? We can escape again."

Detective Park erupted with a hacking cough, spittle trembling on his lower lip. "Just a few more," he said. "Can you think of any reason why Yu-jin would end her life, and did you notice anything out of the ordinary yesterday? Sudden change of mood, erratic behavior?"

"No. Nothing," Min said, assured by the veracity of his statement. He'd spent nearly a year with her. She would have confided in him, leaned on him. And even if something had been wrong, he would have recognized it, especially pain or suffering. We were happy, Min thought. She'd been happy. Of course it wasn't the kind of relationship either had expected to go beyond his time in Seoul or her graduating from university. They'd been honest about their futures, the separate ways they'd go when the time came. Somehow that fact had made their time together more intimate, more meaningful. There'd been no subterfuge, no agenda. At least that's what he'd thought.

Detective Park stood, buttoning his worn suit jacket across his belly. "Do you have someone that can vouch for your whereabouts last night?"

"You think I had something to do with this?"

"I have to investigate every lead, no matter how implausible."

"After our date I went straight home. I only left once to get a snack from the convenience store in my building around midnight."

"That'll work," Park said. "We can check their tapes."

Had he been awake, blissful and breathing, at the precise moment she'd died?

Park rested a hand on his bad shoulder. "It's not abnormal."

Min barely registered his touch, unable to hold back the tears. "What isn't?"

"To not know what's going on inside someone else's head. Trust me. I see it a lot. Sometimes it's the people who seem perfectly fine that are going through hell on the inside. Somehow they're the best at hiding it."

"You don't know what you're talking about."

Yu-jin wouldn't hide something like this, Min thought. We were always candid with each other. She had no reason to keep anything from me. I would have understood.

But even as Min affirmed this to himself, he couldn't ignore the nagging suspicion that he *had* missed something. Something had been going on in Yu-jin's life that he hadn't known about. Someone had done this to her. It was the only possibility.

"Is this your address?" Park said, showing Min his notepad.

"Can you at least tell me what your working theory is?"

"I'm really not supposed to—"

"I'm just asking for any information."

Park frowned, working his lower lip between his teeth. "Right now, the evidence points to suicide."

"But you haven't ruled out foul play."

"I'm not going to speculate, Mr. Ford. I have protocols to follow. I'll go where the evidence takes me."

"I'm telling you Yu-jin wouldn't harm herself. What possible reason would she have for ending her life?"

"Most cases I see are due to social or academic pressures. Like I said, it's too early to say with any real certainty, but given her age, demographic, and socioeconomic status, I'd say stress related to school."

"That's impossible. School was easy for her. She had good friends. People that cared about her. She was graduating in a few weeks."

"I'm not arguing with you, Mr. Ford. If you think of anything, give me a call," Detective Park said, handing a business card to Min, who held it loosely, then tighter, digging the stiff, hard edges into his palm.

"You're making a mistake. If you knew Yu-jin, you'd know she'd never do something like this. Someone must have done something to her . . ."

"You're in shock, Min. Can I call you Min?"

"You still haven't told me how she died."

Detective Park stopped and turned. "I don't think you need that information right now."

"Knowing something is better than nothing."

"Asphyxiation," Park said, his face twisted into a grimace.

Min had thought he'd feel better knowing, but now suddenly all he could think about was his breathing, in and out, how easily it came, smooth and mocking in his ears.

Before leaving, Park offered his condolences once again, all a distant murmur to Min, who sat for a long time after the door closed, going over their last moments together, again and again, rewinding them, searching for something, a hint, a clue, a chink in her armor, a run in her stockings. Yu-jin was strong. She wouldn't have taken her life because of stress or pressure. It wasn't like her. No—someone had done something, threatened her, harmed her. But who? Min thought about what Detective Park had said. Maybe some people were utterly unknowable. Maybe he'd never really known Yu-jin at all.

FOUR

YU-JIN

You're just the perfect girl

I was waiting on the sidewalk with Hae-sook and Hye-jung, all of us shivering in our skirts. We'd worn pants when leaving our households and quickly changed once we met up, then piled into a taxi, the cabdriver's eyes flickering across our bare legs.

Some older boys had invited us to hang out at a multi-room downtown. They'd graduated last July and had spent four grueling months cramming for the CSAT. Their strategy had paid off with strong scores, and they wanted to celebrate. I couldn't imagine waiting like that, delaying my departure from Gyeryong for a second longer than necessary. But they didn't seem to mind. Boys are like that, nonchalant, all confidence and easiness.

They knew of a place where we could bring alcohol, where the owner would let us do whatever we wanted. It was something I expected older boys to know. Where you could drink, what stores would sell you cigarettes. I'd had my moments of indiscretion, but they were fairly tame: sneaking a cigarette during lunch, snagging a spare bottle of *makgeolli* at holiday parties with my cousins. Don't get me wrong. I wanted to break curfew, cut class, get fall-down drunk with the kids who already knew university wasn't for them. But rebellion meant ruining any shot at Ewha, at Seoul. Only now, after acing the exam, could I let my eye wander from the target, however briefly.

I teetered in my heels, the sneakers in my handbag already calling to me and it wasn't even nine. Hae-sook took out a cigarette. I noticed she looked more done up than usual, hair straightened, shingles of onyx, fingernails a scarlet red. "Who's coming tonight?" I asked, wondering what boy she was trying to impress.

Hae-sook fumbled with the lighter. "Don't worry, you know one of the guys."

Even if she wasn't a very convincing smoker, I had to commend the effort. She could actually pass for a university girl, whereas Hye-jung and I still had that awkward look about us, like we were still getting used to our bodies, forever changing, never allowing us to get comfortable.

But she always tried too hard, Hae-sook. She'd ditch us at even just the scent of a boy. She often did, weeks at a time, chasing some new infatuation. Then she'd resurface, brokenhearted, wondering why the guy had dropped her. None of us told her why, but we knew. She gave it up too easily. I was young, but I knew boys liked to play the game, even when they said they didn't.

I was still a virgin, as was Hye-jung, I suspected. True, she spent a lot of time with Hae-sook, but I still caught her looking lost with boys. Should she ignore him? Compliment him? Make him feel wanted? She was like me, unsure of how to wield this power we possessed.

Boys had always been a distraction, a diversion. They were easy to ignore, especially when they realized you weren't interested. So my social life had suffered throughout high school—a small price to pay for perfect grades and exemplary test scores. Even those who I considered my friends, girls like Hye-jung and Hae-sook, were kept at a distance by the intense fear that I would be forced to sacrifice my own time and energy to help them through breakups or console them after a bad grade. My goals and aspirations, they'd always been bigger than friendship.

But not tonight, I thought, borrowing Hye-jung's makeup mirror and checking my eyeliner; tonight I'm free, no more grades, no more percentiles. I'd done what was needed. I could push against my self-imposed guardrails, revel in the present.

Eventually the boys showed, lanky and self-assured in their jeans and faux-leather jackets, no doubt buoyed by a few drinks beforehand. Hae-sook and Hye-jung squealed at the sight of them. I stood awkwardly and waited to be introduced while they hugged. The only one I knew by name was Si-woo, a dour-looking boy from one of my advanced math classes the year before. I thought I recognized the other two but had never spoken a word to them. I'd passed them in the halls, watched them from a distance. I was more curious than attracted, intrigued by their gangly legs and unkempt eyebrows, the way they existed, oblivious to the space around them. I wondered what that must be like: to have the world move for you.

"Everyone," Hae-sook said, twirling on her toes and pointing at me like I was the grand prize on a game show. "This is Yu-jin. She's decided to honor us with her presence tonight."

I pulled my face into a pleasant, welcoming smile.

Hae-sook grabbed the elbow of the boy closest to her. He was tall and slender with high cheekbones, totally her type. "This is Do-yun," she said, "that's Hyun-woo, and I think you know Si-woo."

Crammed into the small elevator, I quickly found myself shoulder-to-shoulder with Si-woo. I tried catching his attention with a glance, but he didn't seem to notice. Hae-sook was already giggling and whispering something in Do-yun's ear. Hye-jung tried to follow suit, leaning against Hyun-woo flirtatiously. Legs jittery, palms damp, I studied my blurred reflection in the scuffed elevator doors.

The multi-room was spacious: two couches and a love seat, all angled toward a massive flat-screen TV. We had our pick of karaoke, video games, and movies. While the boys took out the *soju* and mixers from black plastic bags, Hae-sook, dissatisfied with the streaming options, sent Hye-jung and me out to peruse the DVD collection. "Get an action movie," she said, tossing her gold sequined handbag on the sofa.

She never wasted an opportunity. Always catering to the boys.

With Hye-jung leading the way, we went to the front desk. An old man gave us a nod as we approached, pointing to the wall of DVDs behind us.

"What do you think she's telling them?" I said.

"Probably how we've had crushes on them forever. She's been looking forward to this for weeks. Kind of pathetic really."

Hye-jung's forthrightness was surprising. Usually everything was misdirection with these two: everything said by a look, a wink. I picked up a movie and perused the back.

"That was mean, sorry," she said. "We snuck some *soju* before coming out. I always say dumb stuff when I drink."

"We all do."

She gave a half laugh.

"What?"

"*You*, get drunk and say dumb stuff? See, there I go again."

"No. You're right. I don't know what it's like," I said, refreshed by Hye-jung's honesty. "I don't know why I said it."

"It's cool," she said, her voice airy and slack.

We stood outside our private room, raucous laughing within. The Hae-sook show had already begun.

The last to sit, I settled into the love seat with Si-woo. The pairing off had happened so quickly, I'd hardly known what to do. It seemed Hae-sook and Hye-jung had a plan after all, as I watched them divide and conquer the other boys.

Had all of this been decided earlier? Maybe Hye-jung had been playing coy before. Girls were like that, two-faced. But even as I settled into the surprisingly uncomfortable seat next to my arranged date, I was left feeling like it had been a real moment with her, a second where we'd talked as girls—anxious and insecure.

Drinks were passed around in the semidark, the TV screen dousing us in electric blue. I asked Si-woo what we were drinking and hoped he wouldn't laugh at me.

"It's just *soju* mixed with Sprite. It's not bad. But don't drink it too fast."

I sipped it judiciously, annoyed by his concern for my sobriety. I wanted an older boy, all confidence and swagger, not parental advisory.

Hae-sook jumped up from the couch. "Someone help me put the movie on. I can never figure out these entertainment consoles." Always helpless, needy. She wasn't really, of course, but she knew how boys worked, how they liked to feel smart, in charge.

Maybe it was knowing I'd aced my exam or the alcohol, but I

found myself relaxing, letting my shoulders slump into the crux of Si-woo's arm, which curved ever so slightly around me. Small movements could betray so much. A look was an invitation, the graze of a hand a provocation. That night I imagined my body a beacon, signaling out to the darkness. The thought thrilled me in a way I'd never allowed myself to feel before. Then the movie was playing, a generic action scene. I watched with passive indifference, listening to Hae-sook and Hye-jung in the darkness, giggling and cooing. Si-woo seemed genuinely interested in the movie, with its deafening explosions and zinging bullets.

Thirty minutes later and the room was a blur, spinning out in every direction.

Si-woo's hand was still on my knee, frozen in place. I'd tried willing him to move it closer, to slide it. I'd tried shifting my weight, to the right, to the left. Nothing. Between the screeching tires and gunfire, I heard lips against lips, a zipper singing down a fly. I was missing my chance. Couldn't Si-woo hear these sounds? This was his cue.

Blood thumping in my ears, I took his hand and slid it up my leg, under my skirt.

A quick jerk backwards and he was looking at me, the TV's reflection playing across his estranged face. "What're you doing?"

"I just thought—"

"I'm only here because of my friends." He turned back to the movie. "I told you not to drink that stuff so fast."

Embarrassment broke out like wildfire across my chest, up my neck, the flames licking my cheeks. I sat still, bewildered at what to do or say. Nothing seemed the only option. A day scene in the film illuminated the room. I watched Hae-sook kissing Do-yun's lips, her head tilted, hair tumbling. Her eyes flicked open, and she looked at me. She wrapped a hand around his neck, pushing her fingers through his fine black hair. This is how you do it, she was saying. This is how you get them.

Then I was standing up, announcing that I was going outside to have a cigarette. I never smoked, but no one was listening. Si-woo stared at me dumbly.

Swaying on the sidewalk, I watched a group of kids playing an arcade crane game, trying to snatch an oversized stuffed animal. They shouted at one another, jostling for position over the joystick. I put my hands out in front of me, splaying the fingers apart. I watched them tremble, hating that I couldn't control them. I took a deep breath and jammed them back into my jacket pockets. I thought about Hae-sook and the way she'd looked at me. I didn't know what it meant, any of it.

After giving the kids some money to keep playing their game, I headed back up to my friends. I wasn't going to let Si-woo ruin my night of freedom. I didn't need him. I checked my makeup in the bathroom mirror and collected myself. I nearly dropped my eyeliner in the sink when I heard someone in the stall behind me. I'd thought I was alone.

Whoever it was seemed to be having trouble with the lock on their stall. Then a purse dropped, a cell phone skittering across the floor, followed by lipstick. "Shit."

"Hye-jung?" I said, recognizing the phone case. I tried the latch. "Open up."

After some fumbling, the door swung outward. Hye-jung was kneeling on the floor, tights torn, her elbows resting on the toilet seat. She looked up at me, eyes red, mascara dirtying her cheeks. "I'm gonna be sick," she said to me, before turning away and vomiting.

I held back her hair. After it seemed like she was done, I got some paper towels and ran them under the faucet. I did my best with her mascara and wiped her lips and the corners of her mouth. Everything was beginning to smell foul, but I tried not to let on. Si-woo had been right about the *soju*.

"Are you okay?" I said, dropping the paper towels in the toilet and flushing.

She ran a hand across her mouth and nodded.

"Do you want me to get some water?"

She started to say something but broke down crying instead.

"What's wrong?"

Hye-jung shook her head, waving away my attempts to give her the tissues I'd found in her bag.

"Is it about the boys? Did Hae-sook say something?"

She laughed and sniffled, wet hair glued to the sides of her face. "I bombed the CSAT."

"But you said you'd heard great news. We're all out celebrating."

"I lied. And the worst part is, even my parents are lying, to our extended family, all their friends. I'm gonna feel like such an idiot when I have to retake it next year."

I'd always been jealous, even in awe of Hae-sook and Hye-jung's ability to excel both academically and socially; it was an art I'd yet to master. But with Hye-jung in tears, vulnerable and helpless, that vision was no more.

"Tons of people take it twice, even three times. You've got nothing to worry about," I said.

"Easy for you to say."

"What's that supposed to mean?"

"Everyone knows you're the smartest. You're going to have your pick of schools. You don't give your friends the time of day, and we still invite you to stuff. I don't know why. It's not like you've ever cared about what we thought or what we were doing."

"That's not true," I protested weakly.

"You've got everything figured out. Pretty. Smart. The boys want you even more for ignoring them. You're just the perfect girl, Yu-jin," she said, brushing me aside and staggering out of the stall. "There, I said it."

When she'd gone, I wiped the toilet down and flushed again. Was it true? Was I wanted, envied?

That was the last time I spoke to Hye-jung. She didn't return to school after winter break. I think her parents moved, out of shame.

FIVE

MIN

Something you might have missed

Growing up in Los Angeles, Min had often felt like a stranger to himself, adrift between worlds. There was the Korean church he attended with his mother, where rumors spread quicker than the word of God himself: she'd married a white man; she'd divorced a white man; she wouldn't have any man. It didn't help that she treated church as a mere social affair. There was never any talk of God in their home. How Min wished he could be like his mother, strong and resolute, dispensing of petty gossip with a roll of her eyes, dressed in her Sunday best. "They still eat my *mandu*," she'd say with a smile. Min prayed for her indifference, her assuredness, when kids from Sunday school eyed him suspiciously.

With his father it was worse. He was all blue eyes and immaculate blond hair. Min looked nothing like him, and wherever they went, so followed the sympathetic looks of strangers. "We could never adopt," they'd say. "But good for you."

Min would later wonder why his mother had married someone so different from herself. This Stanford graduate from Orange County, full of rare and unrelenting waspy optimism. Whatever had pulled them together hadn't lasted; ten years and they'd called it quits. Min had just turned nine and stayed with his mother, telling his father he'd rather die than live in San Diego, where there were more country clubs than taco trucks.

His parents' separation was just another oddity, another peculiarity pushing him into a place without a name, a place where you split your holidays between households, where you were the conduit through which your parents spoke, where you took the sharpest thing you could find and split your love in two, no matter how unevenly. After a few years Min didn't think it was a place at all; it was simply the absence of something whole.

Seoul felt like that now with Yu-jin gone: empty, Min thought, as he exited the Samsung building and walked toward the metro station. In the street, buses, taxis, and motorbikes converged into a river of controlled chaos. Surely Yu-jin's roommates could tell him more than Detective Park. Overhead, dust and sand from the Gobi Desert stretched out across the sky, clouds tinged orange and amber by toxins from Chinese factories—the last yellow-haze storm before summer. Throat itching, eyes watering, Min pushed on, cutting swaths through the waves of surgical-masked pedestrians. He'd needed to get away from the office, switching his monitor off and sweeping documents and folders into his desk drawer before striding to the elevator, head down, eyes fixed on the carpeted floor. He jammed the smooth lobby button again and again, possessed by some mad hope that it would give him the answers he required. Even after he'd burst through the heavy glass doors and out onto the street, he imagined his coworkers were all watching him from the windows, waiting for him to fall, crumple, unable to bear the weight of his loss.

His boss's words still sang in his ears like a cheap pop melody—superficial but irresistibly true. "It's nothing to be ashamed of. To feel like you missed something," Sun had said. "Take a few days off. See how you feel. Work might take your mind off things."

Down an escalator, a staircase, Min caught his breath in the underground coolness, hands to knees, neon tears streaming down his cheeks. What had he missed?

At Yu-jin's apartment Min hit the buzzer, a digital screen next to the door illuminating his face, ghostly blue. He buzzed again. There was some shuffling and then a pause. After a moment the door swung inward. Misaki stood in the doorway wearing tweed capri pants, a short matching blazer, and an oversized white button-down shirt. Min was surprised to see she'd dyed her hair. Just last week it had been blond, a hay yellow. Now it was a tawny brown, curving snugly under her chin, bangs obscuring her eyebrows. Min wondered what had prompted the sudden change.

"You missed him," she said, ushering him into the living room.

Min slipped off his loafers and put on a pair of visitor slippers. "Who?"

Misaki sat on the floor by the coffee table strewn with Japanese and Korean street-fashion magazines and balled-up tissues. She always had her nose buried in something, like a deterrent against unwanted conversation. "A detective," she said. "He came this morning."

"He visited me at work. He said . . ." Min stopped himself, afraid he'd falter. He wanted to let it out, but not here, not in front of Misaki. She was practically a stranger. To him she was simply the roommate—someone who'd occupied a physical space in the apartment. She was the sound of running water, the padding of slippers.

"Who found her?"

Misaki was flipping through glossy pages too quickly to be looking at anything. Japanese hip-hop blared from headphones around her neck. Min couldn't help but admire her ability to flaunt her own culture in a foreign land. He was far too self-conscious, always worried about drawing attention to himself as an American.

She looked up at him. "No one found her. I wasn't here. So-ra was. She said paramedics and police came early this morning. They had a stretcher. They wouldn't let So-ra see the body."

"But how did they know to come? Someone must have called them."

"I'm just telling you what I know."

Nothing made sense, but Min didn't have time to dwell on it. "Where's So-ra now?"

She was the one he needed to speak with. Yu-jin's closest friend and confidante. They'd been roommates since freshman year.

"She went for a walk. That was about two hours ago."

"Why didn't you go with her? She shouldn't be alone."

Misaki shrugged, drawing herself inward, the shoulder pads of her blazer threatening to consume her. "She didn't want company."

How could So-ra want to be alone at a time like this? Min was stupefied, and even as he saw Misaki wilt under his accusatory tone, he unleashed the torrent of questions Detective Park had been so unwilling to answer or entertain: Did she or So-ra believe the theory about stress and academic pressure? Did Misaki notice anything strange last night? Did Yu-jin look sad or nervous? Did she mention him, their date?

"I don't know anything, Min, really," Misaki said. "I didn't even see them. I was already in bed when So-ra got home around ten. I heard Yu-jin come in much later, must have been around midnight."

Why had Yu-jin gotten home so late? It hadn't even been dark when they'd said goodbye. Why had it taken her so long to get back to the apartment?

Min pressed on. "How could you not know anything? You live here."

Misaki winced and looked down at her magazines. She picked up a used tissue and clutched the mass in her pale fist.

"I need to know what happened," Min said, on the verge of apologizing for raising his voice.

Misaki switched off her music and looked at Min, eyes rimmed red, lips trembling. "How would I know? The only reason those two let me live with them was because I could pay more rent."

From what Yu-jin had told him, it was mostly true. Both Yu-jin and So-ra alleged she came from a wealthy family in Tokyo. They'd sent Misaki off to Seoul for unknown reasons. Min had never been able to confirm the rumors, but it was obvious she came from money, the way she floated between rooms, aloof and indifferent to others. Whenever Min had spent time at the apartment, she'd scarcely said a word to him, too busy with a book or her phone. Her social calendar seemed limitless. She was always out somewhere, with someone no one had ever met. She'd return the next day, wearing the outfit she'd worn the previous night, oversized sunglasses sliding down her slender nose. Min had been curious about her whereabouts on those nights. She was a foreigner, like him. How'd she know so many people? Where was she spending all her time?

"Yu-jin loved having you as roommate," Min said, seeing he'd opened a wound.

Misaki's cheeks flushed underneath her makeup. "You don't have to lie. I know what they thought of me. The only reason they tolerated me is for this." She looked around at the apartment.

It was an impressive space, expansive street-facing windows, marble countertops, hardwood floors. The technological gadgets alone made the apartments in America seem medieval. Most university students were stuck in dorms, but they had this spacious three-bedroom apartment in Daehangno, one of the trendier neighborhoods in Seoul.

Min wanted to ask Misaki more questions, but he'd upset her, and he wasn't capable of comforting anyone, especially someone he hardly knew. He took a few steps down the familiar hallway. "I need to get into Yu-jin's room. I need to see if she left anything."

"You can't. They said no one's allowed."

"Who?"

"The police. They said it's an active crime scene. They put a lock on the door. They wouldn't even let Yu-jin's dad in."

"Why would he come here? Wouldn't he have gone to identify the body?"

Misaki shrugged, pulling her knees to her chest. "I don't know," she said. "I don't know what people are supposed to do in situations like this."

A digital lock had been installed. When Min punched a number, the keypad glowed to life. He tried a few combinations, but nothing happened. He pressed his head against the door, hoping that if he surrendered himself to Yu-jin's death he might become a ghost and slip through the walls, into her bedroom. More than anything, he wanted to lie in her bed, rest his head on her pillows. Palms against the door, he imagined melting through to the other side. Open up, he thought. Open up and let me in.

After a moment, Min collected himself and returned to the living room. "You really believe that detective? A total stranger?"

Misaki looked at him. "I don't know what to believe."

He despised her in that moment for knowing so little. Min went to leave, shucking his slippers off in the entryway.

"Wait," she said, standing up. "I'm sorry this happened. I can't imagine how you're feeling."

"I'm going to find So-ra," he said, slamming the door behind him.

He walked south toward the river in search of So-ra, his jacket flapping in the wind, tie loose around his neck. How had she died? Asphyxiation. Something around her neck. Min caught a sob halfway in his throat and choked it down. He messaged So-ra. He called her. But there was no response. He walked on, clutching his phone, hoping desperately to feel its slight vibration, its beeping notification. Any sign of life.

·||·

Hours later and still no word from So-ra. Min paced the rain-darkened sidewalks in the direction of Insa-dong. Desperate for clues to Yu-jin's death, he'd decided to retrace their steps from the day before, hoping something might jog his memory. Someone they'd bumped into, something she'd said hinting at some deeper unhappiness. His mind slipped from fear to paranoia. The wash of tires in the rain, pedestrians chattering on cell phones as they passed, watching his every move—blurred faces smeared with suspicion and doubt. Was this real? It felt so much like a dream, a hazy picture of the world breaking down into a thousand trembling granules.

The neighborhood was popular among tourists, speckled with independent art galleries, tearooms, and shops selling traditional Korean souvenirs. It was one of Yu-jin's favorite areas in Seoul because of the foreigners. "Foreigners come in all shapes and sizes. They all look so different," she'd said while they sipped coffees on a bench outside.

Standing in front of the same café a day later, Min tried to remember anything significant from the conversation, but there was nothing. It had all been superficial; like a catamaran skimming the water, their conversations never seemed to delve too deep. It was one of the qualities he'd come to value most in their relationship, the ease with which it moved. But now it seemed that comfort had been an illusion, a lie.

After coffee they'd gone to Gyeongbokgung, the main royal palace in the city. Most of it had been destroyed by the Japanese, twice—once in the sixteenth century and again in 1915. It was all rebuilt now, the buildings and pagodas oddly vibrant and colorful with fresh coats of paint.

More ominous clouds threatened overhead, so Min bought an umbrella from a convenience store before entering the palace grounds. The main courtyard was nearly empty. He only had twenty minutes before it closed to visitors. A few brave explorers tromped through the puddles, stopping every few moments to snap photos, their plastic ponchos gusting around their legs. The throne hall stood ahead, its doors wide open. Inside, a warm darkness lingered. A light rain began to fall, pattering on the tombstone-like markers rising from the courtyard, designating where each court official was meant to stand. Without the rain, the silence would have been almost unbearable. Min thought about calling his mother. But what would he say? He'd never told her about Yu-jin.

Outside the palace walls, Min tried to locate the place where they'd eaten lunch, weaving his way down serpentine alleyways through the growing dark. Yu-jin had suggested it, a small porridge restaurant in Gahoe-dong. She always liked going to mom-and-pop places, holes in the wall. She appreciated coziness in a restaurant. "I feel so alone in those big restaurants, even when I'm surrounded by other people," Min remembered her saying.

Was that something worth noting, that she felt alone even when surrounded by other people? Had she felt unsafe? Threatened?

He checked his phone again—nothing. Looking for answers without talking to So-ra felt pointless. She was with Yu-jin nearly every day. Most likely she already knew why this had happened.

The rain came hard, wind snapping Min's cheap umbrella inside out, bending the metal poles like broken ribs. All around him neon popped in the darkening light, running brilliant reds and greens through the puddles and rain-streaked streets. He was lost, but he pushed on anyway, stopping at a few small storefront windows and peering inside. Everything melded together, all detail lost in the rush of rain, gutters surging, stray cats watching him tentatively from darkened cover, eyes like yellow gems in the night.

Ahead, shelter in the form of a barbecue restaurant beckoned. Smoke from smoldering charcoal and cigarettes billowed from the outside tables, where customers—couples and coworkers—sat, bent in concentration around barking grills and steaming soups. Menu in hand, a waitress appeared, offering Min a seat. He pointed to the awning. Looking a bit hurt, the girl disappeared back inside.

Min pushed his hair back from his eyes before repairing the umbrella and heading back into the rain. He needed to find something, a reason that made sense. He couldn't return home empty-handed. He didn't want to be in his apartment, with its solitude and quiet.

After another hour Min had lost hope and was walking in the direction of Anguk station when he found the restaurant. It looked identical to all the rest, except it was across the street from a burnt-orange garage door of a metal scrapping yard. He remembered being transfixed by the door when he'd sat down to eat with Yu-jin. This was the place.

Min was relieved to see the same waitress on duty. Finally, some good luck. He ordered *naengmyeon* and dried his phone with a napkin. He wasn't hungry, but all he'd had today was coffee. Better eat something, he thought, doing his best to smile as the waitress approached.

"Excuse me," he said after she put the bowl down. "Do you remember me? I was here yesterday."

She was an older woman—early sixties. "Yes, of course. Where's your girlfriend?"

"How'd you know she was my girlfriend?" Min said, sounding more suspicious than he meant.

"You can tell these things when you're my age," she said with a chuckle. "Where's she now? You shouldn't be walking around in this weather, especially with the yellow dust. It makes the rain acidic."

"That's actually what I came here about. Something's happened to her, and I'm trying to find out if there was something I missed while I was with her yesterday."

"Something you missed."

Min didn't want to say much more. What else could he say?

The waitress dropped her hands into her apron with a smile. "Not returning your calls?"

"Something like that."

"You two seemed happy. I didn't notice anything," she said before leaving the table.

We were, Min thought, bringing a spoonful of broth to his mouth. He didn't touch the buckwheat noodles or the hard-boiled egg. He wasn't sure his stomach could handle anything solid. But the beef broth was good, diluted by the melting ice chips. He checked his phone again—nothing from So-ra. Why was she shutting him out?

The rain let up while Min waited for the check. Through the window the orange door caught his attention. It seemed out of place in the muted blue of Seoul. He wondered if it was a doorway to a different reality, an escape hatch. All he had to do was walk through and be gone forever.

As a kid, he'd often done such things, spaced out, mesmerized by some object. An unripened banana, the worn tread of a tire, a naked billboard freshly stripped of its advertisement—these things fascinated Min, pulled him from his current state. "Earth to space cadet," his father would say in those moments. "Earth to space cadet," he'd repeat from across the dinner table, fork in hand, sleeves rolled to his elbows.

His father had the opposite problem, Min would realize later, an inability to see anything beyond his experience, no imagination. A neurosurgeon, he couldn't afford to imagine. His livelihood depended on it. To a maddening fault his father was logical and realistic; he did what made sense. Leave a family, start another, this time with the right woman, a white woman, a doctor from Anaheim. Min had reacted with open hostility, refusing to fly down to San Diego, even for the perfunctory holiday visits. Eventually they'd patched things up when he'd gone to college, his father footing the bill, per the divorce agreement. Min thought he was getting off easy since he qualified for in-state tuition at UCLA, but he never said anything. It was easier to keep the peace, agreeing to disagree, maintaining their truce of a thousand unsaid grievances.

A few emails or texts a month had seemed to work for them, corresponding like old pals, two actors reading their lines. But that was then. Since coming to Seoul, Min had frozen his father out, retribution for his vehement disapproval of Min's trip to Korea.

The orange door came back into focus. Yu-jin's death had put something into motion. Old memories, conjured from the depths.

Check in hand, the waitress paused by the table. "I do remember something," she said. "Something you might have missed."

It was true then; he'd overlooked a detail, a sign.

"Yesterday. When you were in the bathroom. Your girlfriend seemed sad. I only noticed because I was delivering your food at the time. She was upset. She looked shaken."

"Shaken?"

"She might have been crying."

"But when I came back," Min said, leaning closer to the waitress. "When I came back, I never noticed anything. She was fine."

The waitress frowned. It was the same face Detective Park had made when he'd said "asphyxiation."

"Women are good at hiding things," she said. "Especially from those we're closest to."

SIX

YU-JIN

Is this the way it's supposed to feel?

Through flickering pine trees the ocean slipped in and out of sight from the backseat of the car. My parents and I were heading to the beach, where we'd rented a house for the week, a reward for my admission to Ewha and my father's promotion. It was the first time I could remember that we'd gone on a lengthy vacation. In previous summers there'd been weekend camping trips or day excursions to the mountains, but we'd always hurried back on Sunday.

I tried to relax and enjoy the scenic view, the sweet aroma of *gimbap* filling the car as my mother unwrapped the rolls from the tinfoil packaging. She handed a few perfectly cut slices back to me on a paper plate and fed the rest to my father, deftly carrying each one to his mouth with wooden chopsticks while he drove. He grunted with approval, which seemed to please her. I ate a piece and chewed, the rice still warm, a hint of sesame oil sweet in my nose. Even with the prospect of an entire week at the beach ahead of me, I was restless; I couldn't get to Seoul fast enough.

All I found was freedom that week. Hours upon hours of the day when nothing was expected of me. No classes, no tutors, no cram sessions. But even as I swam in the ocean and dozed in the sun, I was restless. There was always something I could do to improve my chances of success at Ewha. Being from Gyeryong would put me at a disadvantage socially. I didn't know the first thing about becoming popular or attracting boys. University wasn't like high school; stellar academic performance wouldn't be enough. I needed to make friends and connections; I needed to be noticed and wanted.

Lucky for me, there was a boy my age at the beach that summer staying in the house next to my family's. We were sitting in rainbow-striped beach chairs, digging our heels into the sunbaked sand. With his browned skin and wind-tousled hair, it was difficult not to stare. I looked out at the ocean in mock rapture, feeling awkward in my ill-fitting one-piece bathing suit. Unlike me, this boy seemed comfortable in his skin, with his bony knees and jutting edges. While I sat rigidly in my chair, afraid a shift in position might reveal some unbecoming angle of my legs, my stomach, or chest, he seemed content to flaunt his imperfections: an oversized clavicle, a pinkish birthmark on his thigh.

Maybe it was the warm summer sun or the unblemished sky, but I found myself speaking with him freely, unencumbered by watchful eyes. It was just us. His name was Jung-woo. It turned out we were the same age, both finishing up our senior years. But when I sat next to him, heat on my sunblock-slathered cheeks, wind in my eyes, he seemed older, almost wise, nothing like Si-woo.

The ocean dazzled before us like shattered glass. Blinded, we squinted and walked down the beach, doling out tidbits of information about ourselves, rationing, making sure we didn't run out of anything to say. Even as nerves threatened to paralyze my feet in the hard-packed sand, I focused on the future: dancing at clubs with girlfriends, dates with boys from Yonsei and Korea University. I hardened my resolve and kept moving. Somewhere along the way we crept back from the water and found a hideout among the black volcanic rocks, tasting salt on each other's lips. A complete stranger, I felt oddly safe in his arms, his hands clinging to my back and hips. It was this anonymity, I knew, that drew me to him. He wasn't from Gyeryong. He'd never tell anyone if I was a bad kisser or terribly awkward. He didn't go to my school or know any of my friends. I'd never see him again; it was perfect.

"Where's it gonna be for university?" he said, leaning back against the rocks. We'd taken a moment to catch our breath. My lips tingled, the skin around my mouth raw. "I bet you're going to one of the big ones in Seoul, right?"

I didn't want to say anything, afraid any dissemination of information would disturb the fragile atmosphere we were building. I could feel it, our energy coalescing, pushing outward, surrounding us, shielding us from out there.

"I don't care where I end up," I said. "I think it's stupid. How crazy everyone gets about university. It isn't everything."

He raised an eyebrow, like he didn't believe me. And why would he? No one spoke this way; no one thought this way. At least not anyone who had a shot at going to university in Seoul.

Whether he knew I was putting on airs or not, he played along. "What's the plan then?"

"Maybe I'll become a farmer, or a movie star. You don't need a college degree for that," I said, leaning into him, his body warmed by the sun. My fingers played over his impossibly hard stomach, rising and falling like sand dunes. "What about you?"

"Same actually. It's always been my dream to be a farmer."

We laughed together, each egging the other on with the prospects of rice fields and ox dung. I didn't ask what his plans were, and we never did say where we wanted to attend university, what we wanted to study, who we wanted to become.

That night I helped my mother steam the crabs we'd picked up for dinner. We stood shoulder-to-shoulder, washing the rice and preparing the *banchan*. I was happy I could help her. During the school year I wasn't allowed in the kitchen; my only responsibility was to study. My earliest memories were of my mother cooking, hair collected in a messy bun, apron slung over her petite frame. It seemed there were endless items that required washing and dicing, pickling and braising. She worked with a silent grace, producing delicious meals for our family, never uttering a single complaint. If my father was the engine, willing us forward, forever further, my mother was the sturdy steel tracks, guiding us to safety. Whenever my father pushed too hard or lost his temper, she was always there with a mug of tea and a sweet piece of *yaksik*. Most of the time I was deserving of my father's admonishments. But there were other moments when I struggled to understand his anger, when it seemed provoked by unseen forces. There was the time at a family barbecue when I was in middle school. We'd just come back from one of our fishing trips; my father loved to take me fishing in the mountains.

Everyone was in our side yard, hovering around the grill. The men sat on plastic chairs, smoking and drinking *soju*. The meat smelled delicious, and I stayed close, hoping someone would let me try a piece before my cousins. My father seemed in good spirits, at ease in blue jeans and a white T-shirt, an outfit he rarely wore. He was listening intently to my uncle on my mother's side.

"It's great that you take Yu-jin on those trips," I heard him say, his words loose and slurred. "It's impressive she can keep up."

"What do you mean?" my father said, back straightening, neck taut.

A slack smiled formed on my uncle's lips. "You know what I mean. For being a girl and all."

The sound of my father's open palm against my uncle's face cut through the humid air. Conversation ceased. The meat sizzled. "You're not to speak of my daughter that way," my father said, his voice low. He stood, towering over my uncle. "I'd knock your teeth out if you weren't family."

My uncle glared up at my father, eyes bleary. Before he could say anything, my mother stepped between them. My father turned away, disgusted by whatever he saw. I followed him into the house and watched him fill a glass of water from the kitchen faucet. He drained the glass in one long gulp. I went to take his hand; I didn't want him to be upset.

"Why did you hit Uncle?"

"That's none of your business," he said, turning on me, eyebrows arched, finger in my face. "Disagreements between adults aren't your concern."

My lips trembled. "I just—"

"Just nothing!" my father hissed. He seized me by the shoulders and spun me to face the door. "Now go outside with the rest of the children."

I did as I was told, holding back tears while I returned to my cousins.

There were other times, too, like when I'd left my new bike out in the rain. To teach me a lesson, my father made me stand outside next to the bike while it poured. He joined me, enormous raindrops splattering the shoulder pads of his olive-green uniform.

"Toys were a luxury when I was a kid," he said after fifteen minutes. "And when we did get a toy, we didn't leave it out to get ruined; we took responsibility for it. Understood?"

I nodded, socks soaked, hair heavy. "Yes," I said.

My mother never apologized for my father's outbursts or his erratic punishments, but she helped me understand: he just wanted the best for me.

In the foreign kitchen, we had trouble finding the pots and pans we needed. My mother complained, opening drawers and cupboards—nothing was where it was supposed to be. Out on the deck, my father read his newspaper, stopping only to slap an insect that had lingered too long on his knee.

My mother began filling a large pot with water. "How can anyone relax in a stranger's home? What an odd thing to do—rent a home that isn't yours."

"I kind of like it. The beach is nice."

My mother turned off the faucet and faced me. "I'm glad, Yu-jin. I don't mean to complain. Sometimes your father just goes overboard. He got it in his head that we needed to do some big thing to celebrate."

"It's better than being in Gyeryong."

She smiled and shook her head. "You mustn't think so little about the place of your birth. True, it's not a wonderfully cultured city. It's not cosmopolitan, but it's safe. A good place to raise a family."

"What do you have against Seoul? I mean, you went to school there."

My mother glanced behind me to where my father sat. "Seoul is great," she replied wearily. "It was an exciting place to be as a university student. But it can be disorienting. It's easy to get lost, that's all."

"I don't understand. A university in Seoul was always the goal. Since I can remember, that's what we've been working toward."

"It still is. Just remember to stay focused on your studies. That's all. I want you to have fun, but academics should be your priority. It's easy to fall in love with the city and get swept up in it all."

"How would you know what it's like? You and Dad are always going on about how different everything was back when you were my age."

She embraced me. I accepted her hug, begrudgingly. "You're probably right, Yu-jin. But you're my only child, so you can forgive me if I worry over you. It's a big change, for everyone."

She released me and turned up the flame, blue and orange licking steel. I opened the bag of crabs and rolled down the crinkled sides; inside, the thorny crustaceans stirred from their frosty slumber, bound in thick rubber bands.

"Have you given any thought as to what you'll study?" my mother said.

Was she driving at something? I didn't mention how I'd promised Father to pursue the majors of his choice in exchange for my independence. "I was thinking Political Science and International Relations. But I'm not sure."

"Following in your father's footsteps then."

"It was just an idea. I don't have to declare until the end of my second year."

"Well, the hardest part's getting in," she said. "You can study whatever you want, as far as I'm concerned."

I was taken aback. With all she'd done, how she'd pushed me in everything: academics, extracurricular activities, test prep. And now here she was, saying I could study anything I wanted. "Really?"

"Within reason, of course. You still represent this family, and we expect you to act accordingly. Now get your father. Tell him I need help with dinner."

Moments later I was doubled over laughing, watching my father chase my mother around the kitchen with one of the crabs. Rubber bands removed, the claws snapped angrily at the air. "He's on the move, he's coming for you!" he shouted gleefully, lunging toward her.

With a yelp my mother ducked under his arm and ran into the living room. "Don't you dare! Don't you dare come near me with that thing," she shrieked.

Then he was coming at me, waving a second crustacean in my face. Fleeing to the living room, I tumbled to the floor in fits of laughter, cheeks aching. "Save me," I cried dramatically to my mother, who cowered in the doorway. She was deathly afraid of anything with claws. I, on the other hand, didn't mind crabs so much. Sometimes I envied them, scuttling across the silent ocean floors.

Having induced the desired effect, my father dropped his accomplices in the steamer, humming a tune to himself. With the prank over, my mother returned to the living room and sat on the couch, throwing a playfully disapproving look toward the kitchen. "You nearly scared us half to death."

Face red, eyes cheerful, my father gave her a kiss before collapsing next to me on the floor. "Only one of you, I think," he said, patting me on the head. "Yu-jin here doesn't scare easily. She was just trying to make you feel better about your phobia."

"Don't start with that again. I eat them after all, don't I?"

He held up an imaginary sword. "Only after I've vanquished them!"

It was a rare moment, perhaps brought on by the ocean air and sunshine, when my parents were completely at ease, especially my father, who spent nearly every waking hour at his office. I remember feeling grateful for their love. I knew they'd do anything for me, no matter the cost.

The good mood was short-lived. While we ate our crabs at the dinner table, my father sliced his finger on a jagged shell, bright red blood trickling into his palm. Cursing under his breath, he snatched up his whole plate, crab and all, and stuffed it into the garbage.

He was like that—slipping from amusement to anger in an instant. I could never predict which version of my father I would get. I don't remember what my mom said, if anything. What I do remember is sneaking out of the house while my parents slept, astounded by my own daring, shocked at the girl I'd become. And while I slipped through the darkened rooms and eased the front door closed, I wondered whether my mother had meant what she'd said. Could I really study whatever I wanted? And why was she so afraid of Seoul? It was just a city after all, a place to live, no matter how intoxicating.

Adrenaline propelled me down the beach, my way lit by the half-moon. Waves rolled in the semidark, and at the water's edge the sand breathed, dimpled like pancake batter. I ran faster, thinking of Jung-woo's half-naked body aglow in the buttery afternoon sun, hair like straw from the salt water. It didn't matter what I did in the here and now; soon I'd be gone forever, leaving Gyeryong behind like a bad dream, misremembered, forgotten with each passing moment.

For a brief second I thought I'd gotten the wrong spot, stopping to look around, the waves sucking sand under my feet. I was breathing hard, blood in my ears. A whisper from the rocks. Jung-woo emerged.

"You came," he said, holding two sweatshirts and a blanket. "I didn't think you were going to."

Me either, I thought to myself, slipping my arm through his.

I lay on the blanket, the stars winking in and out of view behind Jung-woo's head, his lips soft against my neck. Everything happened so quickly. It was how I wanted it to happen after all, wasn't it? Even Jung-woo seemed surprised by my willingness, my urge to have it over and done with. Did he know this? Could he tell? Fumbling with my underwear, his hands clumsy and uncertain. Sand in my hair, between my toes.

The wash of waves, skittering of hermit crabs, Jung-woo's heavy breathing—it all spilled together. Is this the way it's supposed to feel? Someone had put seashells on my ears. There was nothing but the ocean again and again, countless, immeasurable waves. Why was I holding my breath?

The first thing I thought about when he'd finished was that I'd finally done it. I'd done something of my own free will. No one had told me I *could* do it or *should* do it. I'd wanted to. I'd wanted Jung-woo. And when he asked if I was okay, I said yes, because I was. I was more than okay. For the first time in my life I knew what it was like to transgress, and it had felt better than anything I'd ever done.

SEVEN

MIN

Anywhere but here

For as long as he could remember, Min had harbored the sneaking suspicion that he didn't belong anywhere. In kindergarten, teachers puzzled aloud over his name during attendance. "Min-jun Ford, what a lovely combination." What was it that had been combined? Where did his mother start and his father end? Lance, a black boy from Culver City, was his only friend, and Min marveled over the darkness of his skin, the absoluteness of it. How he wished to have a canvas so definite, so clearly one thing.

On a middle school camping trip he'd refused to kiss a girl during a game of truth or dare, seeing the look of anxiety and fear in her eyes. Whether her trepidation was from the idea of a kiss with tongue, or simply because it was him, he would never know. Even with some ribbing from his friends, he'd refused. He grew wary of girls, unable to believe they found anything attractive about him: his slender, almost feminine hands; his straight, boring hair; his eyes that tapered ever so slightly. He was not, as the high school girls said, "hot" or "dreamy." Those terms were reserved for the few (the many).

Things changed in college. Surrounded by forty-five thousand other students at UCLA, Min quickly found he was considered worthy of attention, even attractive, by women. He started dating casually. He'd begun lifting weights, and soon his framed filled out. Gone was his round, boyish face. The bridge of his nose had grown prominent, his jaw square, like his father's, like a white man's. He played intramural sports, attended parties, aced his classes, all while straddling two lanes, distinctly aware he had both white and Asian friends. The collision of these two worlds was something Min never had to worry about. Everyone stuck to their groups, their comfort zones. Except for Min, who happily occupied the in-between for the entirety of his freshman and sophomore years. He saw no issue; it was his biology after all. Then friend groups became more serious, couples formed, spring break vacations were planned, internships sought, and soon Min found himself stuck, forced to choose an identity, a single spyglass through which to gaze.

While attending a party for Young Asian Entrepreneurs, he overheard a group of girls bemoaning his unavailability. He only went for "blond bimbos," as they called them. At the time he was dating a girl from Orange County. Tiffany was blond; bimbo she was not. They'd met during an indoor club soccer game. Everything had been going well between them, except that he'd recently visited her during their winter break, which resulted in an awkward moment when her father thought he was the gardener's son.

A year later he was dating a Korean girl from Tiburon who adored him for his "not-so-Korean-ness," as she called it. He was the perfect combination: Korean enough so she never had to explain herself and

American (white) enough that he didn't expect her to wait on him hand and foot like all the other Korean guys she'd dated. He had progressive ideas about gender roles; he was a feminist! Things had gone well until Min revealed he was agnostic. During their protracted breakup, Grace said her parents would never approve of a marriage to someone who didn't believe in Christ. It seemed there were limits to how much "not-so-Korean-ness" Grace could tolerate.

Afterwards, Min couldn't avoid the fact there'd always be some underlying issues with whomever he dated. Not because of them, but because of him, because he'd never wanted to decide which world to occupy. He'd never wanted to choose which half to be.

So with the vaguest of desires to leave Los Angeles—because leaving at least gave him a chance to reinvent himself, to shed the skins he'd inhabited for too long—he got a job in New York City after college, no small feat considering he'd graduated into what his aggrieved classmates were referring to as the Great Recession. Despite the dearth of entry-level jobs, Min had been presented with multiple offers, which he credited to his near-perfect grades and maddeningly useful Economics and Marketing double major. After brief consideration he'd decided it was time for a change. Growing up, he'd often thought Los Angeles fake, unnatural, a place where no one should be living; whereas "the City," as everyone referred to it, felt authentic, rich with history. And he might have survived the first year out of college—living with two roommates in Murray Hill—if it hadn't been for his job.

What Min failed to account for was the backwardness of the East Coast, with its archaic traditions and old-monied ways. He quickly realized New York City would pose the same challenges he'd experienced at home, except they were more intense, more troubling. On crowded sidewalks or subway platforms, he was safe, one with the masses. But once he entered the office on Monday morning, he felt like a different species, one to wonder at in a museum, pick over. His job at the hypercompetitive marketing firm immediately proved difficult. The slights from his colleagues were never major, nothing he could report to human resources. It was always small stuff. Moments that, upon reflection, appeared harmless or unintended. The disappearance of his coffee mug from the break room, receiving interoffice memos addressed to the only other minority on the floor, people on his team forgetting to cc him on emails.

Not one to complain, he'd taken it all in stride, telling himself that none of it was personal. It was work after all. It was important to keep things professional. But it was worse at social events: happy hours and holiday parties. His colleagues spoke about college a great deal; it seemed they'd all gone to boarding school together, that they'd known one another from birth. He learned an entire new vocabulary. Words like "Nantucket," "Choate," "après-ski," "Delta Kappa Epsilon," "Barbour," and "bocce." After hearing a phrase or word he didn't recognize, Min would excuse himself to the bathroom and write it down in a slender black notebook so he could look it up later, wondering if his mother had done the same thing after meeting his father. He was astounded by the sheer amount of information he didn't know. He hadn't led an overly sheltered life; his parents weren't poor. Until New York, he'd considered himself privileged.

This, however, wasn't the case, proven by his inability to produce a vacation destination or trendy restaurant recommendation that impressed his peers. When people asked him where he was from (no, where he was *really* from), or where he'd gone to school, they didn't seem to know what to make of it, of him. Mostly they just shrugged and said they liked the East Coast better. Everyone was too relaxed out West. No one worked. They'd go crazy if they ever lived there. Sure, it was good for a vacation, but nothing else. Min found himself growing defensive despite agreeing with the criticisms. They were the very reasons he'd left.

In his job, his diligence and hard work seemed to alienate rather than endear him to his peers. He was too severe. Too assiduous. Too meticulous. On more than one occasion he heard his fellow team members bemoaning his inability to relax. Have fun. Did he ever smile? Some nights Min would spend hours in front of the mirror, cursing his mother's solemn Asian face.

After a year, it was almost a relief when human resources called him in, letting him know a complaint had been filed against him. From whom, they couldn't say. Involving what, they alluded to an instance where Min had made a joke they said crossed a boundary. Having no recollection of the moment, he asked a few clarifying questions, but the HR officer, a young woman with black hair pulled into a serious-looking ponytail, could only say he'd made some of his team members deeply uncomfortable.

Min didn't bother to ask what would happen next and quit on the spot. After clearing out his desk, he thanked his boss for the opportunity and didn't look back. He was tired of trying to fit in, pretending to be someone he wasn't, or worse, someone he loathed. He didn't know what he'd thought New York would be like, what marketing would be like, but it hadn't been this.

He'd saved up enough money to take a few months off and figure things out, but even as he packed up his room and bought a plane ticket back home, he wondered if he was just running again, hoping a change of scenery would change him. If his mother shared his trepidation regarding his return, she didn't show it, greeting him with home-cooked meals and motherly attention. If she was anxious about his unemployment, she kept it to herself, spending the majority of her time shuttling between community centers in Koreatown.

Predictably, his father's reaction had been more alarmist. "You can't just give up when something gets difficult," he'd said, in a rare phone call. "You know how many times I wanted to quit in medical school?"

Min didn't have the energy to explain that he wasn't giving up; he was just trying to figure out his life. But soon enough he felt trapped again, hemmed in by perfect palm trees, surrounded by familiar faces from high school and college. New York City had been the farthest point possible from what he'd known, yet it had rendered the same result. There was some deficiency in his character, Min concluded. Why else would he have failed so spectacularly in New York, struggling to make friends, dreading Friday and Saturday nights? Why else would he have insisted on playing football, a sport he was never any good at? Why else would he have resented the foul-smelling *kimchi* in the school lunches his mother packed for him, the Korean language lessons she insisted he take, every white-and-Asian couple he'd see?

So, with a ninety-day tourist visa freshly pressed into the pages of his passport, Min boarded a one-way flight from LAX to Incheon International Airport. It was his mother who'd encouraged him to finally take the trip: he could see where his great-grandfather was buried; he could finally put those language lessons to use. She didn't speak Korean herself. Her father had seen to the gradual scrubbing away of the family's heritage, all in the name of assimilation. But that's the way it had been for the first wave of immigrants. You either bought into the American dream and survived, or you clung to nostalgia and died—at least that's what Min remembered his grandfather telling him on their drives up Route 1, the Pacific on their left, California sunshine dancing off the hood of his freshly waxed Thunderbird. He'd loved America: the cars, the beaches, golf, tennis, cheeseburgers, and drive-throughs. And when he got around to raising a family in Los Angeles, well, speaking Korean was the last thing on his mind.

It was strange, to realize the language had somehow skipped a generation—his mother and her two sisters—and picked back up with Min. Nobody from his mother's generation had ever been to Korea. It wasn't that they weren't interested; the interest had just never been cultivated.

Min wanted to do what his mother had not: see the birthplace of this language he spoke, consume the collective culture he'd hated like bittersweet chocolate. He wanted to understand the parts of himself that made him so decidedly un-American.

When it came time to tell his father about his plans, Min had waited until the last possible moment to call him, just before takeoff. Fearing he wouldn't understand why he was leaving, Min tried to frame his trip as a career change. "There are a ton of professional opportunities in Seoul," he'd said as announcements echoed through the cabin.

"What's wrong with the jobs here? What's this really about?"

Min struggled to find the right words. How could he explain a feeling his father had never felt? "I want to see what it's like in Korea," was all he managed.

"You're too old to be gallivanting around Asia, Min," his father said. "It's time to get serious."

"I am being serious," Min said, wincing apologetically at the stewardess for raising his voice. "This is the first serious thing I've done in a long time."

"Well, it's irresponsible, if you ask me."

Min had hung up on him, bitter and aggrieved. He hadn't expected his father to understand why he needed to go, but that hadn't stopped Min from hoping he might. And so he'd arrived in Seoul possessed by a desperate hope of finally belonging to something, a place where his defects weren't defects at all, but qualities he might share with an entire country. He quickly found a job, ensuring he could stay well beyond his ninety days. And after meeting Yu-jin, a local, a woman content in her skin, in the places she inhabited, Min shook off the memories of his supposed deficiencies, his shapeless existence. With Yu-jin, everything was different. He was American through and through for her, no matter how well he spoke her language, no matter how flawlessly he used his chopsticks. And Min found relief in absolute classification from this woman with thick black hair and a perfectly rounded face. They were honest with each other about their expectations, their situations. They were realistic with each other about the expiration date of their time together. It wasn't love; they'd never pretended it would be. And from this came a deeper understanding, a companionship, an honesty about who they were, who they wanted to become.

But perhaps he'd been mistaken, about everything. Perhaps there was still something wrong with him, a deficiency. Why else would this have happened? Why else would she be gone? Min wondered standing outside Yu-jin's apartment building.

It felt like years had passed since he'd been there that same morning, like time had rushed forward. In the streetlight-dappled darkness, he hardly recognized the edifice, looming and treacherous.

After punching the eleventh-floor button, he leaned into the corner of the elevator, heavy with fatigue. I know better than some waitress, he thought. I would have noticed if something had upset her. More baffling, he'd never seen Yu-jin cry, except during the occasional movie. But she'd never let it all go in front of him, a fact he now remembered very clearly.

On the walk over he'd messaged So-ra, tired of her avoidance: You can't ignore me. I'm coming over. I've got a right to know what's going on.

I won't be shut out, Min decided, floors dinging by like a pinball machine. I was her boyfriend. That has to amount to something, even if I never met her parents. It wasn't a fling. Something's gone very wrong, and I'm the only one taking it seriously. No one's asking the right questions, looking in the right places. And where is So-ra in all this? She should be looking for answers, too.

Fluorescent lights flickered in the hallway, walls a sickly green, floors immaculately buffed, Min's footsteps unnervingly loud. Ear to the door, he heard the brush of slippered feet moving inside the apartment. He knocked and listened. "I know you're there, So-ra," he said, knocking again. "Open up."

The shuffling stopped.

"I'm not leaving until you open the door."

Min rested his full weight against the door. Dealing with the incompetent detective, trying to extract information from Misaki, searching for nonexistent answers in the rain—Min found himself with only more questions, more doubt than certainty.

He remembered Detective Park's business card, how he'd dug it into his palm. He remembered Yu-jin's wry smile, her voice in the rain, her legs between his sheets. He remembered he'd never know her like that again. He remembered he might have never known her at all.

Fists balled, he pounded on the door, a stranger's voice churning in his chest. "What kind of friend are you? How can you believe what the police are saying?"

Back against the door, Min slid to the linoleum floor, favoring his good shoulder. He shook out his hand, already purpling, broken capillaries blinking through the skin. Heavy with fatigue, Min submitted, head throbbing, feet aching as he unlaced his shoes and peeled off his socks, toes pale as paper. Legs pulled to his chest, he rested his head on his forearms. If So-ra wasn't going to answer the door, he'd wait for her. She'd have to leave eventually.

※

A sharp pain in his side jolted Min awake. Someone was trying to open the door. He struggled to his feet and turned around, only to find Misaki's frightened face in the slit of the doorway. He reached for the handle, but she yanked the door shut.

"So-ra isn't here," she said, her voice muffled and small. "I already told you. Please just go away."

It hadn't occurred to Min that So-ra wasn't at the apartment. He suddenly felt foolish for making a scene. "Where is she then?"

"She's staying with someone at Ewha," Misaki said.

He imagined Misaki on the other side of the door, fingers tugging the cuffs of her tweed blazer. "Will you be okay staying by yourself tonight?"

"Why wouldn't I be?"

"I just thought you might feel funny about sleeping in the apartment."

"Just go away. Please."

Min was ashamed for the way he'd treated Misaki. Here she was alone in an apartment where one of her roommates had died, and he'd left her, caught up in his grief, his quest for the truth. And now he'd come back, banging down the door, asking for someone she wasn't, demanding answers she didn't have. He quickly gathered up his socks and mumbled something like an apology.

On the way home he stopped at a bodega. The cashier, a young high school kid, ignored him, glasses aglow from his cell phone, thumbs drumming furiously on the screen. Selecting two twenty-four-ounce cans of Hite—the best beer Korea had to offer, which wasn't saying much—he perused the clinically clean aisles, hints of bleach blooming underfoot. In addition to the beers, he got a bag of dried squid. At the cash register the kid rang him up with one hand, lightning quick.

"Can I get a pack of Cloud 9s, too?"

Min never smoked, but Yu-jin had occasionally. Cloud 9 was the only brand she'd ever bought. He'd never bothered to ask her why; he'd merely tolerated the habit.

"Those are women's cigarettes," the boy said, turning up the volume on his phone.

Min didn't say anything. Too beat to be angry. He was just a teen-ager, off in his own world. Min was jealous in a way.

With exaggerated effort the boy paused the game and turned around, craning his neck to find Min's request. Locating the box, he took it down and rested it on top of the beer cans. "That all?" he said, glancing at his phone.

At home, Min opened a beer and spread the dried squid out on its plastic packaging. The studio felt more claustrophobic than usual, just four steps from the bed to the stove. He still hadn't gotten around to decorating the peach-hued walls. With his salary from Samsung, he could have afforded a much nicer apartment, but he hadn't seen the point. He'd never spent much time at home, especially after meeting Yu-jin. She'd always joked that the place looked like a prison. That didn't feel far off now.

Min thought about Misaki, alone in that apartment, surrounded by darkness. He wondered what she was doing at that exact moment. Yu-jin's death had shifted something inside him. An enormous steel lid had lifted, beneath it a dark and cavernous opening.

He unwrapped the Cloud 9s from their packaging and tugged at one of the pencil-thin cigarettes. *Just one, and you can go anywhere*, the slogan read on the front of the box in cyan script. Anywhere, he thought. Why had he never smoked one with Yu-jin? Why hadn't he asked her why she smoked them? He lay in bed, unlit cigarette be-tween his lips. Inhaling. He imagined tasting the menthol and floral smoke. Imagined the smoke curling up from his lips, her lips, around his nostrils, over his eyes, her eyes. So this was Cloud 9. This was how she'd felt. Just one, and you can go anywhere. Anywhere, he thought, exhaling, perfumed smoke swirling around us. Anywhere but here.

Min closed his eyes, brief moments of blissful nothingness, only to find himself on top of his sheets an hour later, mouth dry and stale, moonlight pushing through the shade, his phone vibrating. The message was from So-ra: Sorry, I just saw your calls. Let's meet at that café near Ewha around 11. The one we usually go to.

EIGHT

YU-JIN

My light, my flare

Seoul was everything. The city churned with a kind of Technicolor effervescence, a civilization in orchestrated chaos. For the first time I was a part of something bigger than myself. I was a microscopic organism, a molecule, a speck, a chip on a motherboard, blinking away with all the other lights, burning up the grid. And I imagined that grid of lights witnessed from space. A yellow crossword puzzle glittering with brilliant expectation.

I was where I was meant to be, living the life I was supposed to live. I began looking back on my time in Gyeryong as a mistake, a mix-up in the sorting. Here, in Seoul—this was where I belonged. And it wasn't just the city itself. It was Ewha, with its expansive quads framed by lush foliage, turning brilliant oranges and reds, the entire student body buzzing with a sense of purpose. But it wasn't merely for the grades like in high school. These women seemed driven by something bigger, something more abstract: a quest for power, strength. And I was in the middle of it all, with So-ra.

A few weeks prior to my arrival on campus, I'd received an email letting me know I'd matched with So-ra. According to a survey we'd taken earlier that summer about our living habits, we were a 98 percent match, which seemed impossibly thrilling. Since we were both already in Seoul, we decided to meet for the first time the night before orientation. So-ra had nixed my suggestion of meeting in the student center for a bakery off campus. By the time I arrived, it was nearly deserted, pale storefront light leaking out into the darkness. Through the window I could see So-ra seated at a small circular table, chin resting in her palm while she read a book. My throat tightened. What if she didn't think I was cool? What if she realized I didn't know the first thing about living in a big city?

So-ra stood up when I entered, fixing me with a pensive smile. "I hope this place is all right," she said. "I got you a croissant."

I thanked her and sat down. "What're you reading?"

"Poetry. Have you ever read Elizabeth Bishop? I've been on a real American-and-European-poet kick lately."

My back stiffened. Within seconds of our meeting, I was already going to prove my illiteracy. "I haven't. Are you reading it for a class?"

If So-ra thought I was uncultured, she didn't let on. "Just for fun. I've always wanted to get out of Korea and travel. This is as close as I can get right now," she said. "I'll lend it to you when I'm finished."

I'd never met anyone my age who read things for fun, let alone poetry. We read for comprehension, for essays and exams. Sitting down, I tried not to feel intimidated. Like me, she was on the taller side, but that's where the similarities stopped. Her body was a compact spring, tightly wound; not an inch of space had been wasted in her creation. Under her black jean jacket, her shoulders were broad and imposing, held aloft with perfect posture, as if a steel rod ran up her back. Across from her, I felt insignificant, wafer-thin. "I haven't read much poetry," I mustered. "It would probably go over my head."

So-ra arched her neck and laughed brightly. "Who cares," she said, looking around at the customer-less tables. "That's not the point. I'd go crazy if I stopped reading or doing things just because they didn't make sense right away. Plus, we got into Ewha. We're smart!"

Her laugh seemed to break the spell. I relaxed in my seat and took a bite of the croissant, buttery and rich. We stayed in the bakery until closing time, speaking freely about our expectations and hopes for the coming year. So-ra was ecstatic when I told her I was from Gyeryong. People from Seoul were stuck-up, she said. She was from Busan, and even though it was a metropolitan city, she'd already been teased for her southern dialect. We were both outsiders then, striving to find our way. So-ra was convinced that destiny had placed me at Ewha, in Seoul, rooming with her. There was no chance or randomness. Fate—that was all. So-ra, with her bold confidence, those dark, untroubled eyes. She was my guide, my bridge across the terrifying chasm that was freshman year. And during those first months of school, I found myself confiding in her, all my doubts and fears late into the night, the words flying from me, up to the top bunk where she lay quietly, listening. And slowly, cautiously, So-ra opened up to me. Told me the future she saw for herself.

Me.

Someone who'd never known friendship, true friendship. I'd been all-consumed, zeroed in, a bullet train flying down the tracks. But

I'd reached the station. I could afford to slow down, see what lay beyond the glass.

From a big city, So-ra was at ease in the endless bustle of Seoul as we explored together, piece by piece, nook by nook. The metro, with its infinite serpentine, crisscrossing lines, the staggering office buildings that negated all sense of direction, the hordes of silver taxicabs and screaming scooters. More than once she took my hand, plunging down an escalator to catch a departing train, burrowing through the masses, plowing ahead, landing us safely inside the car, the doors sucking closed behind us.

"Are you sure this is the right direction?" I said, a few weeks into my time at Ewha. We were exploring a new neighborhood that So-ra had heard about from a classmate.

"And if it isn't?" she said, catching her bag before it slid off her shoulder. "Then we get lost. Worse things have happened."

My anxiety dispersed, dust in the air. Any fear, any trepidation I had about the city I'd moved to, evaporated with So-ra. Her spontaneity and willingness to make mistakes—it was a quality I'd never known. And we did get lost—that day and many others. But we always found our way.

That brisk October day in Seongsu-dong, we discovered a café that had been converted from an old printing warehouse. We sat at one of the outside tables with our coffees and watched the passersby. It was quickly becoming one of our favorite activities: people watching. So-ra was more accustomed to the large crowds, whereas I was still impressed with the limitless energy that seemed to leak from every pore and crack of the city.

"Have you found someone to mark you present for chapel?" So-ra said.

I hadn't. The daily chapel services were required by Ewha, as we were technically a Christian institution. It seemed like the services were just a formality. Despite being vaguely Buddhist, my parents hadn't considered religion an important part of my upbringing. Family was what mattered most, the unit. Still, my parents, especially my father, seemed to think Ewha's Christian affiliation was a plus, even if it was only superficial. I think he thought it would make the students more conservative. It didn't.

So-ra smiled mischievously, taking a long sip of her latte, keeping the white foam petal intact. "What. You've been going to all those?"

"I thought it was required."

"It is, but you can always find someone to check your name off. I can't stand those sermons. They're so dull."

I hadn't exactly enjoyed the morning services, although there was a social aspect I appreciated. I didn't think anyone attended them expecting spiritual enlightenment. It was all pretty vanilla: be mindful, be nice, be respectful. But skipping out, well, that was something I'd never considered.

So-ra was like that, bold and daring, even reckless. I was drawn to it, this strange new way of looking at the world. "I better find someone," I said, thrilled by the idea of skipping something mandatory.

So-ra slid her sunglasses down her nose, fixing me with a dramatic stare. "So easily corrupted," she said, before breaking into a laugh.

The more I got to know her, the more impressed I was with her imperishable desire for something else. Never satisfied with how things *were* or how others thought they *should be*, she was always interested in what was yet to come, what could be, the impossible.

I was surprised she was willing to risk any sort of probation for skipping service, considering she was on full scholarship at Ewha. An accomplished dancer, she'd attracted several offers from top university dance programs. Her parents had pushed her to dance, much in the way mine had pushed me to study. I'd never met anyone who'd focused so singularly on something other than academics, let alone dancing. I found myself struggling to imagine what exactly it was that So-ra did. Images of ballerinas in frilly tutus came to mind, but she assured me her brand of dancing was something entirely different. "It's modern dance," she said, which still didn't help me very much.

How different her life had been from mine! Honing her natural abilities, pushing her body to its physical limits. She knew what it meant to feel alive, to declare one's existence to the world, emphatically. I'd done the same, but my process had been cerebral, invisible to the casual observer. Still, in our own ways, we'd dedicated our lives to the single pursuit of something. And I imagined So-ra felt exactly like me in those first months of university, that we'd passed into some golden, undetermined sphere of our friendship where anything was possible.

We spent the rest of the day sitting outside the café, watching the best of what Seoul had to offer stream by: the businessmen and -women in their sharply tailored suits, the couples in matching outfits, the street sweepers and the occasional beggar. All of it was simultaneously glamorous and crude, overwhelming my senses. Fresh colors had been splashed across my palette, and I saw just how bland and boring my life in Gyeryong had been. But that was all going to change now, I thought, with So-ra alongside me. With her, I'd experience it all. She was my guide, my light, my flare.

A few weeks later, my parents took us out to dinner; they'd said I should bring So-ra along. They were living in Pyeongchang-dong, a small, upscale residential neighborhood at the foot of the Bugak Mountains. According to my mother, it was a quiet, wooded area with large, single-family homes, a rarity in the city. I hadn't visited, mostly in the hope that I'd forget they, too, lived in Seoul. Sometimes when I was out walking the streets with So-ra, I'd be seized with the fear they were watching me, surveilling my every move. It was paranoia, of course. With nearly fifty million people in Seoul, I was secure in my anonymity.

"What should I wear to dinner?" So-ra said, toweling off her hair in front of the mirror.

I rolled over in bed, slinging my arm over the side. "Whatever you want."

"You can't be serious. Do you even know where we're going?"

"Somewhere in Gangnam."

"Then we definitely aren't wearing whatever," So-ra said, moisturizing her toned legs.

I envied them. No matter how much time I spent running, I wouldn't get those legs. It was genetic, the way her muscles responded to her commands.

"What does your dad do again?"

"Something in government," I said. What could I tell her? He'd been handpicked by the President? He was responsible for every military branch in Korea? In truth that was all I knew. My mother had forbidden me from pestering him with questions.

"You don't even know what he does?"

"What's with all the questions?" I said, sitting up. "I don't know anything about *your* family."

So-ra focused on her makeup. "I just thought I should know some stuff. They're paying for the dinner after all. And seriously, you're not wearing just anything. It's in Gangnam. It's gonna be a fancy restaurant."

She was right, of course. She always was.

When we walked into the upscale, Western-style steak house, I was infinitely thankful to her for making me change out of my jeans and shabby flats. Teetering on ten-story wedges, the hostess led us to the back of the restaurant, through the black-and-silver twinkle of Seoul's most ostentatious couples, sipping their Italian reds, savoring their Kobe steaks. No such place existed in Gyeryong. I'd never been so close to such glamour and opulence.

Joining them in a rounded booth, I was astounded at the change in my parents from only a few months ago. My mother was radiant, her cheeks a tawny bronze, shining out against the impenetrable blackness of her freshly dyed hair. With matching diamond earrings and necklace, she was almost unrecognizable—vibrant, full of life, like she'd been supercharged by the city itself. My father's transformation was of a different kind, everything in his features more severe and gaunt, chin jutting, jawline angular. His once gray-speckled crew cut had gone completely silver. Deep creases streaked across his forehead. Despite his weatherworn features, his eyes were piercing as ever, resting deep in their cavernous sockets.

None of this registered with So-ra, of course. To her they were just my parents. They were as they seemed. What had changed them? I wondered, as the hostess took our jackets and presented us with a hand-typed menu on dreamy, eggshell-white paper.

As I introduced So-ra to my parents and droned on—about my challenging classes, the dorm, the beautiful campus, the impeccable professors—a gloomy suspicion slunk around me, a startling realization that my parents had always been this way, and I was only noticing now for the first time. I had changed, not them. Perhaps now that I had lived in Seoul, away from them and Gyeryong, I was seeing them, really seeing them, for the first time.

I don't know how we got on the subject during our dinner conversation. I don't know why there was suddenly a seismic shift, a fissure running down the center of the table, So-ra and I on one side, my parents on the other. I was torn, wondering where my loyalties should lie.

"Excuse me?" my father was saying, his eyes gone wide, tucking his napkin into the crisp collar of his button-down shirt.

So-ra put down her knife and fork and looked at me. Was it an *I'm sorry*? Or a *Watch this*?

"I just don't see very much use for a university education. I'm grateful. But it seems that if parents really wanted the best for their children, they'd let them do whatever they wanted."

My mother sipped her white wine.

"That's ridiculous. Preposterous even," my father said. "As parents we are responsible for our children. It's our duty to look out for them, to give them everything they need to succeed. To help them make decisions. Certainly your parents feel the same way."

"I think they do," So-ra mused. "They just went about it differently. They never made me do anything I didn't want to. I mean, sure, they introduced me to dance, perhaps even pushed me, but it's my passion. If I said I didn't want to do something, that was it, end of discussion."

I'd never heard anyone say these kinds of things, let alone to an elder. So-ra was brash, even defiant. She was, of course, criticizing my parents, not openly but implicitly. I couldn't remember telling

So-ra much about my family life, but she must have picked things up. Tidbits. About how I'd always been on a path, a ladder, each step honed and crafted.

But why was she saying all this now? What did it matter how I'd been raised?

Taken aback by her tone, I hardly had a chance to be angry with her. And even if I was upset, I couldn't take my eyes away from whatever was happening: my father quietly incensed; my mother blithe, even entertained. I wondered if something had shifted between them since their move to Seoul. They regarded each other like politicians on a debate stage, guarded smiles, politeness painted across their faces. Absent were the knowing glances between them, references to some past intimacy I could never know. Were they just each other's ladders now, steps to power and fortune?

"Education is the bedrock of this country," my father was saying, skin taut over his cheekbones. "We have one of the highest percentages of college graduates of developed countries. Because of education, because of our striving, we've raised ourselves out of economic ruin. Because of our parents and their parents before them, we overcame war, poverty, famine—hardships you can't possibly begin to imagine."

I'd rarely heard my father speak of his adolescence, growing up in the rubble of the Korean War, bearing witness to his country's destruction and the formalizing of its division, a fracture initiated by the Soviets and Americans after World War II. The two superpowers drawing a line across the peninsula like children in a sandbox, demarcating North and South, right and wrong, righteous and wicked. Previously I'd only heard snippets, fragments, but So-ra had angered him, pulled the pin.

"Forgive me. I didn't mean to be disrespectful."

"It's not about respect," my father said, looking at So-ra. "It's about understanding your history. If you don't know what's come before, you cannot speak with any authority on the current state of the country."

Everyone at the table was quiet. I was thankful when the servers brought our entrées. My father seemed to welcome the opportunity to recuse himself from the conversation when his steak arrived, bowing his head in concentration, meticulously shearing the fat from his porterhouse.

"So how are you two getting along at Ewha? Do they still have those tedious services in the morning?" my mother said, her smile full of mischief.

Even though he remained silent through the rest of the meal, I couldn't ignore my father's presence. Silent and brooding, his menacing silhouette lingered in the dimming candlelight and hushed table talk. Gone was the cheerful man who'd treated me to ice cream. My mother paid him no attention, buoyant on her plush cushion, luxuriating among diners' flirtatious whispers and silverware clinking to long-forgotten rules of etiquette.

I realized my father and perhaps my mother had always wanted this: Seoul, the status, the wealth. He'd hated Gyeryong, with its common dinginess, just as much as I had.

When he went to the restroom, my mother scanned the tables around us before speaking. "He's under immense pressure, you two understand. National Minister of Defense is no small undertaking. The job comes with unthinkable responsibility. Every day he makes decisions that impact every one of us. He even has his own security detail."

"His own security?" I said, feeling foolish. My father was even more important than I'd thought. If So-ra was eager to say, I told you so, she didn't show it.

When he returned, my father seemed more relaxed, smiling and jocular. He even asked So-ra a few questions about the dance program at Ewha. At the end of the meal, we ordered lavender crème brûlée. So-ra talked about her dance classes and upcoming show. I told my father about the introductory classes I was taking in government and political science, which pleased him. By the end of the night we were ready to burst, brimming with wine and steak. Outside the restaurant we said our goodbyes. I looked for my father's security team but couldn't make anyone out in the darkness. My mother hugged So-ra first, then me, wishing us luck in our classes. My father stood a few steps away, observing us. "Be good," he said, "and a pleasure to meet you, So-ra."

"Thank you for dinner, and sorry again about . . ."

My father waved down a taxi as it was passing. "Let's speak no more of it."

Unaccustomed to the heavy food, I felt drugged and leaned on So-ra as we piled into a cab, giggling in delirium. The car whisked us off, back to the dorms, into the deepening night.

NINE

MIN

Two boulders in a stream

Min woke to a memory. He was flying down a mountain, skis strapped to his feet, wind in his face. Ahead, Yu-jin and So-ra weaved back and forth down the snowy mountainside, moving in tandem, curving figure eights in the fresh powder. Min struggled to keep up as they sped ahead. "Come on," Yu-jin had shouted, before diving out of sight.

He'd never realized what good skiers they were until that weekend in late December. They were waiting for him at the bottom of the hill, goggles atop helmets, noses ruby red. Yu-jin was laughing at something So-ra was saying, puffs of steam rising from their black mufflers. Min offered to stay behind at the lodge while they got in some runs on their own. While So-ra seemed grateful, briskly skiing off to the chairlift line, Yu-jin hesitated, poles thrust into the hard-packed snow. "You sure? We can call it a day."

"Go, go," Min said. "I've slowed you down enough already."

He watched them catch the lift together, side by side, whisked up into the flurries of snow. That night in the lodge, Min and Yu-jin lay in bed, the moon casting winter light across the floor of the bedroom. From the other room, So-ra's snores punctuated the silence. Beyond the walls and roof, only the wind in the snow-covered pines. Accustomed to the chaotic noise of Seoul, Min was wired, unable to sleep.

"You know," Yu-jin whispered, sliding her leg between his, her skin soft as soapstone. "Even by Korean standards, we've waited a long time."

"Have you ever waited this long?"

Yu-jin laughed into his neck, her lips wet. "God, no. I'm not some kind of prude." On top of him, she gathered the sheets around her shoulders, lowering herself. "I just didn't want you thinking I was easy."

"I wouldn't have."

"I know," she said, kissing him. "But I wanted to make sure."

What had that meant? The memory disturbed him, looking back through the prism of her death. It hadn't bothered him at the time. But now, it seemed odd. She'd gone out of her way to present herself a certain way.

Min read So-ra's text message again: Sorry, I just saw your calls. Let's meet at that café near Ewha around 11. The one we usually go to.

No acknowledgment of what had happened, just a cursory apology and a poor excuse for ignoring him.

Out the window, the moon lay high in the sky, a glaring white spotlight against the night. Min thought about Misaki and how terribly he'd treated her. It pained him to remember her face through the crack in the door: terrified and bewildered. Consumed with grief, he'd never stopped to consider Misaki's well-being. Guilt pooling in his chest, he scrolled through his phone for her number—he needed to make amends—only to realize he didn't have it. There'd never been a reason to contact her.

He slept fitfully, sweating through his sheets, the sounds of the city penetrating his dreams. In the early hours of morning he awoke again, gasping for air, clutching at his throat. Maybe this was how Yu-jin had felt, shrouded in darkness—an endless sea of black looking back at her. Where was she now? Was there a moon for her to look at?

⫼

Before meeting So-ra, Min decided to stop by the apartment to see Misaki. In the sobering midmorning sun, he saw the ugliness of how he'd treated her. He needed to make things right. To his surprise, she let him in right away when he buzzed the apartment, opening the door and motioning him inside while she chatted away on the phone. Min could hardly believe her transformation. She wore high-waisted black dress pants and a tight black turtleneck. Gone were the funky street clothes, the endless mishmash of layers and fabrics. Her hair had changed color again, too: black, to match her outfit. While he sat on the couch, Misaki was a blur as she moved through the apartment, taking a yogurt from the fridge, tossing a phone charger, flats, and makeup case into a handbag, all while carrying on in Japanese. He struggled to square these two versions of Misaki.

"Sorry," Misaki said after she'd hung up. "My brother's always checking up on me. He thinks he's my protector or something. Do you have any siblings?"

If she harbored any ill will toward Min for the previous night, she didn't show it. "Only child, I'm afraid."

"I guess that makes sense," Misaki said, turning her attention to the shoe closet. After some rummaging, she emerged with a pair of black high heels.

"What does that mean?"

Shoes dangling from her fingertips, Misaki considered his question. She looked him up and down, as if she might discern the answer right then and there. "I just got a vibe. You seem independent."

"You're living in a foreign country on your own, too."

"It's different for you," she said, slipping on her heels. "I have to get to work. The lock is still on Yu-jin's door if that's why you're here."

Min stood up, oddly nervous. "I actually came to apologize for last night. I didn't mean to freak you out. I never even asked if you were okay. I was just fixated on Yu-jin."

Misaki looked down, toeing the entryway tile. "It's okay. I'd be upset, too, but I really have to go. I can't be late. I'm opening the store this morning."

As they left the apartment and rode the elevator down together, Min grew more curious. He'd never realized Misaki had a job. He watched the illuminated numbers flicker and die, each floor swooping by. Why was she working? She didn't need the money. Yu-jin and So-ra had told him she came from a wealthy family in Tokyo. It didn't make sense. She wasn't even legally allowed to be employed in Korea on a student visa.

At the metro station they said their goodbyes, standing still in the crush of commuters, like two boulders in a stream. "Like I said before," Min said, "I'm really sorry. The way I acted—it wasn't cool."

"Really, it's no big deal," Misaki said. "You don't need to apologize, but I appreciate it. You're so considerate. I'm sure that's why Yu-jin liked you so much."

With that she was gone, and Min was left to ponder the growing mysteries of Misaki. On his way to meet with So-ra, he tried to recall in perfect detail everything that had occurred with Yu-jin the night before her death. It was important his mind was clear. And yet, standing in the crowded subway car, jockeying for position between business suits and grungy sweatshirts, dog-eared newspapers and swinging headphones, he struggled to keep everything straight. Like a perfume, his conversation with Misaki clung to him. Even while he went through his list of questions, the obscurity of her origins, the discovery of her job, dropped a veil over his recollections. She'd said his situation was different, even though they were both foreigners in Korea. What had she meant?

Approaching his stop, Min pushed Misaki from his thoughts and focused on the task at hand. He was eager to speak with So-ra. Things were finally going to start making some sense.

Upon entering the café, Min struggled to reconcile the So-ra he'd known with the So-ra sitting before him. In skinny white jeans and an oversized T-shirt, she looked tired and worn down, her eyes twitching and frantic under a straight line of black bangs.

"I'm sorry about yesterday," she said. "I needed to be alone. I don't think I have the energy to cry anymore."

"Me neither," Min said, relieved. There was an explanation for her behavior after all. She was in mourning.

They sat, not saying anything, watching the Friday crowd spill past. It was difficult for Min not to stare at her, hair knotted, eyelids nearly swollen shut, fingernails chewed to nothing. It seemed he wasn't the only one who'd had trouble sleeping.

"You must have a lot of questions," she said after looking around the café.

"Don't you? The police have some crazy theory about stress and academic pressure. I tried to tell them that wasn't possible, but they wouldn't listen, and Misaki claims Yu-jin didn't get home until past midnight."

Straw between her chapped lips, So-ra took a long sip of iced coffee. She seemed to be concentrating on something. "Misaki told you that?"

"When I stopped by the apartment yesterday."

"Figures. She's always getting into everyone's business."

Min wasn't sure what she meant.

So-ra brushed away an imaginary haze. "I met Yu-jin for drinks that night. After she saw you. But then she said she needed a book from the library to study."

It wasn't like Yu-jin to forget about required reading for an exam. She was meticulous in her preparation when it came to her academics. "She was planning on going home and studying for her final. She never said anything about meeting you," Min said.

"It was kind of spontaneous."

"What time did you say she left again?"

"Around ten."

Then there's a block of unaccounted time, Min thought. More than two hours when Yu-jin could have been anywhere. "You're positive she came home around midnight?"

So-ra ran a finger under each eyelid. "Yes. I heard her."

"You didn't see her?"

"No. But what does it matter? Shouldn't we be mourning her, honoring her?"

"Don't you see!" Min said. "She tells me she's going home to study but hangs out with you. Then she tells you she's going to the library just to pick up a book and somehow that takes almost two hours. Don't you think that's a little strange? She must have gone somewhere else. Something might have happened that could explain all this."

So-ra pushed the iced coffee away. Her shoulders shook, her breathing ragged.

"How can you believe what the police are saying? You knew her, So-ra. Yu-jin had perfect grades, she had a promising career, she had us, people who cared about her."

So-ra nodded. Her lips moved, but no words came.

Min leaned closer to her, the table teetering under his weight. "You were the last one to see her. Did she seem upset, depressed?"

"Please," she sobbed. "Please stop."

"Don't you want to know the truth? Don't you want to know what happened?"

So-ra stood up and rummaged through her tote bag. "I thought I could do this, but I can't." Coins, a few crumpled bills fell to the table as she stood.

Min grabbed her wrist before she could leave. "None of this makes sense," he whispered.

"Maybe not to you," she said, yanking her hand away. "Maybe you didn't know her as well as you think. Ever consider that?"

Min looked around at the other café patrons. Some stared, like witnesses to a car crash, unable to look away; others avoided his gaze entirely, feigning immersion in their newspapers and phones. "So-ra. Please."

Her face softened. "I didn't mean that," she said. "You knew her, Min, so did I. We were close friends. But I have to go now, I'm sorry."

Before he could say anything else, she'd put on her sunglasses and left, walking east. He followed, refusing to let the conversation end there. Behind him, the cashier yelled something about paying for his coffee. She was only a few steps ahead. At an intersection where summer wind eddied and spun down the blocks, she stopped, waiting for the light to change.

"Why won't you listen to me?" Min said between breaths. "Admit it. There are things that don't make sense. This isn't who she was. Why are you pretending like it was?"

So-ra turned on him, sunglasses pushed into her hair. "I know you're hurting right now, Min. I am, too. But I don't have time for this. I've got to meet Yu-jin's parents at the apartment. There are practical matters to take care of."

Min couldn't tell whether she was trying to hurt him or just stating facts. But what did it matter? She was pointing out an important difference in their relationships with Yu-jin. She existed to her parents. He did not.

So-ra was right; there were practical matters to consider. There'd be a service of some kind honoring Yu-jin's life. And her parents—he tried to picture them, standing over what, something he couldn't imagine. He'd never been to a Korean memorial. A casket? An urn? He watched So-ra go. A piece of him had come unglued, unhinged. Nothing made sense. Her allusion to Misaki's intrusiveness, her unwillingness to consider any other reasons behind Yu-jin's suicide. What was she hiding?

In search of shade, Min ducked into an alleyway, pigeons cooing, AC units alive with a metallic whir. Straddling a trickle of sewage, Min dug into his pocket for Detective Park's business card.

TEN

YU-JIN

My mind always came back to her

It was all too easy with So-ra; we did everything together. The all-day study sessions in the library, books and empty coffee cups strewn across the dark mahogany tables, brunch at our favorite café, the Sunday morning talks in the dorm, our room filling up with pure bright light. Concerned that I was limiting myself socially, I made a few half-hearted efforts to make other friends. I joined the International Law Club, thinking I'd meet some like-minded girls. I did, which was the problem. They reminded me of my old self, the one I'd left behind. After the first two meetings I stopped going, incurring the disapproval of the senior members, who shot me dirty looks whenever we crossed paths on campus. It was easy to ignore them. Each glare only made me more steadfast in my friendship with So-ra. Still, making only one friend your first year of university—wasn't that the one thing you weren't supposed to do?

Fearing I'd regret not trying to meet more people, I joined the Mountain Climbing Club in late November. The hiking reminded me of the camping trips I'd taken with my father when I was younger. But even while I navigated a rocky ledge or zigzagged up a rutted dirt path, I couldn't help but wonder what So-ra was doing. No matter where I was or who I was with, my mind always came back to her. Once winter descended on the city, driving everyone indoors with its knifing winds and snowy squalls, the hiking club went into hibernation. I never went back when they started up again in the spring. By then I'd surrendered to the inevitable. Every effort I made to meet more people and make more friends only affirmed the truth So-ra had proclaimed from the beginning: we were meant to be friends.

That spring, Seoul was our very own amusement park. When I wasn't studying and So-ra wasn't in rehearsal, we'd spend whole weekends off campus, exploring every inch of the city, from its museums and outdoor markets to shopping centers and endless street food stalls serving up spicy *tteokbokki* and sweet *bungeoppang*. No matter how many subways we rode or city blocks we traversed, the city revealed itself anew, like a flower perpetually in bloom. As the weather warmed, we made a habit of picnicking by the river or in Seoul Forest, one of So-ra's favorite parks.

The proximity of our birthdays—which fell within a few days of each other in April—only strengthened the sense of our cosmic bond. Technically So-ra's came first, but she delayed her celebration so we could have a joint birthday party. "Get-together" was probably a better description; a few girls from So-ra's dance program had found a seedy bar near campus known for its lax ID policy. We were still a year away from twenty, which meant no dancing and drinking at Gangnam and Hongdae's legendary clubs.

"Don't worry," So-ra said before the party. "You aren't missing much." We'd just spread our picnic blanket out on the grass. We'd decided on Hangang Park, even though it was a long metro ride from Ewha. There were other picnickers nearby, mostly families with their children and younger couples. Ahead, the river lay flat and calm, a glassy mirror broken only by the occasional ripple from a passing boat.

I tried to temper my excitement. "You've actually been inside a club in Seoul?"

So-ra stretched out on the red-and-white gingham blanket, shading her eyes against the sun. "A dancer friend went on a few dates with this bouncer. He snuck us in."

"When was this? I can't believe you didn't invite me."

So-ra waved me off. "It was a last-minute thing. You didn't miss anything."

"You can't be serious. Everyone knows Seoul has the best clubs. What about the music? The guys? You can't tell me there weren't cute guys."

So-ra sat up and took her jacket off, shoulders taut and defined, like she'd been cut from marble. "Sure, there were some handsome guys, but honestly, they bore me. Men are so single-minded. They can never consider multitudes."

"What do you mean?"

"Some people just don't like contradictions or ambiguities. They have no imagination."

I still wasn't quite sure what she meant, so I busied myself with unpacking the snacks and drinks we'd brought along. I wished I could be like So-ra, so blasé and cool. She didn't care what men thought of her, a talent I'd yet to master. Still enamored with my newfound freedom, I couldn't help but feel a thrill whenever a university boy gave me attention.

So-ra was digging around in her bag, unearthing notebooks, tangled headphones, and crumpled receipts. She handed me something wrapped in brown paper. "I got you a birthday gift."

"You liar. You said we weren't doing presents."

So-ra dropped the package in my lap. "Just open it."

I tore off the paper, revealing a slender book. I'd have to find something for So-ra before our party.

"You said you haven't read much poetry. Rimbaud is a good place to start. I marked a few of my favorites. Just thinking about his poems makes me want to run away to France or Italy, somewhere far away from here."

More poetry. And this time I'd be expected to give my opinion on it. My face must have revealed my anxiety.

"You don't give yourself enough credit, Yu-jin," she said. "You just haven't been exposed to the arts, but you're brilliant. Trust me."

And I did, wholly. For whatever reason, So-ra's faith in me felt different from the support my parents had always given me. While they fervently believed in my ability to overcome any obstacle, to bend fate in my favor by sheer determination, So-ra's belief in me felt bigger, almost selfless. It wasn't about my aptitude or my potential; it was about who I was in that singular moment. It was acceptance.

Observing So-ra in the sun, leaning back on her elbows, black blouse falling off one shoulder, I realized I felt something for her, something that went beyond friendship. I yearned to occupy the unknown caverns of her heart. This feeling, nameless and strange, collided with my own understanding of myself. That Yu-jin, ambitious and single-minded, impervious to external whims—an image I'd crafted tirelessly—stood in jarring opposition to who I felt like now, vulnerable and weak. In a panic, I turned away and focused on two young mothers standing in the distance, idly pushing strollers back and forth. I clutched the book So-ra had given me until my fingers ached.

Later that night in the smoke-filled bar, I nudged the memory of my afternoon with So-ra from my mind. Shoulder-to-shoulder with other university students, the sour smell of spilled beer and *soju* in the air—the hours I'd spent by the river with So-ra belonged to a different person, a different time and place. I didn't want to think about what any of it meant. Tonight was for celebrating.

So-ra's friends had arrived early and staked out a booth. We squeezed into the faux-leather seats, sitting three to a bench, a plastic pitcher of beer between us.

"Better drink up," So-ra shouted over the din. "Curfew is midnight."

I gulped my beer and tried not to make a face. All the dorms at Ewha had curfew on the weekends. If you didn't make it back, you'd receive demerit points. The rule hadn't bothered me until that night out, but now I couldn't wait to live off campus in an apartment of my own. Someone opened a bottle of *soju* and poured shots for everyone.

So-ra leaned into me. "You don't have to drink it, you know."

"Just because I'm not from a city doesn't mean I can't hold my liquor."

It wasn't long before we'd abandoned the booth. Some girls were dancing together; others were talking with people I didn't recognize, raucous laughter and frenetic chatter pressing in on me. So-ra was having what looked to be an intense conversation with a girl from her dance program, pointing wildly while she spoke. I couldn't fathom where she got the energy to be so passionate about everything. Sometimes it frightened me, how quickly a fire could rise within her.

Eyes burning from the secondhand smoke, I shimmied through the crowd. Out on the sidewalk, I took deep breaths, my face somehow tingling but numb. Hordes of jabbering students and clubgoers streamed by, hailing taxis, shouting out directions, pushing and pulling their groups to the next destination.

A guy wearing a white linen shirt and black jeans stood near me smoking a cigarette. He looked like a university student, maybe a few years older. I felt a sudden urge to speak to him, to flirt like all the other university girls did.

I asked him for a cigarette, and he obliged. I'd never really seen the appeal of smoking, but in my tipsiness, there was something exhilarating about it. I felt more alert, the softness of the world coming back into focus.

It turned out he was a junior at Yonsei University, majoring in International Business. His name was Sung-do. He was hoping to get a job in Europe when he graduated, maybe Switzerland or Germany. He didn't get condescending when I told him I was a freshman, which seemed encouraging. "Maybe I could call you sometime," was all he said, pinching off his cigarette and dropping it to the sidewalk.

Giddy, I gave him my number and left it at that, telling him I had to check on my friends. If Hae-sook had taught me anything, it was this: always leave them wanting more.

·|⊦·

At the end of the year, I attended So-ra's spring dance performance. I brought Sung-do, or Yonsei Guy, which was what So-ra always called him. We'd gone out a few times, and while he seemed nice enough, I'd found myself resisting his invitations on dates where we'd be drinking or going somewhere late at night, fearing he might expect something more. Still, I wanted to impress him with my cultured taste, and what better way than to take him to So-ra's show?

I'd never been to a dance performance, much less a modern one, which, according to So-ra, was very different. How exactly she wouldn't say.

After we took our seats in the surprisingly full auditorium, the lights dimmed, the audience sliding into a collective hush as the black curtain shimmied upwards, revealing a king-size bed center stage surrounded by manual typewriters suspended in the air by thick twine. Six circles of light grew in intensity onstage.

The stage was empty, void of bodies; all that could be heard was noise, not music but a rapid cacophony of clacking, struck keys, metal to paper, multiplying, the room ringing with manual typewriters pressed by a thousand fingertips. And then a humming, too. A whir. What I imagined to be electric typewriters. Still, nothing onstage. Only a bed. The spotlights. The ominous metal typewriters dangling precipitously in the air.

Finally there were bodies. Six to be exact, dressed in black leotards, streaming in from stage right and left, three to a side, their bodies white and exposed under the harsh light. Each dancer took her place under a typewriter. The machinelike sound grew to a fervor with beeps and clicking, plastic keyboards and blinking monitors. One by one the dancers flashed by, none like the others, their legs stabbing sideways and upwards, backs arching away from the audience, rib cages jutting. I watched them, fixated.

I recognized So-ra as she reached upwards to a typewriter floating above her, arms straining, fingertips longing, and then she crumpled to the floor in a silent wail, like she'd been shot, but then she was moving again, on her knees, facing us. Me.

Bending forward, her chest close to the ground, elbows, fore-arms, shoulders, all bending to me and then circling around her, fin-gertips grazing the stage. Making a ring around herself. She whirled and whirled, a dervish of flesh and bone. The light beating, shining down on her. This body of wonder.

Then all the dancers were up, in unison, mirrors of each other on either side of the bed, taking turns diving, rolling, and tumbling over it. One after another, blurred figures brimming with feverish delight.

I focused on So-ra only. Her face fixed with anguished concentra-tion as she threw herself with graceful, reckless abandon to the floor, her stomach heaving for breath, her eyes bright, focused. With her every move, my chest tightened, my shoulders ached. I held my breath with every twist and tumble. She wasn't there, I realized. She was somewhere else, next to me, watching the performance. Disem-bodied. I wasn't watching So-ra, but some pure essence of her spirit.

One by one the dancers left the stage. Yanked, propelled, swept, compelled—each body exited with a flourish, disintegrated into the darkness, cosmic dust. Until there was only one—So-ra. The four-poster bed receded backwards, pulled by invisible ropes. One by one the lights went out, until it was only her under a singular spotlight. The noise gone, the typewriters disappeared. Just us and her. Me and her.

With a running start she barreled toward the front of the stage jumping high into the air, her face twisted into a joyful grimace. She landed, a resounding *smack* on the floor, palms flat, feet flat, and then we were in darkness, and the auditorium erupted in applause.

When the stage illuminated and the six dancers came forward to bow, I didn't know what I'd seen. I didn't know whether it was good or bad modern dance. I didn't know who this boy was next to me, standing up, clapping, leaning closer to me. He was a stranger, a flirtation. He wasn't real. He didn't matter. He wasn't what I wanted.

No.

What I wanted, who I wanted, everything I'd ever wanted was up on that stage, smiling, beaming, at me.

What I wanted was So-ra.

ELEVEN

MIN

You can always think of me

Known more for its nightlife, Sinchon was unrecognizable during the day. Flyers and business cards for massage parlors, karaoke rooms, taxi services, and hostess bars littered the sidewalk outside the bar where Park had agreed to meet Min. Woodstock was one of a handful of LP music bars in Seoul. For the price of a few drinks, you could request songs—American oldies, mostly—to listen to while you drank. If you got a whole bottle, that bought you a few albums. Min had gone to this particular place on numerous occasions with Yu-jin, but never this early.

The bar was small, a narrow building stuffed between two much larger nightclubs. Naked lightbulbs hung from the ceiling, their incandescent filaments burning yellow. Vintage posters of Hendrix, Marley, and the Stones lined the wood-paneled walls. Despite the lack of customers, smoke still seemed to hang in the air.

Detective Park sat at the bar, facing a wall of alphabetically organized records. The bartender was still setting up: sweeping under tables and chairs, stopping occasionally to slap the padded benches along the far wall.

"Cigarette?" Park said, flipping open the pack. He looked worse than he'd sounded on the phone. Stubble patchy and uneven, like he didn't own a mirror.

Min declined, taking a closer look at the detective. He'd been so preoccupied with the news of Yu-jin's death, he'd barely registered anything from their last meeting. Park's fingernails were yellowed and brown from smoke. He had curly hair for a Korean. It was pushed to one side, partially covering his round face. With his wide-set eyes and bridge-less nose, Min imagined he was shockingly ugly by Korean beauty standards. Although he doubted very much whether anyone would agree with him, Min thought there was something charming about his appearance. He resembled a flounder, sitting at the bottom of the seafloor.

"What is it you have for me? Remember something?" Park said after Min settled onto his barstool.

"How about a drink first. I'm buying."

"Bourbon," Park said, waving an indiscriminate finger at the bottles behind the bar.

Unsure of which brand Park liked, Min deferred to the bartender, who quickly returned with a bottle and seaweed squares for them to snack on.

"Big spender, huh?" Park nudged Min. "Samsung must pay well."

Min unscrewed the bottle and held it out with two hands. Park offered his glass the same way. This was custom in Korea—younger pouring for older, always using both hands. "Pretty good manners for a *kyopo*," Park said, returning the favor.

Min didn't care for the term, which was loosely used for Koreans who hadn't grown up in Korea, but he refrained from saying anything. Detective Park was his only option. He needed to stay in his good graces.

Park requested Bruce Springsteen's *Born in the U.S.A.* from the bartender and gave Min a wink. The needle cracked and popped overhead. Eyes closed, Park moved his head to the synthesizer, drumming on the bar with his thick fingers. His head bounced and rolled, curly hair dancing off his forehead. The bartender looked on, nonplussed.

"Lemme ask you a question," Park said, leaning closer, brow speckled with sweat. "What're you doing here anyway? Samsung's a great job. But couldn't you be doing the same thing in America?"

Min considered all the answers he could give Park. He could tell him about New York City, about the notebook filled with words he'd never known. He could tell him about college, when he'd pretended he didn't speak Korean, just to avoid being invited to church groups. He could tell him about how he'd cried when his mother had explained why he'd never have blond hair like his father. But he didn't.

"My great-grandfather's buried here," he finally said.

"Paying your respects then," Park said. "Admirable."

"In the National Cemetery. He was part of the independence movement."

Park raised his glass. "Even better then. A patriot. So you thought you'd come back to the motherland, pay tribute. Get in touch with your long-lost culture?"

"Something like that."

"Don't be so glum. Plenty of *kyopos* here in Korea. They come from all over, fly in from Sydney, Vancouver, Los Angeles, even met a guy from Iran. They're all looking for the same thing. Rarely happens, of course. In your case I imagine it's been even more difficult."

The idea of others, just like him, traveling to Korea in hopes of finding a place where they belonged made Min feel foolish. Was his situation not unique? This realization should have made him feel better, but it didn't.

Park shifted in his chair, hands hugging his drink. "About the case. What else do you know?"

Min went over his growing list of Yu-jin's suspicious activities leading up to her death. On their last night together, she'd left him under the pretense of studying, but then she'd ended up meeting So-ra for a drink. Then, according to So-ra, Yu-jin left her because she needed a book from the library for her exam, which was implausible, given her preparedness and stellar study habits. Even more mysterious were the two hours it had taken her to retrieve the book and come back to the apartment. Why would she have lied to him about meeting with So-ra in the first place, and why had it taken her so long to run a simple errand?

Park didn't seem particularly surprised. "We already know all that. It doesn't change the working theory that this was a suicide, and we have no reason to believe she was murdered."

"But you can't rule it out. You said so yourself."

"We haven't received the official coroner's report, but foul play is highly unlikely, unless you're implicating one of her roommates. They were the only ones in the apartment that night."

For a brief moment, Min entertained the possibility, but then he stopped—ashamed. So-ra was Yu-jin's best friend, and even though none of them liked Misaki very much, that didn't make her a killer.

Something slick like molasses rolled in Min's stomach. His mind suddenly thick with drink, he struggled to lay out his words in a straight line. Dull light banged through liquor bottles and beer necks. Vinyl scratched; bass thumped. He was missing something, some detail. Then he remembered what Misaki had said: no one had called the police; they'd simply arrived.

"If no one discovered the body, how did the police know to come? Who called you?"

Park put a square of seaweed in his mouth and chewed, noisily. "Hey, what're you serving us here? This isn't Korean seaweed."

Min took a sheet of the crispy algae and let it dissolve on his tongue. "Tastes fine to me."

"You're a *kyopo*. You probably can't even tell a Korean from a Japanese."

Min ignored the barb. "Who told you to go to the apartment?"

Park let out a heavy sigh. "My boss gave me the address to Yu-jin's apartment and said to check it out. He said it was an apparent suicide."

"But who told your boss? Who called it in? So-ra and Misaki both confirmed that police and paramedics showed up at the apartment before they knew Yu-jin was dead."

Park brushed dark green flakes of seaweed from the bar and stared grimly at the floor. "You really don't know who Yu-jin's father is?"

"I told you I never met him," Min said, wondering why Park was bringing him up again.

"She never introduced you," Park corrected him. "Didn't want his precious daughter having any distractions."

"Something like that."

Park looked around the empty bar. "He's the Minister of National Defense."

Min must not have had the appropriate reaction because Detective Park moved closer to him, breath warm and stale. "He's a big deal."

"So he's a high-ranking politician?"

Park ran a big hand over his face. "You aren't hearing me. Her father oversees every military branch in Korea. This is the guy you go to if you want people under surveillance, phones bugged, emails hacked. We're talking deep state stuff."

Min tried to fathom what Park was saying, but his mind raced back to Yu-jin, who'd asked him questions about his family, but hers—she'd made things sound so boring, so ordinary. He'd never felt compelled to ask more than the cursory questions; it was exactly what she'd wanted, he realized.

"So it wasn't just anxiety or stress, her father is trying to cover it up, or worse, he's somehow responsible," Min said, forgetting etiquette and pouring himself a drink.

Park slapped his hand. Min put the bottle down and took his glass in both hands, holding it out like an offering. Park shook his head and poured. "You're not listening. I'm telling you not to involve yourself. The politics around the case are already making things difficult. I'm getting all sorts of pressure to close it quickly, no doubt because she's the Minister's daughter. Think about it. The publicity, the press. It would be a circus. I need to keep all those external factors away from the case in order to solve it properly."

"Yu-jin never mentioned anything about her father."

Swiveling his stool, Park faced Min, eyes white as alabaster. "You don't mess with these people. My boss is a pretty tough guy, and someone's got him on a string. I don't know what her father's capable of, but you don't want to piss him off." Park drained the glass and ran a sleeve under his mouth. "I get that you're upset. Truly, I know you're confused and hurting. I'm sure you were a good boyfriend. We looked into the tapes from the convenience store. Your alibi checks out. I'm sure you didn't have anything to do with this. And I know you've got questions, but right now, the most important thing is solving the case. I know you don't believe Yu-jin took her life, but you need to let me do my job. My gut says suicide, but there are still some clues and other loose ends that point to her case being more complicated than it seems. But I can't investigate them properly if you stir things up. It's only going to complicate matters, and I can only keep the higher-ups away from it for so long. Some very powerful people want this to go away as quickly as possible."

Min tried to focus on what Park was saying but felt himself fall back into familiar doubts. If only he'd been more attentive, asked more questions, maybe Yu-jin would still be here.

"Why meet me then?" Min said, realizing there was no convincing Park of anything. "You clearly don't believe Yu-jin was murdered. Why give me details of the case? Why tell me about Yu-jin's father? Why warn me?"

Park relaxed back into his seat, his gaze wandering across the records and liquor bottles. "I grew up in Gangwon, in the countryside, right across the border from North Korea. Sometimes I could even hear the propaganda speakers on my way to school. My childhood friend and I, we both wanted to be police officers. That was gonna be our ticket out. He was a real joker; he'd do anything for a laugh. Our families never had much money to do anything for fun, so he was always coming up with jokes and pranks to entertain us. No matter how difficult things got, he always found something to laugh about. Some people are gifted that way; they can see the absurdity of everything," Park said, tugging at his tangled locks. "The night before our high school graduation, he committed suicide. His family found him in the toolshed, dead from carbon monoxide poisoning. For months, he'd been collecting *yeontan*, those small briquettes for cooking and heating. He'd stuffed rags and blankets under the door so no oxygen could get inside when he burned them. No one ever found a motive. He didn't leave a note. He'd never said anything to anyone, no cries for help. To this day it still haunts me. I still wonder why he did it; I wonder why I never noticed anything. I don't wish those doubts and misgivings on anyone. That's why I'm telling you. Because I know what it feels like when you start doubting your ability to understand another human being."

Park finished his drink, ice cubes rattling. "Just steer clear of Yu-jin's father. Go on vacation, take some time away. Mourn. Reflect. But let this be. I'll get to the bottom of it."

⫶⫶⫶

Long after Detective Park had left, Min stayed at the bar, thinking about his story. By then the air was choked with cigarette smoke, patrons hovered and hummed around him, the fan above working double time. Maybe Park was right. Maybe Yu-jin had buried her anguish deep, kept it from Min, just like she'd hidden her father's job. A couple sat near him, huddled over a record. Yu-jin had loved this music bar; she'd liked the idea of them having an album. "This is ours," she'd said, clutching *The Freewheelin' Bob Dylan*. "This is us walking down the street, arm in arm, bundled up against the cold.

And whenever you hear it, you can think of me. You can always think of me."

Min finished his drink and paid the tab. Detective Park was wrong; he didn't know Yu-jin like Min did. He'd never witnessed her drive, her strength. Giving up, taking her own life, that wasn't who Yu-jin was. What if her father had somehow been involved in her death? Min knew what he needed to do. Now it was just a matter of finding out where Yu-jin's memorial was being held.

TWELVE

YU-JIN

With her, I felt possible

Weeks, then months passed after the dance show, and I said nothing of what I felt. During our lunches, in the silences between our nightly conversations before we slept, I wondered whether So-ra felt the same. She'd made no declarations, no confessions. And yet, on that stage, it had felt like she'd said all that needed to be said, wordlessly.

I looked for answers in her moods, her banter, seeking significance in the trivial. I studied her gait, her perfect posture, hoping her body might once again speak to me. I scoured the book of poetry she'd given me on my birthday, scrutinizing each poem she'd marked as a favorite, intent on finding some hidden message, evidence of her feelings for me. As our first year drew to a close, I grew more desperate. So-ra would be living in an apartment with other dancers (they'd be performing in various dance shows throughout the summer) while I'd be forced to move back in with my parents until the dorms reopened in the fall. We'd already promised to spend as much time together as possible, but I couldn't fathom going into the summer without knowing whether So-ra shared my feelings. She'd said men bored her. They were single-minded; they could never consider multitudes. I thought about that word "multitudes" for a long time, turning it over like a lozenge in my mouth until there was nothing. Perhaps it was simpler than I wanted to admit. I was her friend, nothing more, I decided. And yet I couldn't help but wonder.

On the final day of the semester, So-ra and I stood in our empty dorm room. Gone was the wall-length mirror, the photo-covered corkboard. The mattresses lay stripped and bare on the bunk beds. I stared down at the rug-less floor, sterile and cold. We'd made this room our own, but it wasn't really our room; someone new would be living here next year. I wanted to say something to stop all this, to grind the moment to a halt, but what words could do such a thing?

"We did a good job cleaning," So-ra said, putting the room keys on the windowsill. "I dare them to charge us an extra fee."

I tried to laugh, but nothing came; something like a cry stuck halfway in my throat.

She must have seen something in my face, the agony of a hundred indecisions and revisions. "This won't change anything," she said. "We'll be rooming together next year."

I unclenched my jaw and tried to breathe. "What about us?"

So-ra picked up a roll of paper towels from the desk, then put them back, almost disappointed, as if she'd hoped they might contain the answer to some agonizing conundrum. Lungs ablaze, stomach twisting, I willed her to understand me. She went to say something but caught herself, lips parted—nothing but air.

"I want this to be different," I blurted out, unable to stand the silence.

She looked at me then, really looked at me, dark brown eyes serene. The moment folded in on itself, everything silky and hushed. I watched her weigh my words for what felt like an eternity, time slowing to an unbearable trickle.

Ever so slightly, So-ra closed the distance between us. "We can be whatever you want, Yu-jin. All you have to do is say so."

"I don't think it's that simple."

"It is," she said, taking my hands in hers.

I couldn't look at her, but I could feel her warmth, her breath. "Then show me," I heard myself say.

She took my cheek in her hand then and turned my face. The room seemed to drop away; we stood alone, together. Something escaped from her open mouth, a whispered assurance, a melody I'd never heard. Craning her neck, she brought her lips to mine, soft and searching. Eyes closed, I imagined this was how So-ra felt when she was dancing, limitless, disembodied and alive all at once. Nothing was of consequence, only this humming thread between us, stitched through our very beings.

⊹⊹⊹

So-ra's off-campus apartment quickly proved beneficial to our new-found relationship during the summer. Her roommates were always gone, busy with rehearsals, auditions, and performances, which gave us a sense of security. We were safe to do as we pleased. And while I had my own responsibilities (summer English classes), the workload was minimal, leaving plenty of time for So-ra. Compared to the dorms, it was heaven. No curfew, no officious hall monitors or security check-ins. For the first time, I felt like I was getting the life I'd always dreamed of. And while my parents insisted I spend most nights at home, they made exceptions on the weekend. I'd received perfect marks during my first year; I was taking academic summer classes—what could they say? What possible objection could they raise with my best friend?

To label what we were, what we had, as something specific—a quantifiable moment, an entity, a transition—was impossible. Like a newly discovered planet, a burning star, we were nameless, untouched by those who might seek to understand.

No words passed between us when we lay together in her room during those long weekend nights, intertwined, marveling at how our bodies could be simultaneously identical and dissimilar. The curve of a belly button, the sprouting of armpit hair, a spatter of freckles. I spent hours admiring So-ra's back, a topographical map of muscle—mountains and valleys, chiseled ledges and sanded peaks. I admired what I'd never known, like a blind woman, touching everything to see.

"What do you think it means?" I said one Sunday morning, the bedroom cool and dark.

So-ra slid an arm under my neck, the freshly laundered sheets rough against my skin. "Are you talking nonsense again?"

"I'm being serious," I said, rolling onto my side. "You act like this is all normal. I mean, like it isn't crazy."

Hands through my hair. Her grip, strong and resolute. "You know where I stand on all this," she said with a smile.

"Easy for you to say. I've never had this feeling. I've never wanted anything like this. With someone like you."

"A girl like me?" So-ra exclaimed in mock ecstasy, resting a palm on her chest.

"You know what I mean. This is simple for you. It isn't confusing."

She was quiet for a moment. It was only us. The world, preoccupied.

"You're right. I've always known who and what I wanted."

"But what if that's not me? What if I'm still attracted to guys like I've always been, but I want you, too? What if you're the only woman I ever want?"

So-ra kissed me quickly on the lips before springing out of bed. "I'd say who cares. I'd say who gets to determine this stuff anyway. I'd say that's fine, even normal. Who you want to sleep with, who you find attractive, these things aren't as concrete as we'd like to think."

I lay in bed while So-ra wrapped herself in a towel. After she'd shuffled down the hall, I sat up, pulling the covers around my shoulders. If my desires could change, if they weren't as fixed as I thought, what did that make me?

More pressing questions quickly emerged when we returned to Ewha for our second year. What had once filled me with excitement and anticipation—the beautiful campus, the ambitious students—now only brought dread. Every interaction with So-ra outside the privacy of our dorm room was a risk, an act of quiet defiance. If we were found out, exposed, it would mean social ruin; we'd be teased and ostracized. To be whatever So-ra and I were, to be anything but straight, was to be an anomaly, a target for attention and scorn. I'd heard stories: parents disowning their children, people taking their own lives out of fear and hopelessness. Even in a city as cosmopolitan as Seoul, with its Pride parade and Queer Culture Festival, I only heard the thousands of demonstrators from Christian groups marching in protest. So-ra was quick to point out the flourishing gay bars and clubs in Itaewon and Jongno, but I only saw how people willed them into obscurity, pretending they didn't exist.

Even as we pushed the boundaries, grew bold in our affections for each other, I became consumed with fear. If discovered, I'd bring unwanted attention and shame upon my family. Public humiliation would be my repayment for their generosity and sacrifice. And as So-ra and I moved through the year surreptitiously, cloaking our longing and desire under the guise of friendship, there were times when I felt deserving of disownment.

The year passed in a paranoid blur, punctuated by moments of pure ecstasy, when So-ra and I retreated to the privacy of our dorm room, unencumbered by prying eyes. And when we grew claustrophobic or frustrated with our confines, there was always Seoul, with its endless bustle and stupendous anonymity. Lost in the city, surrounded by faceless pedestrians, we could let our guard slip, clutch hands under café tables, rub hips on a jam-packed metro. Every act brought a thrill, an intoxicating sense of freedom.

One warm, spring day, So-ra and I were in Dongdaemun, wandering through snaking alleyways, where we perused cluttered shops run by gray-haired men stooped with age. While most people were at Dongdaemun Market, bargaining with wholesalers and gobbling down steaming *sundae* and *mandu* from crowded food stalls, we felt less conspicuous among these low-slung buildings and dimly lit stores.

As we strolled down a narrow street, our elbows grazing, skin to skin, So-ra stopped to show me the secondhand bookstores stretching the entire block. Stacks of books spilled out onto the sidewalk, some threatening to topple over from the slightest provocation. We took our time, showing off our discoveries: comics, archaic instruction manuals, and a few rare books in protective sleeves. Among strangers, I felt myself relax, my smile a bit wider, my lean a bit closer. Craving something cold, we set off in search of iced coffee, holding hands, sunglasses shielding our knowing glances.

Caught up in the moment, I only turned around after hearing my name for the third time. A girl wearing a floral sundress approached us, waving frantically. Only when she'd gotten closer did I recognize Hae-sook.

I quickly withdrew my hand from So-ra's.

"I can't believe it's you," she said, enveloping me in a hug.

My arms hung limply at my side. How long had she been behind us? "I didn't realize you were in Seoul."

"Don't be ridiculous. You knew I got into university here. Aren't you gonna introduce me to your new best friend?"

"Sorry. This is my roommate, So-ra," I said, trying to collect myself. "Hae-sook is a friend from high school."

"Were we even friends?" she said with a laugh. "You never held my hand like that." She glanced at So-ra. "Watch out for this one. She's a real gunner—she'll leave you high and dry if she's got a big test coming up."

I tried to smile, but my face was frozen. "We were good friends," was all I managed to say as we stood awkwardly together on the sidewalk.

Hae-sook poked my shoulder. "I'm only teasing. Lighten up."

I could feel So-ra looking at me, trying to gauge the situation. Hae-sook seemed like she was expecting us to invite her along to wherever we were going, but that wasn't going to happen. I'd always dreaded running into someone from Gyeryong in Seoul, but having it happen while I was with So-ra was catastrophic.

"We have to get going. We're late for a movie," I said.

"That's cool," Hae-sook said.

Hoping to stay on her good side, I asked for her number so we could hang out sometime.

"It's the same from high school. You should still have it."

"Of course," I said, before saying goodbye.

We promised to get together, a promise I would break. I'd deleted her number, along with all my other Gyeryong contacts, the day I'd moved to Seoul.

I was silent the entire way home, thinking about Hae-sook watching me and So-ra together, sharing a tender moment. She'd wanted me to know she'd seen us. How could I have been so reckless? Hae-sook could tell anyone what she'd seen. All she had to do was say something to her mother or her father, and somehow, someway, the news would reach my parents.

After that day in Dongdaemun, I reminded my father of our agreement and my desire to live off campus. Fearful that he might renege on the deal, I told him living in the dorms was a distraction; the residential students weren't serious enough about their studies. I told him everything except for the truth: So-ra and I wanted a place to ourselves. No more shared bathroom down the hall, no more bunk beds, no muffled exclamations whimpered into pillows, into balled-up sheets, into nothing.

What I really wanted, what *we* really wanted, was privacy, to be shielded from prying eyes, real or imagined. The threat of discovery lingered around me, around whatever *this* was, like a poisonous cloud of malicious intent.

So with my second year coming to an end, I told my parents everything that it wasn't. And when we found a place in Daehangno, it was too good to pass up, even if it meant eventually finding a third roommate to make it affordable.

‑‖‑

The summer we moved in together and the start of my third year marked the happiest time in my life, when the apartment was still barely furnished and we were free to do as we pleased. It marked a deepening of our relationship. So-ra unlocked something inside me: a thirst. A deeper yearning I'd never known. Not for grades or a job, but for experience. How little of the world I knew, I came to find. But with her, beside her, I possessed the deepest desire for truth, for some unspeakable certainty, burning, everlasting. Within the walls of our apartment—ours, because that's what it felt like—I was able to exist as I wanted, think as I wanted, unchained from the rigid expectations of all that sought to control me.

She lent me books on French existentialism, laughing when I asked whether she believed in something so ridiculous and wrongheaded. We watched old recordings of Martha Graham, contorting and manipulating her body in a profoundly new way. I'd never known we were capable of such movement, such beauty. She introduced me to Emily Dickinson, read me her poems while we lay in bed, panting, sweat drying on our tongues.

With her, I felt possible.

Despite my workload that semester, So-ra encouraged me to audit an introductory film course, an idea I'd mentioned offhandedly. "It might be interesting. You like movies," she said. "Plus, you'll die from boredom if you only take those required courses for your major."

We were stocking the kitchen with some secondhand utensils and dishware we'd bought at a flea market.

"Don't be ridiculous. I don't know anything about film. What do you even do in a class like that?"

"It's just an introductory class. Plus, you don't have to do or say anything. You're just auditing. You're more creative than you think. Give yourself some credit. It's on Thursday nights from five to ten. The first part is lecture, the second is a viewing session." She closed the cabinets and walked behind me, slinging her arms around my neck. "No one needs to know," she said.

"No one" meant my family, specifically my father, who was against all things "impractical," as he called them. Photography, drawing, film, writing, dance—these were not the serious pursuits of a serious student. As hobbies, he would tolerate them. But anything else was unwelcome. If he discovered I was taking any extra classes, let alone a humanities course, he'd be furious.

Still, So-ra had unearthed a curiosity, and on the first Thursday of the semester I found myself sitting in the back row of a modest lecture hall, notebook open, textbook in my bag, listening to a young female professor talk about her expectations for the course: Introduction to Film: A Survey. Professor Lee stressed that during the semester we would develop a language for talking about film. She was adamant that the study of film, like any other discipline, required a specific vocabulary, a mastery of terminology. Without the language, we wouldn't be able to articulate our observations of the films. "But since it's the first day," the professor said, lowering the projector screen and clicking off the lights, "we will simply watch a film. Perhaps some of you know it. It's quite famous. Either way, don't try to analyze it or dissect it just because we are in an academic setting. Let the film unfold before you."

I settled into my seat and tried to do as the professor had instructed. I'd never seen *Tokyo Story*. It might have actually been the first black-and-white movie I'd ever watched. My parents might have shown me one when I was little, but it seemed unlikely. They didn't think about art in the same way So-ra did, or this professor apparently. Art was entertainment to them.

What was I watching? An enormous granite pagoda by the sea; children walking to school; a black train barreling between rooftops, puffing smoke. I'd never seen anything like it. Everything seemed in slow motion: the way people moved, spoke. The camera lingered on empty streets, smokestacks. I found myself feeling both annoyed and intrigued. I wanted things to move faster. An old married couple was packing for a trip. The camera was angled up at them, like it was sitting on the floor. What was the point of that? And why was their conversation so dull and boring? How could So-ra have thought I'd be interested in this?

That was the last thing I remembered thinking before the lights came up.

Was the film already over? Was that how it ended? I was devastated, heartbroken, unsure of whether to laugh or cry. What I'd watched was not a movie, not even a film. It was art; it had rendered something anew inside me.

The story wasn't anything revelatory: parents go to visit their children in Tokyo. The characters weren't particularly unique or exceptional. On the contrary, they were ordinary. This quality, however, made them more relatable, I found. I recognized them. I knew people like this, in my own life. And yet I was left feeling as if I'd never seen a better portrayal of human imperfection. I looked around at my classmates to see if they were having the same reaction, but most were just waking up. The movie had put more than half the students to sleep.

"Come ready to discuss the film next week. That will be all," the professor said. "We'll also be screening *Metropolis*."

I waited for everyone to filter out before approaching the podium, where the professor was locking the media console. Despite being an upperclassman, I felt on edge. I was worried someone from my government or political science classes would see me and have all sorts of questions. It was weird for a third-year to be taking an introductory course.

Professor Lee was young, perhaps mid-thirties. To compensate for her age, she was dressed in an ankle-length black dress and gray cardigan. I imagined it was hard to be a young female professor, even at Ewha.

"Can I help you?" she said, packing her black Longchamp bag.

"I wanted to see if I could audit the course."

"What did you think of the film we just watched? You stayed awake, yes?"

I hesitated, unsure of what to say. "I'm not sure. I'm not an expert or anything.

"I just want your reaction."

I took a moment to think. "I guess I thought it was sentimental without being sentimental. I can't really describe it. But the film was emotional without becoming melodramatic. It was minimal. The complete opposite of Korean movies."

"That's a very insightful observation. I'd be more than happy to let you audit the class."

"So that's it? I can come next week?"

She turned off the lectern light. "That's it. See you next week."

That's it, I thought, smiling to myself.

So-ra was waiting for me when I got home. She'd stayed up, even though she had dance rehearsal at six the next morning. "So how did it go?"

"You wouldn't believe it," I began, unable to control my excitement. "I was so nervous. It was silly, really. I felt like it was my first year all over again! The professor is this amazing woman, and all we did was watch *Tokyo Story*. Have you seen it? I never imagined movies could be like that."

"Like what?"

I kissed her. "Don't tease. Not all of us can be so articulate about art."

"I saw it a long time ago. Tell me what you thought."

That night we stayed up well into the morning. We spoke of what made us happy, what we owed to our parents and to ourselves. For the first time, So-ra expressed anxiety about her career. The window was small for a dancer. If she wasn't successful in the next few years, there was little chance she'd ever be discovered.

I was less forthcoming, if only because most of my fears involved her, us, whatever we were. Every other part of my life was secure and safe. It made sense. I could see it, all the dots connecting. I'd continue to do well academically. After graduating I'd go to law school or work for a nonprofit, maybe as a community organizer. Something that looked good on my résumé for a career in politics and government. It seemed like a good plan to me. It made sense. Except that once I really started considering everything, the lines between each dot grew hazy and less defined, each time I thought about So-ra and what she meant to me.

·⊪·

By October we'd fallen into a kind of routine. We'd tried, half-heartedly, to find a roommate but never followed up with anyone who showed interest. My parents were willing to pay double my usual rent for the first two months once I'd exaggerated our difficulties. Stellar grades and promising job prospects continued to earn me certain leeway with them.

Free of our inhibitions, liberated from the worries of other students and their petty social concerns, So-ra and I turned inward, crafting a world in which we were the only inhabitants. What we thought was the only thing that mattered. What we desired was only each other. With the external forces of my doubt and insecurity eradicated, I freely accepted us as something real and tangible. There was no one to question the direction of my heart. There was only So-ra, always supportive, affirming what I felt, what I wanted.

She was right about the film class, like so many other things. It liberated me, gave me a new looking glass to view the world, myself. I'd never considered that one could study film. I was astounded to hear you could even receive a PhD in the discipline. It seemed impossibly frivolous. And yet I went to every class. I found myself immersed in a world and language I'd never known. For the first time I was excited about school. Even though I wasn't receiving a grade or credit, I worked tirelessly, treating it like a required class. I wrote papers on *The Great Train Robbery*, *Casablanca*, and *Rear Window*, not for a score but for the pure joy of exploration. I watched and re-watched *Tokyo Story*, gaining an appreciation for the creation of something, the attempt to bring a vision to fruition.

And then, one day in November, my father came to visit the apartment unexpectedly. He was installing some blinds over the window in the living room when I walked in. I'd just come back from a political science class. It was startling to see him in the apartment, but I tried to hide my anxiety. I'd forgotten he had a key to our place.

He put his cordless drill on the island.

"I didn't know you were stopping by."

"I was in the neighborhood, and I had a feeling you two wouldn't get around to installing them."

"Things have been so busy with school."

My father looked down the hallway to the bedrooms. "Where's So-ra? Still dancing her way to fame and fortune?"

Ever since their first dinner together, my father criticized So-ra whenever possible. Most of it was lighthearted, but I was beginning to tire of it. He didn't approve of her or her lifestyle. I knew that. I didn't expect him to. But he seemed increasingly aware there was a connection between us.

"I'm not sure where she is," I said.

"Who's taking the film class?" My father leafed through my textbook. I'd left it on the island that morning. "Is this what they're teaching at university these days? Wait until your mother hears."

Reflexively I snatched the book from him. "It's So-ra's."

"That's odd," he mused. "You'd think she'd be pretty busy with her dancing."

I slid the book back to him. For the first time since I'd been a child, when he could snap at anything—an offhand comment, a chipped dinner plate—I was afraid of him, afraid of what he knew, afraid of what he would do if he discovered the full extent of my transgressions. That's what they were after all.

"Well. I'm pretty much done here," he said, as he packed up his drill.

I walked him to the door.

He slipped on his loafers. "It's about time you get that roommate, don't you think?"

"We've been looking."

The door open, he turned to me. He'd aged immensely in the past two years since we'd arrived in Seoul. Still, there was a presence about him, a quiet energy. It had always been there. A coldness. "Let's say by the end of the week. Can't have you two living alone together. Who knows, she might be having a bad influence on you."

Once he'd gone, I hurried into my room and checked to see if anything was amiss. I wasn't sure what I was looking for: a half-closed desk drawer, a notebook askew. Nothing appeared out of order except for a blouse that had slipped from a hanger in the closet. After three passes through the room, I spread out on the bed, confident no one had gone through my things. Still, I couldn't shake the feeling that my father had been looking for something.

THIRTEEN

MIN

Why do they hate us so much?

Even if it meant delaying his search for the whereabouts of Yu-jin's memorial, Min was relieved to return to work. So-ra wasn't returning his calls, Park had made it clear he didn't think Min should pursue things, and Min was hesitant to enlist Misaki's help. Ever since he'd learned about her job, nothing about her seemed to align with what Yu-jin and So-ra had told him. He'd once thought Misaki spoiled and aloof, but maybe he was wrong. What was she really doing in Seoul? There was another question, too, one he was disinclined to consider, one set in motion by Detective Park's insistence that if Yu-jin had indeed been murdered, the guilt would fall on one of her roommates. And while Min didn't believe Misaki was capable of such an act, he couldn't shake the feeling that she knew more than she was letting on. No one seemed to know the real Misaki.

Work helped pass the time, helped Min forget the questions he dared not ask aloud. And no matter how inconsequential, how shallow the job was, it felt good to be needed, as the projector hummed a singular tune. Laser pointer at the ready, Min stood in the darkened room. This was his arena, his area of expertise. Even if he'd yet to prove himself capable of uncovering the truth behind Yu-jin's death, at least here he still felt somewhat useful.

As a cultural specialist, Min was tasked with explaining the nuances and complexities of American culture to upper-level Samsung employees who were traveling to the United States to close various corporate deals on behalf of the company. At the moment, Min was using clips from *The Bachelor* to explain the basics of American beauty standards.

From somewhere in the audience, Min's boss, Sun, could be heard chewing gum with boss-like authority. The other two members of Min's team, Woo-jin and Su-bin, sat in the front row of folding chairs, dutifully taking notes.

With the video screen paused on twenty-five hopeful women sitting on a heart-shaped couch, Min began. "As you can see, there's a wide range of what might be considered attractive in America. Most foreigners mistakenly assume that only people with blue eyes and blond hair are considered beautiful, but there's actually quite a range."

Su-bin raised her hand. Straight from Seoul University, she was the cold, hyperefficient type with high aspirations. Sometimes Min thought she was a cyborg, shunning all food and levity. "Doesn't look like much of a range to me."

"Would you care to elaborate?"

"All we talk about is how America is a country of immigrants, how it's so heterogenous compared to Korea, but almost all these women are white. I don't see any evidence to support that melting pot theory you were talking about last week."

Min wasn't being paid by Samsung to explain the complexities of race and beauty. They wanted their employees to have basic cultural competencies when they worked in America—that was all. Plus, he didn't feel like getting into it with Su-bin; she was constantly needling him, as if he weren't the cultural specialist on their team. "Obviously this show isn't representative of everything in the US. We're just watching it to get a general idea of things," Min said, running the video.

He actually agreed with Su-bin. He found most of these cultural learning sessions reductive and offensive to everyone's intelligence, but this was what Samsung wanted. Who was he to complain?

The bachelor emerged, brown hair ruffled, blue eyes piercing. The ticker let the audience know he was a real estate agent in Ohio. The camera cut to the female contestants whispering to one another.

Woo-jin's hand popped up, a mop of black hair shaking with anticipation.

"Are the women actually excited to see him, or are they just acting? I don't see how this man could be attractive by American standards. Are we really meant to believe this man has sex appeal? His eyes are too close together. His hair is messy. He has freckles. His ears are too big."

Min played the video, waiting for a close-up, then hitting pause when the bachelor's boyish, Midwestern face appeared, smiling unwittingly.

"Don't ask such stupid questions," Su-bin said. "That's the entire point of this session. This man is attractive by American standards, even if he doesn't fit the stereotype. There's a range. Weren't you listening when Min was talking?"

Min felt the desire to defend Woo-jin, although he did ask incredibly stupid questions and never added much to their meetings. His father was a higher-up at the company, rumored to wield a great deal of power—the only reason he was tolerated.

Min hit play. The women were introduced, their names, ages, and occupations scrolling across the bottom of the screen in shimmering gold cursive.

Woo-jin's plump hand shot up again. "Why would the producers allow a hairdresser or a physical trainer on the show? These aren't attractive professions. Why would the bachelor pick them? People don't care about social class in your country?"

"It's quite the contrary actually. Most Americans are fixated on their social standing in society. In this case, the bachelor's profession and geographic origins place him firmly in the middle class, so he might be quite comfortable marrying someone from a similar background."

"What qualifies as the Midwest again?" Woo-jin asked, looking more confused than ever.

"Don't worry about that," Min said. "You'll be in California for any meetings, so it's not pertinent. That reminds me. When attending these meetings in Los Angeles, be aware of people with alternative lifestyles. As we've discussed, most coastal cities in America are progressive and open-minded. You're bound to meet people who are openly gay or nonconformist in terms of gender and sexuality. It's imperative you're respectful and professional with everyone you interact with."

Min could see Woo-jin struggling over something. He thought it better to have it all out now. "Question, Woo-jin?"

"Just one," he said, reading from his notes. "How can these people be so open about their sexuality? Aren't they worried about social or professional repercussions? A revelation like that would get you fired from your job here, not to mention the teasing and bullying."

Sun gave Min the wrap-this-up-quickly look from where he was sitting. "It's complicated, and a lot depends on where you are exactly. All I can say is that in places like Los Angeles, there isn't the same kind of stigma concerning homosexuality you have here."

Woo-jin nodded knowingly, but it was unlikely anything was getting through to him.

Sun popped up from his seat, rubbing his hands together as he made his way to the front of the room. After flicking on the lights, he took the controller from Min and turned off the projector. "The most important thing," he said, speaking slowly and gesturing with his hands, like they were a group of children, "the most important thing is that you familiarize yourself with the American people, so you're not thrown off by any cultural differences. We can't have any mis-communications ruin our business dealings. And remember, if you run out of things to banter about, just think back to all the television shows we've watched with Min here. They provide endless material for conversation. Americans aren't so different from us, they know most of these reality shows are fake or staged, but they still talk about it at work, discuss it with their friends and family as if it's real. It's essential you share their enthusiasm. Remember, you're in awe of the contestants on *The Biggest Loser*. Americans are always impressed by extreme weight loss. You are disgusted by the things people on *Survivor* are willing to eat. Americans are very squeamish about their food; they don't eat anything if the head is still attached. And now that Min has started our unit on *The Bachelor*, we'll be able to remark on the contestants, their personalities and looks. It's essential you discuss how much you like this season's bachelor with the Americans in your meetings. Tell everyone how genuine he seems, a real all-American Joe. You must understand the psyche of Americans today. They love the underdog, a good old-fashioned love story! And once we've shown our deep understanding of their culture, they'll respect us as business partners. Sprint and their representatives won't be able to say no!"

With that, Sun left them, the way a dictator might leave the stage after speaking to the masses. Su-bin followed, no doubt to complain about Min's presentation. She'd studied abroad at UC Santa Cruz and was equally qualified for his job. But she wasn't American, nor was she a man, and in Korea that got you further than any degree.

Woo-jin hung back, looking over his notes. When the door to the conference room slid shut, he approached Min. He was well-intentioned, but suffered from a bad case of low self-esteem, brought on by his weight and short stature. Min had taken a strange liking to him, not least because being paired with Su-bin was enough to evoke pity for anyone.

"If you don't mind me asking," he said, clutching his notepad like a life vest, "what should we do if the Americans ask us about North Korea?"

Min had been asked endless questions back home: Do you think they have a bomb? Why do they hate us so much? Is your family from North Korea? For Americans, it seemed, it mattered where his family originated. Or at least where one half had, the half that defined him. Woo-jin's questions stirred an old memory, when Min was fifteen, working his first job at a Japanese restaurant. What had the question been? He still remembered.

"No, not where are you from in America: Where are you really from?"

Missiles were launching on CNN behind the bar. B-roll of Kim Jong-il spooled across the screen, impossibly straight lines of soldiers marching in unison, their olive-green uniforms perfectly ironed. Next to them, trucks rolled lazily by, mounted with white arrows of death.

North Korea fires missile into South China Sea, the ticker read.

"It's not just these long-range missiles that are scary, Wolf," an expert was saying. "What's scary is their nuclear capability. If Kim Jong-il gets a nuke, there's no telling what he'll do with it. He's a real nut."

Min glanced at his boss, hoping for a cue, but his stoic face gave nothing away, every ounce of concentration given to cutting the sashimi.

"My family came from Korea," he said.

"North or South?"

"South."

"That's good," the customer said, draining his Sprite and handing it to him, giving the glass a rattle. "I'll take another one of those."

Later that night, Min's boss approached him while he cashed out and balanced the books.

"How'd we do?" he said, putting a hand through his slicked-back hair.

"Fifteen hundred total. Not bad."

His boss looked out the window toward the barren strip mall parking lot buzzing with empty light. The unlucky cars of late-shift Walmart employees sat begrudgingly between faded yellow lines, tacking back and forth across the black sea.

"Why'd you tell that customer your family was from South Korea?" he said, looking at Min warily.

"What do you mean?"

"I mean, why'd you tell him you were Korean at all? You see what they say on television. All the bad things they say about North Korea."

"I just told him the truth. What do you say?"

"I tell them I'm Japanese. I own a sushi restaurant after all. The customers don't think twice about it. Being Korean is bad for business. Better to say you're Japanese next time. Americans like the Japanese: Honda, Mitsubishi, Toshiba. They trust the Japanese. They know the Japanese. They bombed the Japanese. They don't know Korea. North or South—it's all the same to them," he said.

Back then, Min had tried to understand what compelled someone to do such a thing. He tried to understand why this man would rather lie than explain. What made him take the easier route? Didn't all that lying, all that erasure, take a toll on a person?

Years later Min would understand completely, repeating the very same self-betrayal. Failing to correct those who mispronounced his name, accepting whatever nationality strangers ascribed to him, feigning ignorance on how to handle chopsticks—he'd done it all in the name of acceptance, hoping that one day who and what he was wouldn't matter.

Then he'd arrived in Seoul, met Yu-jin, and things had slowly, imperceptibly shifted. He'd felt something like acceptance, at least until he spoke or showed his face; then people saw a foreigner, a *kyopo*, and jettisoned him with a steely stare. But in that brief moment before he was identified, labeled, there was a sense that he was closer to belonging to something than he'd ever been. But now, with Yu-jin gone, Min wondered whether he was fooling himself. Was his job here no different from the one in New York? Was he just playing another part? None of this was helpful to Woo-jin, however.

"They won't ask you anything," Min said, thinking it better to keep him in the dark. He didn't seem like the type of person who could handle much adversity. "Su-bin's just trying to scare you."

"But it wasn't Su-bin. Boss said something about it. He said we must denounce Kim Jong-il. He said we must tell the Americans our families are from the South."

"Just because Sun is the boss doesn't mean he always knows what he's talking about. You're going to L.A. No one's going to ask you about North Korea. They'll just think you're another American."

※

Sun's office, like most in the Samsung building, emitted a sense of austerity—everything made of glass and steel. A monitor sat on one corner of the glossy black desk, along with a telephone and an abstract desk lamp that belonged in a museum.

Sun swiveled in his chair. "If everything goes well with Su-bin and Woo-jin in Los Angeles, Sprint's executives will come to Seoul in the fall. But let's not talk about Woo-jin anymore. What do you say we go out tonight? Me, you, some of the other project managers. You've been doing great work for us. We'd like to show our appreciation."

"I'd rather not," Min said, thinking about Yu-jin's memorial. "Coming to work was difficult enough."

Sun stood up. "You're in Korea, remember?" he said, giving him a playful jab in the shoulder. "To reject a social invitation from your boss would be very disrespectful. In Korea you must do everything the boss says. Drink when I say drink, dance when I say dance. But you already know all of this." He led Min out to the elevator. "Go over to Apgujeong, buy a nice suit. Put it on the company card. And be ready by eight."

"But I—"

He pressed the button for the elevator. "No is not an option, Min. Korean boss, remember?" He pointed to himself with two thumbs. "I know how you Americans love to scurry home to your big houses with big lawns and sit in front of your big televisions with your big families, cut off from the world. But not tonight. Tonight we are going to celebrate like a family!"

Min held the elevator door before getting in. "Why'd you tell Woo-jin to say his family came from South Korea?"

"Well, why not? It's a perfectly reasonable thing to advise him on. You know as well as anyone that people are going to ask. Don't be so sensitive. He'll be fine."

Min stepped into the elevator.

"Where did the Korean side of your family come from?" Sun asked before the doors closed.

"The South."

"Good," he said with a smile. "Then you won't ever have to lie either."

FOURTEEN

YU-JIN

The girl with that je ne sais quoi

After my father's impromptu visit, I realized that no matter how insular, how private a world So-ra and I built, it would never be enough. One day or the next, we'd come up against the hard truth of everything around us, and this place we'd built, made of desire and belief, would shatter like fine china. And even if So-ra was strong enough, even if she could withstand the gawking, the bullying, the banishment, I wasn't. To be a spectacle, an oddity, was my greatest fear, second only to disownment. My father would never condone my transgressions; he'd stop paying for my schooling, my apartment. So with a renewed sense of purpose, my father's words still resounding in my head, I revived our search for a roommate.

Misaki didn't happen by accident or chance. Misaki was our do-ing. She was our plan. We plucked her, like a flower, a snapdragon. She was known around Ewha—the girl with fashion and money, the girl with that *je ne sais quoi*, the girl who'd been sent away to Seoul by her rich Japanese parents. Rumors abounded, whispers in the wind: a hateful stepmother; a prescription drug problem; a penchant for bad boys. Regardless of the tale, one thing was certain: she'd brought shame upon her family. Why else would someone leave their country, their home?

So-ra and I agreed she'd be the perfect roommate. She could pay more in rent for the larger bedroom. She wouldn't have a lot of guests. She was an outsider in every sense of the word. She'd be happy just to make some friends.

We found her studying in the quiet section of the library, headphones on, notebooks strewn across the table. We'd been watching her for a few days, from a distance. I'd never seen her socializing with anyone. And while she spent a lot of time on campus, she wasn't a very serious student. From what I'd gathered she spent most of her time flipping through the library's prized subscriptions of foreign magazines: *Vogue*, *Elle*, and *Vanity Fair*.

So-ra cleared her throat, drawing a few scowls from girls at other tables, studying obediently, bent to their work like potters at their wheels. Misaki took no notice. So-ra pulled one of the chairs back from the table and sat down with a confidence that never ceased to amaze me. "Misaki, right?"

A resounding *sssshhhhh* surged around us. A glare from Misaki seemed to silence Ewha's most studious. "Yeah. We had a class together last year. So-ra, right?" she said, sliding her headphones down around her neck.

"Exactly," So-ra said, pulling me down beside her. "Ancient Civilization. God, that class was a bore."

"I didn't think it was that bad."

Her reaction seemed to throw So-ra a bit, but she quickly regained her composure and momentum. "This is my friend Yu-jin.

We've been living in this amazing three-bedroom in Daehangno since the summer. We were so sick of living in the dorms, we just had to get out. But we've been looking for a third roommate for a while, and we thought you might join us."

"Why me? I mean, don't you have other friends?"

"We don't actually," I said, going along with the strategy So-ra and I had devised before speaking with her. "We were roommates the first two years and haven't met anyone else really. A lot of the girls here are kind of lame. We figured you'd be interested. Unless you like the people you're living with now."

"It's not that," Misaki said, weighing our proposal. "I just never considered living off campus."

So-ra slid an index card across the table. "Here's my number. Just let us know as soon as you can. This apartment isn't gonna be available for long."

A dour-looking girl who'd been enduring our conversation stood up from her desk in a huff and was making her way toward our table, no doubt ready to chastise us about the strict library policies on behavior and etiquette, but Misaki shooed her away with a hand. "They're going. They're going."

It took a few days, but in the end Misaki agreed to our proposal. It wasn't until she'd moved her things in and gotten settled that I broke the news to her about paying more rent. I did it with tact, pointing out that she'd gotten the bigger bedroom. I knew she had money, so I didn't feel so bad about it. She didn't seem to have much of a problem with the arrangement, especially when we were all hanging out as a group: clubbing, exploring the city, avoiding our work.

She never mentioned anything from her past, and I didn't pry. I was more than happy to keep things superficial. It reminded me of my friendships with my girlfriends in high school, where we somehow managed to talk for hours about nothing.

At first, we had fun together, the three of us, in that way women can grow close without knowing one another. It was by design, of course. So-ra and I had no intention of letting Misaki into our circle. But we knew making her comfortable, making her feel like she belonged, was important for the transition to go smoothly. But it wasn't long before So-ra and I began to separate from her. At first it was little things: starting dinner without her, forgetting to text when we said we would. Bit by bit we nudged her from our lives. She made it easy for us, too, leaving at all hours of the night. Sleep was not something she seemed to require. Bleary-eyed, high heels scuffed, she'd come back to the apartment just as So-ra and I were waking up.

"Where do you think she goes?" I'd asked So-ra.

She snickered. "Maybe she's moonlighting as an escort. How else could she afford all those nice clothes?"

I stifled a laugh. The idea of Misaki accompanying rich old men on dates wasn't beyond plausibility.

I suspected So-ra distanced Misaki from us because she never had any real affinity for her. She was part of the equation, a requirement. For me, ostracizing Misaki came from a place of fear, a deep anxiety that she'd discover what So-ra and I were. Sometimes I'd notice her watching us from the couch while we cooked breakfast, early light pouring through the windows, everyone in pajamas, messy hair, bare faces. She acted preoccupied, headphones on, fingers flipping glossy magazine pages, but I felt her gaze, wondering why we were so giddy, so blissfully happy.

I hated having this intruder in my house. A spy. Someone I was forced to treat like a friend but keep at arm's length. But she was a necessity. While my father didn't particularly like that she was Japanese, he said she was better than nothing, and her presence quickly relaxed things between us. He was less suspicious of my friendship with So-ra. Still, there were times when I wondered whether she put our secret in more danger.

So-ra told me I was getting paranoid, which I was. The closer I felt to her, the more I worried about discovery. Sometimes Misaki would come home while we were in bed together. We'd giggle, safe behind locked doors. But in my laugh I recognized fear—that I'd be outed, that So-ra didn't care what happened to us. There was a recklessness to her, a disregard for what anyone thought. In the beginning—when everything was new—I'd found the quality admirable, intoxicating even. I'd looked on her with awe, yearned for her closeness, hoping to absorb even an ounce of her courage and strength. But now, as our relationship had grown more palpable, I found myself distressed by the risks she was willing to take at my expense.

"So what if Misaki knows," So-ra said. "So what if anyone knows."

We were in the kitchen. I was trying to study for a government exam. So-ra sat by the open window, watching the sun set, bruising the sky purple. "You can't mean that. Surely you understand why this needs to be kept secret. When I was in high school, there was a rumor, just a silly little anecdote, about two boys being together. They were bullied mercilessly. Both of them eventually dropped out. One took his own life. It didn't even matter if the rumors were true."

So-ra grew somber. "I'm sorry that boy took his life, but that was in Gyeryong. Things are different in Seoul. Plus, people are changing, attitudes are shifting. I've shown you the bars and clubs, even the on-line forums; there's a whole community out there. A real support system."

"I don't even know what community I belong to, and I'm not like you. I can't risk everything for a feeling."

"Are you ashamed of this? Is that what's driving this paranoia?"

"Of course! Of course that's why. What else would it be? This isn't right."

"It's not right?" So-ra echoed, winching the window shut, the chatter and rumble of the city gone.

"You don't understand. My father's career, his reputation. It would be a scandal. I'd bring shame upon my entire family. Can you imagine? The daughter of the Minister of National Defense with a girl. And my own career, my path. Whatever goals I have would be destroyed. Even if I could survive socially, my father would disown me if he finds out what we're doing. He wouldn't be able to under-stand."

"Is it about your family or you?"

"Both, of course. How could it not be?"

"You'd forsake your own happiness for the acceptance and praise of others. For your family's support."

"They've sacrificed everything for me."

"You don't think they're getting something out of all this? Have you ever considered why your father is pushing you into the same career path he took? All you are is another chance to succeed where he's failed."

"That's not fair," I said, feeling my voice quiver. "Maybe they aren't as open-minded or free-spirited as your parents, but they love me. They want the best for me."

"I'm not asking you to advertise it, but you don't have to treat this like it's some kind of unspeakable sin. It's perfectly natural."

I sat at the island with only words I knew would hurt So-ra. If this was natural, if this was normal, why did it feel so wrong, why had the world condemned it otherwise?

"I was foolish to think you could understand what we have," So-ra said, before walking to her room and shutting the door, leaving me in sudden silence.

What more did So-ra want from me? We couldn't declare it to the world, wear it as a badge of honor. We weren't in Berlin or Toronto. Even if Seoul was a big international city, it was still Korea. There were no antidiscrimination laws in place, no legal acknowledgments for LGBT people. As far as our culture was concerned, we didn't exist. It was as if by never openly acknowledging us, they hoped to will us into oblivion. In private, among their closest friends and family, most people, I suspected, expressed how they really felt: we were morally corrupt, repulsive, even mentally unstable. And whatever was between So-ra and me, whatever we were, it would never be sanctioned by anyone: our families, our country. We'd spend the rest of our lives on the margins, moving in the shadows. At least for So-ra it was easier. There was certainty in her desire. In a singular fashion, she knew what she wanted.

But for me, to want another woman—it was a desire I'd keep secret forever. I had to. And no matter what So-ra said about the fleeting nature of attraction, how my situation with her didn't make me one thing and not the other, I didn't see how she could possibly be right. She'd said I was antiquated, old-fashioned in the way I thought about sexuality. It wasn't static or inert. It could move, change. It was true, among all the people I'd found myself drawn to, she'd been the only woman. But none of that mattered out there, to my parents, to anyone. They wouldn't see it like So-ra did. I wasn't even sure I agreed with her. It defied my own understanding.

Hearing the front door unlocking, I scrambled to open my books and dry my tears.

It was Misaki, arms weighed down by black shopping bags. She tossed her jacket on the couch and shook her headphones from her head. Despite knowing she came from money, I was still impressed with the amount of shopping she did. I don't think I'd ever seen her wear the same outfit twice.

"Everything okay?" she said, looking around like she half expected So-ra to be in the room.

"Why wouldn't it be?"

"Never mind," she said, walking to her bedroom.

"Wait a second. Wanna go out? We could grab something to eat."

"Now?" she said, surprised.

"Why not?"

"Where's So-ra?"

"I don't know. But let's go out. Just the two of us."

Misaki looked at me cautiously, eyelids dusted in smoky eyeshadow. "What did you have in mind?"

"You pick," I said, suddenly feeling reinvigorated, excited at the prospect of getting out of the apartment.

Quickly, and without warning, the energy had shifted between me and So-ra. I felt constricted, limited, like she was beginning to have expectations of me, of whatever we were. It was suffocating. And what I'd once seen as independence and strength now seemed to me bitter prejudice, against my parents, my upbringing. However petty and small of me it was, I wanted to get back at So-ra, show that I could strike out on my own.

·⊩·

Misaki brought me to Yeouido, the financial district in Seoul. I'd never been to the small island jutting out into the Han, mostly because there wasn't much there. Unless you wanted to stare at skyscrapers and bankers, Yeouido wasn't very interesting. Misaki seemed to know the area, oddly enough, navigating the wide, boring streets like a local.

At the river we made a right, passing couples and families strewn over the grassy promenade and concrete steps taking in the warm evening. Across the glassy water, downtown Seoul gleamed like a circus. And in the faraway distance, I thought I could see Seoul Tower, mint green against the mountains.

Another right. Then a left. Now I wondered if Misaki even knew where she was going.

"Are you sure the fish is good here?"

We'd agreed on sushi, and I'd been happy to let Misaki choose the place, but after almost an hour on the subway and what seemed like ten never-ending blocks, my enthusiasm was flagging. Proving my independence to So-ra wasn't worth this.

She turned around, walking backwards against the wind, hair flailing on either side of her face. "Bankers have to eat, too."

It seemed like Misaki knew more about Seoul than most Koreans. Being an outsider had its advantages, it seemed. Without a distinct friend group at Ewha, she must have been forced to strike out on her own.

"Best sashimi in Seoul," she said, giving our order in Japanese to the chef with liver-spotted ears. "Not as good as Tokyo, but what can you do."

I looked around the dingy basement restaurant. It was a hole-in-the-wall—that much was evident. I shifted the uneven legs of my stool. I wanted to take a sponge to the bar, stained with grime and whatever else. "I never would've guessed."

"Still, this is pretty good," Misaki said almost wistfully as she poured *sake* for us. "The best food is always where you least expect it."

"Do you ever get homesick?"

Misaki popped open a black makeup mirror and checked her eyeliner. "Not really. It's kind of nice getting away. My parents can be controlling. I wanted out. That's kind of why I'm here. They couldn't object since it's all coordinated through my university in Tokyo."

"I feel like you're never home. Where are you always going?" My tone was more accusatory than I'd intended, but Misaki didn't seem to care.

"Just out," she said. "You should come sometime. There's always random stuff going on in Itaewon. It's cool meeting other expats and hearing all their reasons for living in Seoul."

"Isn't that where all the foreigners live? I heard it's dangerous."

Misaki shrugged. "I haven't had any problems. I guess it's different if you're Korean." She closed her mirror with a snap. "What about you? Do you miss your parents?"

I wasn't sure I was willing to go this deep with Misaki. I'd wanted to hang out somewhere, but now that we were here, talking and drinking, it seemed too intimate. It had been easy to treat her with disdain when I didn't know anything about her.

"No. They live close by."

"Oh, that's right," she said, like she'd forgotten, although I knew she hadn't. Misaki never forgot things. She was always present, listening, watching. So-ra didn't give her enough credit, but I knew she wasn't to be underestimated.

I wanted to ask more details about her nights out. Was she clubbing? Sleeping around? Nothing would surprise me. But I resisted, let my curiosity die. If she confided in me, told me anything, I'd have to return the favor, something I was unwilling to do. I drank my *sake*. Smiled.

"What about So-ra? Her parents aren't around. She's from Busan, right? She must get homesick."

I suddenly regretted getting dinner with her. I wondered what So-ra was doing. She was undoubtedly furious with me. Even my ancestors would be upset with me over this new transgression. Eating with the enemy, they'd whisper. They stole our culture, our art; they raped our women, erased our language, and now you're having a friendly meal with one of them?

The chef presented us with a board of tuna sashimi, each piece cut with precision. "Dōzo omeshiagarikudasai."

Misaki ate with a kind of furious utility, speedily selecting a slice of tuna and grazing the surface of her soy sauce before depositing it in her mouth with blissful satisfaction. "Eat, eat," she said when she saw me watching her. "I'll finish it all if you give me the chance."

Misaki was right about the sashimi. It was the best I'd tasted, ever, buttery and rich. I tried to hide how impressed I was. If she was right about this place, I wondered what else she'd discovered in Seoul. Eventually the conversation got easier, drifting into safer topics.

After dinner we sat and drank more. It seemed Misaki was good friends with the owner. Is this what she did when she was out of the apartment? Chat up old Japanese guys? While they spoke in Japanese, I resisted the urge to text So-ra, apologize for acting like a petulant child.

"He says you're very beautiful," Misaki said, turning to me.

The sushi chef grinned at me, teeth yellowed and worn.

"He's impressed by your height."

"Tell him thanks," I said. "I should probably be getting back."

I was tired of listening to them, these two strangers, speaking a foreign tongue.

Misaki's face revealed no surprise. "So soon?"

"I forgot I have a paper to write. It's due tomorrow."

"That's fine," she said. "Run along to So-ra. You two can't seem to go more than a few hours without each other."

The sushi chef retreated into the kitchen, sliding the flimsy plastic room-divider closed, like a sea-worn mariner battening down the hatches before a storm.

"What's that supposed to mean?"

"It's not meant to mean anything different. Not everything is subterfuge and disguise, you know. Some people actually mean what they say."

So Misaki knew something was going on between me and So-ra. "This is what I get for feeling bad for you. I was just trying to do something nice," I said, struggling to swallow the tremor in my voice.

"Is that what you were trying to do? Because it seems to me like you were trying to make yourself feel better. And I don't need your pity. I'm just fine. I know what I'm doing here. You're the one who's confused."

Would Misaki tell anyone? Would they believe her? My vision

narrowed, darkness tunneling forward. "We've been nothing but nice to you."

Misaki took out her pocketbook and put down some cash. "I don't mind if you and So-ra don't like me. It's not a big deal. But don't pretend to. That's worse."

My thoughts raced ahead, considering my options. Maybe I could salvage things, bring Misaki back into our circle. If she knew everything, I had to keep her close, keep my eye on her. "We weren't pretending. We can all still do things together."

Misaki looked at me, a pitying smirk on her glossy lips. "I'm not gonna tell anyone, if that's what you're worried about. I'm not like you and So-ra, I don't use things against people," she said before pushing the door open. Then she was gone.

I sat for a long time after she left, wondering what to do. How long had Misaki known? Could she be trusted? It didn't seem like I had much of a choice. The sushi chef never returned. A muted television played on the wall. A meteorologist dressed in a hideous yellow dress was strutting in front of tacky weather graphics. I shivered. The state of the restaurant revolted me. Scuffed and broken tiles, a dust-filled fan oscillating to some bygone tune—I had to get out. I clutched my bag and rushed outside. I needed to go home and shower, to wash this filth off me.

I texted So-ra.

I'm coming back. I don't want to fight.

Her response was almost immediate.

Just come home. I'm sorry.

When I returned to the apartment, apprehensively pushing So-ra's bedroom door open, she was all tears and regret, blanketing me in her embrace, pulling me close as she kissed me frantically. We stood for a long time like that, holding each other. I thought about telling So-ra about Misaki, but before I could speak, she took my hand and led me to the edge of her bed.

"Look at me," she said, her face blotchy and swollen.

How had we gotten here? Where was the strong So-ra, the intrepid explorer, the daredevil?

"I'm sorry," she said, interlocking our fingers. "I pushed too hard. I'm asking too much of you, I know that. It was selfish. You're right. There are parts of this that are easier for me." She fell silent, chewing her lip, blood peeking through. "I'm just scared, of how desperate you make me."

"But what does it make me? Doing this, with you."

"It makes you everything you've always been."

"What is this, So-ra? What exactly are we?"

"We can be whatever you want," she said, lips on my neck, tears slipping down my back. "It's fine just the way it is."

I released myself from her embrace, putting space between us. "So we aren't exclusive. We can see other people."

"You know I don't believe in labels. If you meet someone and want to explore things, I'm not gonna stop you. I'd be a hypocrite if I did."

"And what about you?"

"What about me?" So-ra smiled and wiped her cheeks. "I only want you. That doesn't mean we have to confine ourselves to some textbook definition."

I didn't really believe So-ra. I couldn't imagine her accepting a different version of us. Maybe it didn't matter. It wasn't like I wanted to be with anyone else. Still, a small space was opening inside me, a crack, leading to what—a chasm, an abyss. Seeing So-ra this way, cloying, desperate, I recognized something, behavior I'd eventually detest. I wasn't there yet. I remained engrossed, obsessed, with whatever it was we'd built. And yet, as we drew our faces close, cheeks warm, thighs aching, I knew I'd gone too far in my estimation of what I wanted, what I was willing to give up for someone. And the closer she drew me in, the more I felt the rippling, surging desire to resist, to push her away.

FIFTEEN

MIN

Who cares how they look at us?

Min braved the teeming sidewalks, buffeted by shoppers walking three abreast, saddled with bags overflowing with boxes and tissue paper. In brightly lit storefronts, mannequins stood swaddled in the latest fashion from Italy and France. Apgujeong—the Rodeo Drive of Seoul—where celebrities and K-pop stars came to shop, stalked by hordes of adoring fans and picture-hungry photographers. There was no denying the country's transformation into an economic powerhouse in these neighborhoods, where Koreans flocked to cruise the streets in their imported cars and shop at high-end stores, snapping up the trendiest clothes, bags, and shoes. These opulent neighborhoods of Seoul were evidence that Korea *had* thrown off the chains of oppression—they'd repelled the colonizers.

At first sight of a men's clothing store, Min ducked inside, relieved when the heavy glass doors closed behind him. The space felt palatial despite the clusters of shoppers, and he drifted aimlessly from table to table, petrified of examining anything closer, lest he disrupt the swirls of ties and perfectly stacked shirts.

He'd never given his wardrobe much thought before arriving in Korea, where it was immediately clear that how one dressed mattered a great deal. Since then he'd invested in some nicer clothes for work, but apparently he was still lacking.

A saleswoman approached him. "Is there anything in particular you're looking for?"

Min was about to dismiss her help when he looked up. It was Misaki. She was wearing a similar outfit to when he'd last seen her: slim black jeans, a white ruffled shirt with a black blazer. Min could hardly believe this was the same Misaki, surrounded by posh clothing and chic clientele.

"This is where you work?"

She seemed equally shocked to find him standing in front of her. "Yes. But what are you doing here?"

"Shopping. I need a suit."

"Right, of course," she said, regaining her professional tone. She pulled a jacket from the rack. "Let's try this. I'll find you a shirt and tie," she said, walking toward the changing rooms, her impossibly high heels clicking against the white granite floor.

The blazer hung on the door of the changing room. Min stood awkwardly, feet sinking into the plush carpet. "These should work," Misaki said, handing him a white shirt and black tie.

"Isn't this a bit formal?"

She frowned, looking over what she'd selected. "This is standard dress for a Korean memorial. To wear anything else would be disrespectful."

"I'm just buying something for a work function. I wasn't invited to Yu-jin's memorial."

Misaki's cheeks flushed red. "I'm sorry. I just assumed." She snatched the jacket off the hook. "Let me find you something else."

"Wait, hold on!" Min called after her.

If Misaki knew about the memorial, then she must be planning to attend; she could bring him with her. This was his best chance at meeting Yu-jin's father. Then Min could judge whether he was the kind of man who could have been involved in his own daughter's death. It worked to his advantage that he didn't exist to Yu-jin's parents. He could pass as a friend, an acquaintance.

There was a soft knock on the door. She handed him a flashy electric blue suit. "This should be more appropriate."

"I'll try the black one, too. But I might need your help. I don't know when or where the memorial is being held."

"I don't think that's such a good idea," she said quickly.

Nearly reaching for her hand, Min controlled himself. "Please, Misaki."

"Just try on the blue one. I'll get the other," she said, before closing the door.

The suit was a perfect fit. Even the shirt felt right, which surprised Min. He'd never had a jacket fit so well. They were always too long in the arms or too tight in the armpits. Had Misaki sized him up that quickly?

Shivering in the icy air-conditioned changing room, Min slipped on the pants, smooth like silk against his legs.

"How's the fit?" Misaki said from outside.

Min pulled the blazer snug and notched the top button. "It's perfect."

"I'm putting the black suit on the hook. Try it on if you want."

Min was about to open the door, but he sensed that Misaki would prefer to have this conversation without having to see him.

"I can't go without you," he said.

There was silence, and for a moment, Min thought she'd left.

"So-ra really didn't invite you?"

"I wouldn't be asking if she had."

"I see," Misaki said, her voice wavering. "Then I'll go with you. All the information will be up front when you check out."

By the time he'd changed into his old clothes, Misaki was gone. A young man with swooping hair relieved Min of his suits and carried them to the front desk.

The man slipped them into separate bags. "One on the company card and the other on your personal then? Misaki mentioned the blue one is a business expense," he said, as if to allay Min's fear regarding his telepathic ability. He seemed to take great pride in being let in on whatever transaction had occurred in the changing room. "As for the information," he continued, discreetly sliding a card across the counter, "Misaki also wanted you to have this."

On the back was her number, an address, date, and time. The memorial was scheduled for tomorrow.

Min thanked him and put the card in his wallet. The man smiled coyly, head bowing slightly. "No problem at all, sir. She's marvelous, isn't she? I've never met someone who knows so much about Seoul. I've lived here eight years and she puts me to shame," he said, brushing his hair aside with well-manicured fingers. "She's totally plugged in to the underground music scene. She's taken me to some real dives. Places I can't even describe."

"Misaki?"

"You think you're the only guy to buy something just to get a date?"

"She's an acquaintance," Min said, realizing he couldn't really say she was his friend. Was she even an acquaintance? "She's a friend of a friend."

"She's a wonder. A real wonder."

"You said lots of guys come in here because of her?"

The salesman explained how Misaki was paid under the table for her work at the store. Apparently she'd shown up one day, asking for a part-time job. She'd wanted cash compensation only, as she wasn't legally allowed to work in Korea on her student visa. At first the store manager had been skeptical, but after she'd breezed through her training and showed off her impeccably refined style, he never asked any questions. More important, she knew her fashion. She possessed a knack for measurements and could guess a man's suit size within a half-size margin just by looking at him.

As a result, Misaki had accrued somewhat of a cult following among the male clientele. It wasn't uncommon for her to be approached by former customers with the request of a drink, or dinner. They usually bought her gifts, mostly jewelry. Sometimes they came simply to thank her. They'd received positive reactions to their suits, especially the fit, and they wanted to know how she'd known their exact size. "Pathetic, really," the salesman said, dismissing all of Misaki's suitors with a single wave. "No offense."

"None taken," Min said, trying to remember if he'd ever seen her with anyone. There was so little he knew about Misaki. When he'd first started dating Yu-jin, everyone's role was already in place: So-ra was the best friend; Misaki was the strange roommate. He'd never questioned it. He was ashamed to remember all the nights he'd gone out with Yu-jin and So-ra, never thinking to invite Misaki. How many times had they whispered behind her back, laughed at her expense? It was no wonder he'd never really *seen* Misaki. Yu-jin and So-ra had pushed her to the edges well before he came into their lives.

Outside, suit bags slung over his shoulder, Min called his boss to say he wouldn't be joining him for drinks. Something had come up. Sun was indignant, but there was nothing he could say to change Min's mind. With Yu-jin's memorial tomorrow, Min needed to be sharp and alert. He couldn't stay out all night drinking. Sun was abrasive, even threatening on the phone, but they both knew it was all posturing. Min was American, exempt from most social expectations within Samsung.

"Do you want me to return the suit?" Min said once Sun had finished.

"Keep the damn thing. You could use it," he said, before hanging up.

⫸

The next day, Min sat at a table outside a corner bodega, waiting for Misaki. An uncommon cold front had swept through the city, abating the sweltering summer heat and leaving the sky a thin sheet of blue. Dressed in his newly purchased black suit and heavy with grief, Min felt at odds with the beautiful day. Nowhere closer to understanding Yu-jin's death, he felt hollow and adrift, watching families stroll down the sidewalk on their way to the park, children chattering and prancing about, free from their *hagwon* classes. Today was not a day for a memorial, Min thought—a wedding maybe, a picnic.

As the minutes ticked by and Misaki didn't show, Min grew more anxious, hands buried in his pants pockets, pacing the sidewalk. Despite his guaranteed anonymity, he was growing less certain that meeting Yu-jin's family was good idea. After all, Detective Park had told him not to meddle in the case, warning him that Yu-jin's father wasn't someone to be messed with. What had once seemed like a perfectly rational plan now seemed foolish, perhaps even reckless.

Rounding the corner, Misaki appeared, all coolness in a simple black dress and shawl, large sunglasses shading her face. She'd come. He was struck by this gesture of kindness and what he hoped might be forgiveness. He'd been nothing but rude since the day they'd met, yet here she was, helping him. It dawned on him that she was the closest thing he had to a friend at the moment.

As they walked in silence, Min was struck by their steps, perfectly in sync. His legs were much longer than hers, but she somehow managed to keep up, matching him step for step. It defied basic mathematics. Misaki seemed to defy everything.

They stopped outside a nondescript two-story building. When they entered, Min noticed two men standing on either side of the doorway. They wore black suits, but they didn't seem to be attending the memorial. Both were short and stocky, hair sheared close against their pale scalps, earpieces curling over their cauliflowered ears. These men were unmistakably connected with Yu-jin's father in some way, perhaps his security detail.

Bathed in amber light, the lobby imbued a sense of calm. While Misaki talked with someone at the front desk, Min watched the men from the corner of his eye. One put his hand to his ear and nodded, but that was all. There were other people present, all dressed in black; some women wore the traditional *hanbok*.

Misaki pressed the elevator button. "Not everyone here is coming to Yu-jin's memorial," she explained, realizing his confusion. "There are over twenty memorial rooms in this building." The doors opened. "Today is the second day. Most close relatives will have already come. Today is when her friends or anyone who knew her indirectly is welcome to pay their respects."

As they boarded the elevator, an elderly woman approached. Min held the door. When the woman saw Misaki, she stopped and said something under her breath before turning away.

"What was that about?" Min asked.

"It's nothing," Misaki said, checking her makeup in the mirrored wall. "Sometimes older people have problems with me."

"Because you're Japanese?"

Misaki nodded. "I don't blame them. My country did terrible things here." The door screeched shut. "It's just that I love Korea. The history, the culture. That's why I decided to come here for university. Is that selfish?"

"Not at all," Min said.

"I'll always be treated differently here, and that's okay," Misaki said. "I imagine it's harder for you."

They were arriving at their floor, and Min didn't have time to reply to her. He followed her down the hall, a strange mix between a hotel and hospital. Before they went inside, Misaki looked him over. "May I?" she said, taking hold of his tie and straightening it, cinching it into the crux of his throat.

She spoke calmly. "There will be a picture of Yu-jin surrounded by a lot of flowers. Her family will greet us. Take this envelope. Put it in the inside pocket of your blazer."

"What is it?"

"Cash. Drop it in the white box before you leave. You should see it right when you walk in. Don't be alarmed if her mother is crying."

"Why would I be alarmed?"

Misaki took a deep breath. "You know how you're supposed to slurp your soup loudly to show your appreciation? To show your host how delicious it is?"

Min was beginning to doubt the entire endeavor. "Yes."

"Well, crying at your child's memorial is the same kind of thing. Understand?"

"I think so," Min said, wondering why she was going to such lengths to help him.

"Just watch me closely when we get inside and follow my lead."

It was an austere space, simple and functional. A picture of Yu-jin Min had never seen before stood against the back wall; underneath it sat a large urn filled with sand holding three smoldering joss sticks. Half the room was divided by a sliding plastic partition. Min assumed this was where the family relaxed while waiting for visitors. As they entered, Yu-jin's mother and father appeared from a side room and lined up to the right of the portrait.

Misaki approached the photograph and lit a joss stick, sinking it into the ash-powdered sand. Stepping away, she executed a deep bow, her knees, palms, and forehead touching the floor. She held the position for a moment, before standing and repeating the motion. The third was a half bow facing Yu-jin's family. The entire movement was graceful but exacting—swift but compassionate.

As if on command, Yu-jin's mother let forth a guttural wail, clutching at Yu-jin's father's forearm. The wails grew louder. Yu-jin's father stood stoically, supporting his wife, face ashen, jaw set in a firm line.

His steely gaze remained fixed on the blank wall ahead. One glance at him and Min could tell he'd spent his entire life in the military: dense shoulders, a rigid posture. This was exactly how Min had imagined the Minister of National Defense would look. All those years of dedicated service had chipped away every excess, leaving only what was necessary. Detective Park was right; Yu-jin's father was a man to be feared. But was he capable of taking his daughter's life?

Misaki shook their hands, saying something inaudible. She nodded to Min, indicating it was his turn. Yu-jin was nearly unrecognizable in the large photograph, blue blazer over a collared shirt buttoned to her throat, two white ribbons in her hair. It looked like her high school yearbook picture, a pixelated gray background behind her. This wasn't the Yu-jin Min had known. This wasn't the girl who'd listened to Van Morrison with him, strolling the streets. The girl who'd flaunted their relationship to the world, holding hands, kissing him in public. The more disapproving looks she got from men and the elderly, the better; it only emboldened her. This was a Yu-jin he'd never known: a high school girl, buttoned-up, still under her parents' watch.

Hands trembling, Min took a joss stick from a small pine box on the floor and lit it with a match. He focused on the background of Yu-jin's photograph, sinking into the nebulous nothingness. Going through the motions, he closed his eyes and repeated Misaki's movements. His knees cracked loudly as he bent forward and rested his forehead against the floor. The sobs of Yu-jin's mother had lessened in their anguish, only a dull moan permeating the room.

What does someone say at the altar of their dead girlfriend? What do we say to give moments meaning? Perhaps it would have been easier if there were a priest, a shaman, anyone for Min to follow. But here, bent forward, his body slumping, he was ill-equipped to find anything for Yu-jin in that moment. Only a promise: I'll find out why.

Min rose and approached Yu-jin's parents. Her mother, face raw and bare, stared at him with blank eyes. She had no idea who he was. When Yu-jin's father gave no indication of recognizing him either, Min assumed his existence was a well-hidden secret. They shook hands, the Minister regarding him with kind indifference. His skin was like sandpaper, rough and callused against Min's soft palm.

Now that he'd met Yu-jin's father, Min wasn't sure what to do next. He'd been hoping something would be made clear, a clue connecting the Minister directly to his daughter's death. But now that he was here, standing with Misaki, the photograph of Yu-jin expanding exponentially, absorbing everything else in the room, the air-conditioning and Yu-jin's mother's cries mingling into a slow and steady dirge, he knew Detective Park had been right. There was nothing to be done, no answer he could find here, no lever he could pull. He was helpless. And worse, he'd begun to believe he'd never known Yu-jin at all. It was a mistake to be here, paying his respects to a fantasy.

He was about to suggest leaving when So-ra entered. Seeing Min and Misaki, she recoiled in surprise, but managed to catch herself. Min wondered if anyone else had noticed that look of dread. The Minister readjusted the cuffs of his jacket. While So-ra paid her respects, Yu-jin's mother led Min and Misaki to a side room before rejoining her husband. Sounds of weeping soon followed.

They waited for Yu-jin's parents and So-ra to join them. With an outstretched hand, the Minister instructed them to sit around a small table covered with *banchan*: *kimchi*, *kongnamul*, and *saengseonjjim*, still steaming, filling the room with an aroma of fresh halibut.

Yu-jin's father motioned for So-ra to pour everyone barley water. She obeyed, eyes never leaving the tabletop.

They ate in silence. Min watched So-ra intently, waiting for her to betray some reason for her bizarre reaction to seeing him. Why hadn't she wanted him to come? Not wanting to appear disrespectful, he picked at the *kongnamul*, the cold soybean sprouts wet and tasteless. Next to Min, Misaki ate with methodical precision, selecting each strip of napa cabbage and hunk of fish with care before placing it in her bowl of rice. If he didn't know any better, he'd say she'd come for the free meal.

The Minister cleared his throat, loosening the tie around his neck. So-ra poured him more water, her hands trembling. "It's such a pleasure to meet those that were closest to Yu-jin. Our daughter was always a private person, even before she went to college. It's bittersweet to find out in this manner that she was loved by so many."

He spoke to no one in particular, but Min couldn't help but feel like his comments were directed toward him. Who else would these mysterious friends be? He was on the verge of asking So-ra who'd paid their respects, but Yu-jin's father continued speaking.

He spoke of Korea, how it was once a country of homogeneity, not just in race but in ideals and beliefs. But now, he said, because of globalization, the country was under siege from foreign influences. This was no ordinary ideology, he stressed. For centuries, his country had repelled invaders of every kind. They'd come to her shores in their battleships, cut down through her northern borders on horseback and then in tanks; they occupied her skies, giant birds of steel that rattled and screamed, dropping rolling thunder. Invaders, colonizers, proselytizers, pacifiers, allies in disguise. And everywhere she could, she'd fought, even when it was a losing battle. But the country faced something different now, something far more insidious. Now Korea's young worshipped at the altar of Western culture. They cut their eyelids, broke their noses, bleached their hair, hoping to look like anything but themselves.

Min felt the old man's gaze on him. "In our search for happiness, we've come to believe only ideas existing outside of our culture can save us. You understand, don't you, Min?" he said.

Before Min could reply, So-ra stood up, coughing or crying, he wasn't sure, and fled from the room. He almost followed her, but something stopped him. Yu-jin's father was watching him. Even more unnerving was Misaki, blissfully unaware, chopsticks and mouth in perfect synchronization. For the first time, Min wondered if his identity wasn't a secret at all. Perhaps this was all a test to find out who Yu-jin's boyfriend was. The Minister was waiting for him to react, to expose himself.

The Minister broke his stare with a smile. "What I guess I'm trying to say is that we are grateful, my wife and I. Thank you for paying your respects."

This was their hint to leave. Misaki looked up, having just finished her rice. They bowed to Yu-jin's parents and left. In the main room, there was no sign of So-ra. Min told Misaki to go ahead; he'd find her in the lobby. "I just need a minute."

"Of course," Misaki said, leaving him alone.

He lingered in front of Yu-jin's photograph, waiting for So-ra to reappear. Were the Minister's words a warning? An explanation? Was he pointing the finger at Min and saying, You killed her, you did this?

His joss stick was gone, burned to nothing below this Yu-jin he'd never known.

"Who cares how they look at us," Yu-jin had said one night. They were dancing at a club. So-ra was at the bar getting drinks. "They're just jealous." She moved closer, kissing his neck, her body against his.

Min moved back, aware of the men on the periphery, glaring at them. He could almost hear them repeating the phrases he'd heard every time they'd gone dancing: you're stealing our women; she's only with you because you're American.

Yu-jin's eyes flared in the darkness. "What's your problem," she shouted over the music.

"You don't have to turn it into a public demonstration," Min said.

So-ra arrived with their drinks.

"Fine then," Yu-jin said, taking So-ra's hand. "I'll be dancing with her for the rest of the night."

The photograph reminded Min of nothing. But it was her. He couldn't deny it. From behind the plastic room-divider, Min thought he heard someone moving around. Making sure the Minister and his wife were still in the side room, Min peeked behind the partition. So-ra was sitting among bedrolls and folded blankets, staring at a glossy pamphlet.

"What're you doing back here?"

So-ra let the paper fall from her hands. "You shouldn't have come," she said, looking straight ahead. "Especially with her."

"Misaki? I wouldn't have found this place without her. She's been more of a friend to me than you."

So-ra stood and glared at him, eyes bloodshot, fingertips ghost white as they clutched the lapels of his jacket. "Everything, Min. She ruined everything. We were perfectly happy. How could you bring her here?"

Before Min could defend Misaki, So-ra slumped back to the

ground, coming to rest in a mound at his feet, head buried in her hands. "You weren't supposed to be here."

"What the hell are you talking about? What did Misaki do?"

"It doesn't matter," she said, shoulders convulsing, breath jagged. "None of it matters anymore. I didn't want Yu-jin's father to know who you were, what you looked like. I wanted to keep you safe."

He helped her up. "Keep me safe from what?"

"You don't understand. He's a cruel and hateful man."

"Capable of making his daughter's death look like a suicide?"

"It's not what you think, Min. But he's powerful. He can make your life difficult."

"Is that what he's done to you? Scared you into trying to convince me that Yu-jin's death was a suicide?"

So-ra's eyes darted to the main room at the sound of more guests arriving to pay their respects. "I know you want to think what Yu-jin did wasn't like her, but it was. She was under immense pressure," So-ra whispered, tears rimming the edges of her eyelids. She seemed to be pleading for something. The emotionally distant, tough So-ra he'd once known was no more. "You need to stay away from the Minister. He's controlling everything. He knew Yu-jin had killed herself. That's why the police arrived so quickly, why nothing's gotten out about the real reason she took her life. Everyone's in his pocket."

"Let me help you," Min said.

So-ra shook her head. "I have to go. I'll stall Yu-jin's parents. They can't see us talking like this."

"If you really want me to believe Yu-jin killed herself, tell me why she did it. I deserve to know as much as anyone."

"We can't talk here. Meet me under the Hannam Bridge tomorrow at seven A.M. on the south side. I'll tell you everything. But be careful what you say around Misaki. She can't be trusted," So-ra said, before disappearing behind the partition.

Min quickly left the room, but not before picking up the pamphlet she'd dropped and slipping it into his jacket pocket.

SIXTEEN

YU-JIN

Apple on a willow

Everyone always liked to play psychic when I told them I was an only child. "I had a feeling" or "I thought so," they'd say, with all-knowing smiles that hinted at some immutable truth unknown to eleven-year-old girls. What was it about me that betrayed this oddity?

"We only wanted one," my father would say, "and when you were born, well—it wouldn't be fair to your brother or sister to try and live up to you. You were everything we wanted, Yu-jin. From the beginning we knew you were special."

"Everyone was hoping for a boy," my mother said one day when I'd come home from elementary school, distraught from a family tree project, in which I was made even more aware of my unique situation. "But when they told me you were a girl, I was overjoyed. People wish for sons; they pray for sons. But I had brothers. You know your uncles. Spoiled through and through. Sons, especially the eldest, are given everything. They grow up entitled and aimless. I was ecstatic when the doctors said you were a girl. I knew you would be hardworking and honest—never spoiled. Both your father and I knew it. And how right we were."

It was only in high school that I began to consider my parents' answers suspicious, even rehearsed. It wasn't anything in particular they said or did; I just found it impossible to believe they'd only wanted one child. There was nothing they could do or say to disabuse me of this inkling, which only seemed to grow exponentially, spreading out like watercolor paint. Had they wanted more children? Could they have had more? I always suspected they had tried, but my parents never alluded to any difficulties. We weren't that kind of family; we didn't talk about things that hadn't happened. We did not wallow in regret, as my father always liked to say.

When I was young, my father always made me feel grateful for being an only child. I was the center of his universe, meant to be. He liked to take me camping. Just the two of us. He'd pick me up early from school, sometimes still wearing his military uniform, car packed with everything we'd need for a weekend in the mountains: tent, sleeping bags, gas stove, and fishing poles.

Our destination was always Chiaksan National Park, a few hours north of Gyeryong, where the air seemed cleaner and the water colder. I was given full autonomy over the music on these camping trips, sliding in a CD and serenading my father with the latest pop hits. With a particular song on repeat, he'd eventually learn the words, and then we'd sing along together, windows down, as trees whipped green and gold beyond the sunroof.

Beyond the city limits, Gyeryong in our rearview mirror, I could feel my father relax, ever so slightly, his mood unwinding like the mountain roads that snaked between granite peaks. Forgoing the public campgrounds, we'd turn off somewhere—a spot my father had no doubt landed upon in his meticulous preparations—and park the car, hefting packs upon our shoulders, weighed down with bed-rolls and sleeping bags, metal plates and canteens echoing through the solitude with a cheerful jangle.

Even as we made our way deeper into the forest, I always felt safe, following my father's footsteps. Ahead of me, his frame parted all foliage and shrubs for me; they brushed my arms with only a gentle glance. At the sound of water, he would pick up speed, excited by the prospect of finding a good fishing hole. Sometimes I'd stop momen-tarily and peer back from where we'd come, a wall of ferns or bark-peeled trees thrown up to the sky, streaks of blue crossing the canopy. There was magic in those woods, where wet leaves stuck to the soles of my shoes, where moss grew on the smoothest of rocks.

After finding a dry area on high ground, we'd set about getting our camp ready. We worked in steady silence. There was no need to speak. It had grown routine, nearly muscle memory, and I relished using my hands, my weight, a stark contrast from wearing out text-book spines and flipping through smudged flash cards. Hammering tent spikes, gathering wood, digging the firepit—it was all my re-sponsibility. And then, with sweat on my brow and dirt under my nails, I'd head to the water, where I knew my father was, still looking for the perfect place to cast the first fly.

This was the part I enjoyed most. Moving up and down the banks of the river, over wet rocks and mud that sucked at my heels, I searched the water's surface, mottled with sun, for hints of life below. A fish, lurking in the shadowed shoals, treading water, waiting for something to drift downstream.

"The fish works smarter, not harder," my father always said, unzipping his beige passport-size case of handmade flies. "He gets everything that's coming to him."

It was around this time that my stomach would start grumbling, the *juk* we'd eaten at dawn all but a memory. I tried to forget about the *kalbi* and *gimbaps* my mother had packed us in case we didn't catch any fish. Her meal was not to be touched until we'd expended ourselves completely in our effort to fish for our dinner. My father was convinced it brought us good luck.

"It's an offering," he said, eyes scanning where the water slipped and boiled around rocks, the current quick and deep. "It shows you're willing to take a risk, to go hungry if you don't catch anything. It's a leap of faith."

"But who knows we are taking the leap if it's just us?"

"God, of course," he said with a smile, before casting his fly out onto the surface of the water and flicking it back and forth, the line flagellating the crisp air.

Whenever it was my turn, he'd stand to my left, gently critiquing my form and technique. Fly-fishing wasn't about brute strength. In fact, the harder you tried to cast, the more force you put into it, the more likely it was your fly would go nowhere. Casting with distance and accuracy was all about tension and using the rod as a lever.

"Apple on a willow. Apple on a willow," he would whisper in my ear.

It was a simple but effective trick for visualizing your cast. Too fast and you'd lose the apple, too much force and the willow would break. But with just the right amount of balance and momentum, you could fling the apple a good distance.

Miraculously, we almost never resorted to eating the food my mother had prepared. Even when we'd been on the river for two hours straight, the sun slipping behind the mountains, the wind suddenly coarse and cold, we'd always catch something. Even if it was just one or two *keuri*, we were ecstatic. Our stomachs complaining, toes frozen in our waders, we'd scramble up to the camp, where I'd already prepared the fire. All it needed was a match.

While the fire burned, I cleaned the fish under my father's watchful eye. When I'd done a satisfactory job, he'd send me back down to the river to wash them off. I always marveled at the pale white flesh between my fingers, blood swirling downstream. Only moments before they'd been flopping with life, their wet bodies slapping the dry earth.

We always cooked the fish the same way, wrapping them in tinfoil with ginger and scallions, settling them into the glowing embers of the fire. Once dinner was cooked, we'd build the fire back up, a pyre of flame surging into the night sky. We would eat in silence, nothing but crackling wood in our ears.

Usually we slept under the stars, sleeping bags side by side. If rain was in the forecast, we would set up a tent. Those were some of my fondest memories. Sitting inside our shelter, wind howling around us, rain drumming on the nylon. We never talked much while we were in the mountains. It seemed like such a waste to try and communicate anything truer than the warbling birds and restless breeze.

It was on those excursions, where we fished and hiked, set up and broke down camp, heard our shouts echo off pale mountain peaks, that I felt affirmed and wanted. I was my parents' only child, their only daughter. My father insisted these trips were our own special ritual, reserved for only us. I always got a thrill thinking about what my girlfriends were doing: lounging in shopping malls or forced to help their mothers in the kitchen. I was lucky that my parents didn't believe in treating me any different, just because I was a girl. This only affirmed my certainty: they were content, even overjoyed to have me and only me. Still, there were times when I had my doubts. Wouldn't my father have liked to take his son with him, up into those mountains, where icy waters rushed and emerald pines dwarfed all things? Wouldn't he have liked to see his name passed on, to know his line wouldn't end with me? Even in the happiest moments he must have felt a twinge of regret, knowing all he had was me. Sometimes I caught myself daydreaming about what it would be like to have a sibling. With a brother or sister, I'd have someone to split the all-consuming burden of my parents' expectations. But then I'd have to share their attention and adoration, and I wasn't sure I was ready to give that up.

There was another reason why I was never allowed to bring friends on our camping trips. These weekend-long forest treks weren't just about bonding and getting away from the city; they were about survival. I was learning how to become self-sufficient, impervious to setbacks. Everything we did—making the fires, erecting the tents, catching our meals—served a practical purpose, a lesson for the real world. "Nature is unforgiving," my father always used to say whenever I grew dejected with a task. "She doesn't care if you're cold or hungry. Her will is unbreakable. So when you encounter a challenge, you must face it head-on. You can't ever give up. You must be unrelenting."

I felt empowered, thrilled by how much promise my father saw in me. The elation and pride I experienced after constructing my first functioning bow drill or tying my first sheet bend knot was addicting.

But as was always the case with my father, the highs were punctuated by lows, when his temper flashed, like lightning in a coal-black night.

When I was what my father considered a novice, he was quite forgiving about any mishaps I had. "A natural part of learning," he would say cheerfully after I'd forgotten to zip up the tent or left a pocketknife open.

It was once my father thought me an expert outdoorsman that things grew perilous. There was the night I neglected to secure the rain cover on our tent, causing it to break loose during the night. My father snapped awake, somehow already in a foul mood. While he went outside to fix my mistake, he shouted at me gruffly over the howling winds. I pretended to be asleep, not wanting to incur more of his wrath.

Then there was the time I banked our fire incorrectly, leaving us with no coals the following morning. My father stalked around the ashes, prodding the disintegrating mass with a stick. "How many times have I showed you how to do this properly?" he said, shaking the stick at me.

I'd just emerged from the tent and stood with my head down, knowing better than to speak.

"Look at me when I'm talking to you, Yu-jin. This isn't a joke. This is about preparation. Preparation leads to success. The fire died because you got lazy; you thought you could take shortcuts, and look what it's led to."

I could feel the tears coming, my nose a wet mess. Usually when my father saw me cry, he'd let up, but this time was different; my blubbering only further proving my inadequacies.

"Crying isn't the solution, Yu-jin. Tears are for the weak. You aren't weak. Are you?" he said, looming over me, his voice rising to the treetops.

I shook my head, hair pasted to my burning cheeks. I closed my eyes, only opening them when I heard him stomp off through the underbrush, silence descending like an ignominious cloak around my shoulders.

SEVENTEEN

MIN

To choose your own destiny

The granite Buddha towered overhead, garbed in flowing robes, right palm extended outward over a marble praying platform. The courtyard in which the statue stood was nearly deserted, except for a few monks bent in prayer. From the small temple buildings, chants could be heard, a low, persistent call echoing amid the strings of lotus lanterns hung between temple eaves.

Misaki had suggested the place after leaving the memorial. Min hastily agreed to join her, hoping to make sense of what So-ra had said earlier. He needed to know: What had Misaki ruined?

"I usually come here when the weather's nice," Misaki said. "Right now it's perfect because it's empty, but it'll get crowded soon."

Min could see why. Bongeunsa wasn't palatial or awe-inspiring like some of the other Buddhist temples around Seoul—its aesthetics were modest and understated—but as Misaki and Min hiked up a narrow, wooded trail behind the statue, they were confronted by a stunning, almost futuristic skyline. She picked her way along the path in her high heels, walking with cautious confidence. They eventually came to a stone bench in a small clearing. Undoing the thin straps of her heels, Misaki flicked them off and spread her toes in the dirt.

"I thought you might like it here," she said. "It's a good place to clear your head."

Min imagined they looked quite strange sitting together, dressed in black on such a beautiful day. Even with his own vague suspicions and So-ra's reproaches echoing in his head, Min had trouble seeing how Misaki could be connected to Yu-jin's death. Here was the girl who'd brought him to the memorial, taken him to a quiet place to clear his head. She'd chomped her bean sprouts and cabbage as loudly as if she were in a bar, oblivious to So-ra's frenzied demeanor and the Minister's ominous words.

High above, the hackberry and elm trees swayed. Straight ahead, the contours of the Buddha statue cut between the skyline, gazing down on Gangnam; the temple grounds rolled into the congested city streets and Coex Mall, the largest underground mall in the world, a tortoise shell of green glass and tempered steel. Farther in the distance, the World Trade Center glimmered like some tectonic outcropping, an obsidian blade splitting the sky open.

Why had she brought him here? Was this—the monks, the trees, the skyscrapers—real compared to the charade that was Yu-jin's memorial? Misaki's practiced bowing, focused eating, and obliviousness—it was all an acknowledgment that the beautiful wreaths, the theatrical sobbing, and the clinical portrait of Yu-jin were fake. But there was authenticity, realness, in what stood before them, Min realized. This place where the passage of time was most evident, where the boundaries blurred between what had been and what now was.

Misaki took off her sunglasses. "What was it like, growing up in California? It must have been exciting, surrounded by all that sunshine and water, all those celebrities and movie stars."

Min was at a loss for words. Hollywood, surfers, and models with alabaster skin and sun-bleached hair—it was miles away from anything he'd known.

"How was growing up in Tokyo?" he said, buying time.

Misaki only had to think for a few seconds. "Dull. I hated everyone in high school. The girls were so catty, and the boys were only interested in having you one way or another. Japan is a hard place to be a girl, not so different from Korea, really. I remember learning that for the first time. Not where or when specifically, but I do recall this feeling—that the world saw me in a particular way. There was no escaping it. No matter how I acted, no matter what I accomplished, I'd always be judged along certain lines. I think that's initially what attracted me to Korean culture and why I eventually came to Seoul. At least here I'm a foreigner. It's another layer of protection against those judgments."

Min was awed by her self-assurance, the confidence with which she spoke. "I guess I'd say growing up in America was privileged. Sometimes I think about what my ancestors on my Korean side had to go through. They fought for independence, fled the country, and once they got to Hawaii or California, they were relegated to second-class citizens. And then there's me. What am I doing? What struggles am I overcoming?"

"You still didn't answer my question."

Min searched for the right response in the impossibly blue sky. "I guess I'd say it was infuriatingly intoxicating."

"Infuriatingly intoxicating," Misaki repeated.

"America gives you this promise: life, liberty, and the pursuit of happiness. And when you're young, you internalize that stuff. It's romantic, thinking about being part of a country, a collective, all striving. But after I went to college and got a job, it seemed like having a life and pursuing happiness meant forgetting myself completely. It's one of the reasons I came to Seoul, to see if I could be happy without sacrificing who I am."

Misaki spoke slowly. "In Korea, they call it *Han*. It's a feeling of sorts. A kind of collective despair in response to being conquered and oppressed for long periods of time, over generations. To choose your own destiny—that's what an individual, a nation, craves most. *Han* is a result of that most basic desire being crushed."

"How do you know about all this?"

"My country did so many terrible things here. I felt like it was my responsibility to try and understand it."

"Mine, too," Min said.

For a moment, neither of them spoke. Min took off his jacket and loosened his tie. He listened to the wind moving through the trees, the bustle of the city subdued to a murmur.

"So you're saying I have this *Han*, this feeling?"

"I think a lot of people do. There's something almost universal about those feelings. We want to feel in control. We want to believe we have the power to decide our outcome, that we have the ability to make our own decisions. When that's taken away, we're left with this sense of inexplicable loss. But you might feel it more acutely, given your background."

"Is that what you meant when you said it was different for me?"

Misaki nodded, toying with a strand of hair. Looking down, she squished her toes further into the dirt. Her toenails were also painted black. She always matched—no matter the occasion. "That's what I like about you," she continued. "You aren't satisfied with your state of being. You're searching for your place in the world. Most people aren't willing to take that risk; they're too afraid they'll never find it."

"And you aren't satisfied either? That's why you're here instead of Tokyo, why you're working at the store."

"The work is mostly so I don't have to take money from my family. But yeah, I'm here for a lot of the same reasons as you."

Min had never had conversations like this with Yu-jin, or with anyone, for that matter. He and Misaki seemed linked by desire, a ghostly yearning to deflect the world's opinion. There was something more about Misaki, too. The questions she asked, the things she said: they dug deep, tapped his core. And as much as Min wanted to stay like this, suspended from everything that had happened— was happening—he couldn't. Yu-jin's father's eyes hovered before him; So-ra's accusations played on. He couldn't just let go, even now. "Why are you helping me?"

Misaki looked at him questioningly.

Min searched for the appropriate words, ones that would sound neutral and calm. "I just know you weren't close to Yu-jin or So-ra, even me."

"I wanted to make things right."

"But you had nothing to do with this," Min said, feeling like he was close to unearthing something.

"I've been wondering what I could've done differently," she said. "We weren't close. But now she's gone. And I can't help feeling guilty."

Silence opened up between them. The sky was still an impeccable blue—not a single cloud, not even a wisp. It was the kind of day

Yu-jin would have hated. She was fascinated by clouds; she could name all the types. She loved watching the sun drop behind them, splashing the sky with light.

"Did something happen between you, So-ra, and Yu-jin? I mean, was there a reason you weren't on good terms with them?"

Misaki stiffened. "Why? Did So-ra say something back at the memorial?"

"We were just talking—"

"I suppose she blames me for everything, meanwhile they were perfect. They never deceived anyone or misrepresented themselves. It's all my fault, is that right?"

"I'm just trying to find out what happened."

"So that's why you apologized to me, why you showed up at the store and asked for my help. You think I'm the only one responsible for Yu-jin's death," Misaki said, putting her shoes back on and starting down the hillside. "I thought you were different, but you're just like them. You'll use anyone."

"Wait," Min called to her, scrambling down the path. "Misaki!"

They passed through hordes of tourists, Nikons swinging from their necks, noses bleached with sunscreen. Coming to the street, Misaki paused, looking unsure of which way to go, her head already adorned with her pink headphones. All around the air was thick as mud, buses coughed exhaust, heat waves shimmered above the baking asphalt.

Before she could lose him, Min stepped in front of her. "It was wrong what we did. We shouldn't have frozen you out. They told me that's what you wanted. I should have questioned it, but I didn't, and I'm sorry."

"Yet here you are, interrogating me because of something So-ra told you," Misaki said, looking beyond him. "Has it ever occurred to you that So-ra might not have your best interests at heart?"

"How can you blame her? She just lost her best friend."

"I can't do this, Min," Misaki said. "You don't know what you're talking about."

"So it's a lie then, what So-ra told me, that you ruined everything?"

Misaki yanked her headphones down around her neck and jabbed a finger into Min's chest. "If So-ra wants to put the blame on me, I can take it, but you wouldn't be on her side if you knew the truth," she said, her voice knifing through the city bustle. "I didn't know what was on that tape she made."

EIGHTEEN

YU-JIN

Only a dream

After my meal with Misaki, I was rough with So-ra for the first time, dictating what I wanted. My newfound position of power over her was intoxicating as she complied with my every command. Fists of her hair, her fingers inside me, her gasps rapid and desperate, I found new joy in the vast blankness of the bedroom ceiling—a salt flat. When I'd first met So-ra, I'd been the one in awe, the one mystified. But with my back arching from the sheets in a perfect semicircle, with her eyes taking in my breasts, my unadorned neck, I imagined it was she, not I, who'd renounced control, given herself over to desire, to the whims of her breathless heart.

"Misaki knows," I said, hours later.

So-ra was on top of the covers, hair falling across her chest. "How can you be sure?"

"She told me."

The news didn't seem to alarm So-ra. I wondered if it pleased her, knowing someone else knew. "It's not like anyone would believe her if she told them," she said. "Plus, who can she tell? She doesn't have any friends at Ewha."

So-ra was right, but that didn't assuage my anxiety. Little by little, slip by slip, I was losing control. "My father's already suspicious. I told you how he was in the apartment when I came home the other day. I swear he'd been in my bedroom. I can't go on like this. Something needs to change. Being careful isn't enough. Counting on Misaki not to say anything isn't enough."

So-ra pulled the covers around her. "What are you proposing?"

"You said we could date other people, that we aren't exclusive."

"And if you're with a boy, no one will be suspicious of us," she said. "You'll be safe."

I ignored the pain in her eyes, the disappointment in her voice. I knew this wasn't what she wanted. This was killing her. "It won't change anything between us. It's like you said, we don't need to be exclusive—that's just a label."

I was saying everything So-ra didn't want to hear. She wanted all of me. But I knew she'd take half, maybe less. She'd take whatever she could get. At least that's what I needed for her to pretend in that brief moment. I couldn't afford to be some rebel. Being different was too hard. It required something I wasn't willing to find in myself. I wasn't sure I'd find it even if I looked.

That night I woke in my bed, across the hall from So-ra. I lay awake, listening for the sounds of the sea, which was impossible. I was in Seoul—not an ocean for miles. And yet, in the darkness, hands cupped around my ears, I heard it—distinctly. The deep roll of waves, the smack of water against soaked sand, and then silence as the tide receded, leaving in its wake a thousand orbs of glittering sand, scrubbed to perfection.

I saw myself on the beach, Jung-woo on top of me, my legs embracing him, entrapping him. I heard the skittering crabs. I heard my cries. His cries—of what?

What had that moment been?

Through closed bedroom doors I heard So-ra's cries, too, like echoes from my past, murmurs of my youth. I knew I'd hurt her.

·‖·

And then it happened, a month or so after that night. After I'd broken everything wide open with So-ra, told her where I stood and what I wanted, or, more important, what I didn't want. I was at karaoke with some university friends, girls I hung out with when So-ra was busy with dance rehearsal. I'd left our rented room to check my makeup in the restroom when I ran into him.

He was tall and angular, with an attitude I could only describe as American, leaning against the narrow hallway walls of the *norebang*, all quiet confidence. And he *was* American. Or, was and wasn't. What was it that gave it away? Something about his eyes, his slender fingers. I knew he was both: Korean and American. And I thought I'd never seen someone so beautiful, so perfectly handsome, and I knew he was exactly what I'd been looking for. If I was with him, no one would ever presume I was carrying on with So-ra.

How easy it would be, I thought—still forbidden, still risky, just not as much—to hold hands in the streets, dance in the sunshine, never looking over our shoulders, wondering who was watching and what they were saying.

When the first semester of my junior year at Ewha was nearly over, after I'd met Min, I knew he was the someone or at least *something* I'd been moving toward. He was that amorphous, disembodied light in the fog. The previous five semesters at Ewha had been thrilling, spirit-altering, but I was left with a gut-twisting sense that I was mistaking my aimlessness for progress, my stagnancy for ascension. Was I going to wake up one day back where I'd started?

I'd catch myself spacing out in class, notes aslant. I found my government and political science classes boring as ever. My classmates seemed to agree, although that didn't stop them from doubling their efforts, kissing up to professors in the hope of a connection down the line. I didn't know how my future was supposed to look, although I knew what my father expected. I never dared tell any of my cohort who he was. I didn't want them to think I'd only gotten into Ewha because of him.

In the crowded lecture halls, winding cafeteria lines, sardine-packed metro cars, I looked out on my future—beyond Ewha, beyond Seoul—and saw nothing in particular. Only a vague plan I was supposed to want. I was still looking for what made me happy, hoping desperately that it wasn't just So-ra. And just like that, Min became a steadying hand, a whispered reassurance.

I wasn't sure how So-ra would react to the news about Min. Everything had seemed theoretical and abstract up until now. A sickening dread consumed me when I finally decided to tell her. We were working out together at the university gym, an activity we'd taken to since the first snowfall in December. While she ran and lifted, I'd be next to her chatting, watching, passing time.

I was standing next to So-ra while she was on the treadmill. At first she didn't say anything, head bobbing, one earbud swinging wildly as she pummeled the rubber belt. I thought she might not have heard me, eyes straight ahead, lips set in a grim line of determination.

"So-ra," I said, putting my hand on the console. "Did you hear me?"

She increased the speed, keeping stride. "Who is he?"

I couldn't hear myself think, the whir of the belt grating and terrible in my ears. "He's an American. Works at Samsung."

As if to drown me out, she set the speed even higher. Sweat slid down her neck. Her feet pounded harder and harder, eyes ahead, arms cutting through the air, thick with perfumed sweat. "Are you telling me because you really like him?"

I measured my words. Despite So-ra's blessing to pursue something that might provide me with peace of mind, I knew she wasn't happy with this. But why couldn't she see things from my perspective? I wanted her to be happy for me, to accept this was something I needed to feel safe. "We've only been on a few dates."

So-ra pulled wisps of wet hair behind her ears. "You don't have to bullshit me, Yu-jin. I can take it. You can tell me if it's serious. If he's more than just a facade."

I didn't like thinking about Min as purely camouflage, but what else was he? "It's anything but serious," I said. "It's a casual thing. Plus, he's American. He'll go home eventually, and my parents were pretty clear about relationships during college."

So-ra looked like she was going to say something but thought better of it. Beneath the unrelenting brightness of the gym lights, I saw her in a new way: at war with everything around her. She fed off opposition. She found identity in the contrasts, the differences. Her attitude, her aura, even her sexuality was defined against something. I admired her, deeply. She was stronger than I was. She could run forever, fueled by some greater sense of self. True, she'd been the one to tell me my views on sexuality were old-fashioned; she was the one who introduced me to culture: film, art, dance. She'd been my education. But for all her postulations, for all her beliefs in freedom, she was still jealous. She was still human. She wanted me for her own, and I sensed that she judged me for being with a man, for finding a different kind of happiness with Min, no matter how superficial.

"I think you'd like him," I offered. "Not your typical Samsung guy."

Hands on the railing of the treadmill, So-ra popped up, resting her sneakered feet on either side of the whirring belt. "Does it matter if I like him?"

"Of course. You're my best friend."

She exhaled audibly and looked past me, through me, like she was hoping some other version of me was about to appear, a better version, a stronger one. What had she seen in me? How had she thought all of this was going to end? And then she was putting her earbuds into her ears and running, faster, cranking up the speed on the dial.

Faster. Faster.

In the locker room showers, water pounding my face, drumming my eyelids, I cried—where no one would know, my tears becoming water, running down my cheeks, my stomach, between my toes, circling the drain, down into nothing. I was pushing So-ra away. I knew this. It was my doing. And yet I couldn't bear the thought of not having her in my life. She was my friend, my lover, my guide. But it couldn't be. We both knew this. Plus, I liked Min. He intrigued me. There was no pressure, no expectations. I was graduating in a year and a half. He would eventually go home to California—there was no pretense in what we wanted to be.

Even as I cried and cried, steeling my resolve to be with Min, really be with him, without giving thought to So-ra, I felt my weakness, my desire for her.

She was waiting in front of my locker when I came back from the showers, my hair dripping, eyes aching. She looked up from the straddled bench, anger and understanding in her expression. I went to say something but she stopped me, standing up and embracing me, her body against mine. I held her close, breathing her in.

"I'd like to meet him," she said softly. "I want to see you happy."

-ıı|ı-

That same night, I met Min for dinner at a barbecue place in Songpa-gu. It was only our fifth date. We sat at a table in the back corner of the restaurant, close to the kitchen, where the barks of grandmothers filled the air. Young men with grungy faces, darkened with ash from the coals, scurried back and forth. Min had arrived earlier than me, ordering a few different dishes of meat: *samgyeopsal* and *jumulleok*.

"Figured you'd like one of them," he said with a grin.

I didn't particularly like barbecue. I especially hated the way it made my clothes smell, but I didn't want to appear picky. Plus, I was excited by this old feeling of awkward nervousness, something I hadn't experienced since that weekend at the beach with Jung-woo.

"If we don't like it, we can always dine and dash."

"Dine and dash?"

"You know," he said, looking around the restaurant. "Eat and ditch the check. Dine and dash."

"Is this something you do in America?"

He laughed, an unabashed laugh, full of assurance and weight. "An age-old tradition."

"Should we?" I said, feeling the tension release between us, some slack in the line, room to play. I liked this about him: he could laugh at himself, at anything too serious. He was different in this way from other people I'd spent time with, Korean boys, even So-ra.

"Maybe another place," he said, taking up a piece of *dotorimuk-muchim*. "I like this restaurant. I'd prefer not being banned."

I can't say with any certainty what it was about Min that capti-vated me. I suppose like anything it was a combination of things. That night, and many others after, he displayed the capacity to be multifaceted: earnest, self-deprecating, and serious. It was me, he said, my presence that brought out this blitheness. With everyone else he was uptight and edgy, constantly aware of how others might perceive him. I had a hard time imagining the person he described. Min wasn't one thing, one *kind* of person. Like me, he was stuck in the in-between. I saw my own doubt in him, and I latched onto it, reveled in it. And he was fun to be with; he helped me forget.

We ended up ordering more dishes, our appetites growing as we got more comfortable. I hadn't realized I was so hungry, and after two beers I felt like I could eat straight through to midnight, our conversation growing more fervent as the night grew late. I liked the way he asked questions; he let you fill in whatever answer you wanted. He didn't ask what I was going to do when I graduated or what job I wanted. He left it open-ended, like he knew I couldn't care less about my major.

A waitress approached, but he waved her away, taking the tongs and flipping the meat himself, fat popping into smoke, sucked up into the fan above. I asked him about his job, what he liked about it. He seemed at a loss, only saying the work was tedious at times. It wasn't exactly high art he was dealing with, he said. Still, there were mo-ments when he had realizations about the differences between Amer-ica and Korea. He explained how until he came to Korea, he always thought Americans possessed a rigid definition of beauty. It seemed there was only one set of characteristics that were deemed attractive.

But since coming here, he'd realized Americans had a pretty broad definition of what was beautiful, successful, even desirable, not just aesthetically but overall.

I caught myself thinking about So-ra, about her beauty, her elegance, her raw energy. I wondered what she was doing at this exact moment, a twinge of guilt slipping between my ribs as I remembered what I'd told her at the gym. I knew we wouldn't end because of Min. And yet I realized he was more than just a mask. I wanted to be with him, too, and if anyone looked our way, threw a disapproving glance, it was only because he was American, nothing else. How uncomplicated, how easy it all was.

"And what do your aesthetics tell you about me?" I said, pushing So-ra from my mind.

Min watched me. "Are you asking if I think you're beautiful?"

"Yes. Yes, I am."

⊹

After dinner we decided to walk back to my apartment despite the cold, jackets buttoned to our chins, elbows grazing, stomachs warm and full. Snowflakes danced in headlights; traffic slowed to a crawl. Around city blocks, down alleys where late-night patrons spilled out into the night, cigarettes aglow, voices booming. The wind howled, even whistled.

On the way, Min told me about Los Angeles and his reasons for leaving home. I imagined this world of celebrities and palm trees, Beverly Hills and Venice Beach—a place I'd only seen on television. I listened intently, happy I wasn't being forced to answer questions about my own life. When he did ask me something, he never pried. He accepted whatever answer I gave him, however vague and indeterminate.

When we turned a corner, the wind whipped up around us, swirling into my jacket, my skin going goosebumped. I shivered and smiled as Min put his arm around me, holding me loosely.

We said goodbye in the lobby of my building, making plans for the next time we'd see each other. As we were kissing good night, Misaki emerged from the elevator, a blur of pink-orbed headphones and black hair, heeled snow boots thundering on the tiled floor.

"I'm going out for the night," she said, looking at me and then Min, head to toe. "So-ra was wondering where you were."

"This is Misaki. She's one of my roommates. She's from Japan."

"Nice to meet you," Min said. "You're the first Japanese person I've met since coming to Seoul."

"You aren't the first American, but it's nice to meet you all the same."

"My accent is that bad?"

"No, not at all. You just have that American look," Misaki said.

Min laughed. "Not sure that's a compliment, but I'll take it."

I tried to rein in the jealousy careening through me, cheeks hot, fingers tingling.

Misaki gave a playful shrug.

"It's late. Where are you headed?" Min asked.

I couldn't stand watching them talk, even if it was harmless. "Misaki's always got somewhere to be."

Misaki slid her headphones back on. "This is Seoul. There's always something going on."

As she walked away, I entertained fantasies: grabbing her by that frilly fur hood and yanking her to the ground, giving her a shove out the front door of my apartment building, sending her sprawling out onto the frozen sidewalk.

"She seems cool," Min said, oblivious to it all. "Very mysterious."

I knew his comments were benign, but I couldn't help feeling annoyed.

In the elevator, sliding upwards, all I could think about was Misaki—the way she'd flirted with him, looked at him. Would she tell him I was using him as refuge? Would she expose me, out of jealousy or malice?

Misaki had promised not to tell anyone about me and So-ra, but could I trust her?

I decided to say nothing, explain nothing. She was nosy, but I couldn't picture her seeking Min out, telling him the truth. And what was the truth anyway? I did like him. He made me feel safe, comfortable in a way I'd never known. And even if I carried on with So-ra on the side, that was something wholly separate. It had no bearing on whatever Min and I became. Because we were becoming something, a couple, an entity, and nothing Misaki thought would change that.

-|||-

A few weeks later we went skiing for the weekend, me, So-ra, and Min. My relationship with him was going better than I'd ever imagined. We hadn't slept together, but it wasn't for a lack of desire, the decision to wait. It was quite the opposite actually. Whenever we were together, even when So-ra was with us, I felt a desire for his hand on my waist, his stubble against my cheek. So far I'd resisted the urge to fall into bed with him. But that would change on the trip. I'd made up my mind.

Despite her initial promises to accept Min into our lives, So-ra was still resistant, aloof in the subtlest of ways. The slights were so minor, done with such grace, I found it impossible to say anything, lest I sound like the judgmental one. There was the way she always handed me my menu first when we sat down at a restaurant, the way she seemed to shift our conversations back to a time before Min. Even when she glossed over something Min said, diminishing it ever so slightly, I knew he couldn't sense any derision or animosity. But I knew it was there; I could feel it.

She stopped asking for things she knew I couldn't give. We'd reached an understanding. This didn't mean I didn't fall back into her arms, her bed. Enthralled, resisting all sense, I never considered what we did as wrong or disloyal to Min. What I had with So-ra was separate.

Other times I struggled to see our situation as anything but weakness, this carnal desire. The truth was that deep down, somewhere hidden from So-ra, perhaps even from myself, I felt guilty for everything: my relationship with Min, my involvement with her. In the starkest of terms, I was cheating on him, betraying his trust. And yet that feeling, that sense of guilt, was never enough to stop me because I knew there was no helping it, any of it.

That night I took Min, or I should say, let him take me. He was present, gentle even, in a way I'd never known. On top of him, in the darkness, I heard the snow shifting around the cabin. With Min below me I felt myself losing touch with my body, hands on his chest, thighs around him. I saw myself as if from above, drifting upwards, through the roof, into the sky, up the snowy slopes, carved between dark-wooded forests. The frigid winds scraped white wisps from snowy peaks, gray and stoic in the night. Beyond everything storm clouds shuddered in the moonlight, lightning brewing.

Afterwards, Min lay beneath me, both of us shivering, sweat drying cold on our skin. When I came back from the bathroom, he was asleep, his breathing quiet, almost imperceptible. Even as I gazed down upon him, even as I remembered his touch, thought of how he'd felt inside me, I couldn't help but be filled with another memory, another sensation, from just a few hours ago.

So-ra and I, gliding down the mountain, wind in our faces, sun tinted by our mirrored goggles. I could hear her laughter, her shouts twirled in the wind and funneled back to me, matching her every turn, every cut in the snow that sang beneath our skis. So-ra's ski poles danced on either side of her legs, turning powerfully, confidently with the mountain, every bump, every sluice in the powder. I'd smiled under my black muffler, deeply satisfied in that slippage of time—wholly content, even happy. I could have moved forever like that, sashaying down that mountainside, untethered. I wanted that again. I couldn't get it anywhere else.

The moon had shifted, its light sliding downward across Min's face, a mask I no longer recognized. Resolved, I stole from the room, leaving him to sleep. I would join him before he woke. Making my way through the dark cabin, I came to So-ra's room, her door ajar. When I pushed it open, she sat up in bed, making me out, or perhaps just my shadow.

"Can't sleep?" she mumbled, her voice husky with dreams.

I said nothing, throat aching.

"Come to bed." She threw back the blankets. "Come get warm."

When I woke the next day, Min beside me, face serene as ever, it was as if nothing had happened, only a dream.

NINETEEN

MIN

We hope to reemerge with more clarity

Min was up early the next morning. Not wanting to take any chances, he arrived under the Hannam Bridge thirty minutes earlier than the agreed-on time. With no sign of So-ra at seven, he called her cell. Straight to voicemail. He waited a few minutes before trying again. Nothing. Just in case he'd misheard her, Min stuck around for another hour, but by then he knew she wasn't coming. Maybe she'd never intended to show up, or maybe, worse, someone had stopped her.

Min drifted from place to place, despondent and listless. Unmoored, he was barely conscious of this body that moved through his world: the office, the rugby field, his cramped and oppressive apartment. The shock of Yu-jin's death and So-ra's abandonment settled on him like the densest of fogs, obscuring all direction and purpose.

His coworkers spoke to him, encouraged him, empathized with him, their words nearly indiscernible, as if spoken from a great distance. Most nights he stayed up late nursing a beer, waiting for sleep to rescue him. One early morning, just past midnight, he got an email from his father. Bleary-eyed, he double-checked the name. It was their first correspondence since he'd left for Seoul. He deleted the email without opening it. He didn't want to hear what his father had to say, apology or not. He called his mother with the intention of telling her about Yu-jin but couldn't find the words. Where would he begin? Instead they talked about the latest church gossip, the news, anything allowing Min to avoid being the topic of discussion.

⊪

There were brief moments of clarity, searing memories that seemed Technicolor compared to the drab and hazy gauze covering his eyes: Yu-jin's hand around his waist, her defiant laughter, her hair tickling his nose. In his first seconds of wakefulness, Min would roll over, expectant, even aroused, only to find an empty space in his bed, pillow and sheets untouched, as if he was awaiting her return.

Min had never known grief. From his childhood there were memories of funerals for his grandfathers on both sides, where men and women dressed in black sidled up to one another, murmuring condolences. Even the more vivid recollections—an uncle sobbing outside a modest white church, a distant cousin delivering a moving poem she'd written *in memoriam*—were blurred at best. Min had seen sorrow, witnessed it in people around him, but never had it struck at the heart of his being as it did now. For the first time he knew what it meant to lose something, to have a piece of you cleaved away and tossed into the ether.

Waking from nightmares, soaked in sweat, he'd try So-ra's number again and again, finding one early morning that it had been disconnected. More than once he'd dialed Misaki's number, only to end the call before it rang. The way they'd left things, there was no use.

The more days that passed, the louder So-ra's and Misaki's words played in his head: "*He's a cruel and hateful man.*" "*You wouldn't be on her side if you knew the truth. I didn't know what was on that tape she made.*"

Left to its own devices, Min's mind careened through unthinkable scenarios where he imagined So-ra meeting the same fate as Yu-jin. Phantoms haunted him in the form of the security guards he'd seen at Yu-jin's funeral, lurking behind every corner, watching his every move, reporting back, fingers to earpieces. It wasn't just paranoia, Min realized. He started noticing men, never more than two, following him. They all wore the same anonymous black suits, had the same crew cuts. They always kept their distance, never getting close enough for Min to really see their faces. He figured they were gathering intelligence, recording his whereabouts. But what possible threat could he pose? He started entering stores from the back, doubling back down streets, and disembarking subways at the last minute, narrowly missing the doors. This was what Detective Park had warned him about. Plagued by suspicion and doubt, he holed up in his apartment, analyzing every sound he heard outside his door.

He gave in to despair. Without So-ra, Min saw no avenue, no path to ever understanding what had happened to Yu-jin. He racked his memory for anything she might have said or done that would hint at her whereabouts. At times, in the fragile light of morning, he wished the Minister's men would come and take him away, give him respite, save him from this madness. Anything was preferable to this constant state of doubt.

Then he remembered. The paper he'd taken from the memorial. Rifling through his closet, Min found the suit Misaki had helped him pick out. Inside the jacket pocket was the glossy pamphlet So-ra had been so fixated on when he'd interrupted her at Yu-jin's memorial. He'd thought nothing of it when he'd picked it up, but now it was the only thing that might help him find her.

Min sat down at his kitchen table and read.

> HOUSE OF THE LOTUS TREE aims to provide holistic healing to both the mind and body. Only when both have been cleansed can we hope to live, free of our earthly burdens, our impediments, our chains. By re-understanding our most basic concepts of nutrition, biology, sociology, and phenomenology, we hope to reemerge with more clarity and understanding of our world.

The brochure's color palette was calming and neutral. Adorned with austere off-white lettering on a forest-green backdrop, it invited "truth seekers" to come to Jawoldo island. On the back were pictures of sunsets and beaches at low tide. Information was sparse, seemingly on purpose.

The description was so vague that it was unclear whether House of the Lotus Tree was a cult or a mental institution. If it was an active mental hospital, they were misrepresenting themselves. This wasn't out of the question, considering most people in Korea considered therapy and other forms of psychiatric aid a sign of weakness. As a result, great pains were taken by hospitals to give their patients as much privacy and anonymity as possible. Plus, the tone and language of the message didn't make any grand proclamations, made no messianic promise. Still, everything seemed a bit too granola and wheatgrass for the place to be a legitimate medical practice.

But why would So-ra go to this kind of place? It wasn't like her. Unless she'd been forced. When a quick internet search for House of the Lotus Tree revealed nothing, Min grew more panicked, fearing for So-ra's well-being. Grabbing his phone from the bedside table, he called Detective Park.

"What is it?" he grumbled.

"I'm worried about So-ra. I can't get in touch with her."

"That makes two us, although I'm sure she's fine."

"I know where she is."

There was a long pause. "Meet me in Seoul Forest. There's a small playground on the north side, right near the metro stop. I'll be there in an hour."

"Can't we just talk over the phone? It's urgent. I think she's in some kind of trouble."

"Out of the question," Park said, before hanging up.

⊣⊢⊢

Min took extra precautions leaving his apartment. If the men following him were associated with the Minister, he couldn't risk them seeing him working with Detective Park. Instead of going out the front door, he took the elevator down to the trash and recycling room in the basement. From there, he took the stairs one flight up and exited his building from the rear.

With his baseball cap pulled down low and his sunglasses on, Min waited at the bus stop for the 110B. Traffic whizzed by in either direction, kicking up clouds of hot exhaust. Only after he'd taken a seat and no one got on after him did Min allow himself to relax. At least he'd know if he was being followed. On the metro it would have been almost impossible.

Min's relief was short-lived. Two men in suits boarded the bus at the next stop. Matching military-style haircuts, athletic builds. They weren't even carrying briefcases; these were no office workers. Min thought about confronting them, but what could he do? They'd just deny following him; he'd look like a lunatic.

Somewhere between the Oksu and Geumho metro stations, Min got off the bus and started walking. Waiting at a crosswalk, he spotted his tail in the reflection of a storefront across the street. Down the next block, a silver taxi pulled over to end its fare. With the light still red, Min looked both ways before sprinting across the street, arriving just as the car door swung open. He apologized to the flustered exiting rider, a well-dressed businessman, before sliding into the backseat himself and telling the driver to get him to Seoul Forest. He'd pay him double. He was in a hurry. As they drove away, Min peeked over the backseat and watched the Minister's men fade into the distance.

Park sat on a tree-shaded bench facing a playground, arms draped over the back like drying laundry. Burned down to the filter, a cigarette smoldered between his fingers. He watched children on the playground wearily, tracking their spry movements as they slipped down a bright red slide, flung themselves from metal rings.

"Why couldn't we just talk over the phone?" Min said, sitting down. He'd already made up his mind not to tell Park about the men who'd been following him. If the detective was worried about him, he might try and stop him from investigating further.

"It might be bugged, and things have gotten complicated," Park said. "I've been barred from speaking with anyone of interest concerning the investigation. There's also mounting pressure to close the case immediately."

"Yu-jin's father?"

Park nodded. "He's the only person with that kind of influence. But we're safe here. Easy to spot a tail."

Min studied the grandmothers and mothers on the benches, some reading, others watching the children at play, ready to spring into action at the sign of a slip or fall. "With everything the Minister is doing, how can you think Yu-jin killed herself?"

Park flicked his cigarette into the grass, eliciting glares from the playground women. "I'm just looking at the facts, but I haven't ruled anything out. There are still some details that aren't adding up. Until they do, I'm keeping the case open. I just need to find a way to get to So-ra and the Minister."

Park seemed to be suffering from a worse-than-usual hangover, curls of hair clinging to his forehead, yellow rings swimming beneath his desperate eyes.

"What if I can talk to So-ra? I told you, I know where she is."

"I'm not sure that's very wise," Park said, lighting another cigarette.

Elbows on his knees, Min leaned forward, something like a plan forming in his mind. "You said so yourself. You can't approach her. But I can. I'm an outsider. I'm not beholden to anyone. I can talk to anyone I want. I can get the answers you need. So-ra's on Jawoldo. I think she's staying at someplace called House of the Lotus Tree. I did some research but couldn't find anything on them."

A gust of humid air swirled then languished around them. Park picked at the splintered corner of the bench. Min could see he was struggling with something, playing out each scenario, head cocked to the side, like he'd heard a faint sound, a distant warning. "They're a fairly secretive group," he finally said. "Fly very low under the radar. Some say they're a cult, others a religious group, a commune. They've been around a few decades. Lots of cults popped up in this country during the seventies and eighties. At least at the lower levels the police didn't pay much attention to these types of groups. That was until the Odaeyang mass suicide in eighty-seven. That got our attention. Anyway—I don't think House of the Lotus Tree is one of those hard-core cults. It's a scam—there's no doubt about it—but whatever they're doing, it seems pretty benign."

"I think So-ra was coerced into going there. They might be holding her against her will."

"How'd you find out about them?"

"So-ra was looking at their brochure at Yu-jin's memorial."

Park loosened his collar. "I see you didn't take my advice about staying away from the Minister."

"Yu-jin's father played a role in all this. I can't prove he was directly involved, but there's no question he did something. He's got So-ra scared."

"Let me handle him. Just focus on So-ra for now."

Min considered asking Park about the tape that Misaki had referenced, but he resisted, thinking it better to hear from So-ra first. "I'll call you when I get back."

Detective Park stood up. "One more thing. Did Yu-jin have two cell phones?"

"Like a burner?"

Park nodded.

"No," Min said. "Her old one broke a few months ago, so she had to get a new one. Why?"

"When I swept her room, I found two phones. Thought it might be something."

Min thanked Park for the information. The late-afternoon sun slanted through the trees; shadows stretched and stole over the grass.

"Be careful," Park said. "There are invisible hands moving us around all the time, even when we believe we're the ones making decisions."

TWENTY

YU-JIN

Deception was my happiness

During my senior year, deception was my happiness. Auditing a second film course, becoming a tight-knit group with Min and So-ra, entertaining my father with potential jobs for the following year—it was all illusory, imagined, but somehow more real than anything else. It was the reality I wanted for myself.

I had arrived—where exactly, I wasn't certain, but I felt more assured, more comfortable with my desires. I had learned to hold two, even three competing ideas in my head simultaneously. I was no longer dismayed by my contradictions. I accepted them, let them rub up against each other, like vibrating ions. In my heart, in my head, I could contradict. I could waver.

I was still in awe of So-ra, but I no longer worshipped her ability to navigate Seoul, speak her mind, analyze films, books, ideas. I could do those things, too, now. I had the distinct belief my own opinions mattered, carried weight, and I gave them freely. Min marveled at my confidence, telling me how much he admired my strength and independence. So-ra welcomed my transformation, although I couldn't help but observe brief slips, momentary lapses, where she grew taciturn, even acerbic, when her warm and reassuring smile would slip from her face. Wasn't this what she'd wanted all along for me? I was growing and evolving, reaching for the sun.

Bundled up against the wet March wind, sky whisked gray, we would wait for Min outside the Samsung building, watching the businessmen and -women come and go. We were intrigued by them, in their adultness. They seemed resolute and calculated in their existence, measuring their lives in client lunches, reply-all emails, and office birthday parties.

I spotted Min in the lobby. He wore a charcoal suit and a pale blue collared shirt. No tie, which I liked. Korean businessmen always wore the ugliest ties, the preknotted ones you could tighten with a zip. He wasn't bound by the same rules as the other employees. With no interest in moving up or taking on more responsibilities, he didn't have anyone to impress.

"Freedom!" he shouted when he saw us.

I gave him a kiss on the cheek and wondered if any of his colleagues could see us. Did they know who I was? Did he talk about me at work? Was I on his mind when I wasn't around?

Since it was raining, So-ra suggested we go to the Art Sonje Center in Samcheong-dong. I protested, fearing Min would find an art museum boring. I was wary of So-ra suggesting activities that interested only us, nudging Min to the periphery.

"It's not a museum. It's a bunch of different art galleries. It'll be fun. Plus, there are lots of cafés and restaurants, too."

"I'll go if there's food," Min said.

We set off, Min and I walking side by side. So-ra came between us, taking our hands in hers. "Come on. I heard they have some really cool installations up."

We got out at Anguk metro station, So-ra leading the way. A light rain dusted us, pushed by the wind. I kept thinking about their hands, So-ra's rough and callused, Min's delicate and slender. So-ra stopped at various galleries, giving us tidbits of information: what they sold, what kind of artists they promoted. She knew all the most recent trends in contemporary art. Between her dance rehearsals and studies, I wondered when she had the time to discover all of this. When had she snuck off and found this world without me?

Knowing nothing about art or the art scene in Seoul, I could see Min was impressed by her breadth of knowledge. She patiently answered all his questions like a jaded museum tour guide. Coming to a shabby gray building, So-ra stopped. Apparently we'd arrived. I'd never been to a real art gallery. Sure, I'd gone to museums, exhibitions open to the masses. But this was something else entirely. It was intimate. Personal.

Climbing the stairs, we stopped at the fourth floor. A well-dressed young man gave us a simple pamphlet and encouraged us to have a look around. There was only one piece showing at the moment, he said.

The installation was imposing: a massive, life-size house made of blue cloth or thread—I couldn't be sure. It was transparent, but the artist had crafted definitive lines with thicker thread to give the structure a distinct shape. The home looked Victorian, or what I imagined old colonial American homes to look like, something that belonged on the windswept shores of a lonely New England fishing town. As I approached, I noticed another construction made of the same blue cloth. It was a traditional Korean home suspended within the larger, Western-looking one. The structure seemed to gain depth and size. Even the exhibition room was impressive, glowing with natural light, the walls an eggshell white, forever expanding, knowing no bounds. It was hard to believe a room like this could exist in such an unassuming building.

"What's the name of the piece?" Min asked in a near whisper, like he was afraid the entire apparatus might come tumbling down.

So-ra read the plaque on the wall. "*Home Within a Home*."

I entered the structure, walking through the front door of the cloth house. Shaded in blue, I watched Min and So-ra move around me, marveling at the attention to detail. Overhead, the outline of the traditional Korean home loomed, with its curved shingles and up-turned eaves.

"It's marvelous," I heard Min say.

"I thought you guys might like it. This is my third time here," So-ra said.

What was I missing? The sheer size of the installation was impressive. I would never have conceived such a thing. But what did they see? I saw two houses, two homes, one within the other. One Western, one Korean. Was it meant to symbolize the artist's yearning for home? Or was it a commentary on the cultures, their connections? I liked it, I thought it was aesthetically pleasing, but did that make it art?

Min and So-ra were huddled together, studying a corner of the house. I wondered if he was winning her over.

"It says here it's made of muslin."

"I can't believe how much detail there is. The needlework. It must have taken months, years to complete."

I was embarrassed by my jealousy, my pettiness. Why should their shared enjoyment bother me? She was trying to do what I wanted her to do. As usual, she was proving to be the better person, in all facets. And yet I wondered whether this was all an act, an attempt by So-ra to make me jealous.

I was determined not to let on, so I pretended to be enthralled, thinking of questions I could ask Min later about the artwork. After what felt like an eternity, we agreed to get something to eat. So-ra said there was a place that did good burgers around the corner.

"I haven't had a decent hamburger in ages," Min said, pulling me close as we left the gallery. "I'm dying for something greasy."

So-ra playfully slapped my ass. "We can split one. We'll get fat if we eat American portions."

I ran after her, pinching her thigh. She let out a yelp and tried to pinch me back. We went down the sidewalk like that, swerving, pushing and tugging, pedestrians moving aside, annoyed at our childishness, which only encouraged us more.

My moment of jealousy had evaporated.

Min jogged behind us to keep up. Rain fell. My heart grew light. The city went quiet. Muted. Like a hand upon a singing string.

At the restaurant we sat in a window booth and watched the rain, talking about So-ra's upcoming dance recital and Min's coworkers, who we found immensely entertaining. It was mind-boggling, to think he worked with such idiots. I was happy my father wasn't pushing me into the business sector. And while we talked of other things, I was mindful not to stray too far from the present. So-ra knew this, too, and always navigated the conversation away from the future.

It didn't scare me, the future. Min and I had already tacitly acknowledged things wouldn't proceed beyond graduation. Still, I wanted to avoid any awkwardness. So-ra was happy to help, if only because neither of us wanted to think about our own lives after Ewha.

The real world presented problems neither of us were willing to face. So we looped our conversations back to the here and now, to the minutes passing before us.

It was a high-wire act, these dates with So-ra and Min. I was suspended, high up, close to the sun, where the clouds stretched for miles like a downy ocean, where I balanced, arms outstretched, accounting for each bend, each twang in the wire.

Was it the act, the performance that I enjoyed the most? It was confusing, but it was also exhilarating. At least that's what it felt like in the moment, when I had both their ears, both their hearts.

That night, when So-ra had said good night, when Misaki had left for another one of her mystery dates, I lay in bed and watched Min undress. Naked, he flopped onto the bed, burying his face in my pillows. "Like what you see?" he said, his laugh muffled. He was careless with his body in that endearingly childish way. I was shocked the first time I stayed at his apartment overnight, his sleeping in the nude. It was audacious, flagrant. So different from anything I'd known. I'd lain on my stomach, watching him, wondering whether it was confidence, indifference, or both. What was it like to be so careless with one's body?

"What were you talking with So-ra about today?"

He rolled onto his side. "When?"

"At the art gallery. You guys seemed really into the installation."

"About the piece. How cool we thought it was. I never would've guessed there were all those galleries in that neighborhood."

"What did you like about it?"

"What do you mean?" he said, closing his eyes.

I switched off the bedside lamp, leaving us in darkness. "What did you see?"

He was quiet for a while, and I thought he might have fallen asleep.

"I guess I saw homes. I figured the piece was about being homesick. But then I saw one home, one culture trapped within another, consumed by another, and I wondered whether there was some darker meaning to the piece."

"Is that what you were talking to So-ra about?"

"Kind of."

"What did she say?"

"She said she didn't know, but that she could see why I might feel like that." He was drifting off, his voice already tinged with dreams.

I knew I was violating my own rule to keep him at a distance, but I wanted to know. "Do you ever get homesick?"

"Homesick?" he said to the darkness. "Not really."

I lay still until I heard his light snores, felt his body rising and falling. He wasn't homesick; he didn't miss his parents, his friends. Other than working, what was he really doing here? What was he trying to find?

TWENTY-ONE

MIN

It's not my secret to tell

The wind was salty on Min's lips. From the top deck of the ferry he watched Incheon drift into the gray-blue morning, a concrete canvas flecked with red and green cargo ships. He'd caught the morning ferry to Jawoldo. Except for a few fishermen smoking cigarettes, he was the only one above deck. Everyone else was below, watching the sea slip away behind plexiglass windows, only the dull chop of water reaching their ears.

The island was mostly known for its tourism, according to Detective Park, who'd given him some information before he'd left. The House of the Lotus Tree complex was somewhere in the middle of the island. He was looking for something that didn't quite fit among the beaches, holiday pensions, and fishing villages.

Cigarettes finished and flicked into the ocean, the fishermen slipped belowdecks, leaving Min to himself. He tried to make sense of everything he'd learned: the Minister's efforts to impede the investigation, So-ra's disappearance, her accusations about Misaki "ruining everything," and now some kind of recording Yu-jin had made. But he couldn't focus, the hypnotic push and pull of the waves lulling him into a state of relaxation. It was a relief to let all his questions go, if only for a moment. He could drift away, forget it all.

In America there was no proof of Yu-jin, Misaki, or So-ra. They only existed if he spoke of them, remembered them. He could make what had happened a dream, if he wanted. All it would take was a plane ticket back home.

But the sea in his ears reminded Min that your memories always followed you, no matter where you went. He'd traded Los Angeles for New York, and now one hemisphere for another, only to find he was the same person, knotted and tangled as ever, still searching for peace. He'd always occupy this liminal space, no matter how many times he changed the frame of his existence, gilded it with golden leaf, until he stopped running. He saw himself, a nine-year-old running barefoot down the sidewalk, tears swept across his cheeks, running, running. It was the day his parents had told him they were separating. It was the only time he could remember crying about their eventual divorce. Hearing the news, he'd taken off, bolted— where, it didn't matter. "Away" was the only word he heard.

Sometime near dark he returned home and saw his parents standing on the porch of their adobe house, speaking gravely to a police officer. In a white linen jacket, his father's outline gleamed in the twilight, his mother clinging to his arm. It was a picture of shared anxiety and love, but all Min felt was betrayal.

Then he saw himself older, in high school, slide-tackling a boy in soccer, hitting his ankle at just the right angle and speed to break it. He remembered standing over the boy, catatonic, listening to his screams. The boy had said something to provoke him, "gook" or "twinkie," he couldn't remember. But something had swelled up in him, compelled Min to hurt the boy. After he'd been ejected and sent home, his father asked him why he'd done such a terrible thing. Min didn't know how to explain it. All he knew was that the anger was there, always had been, drilled down deep, where it flowed like lava—his *Han*.

All this fury had helped him excel, academically and athletically; he was unrelenting in his competitiveness, in his desire to prove his invulnerability. But Min now saw avoidance in this tactic. Yu-jin's death had exposed his weakness and pain; it had opened his eyes to the escape artist he'd become. Always running and running. Only now was he beginning to understand that everything he thought he'd found in Seoul wasn't as it seemed. A culture he thought his own, a job he thought fulfilling, a partner he thought he knew—it accumulated into a glaring and painful realization that he'd perhaps been wrong about everything.

Where had he been running that night? Gravel underfoot, tears stinging his eyes. There'd never been a destination, only an instinct. It was still his instinct now, even as the ferry came into port, but that wasn't an option. No more running, Min thought, no matter the risks.

⁜

Min was the last person to disembark, making sure no one was following him. Unless the Minister's men had started disguising themselves as fishermen or families headed to the beach, Min was safe.

Finding So-ra's whereabouts on the small island proved more difficult than Min had anticipated. At the dock, taxis queued, waiting for the ferry passengers to disembark. He approached one after another, but the response was always the same: a look of bewilderment, followed by an offer to drive him to the closest beach. No one seemed to have heard of House of the Lotus Tree. Forgoing a taxi, Min decided to walk to the center of town, following the two-lane road that snaked the circumference of the island. He stuck close to the rusted steel barriers, keeping an eye out for any paths that might lead to the island's center, as cars and old pickup trucks carrying squealing livestock and produce whizzed by. Overgrown weeds and thistles clung to his pants. The wind died in spats, the drone of insects filling the silence.

Throat dry, blisters working their way between his toes, it was almost noon when Min reached the first beach. Stopping at a street stall, he bought a bottle of water from a young boy with sun-bronzed shoulders. When Min asked him if there were any paths that led to the island's interior, he pointed down the road, instructing Min to take two rights and a left, until he reached the dead end.

Waves lapped the sand like a cat drinking from a saucer. Families lounged on the beach, adults reading newspapers and paperback novels while children played in the shallows with their inflatable tubes and Styrofoam noodles. Min thanked the boy for his directions.

The path took him deep into the heart of the island. All sound soon disappeared, the roll of waves, birdcalls—only his footsteps remained. Above, a dense foliage blotted out the sun. The silence was unnerving, a gloominess permeating the darkness. At the crackling of twigs underfoot, Min whirled around and peered behind him, into the murk. He stood still, blood in his ears. Was he being followed? He'd taken every precaution before disembarking the ferry. He kept on, fancying himself a brave pioneer, machete in hand, hacking his way through the jungle. Vines and low-hanging branches seemed to close in around him, his line of vision narrowing to a pinhole.

After losing sight of the path, he was forced to double back and retrace his steps, his own footprints unrecognizable. Without guideposts he quickly became disoriented. Every flower, leaf, and bush bled into a camouflage tapestry of greens, a maze of indiscernible details. Min's heart pounded; his knees went weak. And just when he was about to call out, go back the way he thought he'd come, convinced the boy had given him bad directions, he noticed the path brightening. He could breathe again. The canopy opened, showering him with light. In the clearing stood the compound. If he hadn't known otherwise, he would've guessed it was a prison. There were two white buildings, four stories tall, separated by what Min thought to be a recreational yard. The only windows were slender slits running up the sides, like someone had taken a razor to the walls. The building gave off an ominous but calming aura, as if to both intimidate and intrigue its visitors. It wasn't until his second time around the property that Min found the entrance, a long turquoise-tiled hall lit by fluorescent lights crackling overhead. The color inspired a distinct childhood memory of when he'd gone to the aquarium in Monterey for the first time. He looked up, half expecting to see dolphins and manta rays swimming above.

A woman sat behind a sliding glass window at the check-in desk. She was in her early forties, lines beginning to crease across her pale forehead. A gray cardigan clung to her shoulders as she stood up to greet him. Only then did Min realize how cold it was inside.

"May I help you?" she said, sliding the window open.

"I'm here to see someone," he said, surprised by the calmness of his voice.

Clipboard in her dry, cracked hands, the woman flipped through pages. "Name?"

"So-ra. Family name—"

"Just sign in." She slid a thick book with a blue canvas cover to him. As her face met the light above, Min noticed how plain and bare it looked, her eyelashes sparse, lips a dull magenta, like she'd given blood earlier in the day.

"Right there," the woman said, her finger resting on a line. "And I'll need to hold your bag and your phone here."

After signing in, he was led by another woman through a series of hallways, all decorated in the same turquoise tile. All the doors lacked handles—only keypads to gain access, it seemed. Min expected their feet to echo through the hall, but the floor was covered with sound-deadening material. It looked like tile but gave off the sound of a rug each time he put his heel to it.

"If you'd be so kind as to wait out here," the woman said, rapidly tapping a seven-digit code into the keypad. A door opened into a courtyard at the center of the complex. "So-ra will be with you shortly."

Aside from a few metal picnic tables scattered about the yard, there wasn't much. The sun beat down on Min, baking the already dry dirt. The high concrete wall made it impossible for him to get his bearings. He thought he'd entered the clearing from the east, but now he couldn't be sure. The lush jungle path seemed an impossibility under the blazing heat.

Tongue swollen, throat dry, Min drummed a beat on the tabletop. Then So-ra appeared, the door closing slowly behind her. Min was filled with an overwhelming sense of relief. She was okay. She was alive.

So-ra stood in the courtyard, skin like rice paper, hair limp against her bony cheeks, dressed in gray sweats, squinting up at the sun. Even from a distance, it was clear she was unwell. If she recognized Min, she gave no indication.

"It's Min," he said when she didn't acknowledge him, eyes wandering from his face to the walls to the sky. "So-ra."

She forced a smile, her lips drawn and chapped. "Min. So nice of you to come. I didn't think I'd have visitors so soon."

"What's going on? Are you okay?"

"I'm fine. Much better now that I'm on a schedule."

"What do you mean?"

She paused, still taking him in. "I never realized how disconnected I was until coming here. They've got me working in the agriculture pod. Apparently I'm skilled when it comes to planting and growing things. I forgot how good it feels to get dirt under your fingernails."

"But you're so pale."

"Oh," she said, looking down at her hands with embarrassment. "Am I? I hadn't noticed. All our farming is done hydroponically. We only see the sun during our time in this yard. While the sun gives us life, too much can damage us." She reached across the table and squeezed his arm. "You don't have to worry, Min. I'm where I want to be. Everyone's here because they've made a choice."

"But at the memorial. You were terrified. You told me to meet you. Remember? Under Hannam Bridge. You said you'd explain everything."

So-ra puzzled over what he'd said, dull eyes flicking back and forth. "I'm not sure what you mean."

He tried to catch her gaze. "You're saying you don't remember?"

"I was upset. But I'm better now. It's all going to be better," she said, sliding her hands inside her shirtsleeves. Her once powerful frame swam inside the sweatshirt.

Min reached across the table. "So-ra. What's going on? Who brought you here?"

"Yu-jin's father. He thought it best if I got some help. He said I was having a breakdown," she recounted, like she was reading a ledger, all numbers and percentages.

"I had no idea."

"Neither did I, really. But after talking with Yu-jin's family—"

"Her father, you mean."

"Yes, her father. We decided it was best for me to get some help," she said, putting her hands on the table.

Min gently squeezed those delicate fingers, afraid they might dissolve in his grasp. "Are you sure that's what they're doing here? Helping you?"

She nodded vigorously.

"Help me understand."

She pulled her hair back into a ponytail, eyes sunken, like two holes drilled into the moon's crust.

Min waited for an answer, but nothing came, only So-ra's shallow breathing. Around them, nothing. Like the tiles in the hallway, the walls of the courtyard killed all sound. How could she stand it in this place?

Despite So-ra's fragility and diminished faculties, Min blamed her somehow, for everything: Yu-jin's death, Misaki's strange behavior, her own disappearance. He measured his words, weighed their worth. "You said you'd tell me the real reason Yu-jin took her life."

So-ra tugged at her eyebrows, sprinkling the fine black hairs on the table.

"You promised me," Min said.

"I made a promise to her, too," she said quietly, "to never tell you."

"Tell me what?"

Chin to her chest, So-ra moved her lips, but no words escaped. She seemed to be repeating something to herself, a mantra or prayer. Min grasped her by the shoulders and was surprised by how frail they felt. "Please, So-ra. I've come all this way."

"It's not my secret to tell. I know that now," she said, refusing to meet his gaze.

"What secret?" Min said, his voice echoing back to him. "Yu-jin's dead, So-ra. Telling it can't hurt anyone now."

So-ra sank into herself, shrinking further and further away. Arms wrapped around her knees, she rocked back and forth. "I can't," she kept saying, eyes closed. "I can't."

Min released her from his grip and sat back down. So-ra stayed where she was, fingers interlaced. Eventually she opened her eyes, regarding him with a strange calmness. It occurred to him that she was on something: Prozac, Zoloft, maybe something stronger, antipsychotics.

"I get what you're going through," he said. "I wasn't best friends with her like you, but I was still her boyfriend. And I'm not kidding myself, I know it wasn't crazy love, the kind you shout from the rooftop or flaunt to everyone in sight, but we still had something real. I miss her, So-ra. And now all I can think about is whether I overlooked some warning sign or a cry for help. What if I could have saved her?"

So-ra only shook her head.

"I'd give up everything just to have her here with us, alive," Min said.

Chin trembling, So-ra looked at him. "I miss her so much. More than you could ever know."

Min didn't get the chance to ask what she meant, So-ra's face crumpling, tears gathering in her eyes. "I'd give anything." Her voice broke. "I loved her, too. We cared for each other, Min. We were together. Do you understand now? You couldn't have done anything. Shame killed her. Guilt killed her." Her voice rose, piercing the silence. "She's dead because of who she wanted to be. Yes, she liked men, she slept with men, she slept with you. But she was with me, too. And now she's gone because she was discovered. I thought she'd be strong enough, but it was too much to bear. It was always her father's judgment she dreaded most."

It couldn't be. It was impossible. Yu-jin with So-ra. He would have noticed. Why would Yu-jin have lied about such a thing? Why pursue him in the first place? Min tried to steady himself, his chest tight, breath raspy. "Why would you say something like that? You know it's not the truth," he heard himself say.

"Sometimes I wish it wasn't," So-ra said. "Then she might still be with us."

It was true then, Min realized, almost smiling at his own blindness. He'd been the perfect disguise. Yu-jin and So-ra, together the whole time, from beginning to end. And the Minister . . . "You're saying Yu-jin's father found out, that he confronted her."

"He threatened to cut her off—financially, emotionally. He was prepared to forget her completely. She told me. We were with each other after she saw you. But then she said she'd forgotten a book at the library, so we said good night . . . If I'd only known what she was thinking, I never would've left her side. I never would've . . ."

The Minister's reaction wasn't entirely shocking. He was a

politician. Public image, reputation—these were things that mattered to someone in his position. If word got out of his daughter's sexuality, no matter how benign, he'd be destroyed. The tabloids, his colleagues, the country—the wave would crush him. In the public's imagination, there were no gay Koreans. Sure, homosexuality was real; it wasn't some horrible thing, but it existed elsewhere, New York, Bangkok, Berlin, anywhere but Korea.

"She didn't want to hurt you," So-ra said, her voice wavering. "She never wanted you to know."

"How long?"

"It wasn't like that. We weren't a thing. It wasn't exclusive." She looked at him pleadingly. "Yu-jin loved you. She cared about you more than anything. You know that."

Min leaned back from the table.

"She wanted to be with you. But she was also trying to convince herself of something. And when she couldn't anymore, she'd come to me."

"I see," he said, replaying every intimate moment they'd had, trying to find what he'd missed. It had felt real. Could his perceptions have been so wrong? Memories of Yu-jin flooded his thoughts. Moments they'd shared, specks of time that had only existed to them: a moonlit walk along the Cheonggyecheon, listening to old records in smoke-filled bars, her nails in his back, the tremor of her heart. What had these been to her? Had it all been an act?

"She was a confused person, Min. She really did care for you. Yu-jin wasn't the kind of person to do things she didn't want to do."

"But she wanted you, too."

"Yes," So-ra said, lowering her eyes.

"Was it just you? Were there other women?"

"Only me," she said. "There was no one else." So-ra rubbed her eyes with her shirtsleeve. "I know I've hurt people. That's why I'm here. House of the Lotus Tree is going to fix me. Nothing I do can bring Yu-jin back, but maybe through this community I can somehow save myself, heal the relationships I've damaged."

Min looked at So-ra, weary and alone. She'd endured more than he could have ever imagined. Her pain was real, the blame and regret—she was a part of Yu-jin's death in a way he could never be. Intricately entangled, forever tied to the passing of her friend and lover. Even in his anger, Min felt her suffering. "But how did Yu-jin's father find everything out? Weren't you careful?"

"Of course," So-ra said, grimacing. "We took every precaution."

"Then how?"

The words didn't seem to reach her. She regarded the walls of the courtyard wearily, her eyes glassy and cold. "I just realized you can't hear the ocean from here. How strange," she said.

"Someone must have told him."

"Someone. Yes," she murmured, like she was acting and speaking from a sunken cavern deep inside her.

"Was it the tape?" Min said. "The recording you made with Yu-jin. Is that how the Minister found out?"

"It was just a project for her film class," So-ra said, running her nail-bitten fingers over her lips. "That's all it was." A gull flew overhead, its call strange and unsettling. So-ra stared at the bird, mesmerized, like she'd never seen its kind before. "Misaki. I know it was her. She told Yu-jin's father about the film classes and the recording. She knew he didn't approve of Yu-jin taking courses outside her major."

"She did it to get back at you. For the way you treated her."

"She must have overheard us. Yu-jin was so excited about the project and the classes. She couldn't stop talking about them, even in the apartment when Misaki was around."

"So that's what you meant when you said she ruined everything."

"After that, her father started asking all sorts of questions. It was only a matter of time," So-ra said, resting her hands in her lap.

Min leaned in closer, willing So-ra to look at him. "Did Misaki know about you and Yu-jin? Did she ever suspect anything?"

Before Min could say anything, the door to the courtyard opened. An attendant approached them, her white-sneakered feet crunching on the gravel.

"The tape isn't what you think. It isn't what anyone thinks!" So-ra said, gripping down on the metal tabletop, her voice rising. But the momentary burst of emotion had already wilted before she continued, "It was something Yu-jin was proud of. It was a work of art."

Turning her head, So-ra acknowledged the woman with a slump of her shoulders, abdicating all agency as she stood. Min noticed she wore no shoes. Against the sun-bleached ground, her feet, gnarled and battered from a life of dance, were beautifully grotesque. Min couldn't look away. How had Yu-jin seen her? Had she thought these feet beautiful? A testament to So-ra's dedication and drive, whatever it was he didn't have?

The attendant, a middle-aged woman with graying hair, put her hands on So-ra's shoulders. "Recreational time is limited here at House of the Lotus Tree. I'm afraid So-ra's time is up."

She went willingly. Min followed, his vision a swarm of blinding sunlight. The attendant punched in a code. The door popped open from the wall; a medicinal-scented coolness washed over them. So-ra turned and held him close, her bony ribs jabbing his stomach. "I know what we did was wrong, Min. I can never undo what I did to her, what we did to you, but I'm still sorry."

"I don't care about any of that now," Min said. "Why don't you come with me? I can get you out of here. You don't have to stay. You shouldn't punish yourself for this. Think about your future, your dance career."

"This is where I belong," she said, slipping inside, the door closing behind her.

Min stood in the empty courtyard, condemned to some truth he'd yet to discover. Everything inside him fell. Hunched over, head spinning, he groped for shade against the tall concrete wall. A laugh or a scream welled up inside him, fists full of gravel. What a fool I've been, he thought. My girlfriend sleeping with someone else, another woman, my girlfriend on the brink of self-destruction, all while I had her next to me—some happy mirage, a charade for my ego. The sum of his misperceptions seemed insurmountable, a floodlight obliterating everything.

·⫸·

The weather turned rough on the late-afternoon ferry back to Incheon. Doubt churned within Min. The knowledge that every word, every action of Yu-jin's could have been deception, duplicity, sat like a poison pill in his stomach. He saw her smile, felt her touch, but all with shaded cynicism. Had she meant any of it? Had she been present with him? Or had her thoughts been with So-ra, always So-ra? He wanted to believe she'd been conflicted, torn between them. He wanted desperately to know their time had meant something, more than just a passing moment, convenience. Although hadn't she been that for him? A distraction, a way to convince himself he belonged in Seoul?

Min remembered going to an art show with Yu-jin and So-ra, a giant blue house, and something Yu-jin had asked him later that night, in the warmth of her bed: "Do you ever get homesick?" Had she wanted to talk with him in that moment, *really* talk with him, or had it been about So-ra all along? Had their entire relationship been a clever magic trick? Had he wanted to be deceived? Her suffering, her pain, it had all been concealed, out of sight. Or worse, he'd comprehended everything in its totality and turned away. Held his tongue when he knew something lay there, something raw and authentic. Perhaps I saw every sign, he thought, and I ignored it.

As Min sat with his thoughts, a coil of doubt slipped around his ankle, tightening with every wave that slapped against the ferry's hull. Could he really believe everything So-ra had said? She'd been admitted to House of the Lotus Tree for a reason. She wasn't well; she was heavily medicated. However painful it was to admit, Min knew in his heart she was telling the truth about her and Yu-jin, but everything else—Misaki's role, the Minister's condemnation, the tape's contents—seemed far-fetched. Misaki had done nothing but help him since Yu-jin's death. She'd been the closest thing he had to a friend. Was she really capable of such deceit and vengefulness?

The longer Min dwelled on So-ra's confession—the frenzied speech and strange demeanor—the more skeptical he grew. How could the tape be nothing? And was disownment really what Yu-jin's father had threatened? His only daughter, the crown jewel of his accomplishments, his legacy. And even if the Minister had found the strength to cast her out of the family circle, would that have crushed

Yu-jin? Would she have surrendered so easily? She was resilient; she was stubborn. He couldn't fathom Yu-jin falling into desolation with the threat of disownment. She couldn't have taken her life, and even if she had, there must have been something else that had dragged her down, into the murk.

TWENTY-TWO

YU-JIN

A lie, of course

In the coming weeks it grew increasingly difficult to ignore my future beyond graduation, as my father became more dogged in his efforts to find me a job. He provided me with a list of things I needed to do before considering myself ready for the interview circuit he'd arranged for me. First there was the haircut and makeup consultation at a beauty salon in Myeongdong, where a woman fussed over my split ends and scolded me for my unkempt eyebrows. I'd always considered myself fairly knowledgeable when it came to feminine beauty trends and products, especially when compared to So-ra, but apparently I was severely lacking. I was sent away with bags stuffed with lotions, lipsticks, and powders. Afterwards, my father accompanied me to a photography studio, where he'd scheduled me for a round of professional headshots. He stood behind the photographer, a slender man wearing a lavender turtleneck, throughout the shoot, talking on his phone, stopping only to signal for me to keep my chin up and stop slouching. I teetered atop the small wooden stool, buttocks sore, back seizing. With the camera's inexhaustible flash causing temporary blindness every few seconds and my cheeks aching from holding an expression that my father said must exude "serious but not intimidating, hardworking but not difficult," I struggled to remember a more unpleasant experience.

By the time we arrived at the tailor, where I was fitted for my custom-made business suit, I was somewhere far away, watching myself before the three floor-length mirrors, measuring tape pulled taut against my inner thighs and underarms, fabric and cloth dangling from me like a second skin. My father looked at me approvingly. I tried to see what he saw. Once the tailor had recorded my measurements, I was free to go.

The only remaining item on my father's list was the interview coach, which didn't happen until a few days later. I arrived at the office in Gangnam ten minutes early. When I entered, tentatively pushing the heavy, frosted glass door ajar, I was greeted by the coach herself, dressed in a severe black blazer and dress.

"You're late," she said, offering me a seat in front of the desk. "Always arrive at least fifteen minutes early."

"Sorry," I said, trying to compose my face as my father had told me to.

The woman gave me a toothless smile. "Your father thought having a female interview coach would be most ideal for you, and I tend to agree. There are certain challenges women face when interviewing for a job."

"I see."

"Your father thinks you are quite capable, so this will be our only meeting. I don't usually meet with my clients for only one session, but I'm making an exception," the woman said, opening a folder in front of her. "I'm about to tell you some rules. You don't need to write anything down. I'll be giving you this folder before you leave. What I'd like you to do is listen to these rules. Don't just commit them to memory, absorb them into your being, your ethos."

I narrowed my focus, listened to her words, jettisoning all fear and doubt from my mind.

"Most importantly," the coach said, "you must never express an affinity or interest in marriage or children. Employers view this as a lack of commitment to the company. You must vocalize your enthusiasm for group work, even if it means you won't receive individual praise. If asked for your greatest weakness, always say it's that you work too many hours. In addition, there may be an instance where a man makes an inappropriate comment about your clothing or appearance during the interview. If this happens, you must smile and ask for the next question. It's essential that you do not miss a beat. Simply move on."

There were other rules and tips, all seemingly aimed at subservience and decorum. Was this the reality awaiting me after I graduated? Why hadn't my father warned me himself? I thought about what So-ra would do in this situation. No doubt she'd leave, but not before railing against the sexist work culture this woman so willfully perpetuated. I wished I had her strength, her fire.

After the interview coach had finished her lecture, I hurried out of the office, her staccato voice pinging in my head. In the cacophonous lobby of the office building, I took the folder she'd given me and tossed it in the garbage. I didn't need her rules.

My father's car was waiting for me outside. He no longer drove. He had his own personal chauffeur, compliments of his job. Dressed in his blue military uniform, medals glimmering gold on his lapel, he spoke to me excitedly about my potential career while I swam in the expansive backseat of the black Mercedes. Anything involving community service was good optics for a career in politics, and going to law school was always an option if I wanted to make some money before jumping into public service.

With freshly printed résumés and glossy business cards, I met with politicians, campaign organizers, paralegals, executive managers, and community organizers. The sheer number of people who seemed to know my father was staggering. Three interviews went particularly well, but I still couldn't believe these people would consider hiring me in any capacity simply because of my connection to him—it was inconceivable.

It was heartening and terrifying to know how much my father cared for me, how invested he was in my future. He and my mother had always pushed me to become something, and now I was a step closer. Still, I started to wonder if any of this was what I wanted: law school, politics. It all started to ring hollow. These careers inspired nothing in me. But were they supposed to? It was a vocation—it wasn't meant to be inspiring.

"Do you like your job?" I asked him on the way back from a meeting with the Chairman of the Saenuri Party, who'd seemed eager to do my father a favor by potentially offering me a position on his staff.

My father stopped texting on his phone. "What do you mean?"

"Do you enjoy what you do? Does it make you happy?"

He was quiet for a moment. I thought he might be worried the chauffeur was listening. Then he went on, "This job has been a blessing, Yu-jin. It's enabled us to move to Seoul, have a higher quality of life. Your mother doesn't need to work, you can afford to live off campus. These are the things that bring me happiness. They are a by-product of my job. You'll be disappointed if you look to your career for happiness. A job is a job. Work is work. It's one's duty to provide, for oneself and one's family. This wasn't always the case for women. It certainly wasn't for your mother. But things are different now. They're changing for the better. More people in the workforce means our economy will be even stronger. You're lucky to have the opportunity to work at all. Who's putting these ideas in your head anyway?"

I was startled by his direct line of questioning. "No one. All these interviews got me thinking about it. That's all."

"Wouldn't have anything to do with So-ra, would it?" he said. "She's quite the idealist."

I was silent, unsure of what to say, where to step.

"Trust me," my father continued. "Give it five or six years. She'll be wishing she'd pursued something more practical. The world isn't kind to dreamers."

I thought about my film classes, all the hours I'd spent watching movies, writing papers on cinematography, directorial influences, the male gaze. It wasn't practical in the slightest. But it thrilled me, challenged me. I knew it wasn't useful, in the most basic sense of the word, but it still felt like a worthy pursuit, if only because it made me feel worthwhile.

"Your mother and I are lucky we don't have to worry about that with you. You were always focused and driven. Even as a kid." The car stopped; we were outside my apartment. He unbuckled his seat belt and hugged me. "You did well today. Let me know when you hear from them."

I rested my chin on his overpadded shoulder. "Thanks for everything, Dad. You didn't have to arrange all this."

"What, and leave it all to chance?" he said, letting me go. "That's not how things get done."

Before I could get inside my building, he called to me from the descending tinted window: "How's everything working out with the new roommate? Japanese girl, right?"

I tried to recall when I'd told him about Misaki. "It's good. She isn't messy, which is all we really care about."

"You and So-ra playing nice?"

"What do you mean?"

"Three can be a difficult number," he said. "Someone's always bound to feel left out."

I waited for him to say something more, but he didn't. "I think we'll end up being good friends. We're already spending lots of time together."

A lie, of course. So-ra and I were still doing everything in our power to separate from Misaki. She'd accepted her excommunication willingly, which had only unnerved me more.

"Keep me updated. You'll be getting calls in no time at all."

I did get calls the next week. I was offered three jobs, with training beginning in June. A shocking development, considering all the interviews were only meant to be preliminary. It seemed my father's status was opening doors that were shut to most. I never returned any of their messages. I turned my full attention to the final project for my film class. Even though it was an intermediate-level course, Professor Lee was encouraging us to create a short clip, a re-creation of one of our favorite scenes from the films we'd watched so far. She'd already coordinated with the media department to allow us to check out the cameras and other necessary equipment.

"In order to further understand film," she said, "you must attempt to create it. Then you'll see the choices that directors and cinematographers make. This in turn will help you understand how a film's narratives and characters are created."

I knew immediately I'd re-create the famous fountain scene from *La Dolce Vita*, which had quickly become one of my favorite films. I was enthralled by its episodic nature, its movements from day to night, the depiction of Rome, a city that seemed to be dying and blooming simultaneously. With its ancient ruins, cobblestone streets, crumbling buildings, it was the antithesis of Seoul.

All I needed was So-ra's help.

TWENTY-THREE

MIN

Maybe not you, but someone else, someone inside you

After his trip to Jawoldo, Min called Detective Park to tell him what he'd learned. The revelation regarding Yu-jin and So-ra's secret relationship made Min even more suspicious of the Minister's involvement in his daughter's death. Detective Park had said all the arrows pointed to suicide, but for the first time, Min felt like he'd discovered a potential motive for the Minister: a desire to silence his daughter, or make her disappear altogether. When the call went straight to voicemail, he left a message, telling Park to call him back. It was urgent.

While he waited, for hours and then days, Min was grateful for Seoul's twenty-four-hour offerings. Rather than face the awful silence in his apartment, where doubt and insecurity were his only companions, Min frequented *jjimjilbangs*, where he could bathe and sleep for cheap. Everything in his apartment reminded him of Yu-jin, and Min took to getting all his meals from food stalls and convenience stores, scarfing down neatly packaged *samgak kimbap* and crispy *bindae-tteok* while he lingered on the street, comforted by the endless bustle.

A week later and Min still hadn't heard from Detective Park. It was a balmy Sunday night, and he was headed back to his apartment for a fresh pair of clothes when he was cornered by two of the Minister's goons. They'd waited to grab him until he'd turned off the main road, shoving him into an alley bathed in shadows. He'd never seen them coming.

Min didn't recognize either of the men. They seemed burlier and tougher than the last pair who had followed him. One had a chipped tooth protruding from his upper lip, as if it was too long for his mouth. They wore black suit jackets over black turtlenecks, their frames square and menacing. Hands under his armpits, they maneuvered Min into a corner where they were shielded from view by a large dumpster overflowing with refuse. While one man pushed Min up against the wall, nestling an elbow into the small of his back, Chipped Tooth patted him down, turning his pockets inside out and removing his wallet and phone. An overwhelming stench of rotting food filled Min's nostrils.

"He doesn't have it," Chipped Tooth muttered to his partner.

Min didn't understand what they were looking for. When they turned him around, there was a flashlight in his face. Min squinted into the glare. He considered trying to run but thought better of it. If the Minister wanted him dead, he would've been a long time ago.

"Where's the tape?" Chipped Tooth said.

So that's what they'd been after this entire time. Min wiped beading sweat from his brow. "What tape?"

The slap came without warning, quick and flat against his face. Stars joined the glare from the flashlight as Min worked his jaw open and closed, his ear popping.

"We aren't supposed to hurt him," a voice said.

"He knows where it is," Chipped Tooth said. "Why else would he have run from the other guys?"

Min checked his lip for blood. "I don't know what the hell you're talking about."

Chipped Tooth seemed to be debating whether to slap him again. Min tried to control his breathing, ears hot, neck tingling. "Look at my phone. Check my texts, my emails," he continued. "I don't have anything to hide."

Chipped Tooth kept the light trained on Min.

"Nothing," the other man said after a moment.

The light clicked off. Min rubbed his eyes trying to acclimate to the darkness. Chipped Tooth closed the distance between them, breath stale with cigarette smoke. He wrapped a big hand around the back of Min's neck and pulled him close. "Where's the recording? We know it's not at your apartment, we just came from there," he said.

"I'm telling you the truth."

Chipped Tooth exhaled slowly, an unnerving whistle emanating from his mouth. "I'll pass that along to the boss. He seems to think otherwise," he said, before releasing Min from his grip and walking away, his partner already vanished from the alley.

Min took a few long breaths to gather himself, knees weak, hands trembling. He rubbed his cheek, feeling the raised skin, bumpy and tender. He'd taken worse hits in rugby.

Min returned to find his apartment in disarray. The Minister's men had gone through everything. Work files lay scattered across the floor; dresser drawers had been pulled out and dumped on his bed; even his medicine cabinet had been emptied. While he cleaned up, Min called Detective Park again. All he got was a message saying the number had been deactivated. He was beginning to worry. Maybe Park had been removed from the case, or maybe the Minister had taken more drastic measures. If the men following him were any indication, Yu-jin's father was getting more desperate.

Min couldn't waste any more time. He'd find the tape himself. If the Minister wanted it that badly, there must be something on it. And even if it was just a class project, like So-ra said, maybe it would explain why Yu-jin had withered so easily under her father's threats.

Once he'd done his best to tidy up his apartment, Min headed out to the closest *PC bang* to look up Ewha's online course catalogue. To call *PC bangs* internet cafés did them a disservice; they were self-sufficient ecosystems, meccas of respite for the world-weary. With bathrooms, snack bars, and waitstaff, these places catered to those least interested in reality. Most of the patrons were gamers: truant kids and young adults who poured their lives into online tournaments and role-playing games. It was an escape, one that Min understood more than ever as he sat down and logged on.

Settling into his seat in the semidarkness, Min typed away, perusing the course offerings at Ewha for the fall. Next to him, a kid aggressively clicked his mouse while muttering orders into his headset. Empty packets of ramen noodles littered his cubicle. Min pulled his chair closer to the desk and scrolled through the classes. Yu-jin had never mentioned the name of her film professor. Luckily the department was small. There were only six courses being offered by three different professors. Min took down all their names and numbers in his phone before logging off.

·⫿·

At the height of summer break, Ewha's campus was desolate, save for the few unfortunate summer school students lugging books and laptops in half-slung bags. Min traversed the expansive quads and tree-lined paths in search of the College of Liberal Arts. When he finally came across a campus map, he was thankful to find he was only steps from where he needed to go.

The building in which the film department was housed had escaped Ewha's most recent campus renovation. Musty and dank, it was a portal to a lost time, the hallway lights shining the color of yellowed book pages, paint peeling from the walls, the hint of mothballs lingering in the stuffy air. Min stood for a moment relishing the coolness, sweat drying on his arms.

What had Yu-jin thought walking these gloomy halls? Had she felt free, cloaked from needling eyes? When she'd mentioned it, Min had thought the class was a casual interest, a break from the monotony of her required classes, but after speaking with So-ra, he thought it was possible there was more to the decision. Was it the act of watching, of being invisible in the darkened audience, free to observe anything that caught her eye? Or maybe it was the analytical aspect, determining how a scene was constructed, shot, and balanced. There were a million ways to look at something.

With the knowledge of her relationship with So-ra, Min saw every decision Yu-jin had made in a different light. Things he'd dismissed or forgotten now returned twofold under the microscope of his doubt.

Ahead, a slant of light fell across the mildewed carpet. A distant clacking rattled down the corridor, self-assured fingers plugging away on something, a keyboard perhaps. Min found himself in a cozy vestibule at the end of the hall. He counted six offices in total. Only one door was open. Min hesitated, mesmerized by the rhythm of the keys. Checking the nameplate, he was pleased to find a name that matched one from his list. Meekly, he knocked. The typing stopped. Inside, a young woman sat with impeccable posture behind a rectangular glass desk, the laptop's white screen reflecting off her glasses. Aside from the framed diplomas on the wall and the shelf of DVDs, the office was void of decoration. Min tried to hide his surprise. For some reason he'd pictured an old man with horn-rimmed glasses, surrounded by books and cardboard cutouts of *Frankenstein* and *Creature from the Black Lagoon*.

"May I help you?" the woman said.

"I'm looking for Professor Lee."

"I'm Professor Lee."

The professor offered him a seat in a stiff-looking wooden armchair. "What can I do for you? I assume you aren't a student here."

Min sat, unsure of what to say.

"A joke," she said. "We're an all-female institution, as I'm sure you're aware."

"Yes, of course," Min said, trying not to sound flustered. "I just had a few questions about a former student."

After removing her glasses, spritzing them with a fine mist, and cleaning them with a cloth from her pocket, the professor explained it was against school policy to discuss current or former students.

"I understand completely, it's just that I'm a friend of Yu-jin's.

Kim Yu-jin. She would have been in one of your classes last semester."

The professor gave him a quizzical look. "Yes," she said. "I remember her. But as I said, I can't discuss anything with you."

Min waited for her to say more, but she was finished, lips pressed into a thin line. Was it possible she didn't know about Yu-jin's death? Had the Minister somehow suppressed even that news?

He felt strangely comforted. There were others who'd been left in the dark. He wondered if this was how Park had felt delivering the news to him. "I'm sorry I'm the one to have to tell you this," he said, "but she's dead. She took her life at the end of the semester."

The professor seemed genuinely moved. "That's awful. She only audited my courses, but she seemed like an impressive young woman. She really committed suicide?"

"I'm afraid so. The thing is, I came here because I was her close friend, and I know she was working on something for your class, a recording. Her family would like to have it for sentimental reasons, but since her death we've had trouble locating it. I was hoping you might know something about it or its whereabouts."

A tremor flickered over the professor's face. "I can't help you."

Min explained how Yu-jin's parents were really looking forward to seeing the completed project. Professor Lee seemed skeptical, even nervous, as she fiddled with her laptop, clicking and scrolling. The Minister must have already gotten to her. What had it taken, money, threats?

"I really can't tell you anything, not just because of the rules, but because she never shared the project with the class or turned it in. It was the only assignment she didn't submit."

"Could you tell me a little bit about what she was working on?"

This line of questioning seemed more agreeable to Professor Lee, who quickly closed her laptop. She explained that students had been asked to re-create a single scene from a classic film they'd watched in class that semester. Yu-jin had chosen *La Dolce Vita*.

"It's a wonderful film," she continued. "It was actually booed when they showed a rough cut in Milan. It's funny how people, even intelligent people, can fail to see the genius and beauty of something at first. If I recall, it didn't stop there—Fellini was accused of being an atheist and a communist, treasonous even."

Min had heard of the movie but never seen it. Yu-jin had only mentioned the class in passing. She'd never seemed deeply interested in the arts. That was more So-ra's territory. That's what made all of this so strange. It was why Min needed to grasp the film's significance to Yu-jin. Even if it was just a movie, it might further explain her father's dogged inquisitiveness, her death.

"I'm just trying to understand why she would choose that particular film."

"The film is about many things, like any good piece of art," Professor Lee said. "But essentially, *La Dolce Vita* is about our most inherent struggle between the duality of human desire. In the film, Marcello, the protagonist, is torn between two worlds: one of wealth and celebrity, with its fancy cars, beautiful women, and endless parties, and one of the intellectual or artist, with its culture and discourse. Of course this is a bit simplistic—but most great works of art can be boiled down to a single concept or idea. *La Dolce Vita* is no different. It presents the audience with two men, Marcello, the journalist, and his friend, Steiner, a wealthy intellectual, who are trapped by their own desires and fears: Marcello with his love of parties, celebrity, and sex, and Steiner with his want of security and wealth. Both men fear they've lost their ambition: their quest for spiritual fulfillment in a world that is rapidly losing any moral certainty."

Had Yu-jin felt trapped by her desires? Had she felt torn between risk and security?

"Does that make anything clearer for you?"

Min said he wasn't sure and thanked her before walking to the door.

"Perhaps," Professor Lee said. "Perhaps this will shed some light on the questions you have. It's something Steiner says in the film: 'Sometimes at night the darkness and silence weighs upon me. Peace frightens me; perhaps I fear it most of all. I feel it is only a facade hiding the face of hell.'"

The face of hell. Was that what Yu-jin had seen? Had the silence and darkness weighed upon her? Had she seen their relationship, her entire life, for the facade it was?

Min knew now that he had lost Yu-jin long before she'd died, or perhaps he'd never really had her. True, they'd been together, but she'd never wanted to be possessed, by anyone. All that time, she'd hidden an essential part of who she was, who she wanted to be. For the first time, Min understood why she hadn't told him her secret. What had gone unspoken between them, what they'd left unsaid, had allowed them to flourish, even thrive together. They'd found comfort and security in the undefined, never forced to take the leap, demand something, not just from themselves but from each other. In this harsh new light, Min saw his own complicity in Yu-jin's deceits. He'd welcomed their relationship's superficiality, found comfort in the shallow pool of their shared existence, where nothing bottomless and strange could swallow them up.

After thanking the professor one final time, Min made his way back through the musty hallways. If the professor was right, So-ra had been telling the truth. The tape was just a class project, an artistic endeavor. But did he really believe that's all it was? Why then had Misaki thought to use it against So-ra and Yu-jin? Why had the news of it and the film classes sent the Minister rampaging through his daughter's life, and why were his men so eager to get their hands on it?

Without Detective Park, Min felt himself floundering, sinking beneath the weight of unanswerable questions. All the answers lay on Yu-jin's cold lips, forever unspoken. Min stood inside the gloomy entryway, looking out at heat waves shimmering above the water-starved grass. He couldn't go back to his apartment. The quiet, the time to sit and think. Nausea rolled in his stomach. Chewing the inside of his cheek, Min stepped back out into the sultry weather, air like a waterlogged towel around his neck. His pocket vibrated as he exited the building into the sultry afternoon air. It was a text message from Misaki: Wanna come to a party tonight?

⫸

The bar was packed, air thick with cigarette smoke and sweat. Feedback from the microphone crackled overhead as Min pushed his way through the crowd of twenty- and thirtysomethings. There were tattoos, pierced ears, and lace-up boots mixed in a sea of cutoff jeans and denim jackets. Min felt out of place in his plain button-down and khakis.

A voice blared over the sound system: "Fuck the government!" Everyone roared. "Fuck the system! Let's party!" The sound was deafening; a guttural electric guitar power stroke surged overhead like a B-52 bombing run. The crowd pitched toward the makeshift stage, where a band had started playing. The lead singer wore only tight blue jeans, channeling his inner Mick Jagger, hips gyrating, his lean, muscular frame already glistening with sweat.

Around the stage, a few girls thrashed about, sacrificing themselves at the altar of their rock god. One of the girls fell forward, almost hugging the speaker that blew her hair back with every bass note. She wore white Converse sneakers and overalls, one of the buckles already undone, catching the smoky light as it flailed back and forth with each twist of her body.

This was Seoul's counterculture—something Min had only heard about, never seen—churning and writhing like some pissed-off beast. It was a world away from the silent commuter metro rides, the suits and ties, the pencil skirts, the astronomical academic expectations, the conscription, the *soju*, the plastic surgery, the DMZ. These were the rebels, rejecting the patriarchy, the gender pay gap. This was their collective rage against a society and country that demanded perfection, filial piety, and allegiance; rage against the demilitarized zone just thirty-five miles north, running like a jagged scar across their country, cut by milky-faced foreign ministers in Berlin; rage that they still carried this burden, so many years later (all able-bodied men are required to defend South Korea for two years, forming one of the largest standing armies in the world). This was their rallying cry, their lament.

The crowd swelled. Microphone extended, the lead singer beckoned all, his head bent in prayer. The girl in the overalls moved closer, the masses pressing her up against the stage. Flinging back his hair, teeth catching the light, the lead singer reached out and held the girl's chin to the lights. It was Misaki. She was beautiful, in a crazed,

243

uninhibited way. She'd always been like this. But it was only now—under the spotlight, ragged with rhythm—that Min recognized her singular gift for belonging, her unabashed confidence no matter where she was.

It was a feeling he'd always craved, rarely known, and suddenly Min was seeing Misaki in a way he never had before, and he felt drawn to her, captivated, unable to look away.

Misaki gave herself to the music, lunging forward, holding the singer's hand to her cheek, then pushing away, spinning into the crowd, lost among the lurching mass. Min found her at the bar, face flushed, chest heaving.

"You came!" she said, throwing her arms around his neck. Min couldn't help but breathe in deeply, lingering in her hair as long as possible. He was startled by this new sense of yearning. "I didn't think you would, especially after the way I acted after the memorial. I'm really sorry."

"Wouldn't have missed it for anything," he said. "I wanted to see you."

"That's good enough for me." She took his hand. "Come on. Let's dance."

There'd been other reasons for Min's acceptance of her invitation. Since his conversation with So-ra on Jawoldo and his meeting with Professor Lee, he wanted to know whether Misaki knew about So-ra and Yu-jin. Had she really never suspected anything? And more important, why had she told Yu-jin's father about the recording? But now that he was here with Misaki, face-to-face, something stopped him from asking his questions. He didn't want her to be connected to Yu-jin's death. Because if she was responsible for all this—the loss, the pain—how could he explain this need to know her entirely? This growing desire—it was betrayal, a desecration of Yu-jin's memory, and Min tried to douse the shameful want, but there it stayed, smoldering in his chest.

It was a feeling, a connection he'd never felt before. And he found himself infinitely close to her in those few hours, when it seemed the world no longer existed outside their own. There was nothing real except for whatever it was that pulsed between their bodies as they danced long into the night.

When the band finally took a break, they retreated in a haze of euphoria to the bar, where they gulped water from plastic cups and caught their breath, grinning at one another. The lead singer came up behind Misaki and wrapped her in an all-encompassing hug. "Little dancing machine out there," he said, hands on her hips.

Misaki moved out from under his embrace. "This is my friend Min. The guy I was telling you about."

"Chaz," he said, gripping Min's hand and giving him a wink. "I'm sure our little band isn't much compared to what you've got in America. But you gotta start somewhere, right? By the way, we're having an album release party tomorrow night. You should come by. Bring a lady friend if you've got one."

A pain, first imperceptible, then searing, cut into Min, a hot blade down into his heart where it stuck. Min was shocked to find he was jealous—of this man, this poseur musician who, for all he knew, had nothing to do with Misaki. And yet he was jealous of the way she'd danced for him, jealous of the way she coaxed that look from his eyes, a lustful gaze.

Chaz interrupted Min's spiraling thoughts to say he had to prep for the next set, but not before embracing him like they were brothers.

"Let's get out of here," Misaki said.

"What about the show? What about Chaz?" Min said, unable to hide his bitterness.

"Chaz?" She laughed. "He's harmless. Come on."

"Where d'you wanna go?"

"How about your place?" she said.

·╫·

Before Min let Misaki into his apartment, he asked her to wait in the hallway while he tidied up. The place had fallen into disarray since he'd returned from Jawoldo. Misaki just laughed, leaning against the wall. "I really don't mind. How messy can it be?"

Once inside, Min turned the AC on high. After collecting his dirty laundry from the floor, he tossed it in the hamper. He did his best with the bed, straightening the pillows and smoothing out the comforter. Luckily there were no dirty dishes. He made one more pass before opening the front door.

"You really didn't have to clean up," Misaki said after she'd come in and taken her shoes off. "You should see my bedroom. I'm lucky if I can see the floor under all the clothes."

The apartment, her room, Min thought. It all brought him back to Yu-jin. Was he betraying her? If she were alive, would she understand this, just as he understood why she'd kept her relationship with So-ra a secret? He moved to the window and slid it shut, sealing out the city sounds. Misaki turned off the overhead light and moved to him.

In the darkness, Min allowed himself to look at Misaki, tracing the contours of her face with his hand. She was warm to the touch. She was burning up. Heat radiated from underneath her flushed cheeks, like some dormant volcano.

Hands together, they sat on the edge of his bed. The B side of Springsteen's *Tunnel of Love* played around them. Misaki had requested it. "Something American," she'd said with a smile. In Misaki's presence everything washed away. All the questions, the hopes and fears about Yu-jin and So-ra, the tape. They pushed off from shore, drifting into blue oblivion. Eyes closed, Min caressed the soft valleys of skin between her knuckles.

And then they were facing each other, gazing into each other, unafraid of what they might find.

"Do you want me?" she asked, her eyes unblinking.

Min unbuttoned the top of her overalls, fingers grazing her smooth abdomen and hips. "Yes," he heard himself say, pulling her close and unhooking her bra. She slid the straps off her shoulders and flung it to the floor. They laughed together as she tugged his shirt over his head.

The music was still playing, but he didn't hear it anymore as Misaki slid underneath him. Pants were unbuttoned, belt snaked through loops, hips wriggled from underwear. Craning her neck, Misaki looked down at his erection. "It's exactly as I imagined," she said, taking it gently in her hand.

Min laughed into her neck. "You've been imagining?"

"What. You haven't been thinking about me?" she said, hands on his chest.

"I have. I guess I just didn't know it."

She pulled him down by his shoulders, pressing her lips against his. As they kissed, Misaki guided him inside, her eyes open and searching. Wrapping her legs around him, she drew him closer. Min began to close his eyes, but she stopped him. "Look at me," she said. "Don't stop looking at me."

A chaos grew up between them—a rhythmic beat only they could hear. Sheets were discarded to the floor. Misaki opened her mouth in a silent cry, her legs trembling as they clutched Min. The blistering heat from her body engulfed him, flames setting his flesh ablaze. They burned in the darkness of his bedroom.

"Min," he heard her calling. "Min. Come back."

Looking down, he realized he'd lost his erection.

"Is everything all right?" she said, her fingers tracing down his lower back. "What can I do?"

Like an echo in an empty room, he remembered Yu-jin's words: "This is us walking down the street, arm in arm, bundled up against the cold." His mind wandered—along the blank coasts of his consciousness—waves of the abyss crashing against sea cliffs. Why hadn't she said anything? Why had she left him that day in the subway?

He heard the professor: "'Sometimes at night the darkness and silence weighs upon me.'"

Misaki pulled him close, her breath cool and damp against his chest. "Tell me what to do, Min. What do you need?"

Min saw Yu-jin ankle-deep in the Cheonggyecheon, jeans rolled up to her knees, smiling, beckoning him to join her, tanned by the summer sun. He saw her standing on an empty sidewalk, swirling snowflakes dusting her black hair. He heard her laugh in the wind, gusting through him, gone forever.

Taking Misaki's hands, he placed them gently around his neck, one and then the other.

He wanted to feel what Yu-jin had felt, know what she had known during those last moments of her life.

"Are you sure?" she said.

He felt himself nodding. Then, Misaki's voice through the mystic gray—a foghorn in the night: "Tell me when it's too much." She grasped his throat, her grip tentative and frightened. With the slightest touch, Min felt himself awaken. Her body quivered below. She squeezed tighter, the air coming less easily. With each breath more difficult, he grew inside of her. There were stars now, blinking across the inside of his eyelids, white fireworks lighting up the sky. Was this what she had seen? Was this where she'd gone before leaving him?

"Please, Min," Misaki was saying. "Please."

His chest burned. He remembered collapsing onto Misaki, gasping for air, her hair in his mouth. Empty—chest heaving. He kissed her neck, holding her tightly. They lay there together, pillowcase damp, listening to the beating of their hearts, the expanding and contracting of their lungs.

"Is it because of her?" Misaki finally said.

"I don't know."

"Do you miss her?"

"I don't know. I mean, of course I do, but then I think about the way things ended. And I'm not sure what I'm missing was there to begin with."

"I'm sorry I wasn't kinder to you when she died," Misaki said. "I know I was callous and cold. I was just jealous. Even in death Yu-jin was getting your attention. It's a horrible thing to admit, but it's true."

Min struggled to understand what Misaki was trying to tell him. "You mean you liked me? Before everything happened?"

"You couldn't have known," she said with a smile. "But after we met that first night, I've always been interested. But you were with Yu-jin. You seemed content."

"I was," Min said bitterly, an overwhelming question rising to his lips: Did you know about So-ra and Yu-jin? But he swallowed it. He didn't want to know, at least not tonight. "I'm sorry, too," he said. "Not just for the way I acted after Yu-jin died, but for the way we treated you. I never stood up for you."

Misaki pulled the sheets around their shoulders and burrowed close to him. "Are we bad people? For doing this, so soon after everything?"

Guilt and euphoria swirled inside Min. He didn't know what to say or feel. All he could think was that for the first time since Yu-jin had died, he was close to something like happiness. He wrapped his arm around Misaki. "I'm glad this happened."

"Me, too," said. "Just don't make me do that to you again. I don't like hurting people. And I felt like I was hurting someone. Maybe not you, but someone else, someone inside you."

Min held her close, the faintest smell of perspiration on her skin. It reminded him of rain-soaked soil, of backyards and grass. "I won't," he said, inhaling again and again. "I won't."

In the night, Min awoke. At the end of the bed, Misaki's silhouette was huddled, head in her hands. The mattress shook as she cried.

TWENTY-FOUR

YU-JIN

You do them because they go against something

It was in April—the last reminders of winter discarded by the blustering spring air—when my parents invited me to a lake house they'd rented for the month. It was a trial; if they liked it, they were going to buy it, my mother said. I was surprised by the news. My father had made no mention of it during my interviews. When I asked if So-ra could come, my mother politely said no. When pressed, she said in a short, firm voice that it wouldn't be appropriate.

That word, "appropriate," haunted me the entire train ride to Lake Uiam, as I ceded the armrests to weekday commuters with worn-out faces. Had I been discovered? Betrayed? I thought about the recording—safe and sound—on the thumb drive, buried in the toe of my Stuart Weitzman boot in the back of my closet. I'd spread the filming out over three nights, but with So-ra's help, it wasn't too difficult. After getting some shots around Seoul, we'd done most of the filming at the Cheonggyecheon stream early in the morning to avoid any crowds. When So-ra and I watched the final cut, I thought we looked grand. It was just like an old-timey movie. So-ra and I had found our outfits at a vintage store in Yeonpyeong. It was silly to be so protective of this artistic experiment. And yet I was. For most people in my class, it was probably just an assignment. But for me, I felt like my entire life, every secret, every fantasy was contained on that thumb drive.

We chugged along the tracks to Chuncheon station, the carriage stuffed to capacity, brimming with warm bodies. The smell of cigarettes and aftershave coalesced in the stuffy cabin—a noxious scent. I buried my nose in my sweatshirt and put my earbuds in. What percentage of their lives did these commuters spend on this train going back and forth? These were the unlucky ones, the ones who couldn't afford to live in Seoul, making their daily pilgrimage to the capital for higher wages and more opportunity.

The magnetism of Seoul that had once seduced me now seemed tarnished, even repulsive. In the eye of the storm, it was beautiful, majestic, and awe-inspiring. But from here, within the arteries that flowed from the heart, beat an ominous and sorrowful drum, one of duty, responsibility, honor, and money. These commuters no doubt had children to feed, wives and husbands to support, but certainly there were other ways to make a life. What must one do? We couldn't all be like Misaki, living off our parents' money, or So-ra, raging against the world. Brash and brave, incongruous in all facets. But perhaps we could. If we were all strong enough. If I was strong enough.

With each stop, the train emptied bit by bit, a slow trickle of life. I began to feel like I could breathe again. Outside the carriage window, dusk clung low to the rice paddies, stretching for miles. The announcement for Chuncheon garbled over the loudspeaker. My alarm grew when I saw only my mother waiting for me on the train platform, sticking out from the crowd in her white slacks and olive-green parka. She rarely drove. Something was wrong.

As the train slowed, I considered the countless things it could be: So-ra, Min, the film class, the unreturned calls about the job offers. The list went on.

"Only one bag?" my mother greeted me as I got off the train.

"Should I have packed more?"

Under the fluorescent platform lights, moths and insects hovered like a winged collective. The train let out a final call, lurching from the station.

"One is good enough," she said, snatching it from me.

I held on to the handle. "What're you doing?"

She wrenched it from my fingers with a quickness that surprised me. "I can't carry my own daughter's bag?"

"Where's Dad?"

"At the house. He had some calls to make."

I couldn't read my mother's face in the half-light of the parking lot. Something was happening, or had already happened, I realized, as we crossed a two-lane bridge over the wide expanse of unmoving black water, the steel girders of the bridge shuddering around us. Perhaps I was too late; I'd already moved beyond the point of absolution. Maybe it was time to end the charade and tell them—tell them what? How many lies had I told? How many was I living?

Once across, we took a winding tree-lined road that skirted the lake. As we drove, I could hear what I thought were crickets and the whistle of wind on the water. With no cars in front of us my mother increased our speed, shifting into fourth, tunneling us deeper into the dark. Silence engulfed us.

"Do you know what this is about, Yu-jin?" she finally said, eyeing the road. "Your father's livid. He's been in a state ever since he got in from Seoul. He's furious, even despondent, and he won't tell me why. I've never seen him like this."

Was it relief I felt? Did I want to be caught, forced into the light?

I could see myself confessing, hear myself telling my mother everything, the words crashing like an avalanche, roaring toward destruction.

When we rounded a turn, something flashed in front of us. My mother slammed on the brakes, rubber clawing the road, gears gnashing. Then we were swerving onto the shoulder, the car shrieking to a stop. In the middle of the road stood a deer, its tail quivering, nose testing the air. White spots on its brown coat shimmered out in the night as it darted back from where it had come, effortlessly vaulting the metal safety fence. Engine thrumming, we sat, not speaking a word. If I listened closely, I thought I could still hear the deer, dodging between trees and underbrush, careening through the forest. Something must have been chasing it, spooked it out into the open. Run, I thought, run.

Seat belt undone, my mother turned to me, resting a hand in my lap. "If you tell me the truth, I can help you. But you must be honest with me. If you tell me what's happened, I can protect you."

In the mirror I watched the car exhaust boil break-light red. The walls of the car seemed to lean inward, the roof sinking, caving to some invisible force. I rearranged myself, leather clinging to the backs of my arms, sticky with sweat. Nausea blossoming, I put the window down and gulped air. Out in the darkness, where I imagined the lake shimmered like ink, I reached out to So-ra, dancing, leaping, falling, falling into my bed, skin against skin, sheets tucked under our toes. Snowflakes tumbling, then zooming down, funneling around corners, Min's weight on my shoulder, my gloved hand in his. Fresh powder underfoot, our footprints melting into city sidewalks, noses cold, tongues hot, we pushed up against each other, against storefronts and alley walls, anything that would hold us.

Through the windshield I saw myself, my mother, our faces painted in dashboard greens and blues. We did not look like mother and daughter; we looked afraid, even terrified of each other, of what might come next. The engine's hymn—measured and exacting—brought me back, like a knock at the door, the knock of my heart, from the void, where everything I'd wanted, everything I'd done, lay before me. I needed to say something, even if it was half, a third of the truth.

My mind went back to the deer. It had escaped death, at least for another day. It was still out there, still running, still alive. I told her then, about both film classes, how they were infinitely more interesting than the political science and government courses I'd taken. I admitted to never following up with the people who'd offered me jobs starting in the summer.

My mother hit the hazards, dull yellow pleading to the night. I waited for her to say something, balk at the trivial nature of my admission compared to my other transgressions, but she did not. I held out hope that my father remained ignorant of my more serious wrongdoings. But the film class alone wouldn't explain his despondence. More needed to be divulged. More was to be doled out.

"There's one more thing," I said. "I'm seeing someone. An American. It isn't serious. I plan on ending it before the end of summer."

My mother laughed, a genuine, unadorned laugh. It sounded strange, alien. She squeezed my hand tightly. "Love is always the best explanation for things. Once your father told me about your recent behavior, I had a feeling you'd met someone."

"We aren't in love," I said, suddenly alarmed by my mother's giddiness.

"There are varying degrees. You can fall in love many times, contrary to popular belief."

"You're not angry? Both of you forbid relationships while I was at university."

"I never thought you'd actually listen to us. Perhaps your father did, but he's antiquated. Hasn't a clue what young people are like these days."

"You don't care that he's American?"

"I don't. As long as it's casual. I'm glad you're finally enjoying yourself."

"What about the film class and the interviews?"

"We'll speak about it with your father."

My mother seemed satisfied, flicking on the blinker and merging back onto the road, the deer forgotten. I allowed relief to seep in, unclenching my hands. I told myself to relax, even though the worst was yet to come. I wondered what my mother really thought. Was she happy that she knew something my father didn't? Did it empower her, make her feel closer to me?

Eventually we slowed and turned down a gravel driveway lined with tall pine trees; the smell of sweet citrus hung in the air. I imagined the road and landscape could have been mistaken for some Nordic country like Sweden or Norway. The gravel crunched underneath our tires as we came to a clearing that looked out over the lake. On the other side, I thought I could see the dim lights of Chuncheon. To the right stood a jarringly modern home—a two-story rectangle of glass and concrete facing the lake. Encircled by the trees and water, the home seemed at war against its surroundings.

"How'd Dad find out about everything?"

She cut the engine. "He's the Minister of National Defense, Yu-jin. He can find out anything he wants."

"So he spied on me. What did he do, read my emails? My text messages?"

"He loves you, Yu-jin. He only did it because he was worried about you."

Her nonanswer seemed to confirm my fears. My phone, emails. I tried to think. I was auditing the film class, so I'd never received any communication from the professor. I'd never mentioned the recording over text message. With So-ra, I'd always been careful not to say too much when messaging. Even that day we'd fought and I'd gone to lunch with Misaki—our communication would have just looked like an argument between roommates. I'd been meticulous about covering my tracks. Sure, I'd gotten careless with Min while we'd been in public, and we text-messaged enough for it to look romantic. But that had been the point; that was my cover, the least of my transgressions. And being with a boy—that wasn't enough to jolt my father like this. Unless he'd had someone watching me and they'd seen something more damaging. I remembered running into Hae-sook when I'd been shopping for books with So-ra. Had she told my father what she'd seen?

Inside, I tossed my bag on the couch while my mother went in search of my father. The house was a strange mixture of contemporary design and vintage furniture. Hungry, I went to the kitchen, where silver appliances and cool gray countertops glittered with metallic sheen. The house seemed like a display room, immaculately clean, unlived in. I couldn't fathom my parents inhabiting such a place. I thought I'd understand them more as I got older. Why they made certain decisions, how they'd come to be where they were. But I realized then, walking around this strange home, with its enormous plasma television and matching Eames chairs, my parents would always be a mystery to me, as I was to them. What was it they desired from this life? Compared to So-ra, Min, my film professor, there was an emptiness to them. For all their pushing, for all their support and love, what did they see when they looked at me? What did they want for me? Had they considered anything other than the path they'd set me on?

When my mother appeared, she said I could finish the film course as long as it didn't interfere with the maintaining of my 4.0. As for the interviews, I was to call all the offices back and see if any of their offers stood. If any did, I was to accept it with the intention of starting in June. I'd also apologize to everyone in writing. Lecture finished, she gave me another knowing smile. "Let's go up to the roof. It's a clear night. We'll be able to see the stars."

By the time I emerged on the deck, I was light-headed from going around in circles on the spiral staircase. I looked around at the trees and mountains behind us. Above, the sky unfurled like a velvet nightgown. My mother handed me one of the blankets she'd brought up with us. After wrapping herself, she sat down in one of the wicker lounge chairs.

"So, Dad is pretty pissed."

"Don't make light of it, Yu-jin," she scolded me. "He's disappointed. Mostly I think he's in shock. He cares a great deal about you. He went to immense efforts to secure those interviews. It was thoughtless of you not to return their calls."

"You didn't tell him about the other thing?"

"Of course not. That's between us."

The way she said it, I knew she enjoyed having a shared secret.

"But in all seriousness, Yu-jin. You can attend this film class, but you must begin to consider life after graduation. I know there may be temptations to act out or go in a different direction, but you need to remember your future. You've worked incredibly hard to get to this point. You're in such a good position to succeed."

That word, "seriousness." It rang in my head. My death knell. I'd been playing make-believe, fooling myself. No amount of film classes would save me from the future my parents had fashioned for me. It had only ever been about gaining freedom and independence: the hard work, the sacrifice. At Ewha, in Seoul, I thought I'd finally broken free, but it was an illusion; I saw that now. I was always going to end up here, playing the role I was intended for. I shuddered, the weight of my reckoning cold and terrible. Even in my happiest moments, when I thought I was flying, I'd always been caged. I looked upwards. I'd almost forgotten what the stars really looked like. I never saw any in the city. I let my vision go, blur the sky into a deluge of cold light.

"I had an American boyfriend once, too, a soldier stationed in Seoul," my mother said, almost wistfully.

"When? Before Dad?"

She chuckled, pulling the blanket tight over her shoulders and gazing out over the moon-kissed lake. "It was a few years before your father. In addition to going to nursing school, I worked a few shifts at the American embassy, helping them with visa applicants and other things. The Americans were desperate for people who could speak English and Korean fluently. Anyway, he was with the military police, you know, the guys who police the soldiers."

I'd never considered that my parents had lives before they met each other; it had seemed they simply came into existence the day they met. It was all they'd ever told me. "Did your parents know?"

"Of course not. They didn't even approve of your father. He was too poor, had no familial connections. This was before the military helped him through university, of course. At the time, they practically disowned me for marrying him. It would've been my head if they knew I was running around with some American solider, let alone a black one."

I stared at my mother, dumbfounded. Even now, as Korea was diversifying, globalizing, dropping their homogeneity as a rallying cry of pride, it was rare to see any African Americans in Seoul. Indians, Russians, even some immigrants from North Africa, but African Americans still caused a stir.

Why was she telling me this—why now, why here?

"Where was he from?"

"Georgia," she said, very slowly, savoring each letter like a sweet candy. "Atlanta, Georgia."

"What was it like? Did you have to sneak around? I mean, could you be seen in public?"

"It was thrilling. Doing something so forbidden. We kept it a secret from everyone. I suppose if we'd been more serious—if I'd been more serious—we could have made ourselves visible to the world, although that might have been hard. Koreans didn't mix with Americans back then, especially military."

I tried to process my mother's story. Had she really kept this from my father? Were we trading secrets, building our trust with things we could tell no one else? "Weren't you scared?"

"Sometimes, when you're young, you do things not because they're in your best interest, or because they will make you happy," my mother said, her eyes serious in the moonlight. "You do them because they go against something. The greatest fear of a young person is that you're doomed to be like everyone else. So we do things: date Americans, take film classes."

I couldn't help but connect everything she was saying to So-ra. Was it possible she knew more than she was letting on? With every word my mother spoke, I felt a growing sense that she knew everything, and she was giving me this one chance to tell my truth, say it all.

She continued, "I look back at certain moments in my life, and I see that what I thought was independence, even strength, was actually extended periods of self-destruction. I wanted to be caught, reprimanded. I wanted to destroy the life I'd been given. And why? Because, simply put, it was my life, and I yearned to exercise power over it. I'm telling you all of this because I want you to know it's normal. It's okay to feel those things as long as you don't let them rule you."

The urge to let it all go, tell her about So-ra, everything, grew with each passing moment. How good it would feel to say those words aloud, hear them outside my head. It would make everything real. Too real, I realized. Once said, once exposed, everything would evaporate under the harsh sun of reality. "I'm good, Mom. I'm happy," I said. "Just because I'm trying new things doesn't mean I'm dissatisfied with anything. Not following through with the interviews was impulsive and stupid. I'm serious about my studies and my career."

In the darkness I thought she looked almost suspicious, eyes tracing my silhouette in the moonlight, but then she smiled and looked to the stars.

·⋕·

Later that night I awoke in that strange new bedroom, hunger tugging at my stomach. I stretched, arms over my head, palms flat against the cool, tempered glass that was an entire wall of the room. A room anyone could see into—who would make such a thing? I remembered the deer we'd almost hit. I wondered if it was out there, beyond my shadowed reflection.

Eyes still adjusting, I kept waiting to see the lake beyond the trees, only to realize I was facing the opposite direction. All glass and angles, the house had a disorienting effect. Phone aglow, I checked the time, the pillowcase rough against my cheek. Sleep seemed an impossible task without the honking taxicabs, drunken cries of midnight revelers, and distant thump of nightclubs. There were other sounds, but they were stealthy, unseen: droning steel appliances, shuffling leaves. They imbued no sense of comfort, only suspicion.

Then there was another noise, distinct even in its indecipherability: the hum of conversation. Through the door, the low rumble of my father's voice, accusatory; my mother's, defensive, full of knowing. I sat up in bed, straining. I pushed my door open and crept down the hallway, the poured-concrete floor shockingly cold to my feet. Light from the kitchen shone up the staircase. Sticking close to the wall, I stole toward the top of the stairs, descending, step by step, lungs in my ears, every sound a deafening *creak*. From the shadows, I saw my mother and father standing around the kitchen island. In the cavernous house, I strained to hear their voices, distant and hushed.

"He's just a fling," my mother was saying. "It'll be over once she graduates."

So she'd told him. Or perhaps he'd already known. It wasn't just the film class and the interviews.

My father traced a pattern on the marble countertop. "Everything we've done for her," he said. "And now this."

"It's normal for kids her age to rebel, but they always come back to the road their parents set them on," my mother said, reassuringly.

My father was rooting around in a drawer of the island. After some searching, he dropped a large bag of peanuts on the counter. With swift belligerence, he produced a handful of crushed peanuts before him, sifting through them. "And you're so confident why? Because you're a woman? You didn't like the taste of your silver spoon? You know what it's like to grow up spoiled?"

A scornful look flickered across my mother's face, one that seemed to contain an age-old argument that had been waged before my existence. I couldn't hear her reply. I leaned forward, as close as I dared.

"Had a chat with that roommate Misaki," my father muttered, his voice seeping in and out. "Girl's tough, but she told me . . . the classes and this recording. Already had my suspicions when I saw that film studies textbook . . . Something wrong with that So-ra girl . . . Making videos together." His voice rose. "She's filling Yu-jin's head with all sorts of nonsense about art and expression."

My mother appeared to come to my defense. "She's got perfect grades. Her future's bright. She's become the daughter we've always wanted."

"Why didn't she fess up to the tape? What's on it?"

"You're being paranoid. You never should have looked into her private life. Reading her texts and emails . . . Please tell me you didn't have people following her."

"I had a few of my guys keep an eye on her. But we're her parents. We have a right to know what's going on in her life. You didn't have a problem with it when I told you about the American boyfriend. You were worried about her, too. We need to make sure she doesn't sabotage her chances at a successful life."

I caught my breath. I'd never noticed anyone following me. My emails. My texts. And my mother. Everything at the train station, in the car, it had all been a ploy. She'd already known about the classes, my recording, Min. She'd just wanted to see whether I'd tell her the truth.

My mother turned away in disgust. In the empty kitchen, my father hunched over, elbows on the counter, looking at nothing. I tried to swallow, my throat scratchy, knees aching from my crouched position. Every expansion of my lungs, every gurgle of my stomach seemed amplified, shaking the panes of this glass house. I wanted to leave, run, curl into the comfort and safety of my bed, and yet I stayed, glued to my spot.

I stayed still, for how long I couldn't be sure. Something like a dream spun out from my center, every fear, every doubt I'd had intertwined. I rocked back and forth, face pressed between my knees, knuckles bone white.

TWENTY-FIVE

MIN

How little you must think of me

Before the sun crests the mountains, before streetlights power down, before stray cats slink under chain-link fences, there is a fleeting moment, a blue-gray spasm that grips Seoul, paralyzing time. Those who are lucky—the early dog-walkers, the monks, the ever-optimistic fishermen, the curious travelers flying from Bangkok to Sapporo, hoping to catch a glimpse of North Korea from the window of their 747—can imagine the city as limitless, untethered from time. They could see what had come before, royal palaces, stone pagodas, trolley cars, and telegraph lines. They could bear witness to what lay beneath their feet, what towered over their heads. All that had been erased would be made visible to them, if only for a second.

It was at this precise moment in time that Min stepped onto the field in his athletic shorts and T-shirt, unaware he'd missed his chance to imagine. He'd been too busy tying his sneakers and stretching before the game to notice anything. Now that it was late summer, Seoul's heat and smog necessitated the rugby games start earlier and earlier.

Min was eager to play, having missed the last three matches. No teammates addressed his prolonged absence, not even Mark, the friendly Canadian. The opposing team was from Daegu. They'd played before, but Min couldn't remember who'd won, who to watch out for. There were always a few guys who played just to hurt you. He scanned their faces, boxy and white, but nothing came to him. Still, it felt good to be back on the pitch, grass underfoot, tape wrapped around his balky shoulder. It reminded Min of everything he was good at: running, blind effort. The scrum had already started, a whirling mass of shoulders and forearms, calves pumping, eyes bulging. Min watched the opposition, waiting for his chance to steal the ball.

While he played, his mind was empty and clear. There was no time, no opportunity for Min to consider the previous night, when he'd heard Misaki crying. It had seemed a dream at first, her inky silhouette at the edge of his bed. He'd resisted consoling her, fearful they shared the same guilt for sleeping together so soon after Yu-jin's death.

After the game Min was greeted by a slew of panicked text messages from Su-bin. It seemed there'd been an accident involving Woo-jin. With an ice pack secured behind his neck, Min made his way to work, a curious, mud-stained sight on the metro. Luckily Samsung had showers and even beds for employees truly committed to their corporate cause. Min had never been one of those workers, and if his interest in his job had been tepid at the start of summer, it had now bottomed out. The consequences of Yu-jin's death had brought a painful perspective to his job, the superficiality of it, the uselessness. What exactly am I doing? he wondered, throwing his athletic bag over his shoulder and exiting the sardine-packed metro.

In an effort to appear more Western for his upcoming meetings with Sprint, Woo-jin had done something awful to his hair. The most recent bachelor had been his inspiration. And despite the hairdresser's warning regarding the consequences, Woo-jin had still gone ahead with the bleaching and chemical straightening process. The outcome was catastrophic, and one that had led Sun to consider delaying the first round of meetings with Sprint in Los Angeles. Taking Woo-jin off the team was out of the question. If it was the family connection that had secured him the job, it was that same connection that ensured he'd stay on the project, regardless of Sun's wishes.

"What the hell took you so long?" Sun said, pacing around his office. "Have you seen it?" he demanded. "Have you? It's an abomination. He's going to be the laughingstock of the meeting."

From Sun's office, Woo-jin could be seen sitting alone in the break room with what appeared to be a giant beaver pelt on his head. "It looks bad," Min observed.

"You think? It looks like a piece of roadkill. Apparently he was planning on double eyelid surgery before Su-bin stopped him. Can you imagine? Where the hell would he get an idea like that?"

Something stirred in Min. "Isn't it obvious? You've had the team watching nothing but American television for three months. Woo-jin clearly thought looking different would help Samsung close the deal."

"We aren't paying you for psychological insights," Sun said dismissively. "I've already got Su-bin on the phone with some stylists who are gonna do what they can. I need you to go and talk some sense into him. We can't have him like this in Los Angeles. He'll torpedo the whole deal."

"What should I say?"

"Tell him we want him thinking like an American, not looking like one. The whole point of sending Woo-jin is he'll put people at ease. He needs to look authentically Korean," Sun said, taking a drink of water. "Don't look at me like that. You know what I'm talking about. Why do you think Asians have done so well in America? It's because we don't threaten them. They like us, feel like they can trust us. It's essential Woo-jin look the part. We can't have him scaring them off."

It could have been the numerous hits he'd taken during the rugby game that morning, or the way the sky had looked when he'd left his apartment, wondrous and forgiving, or the memory of Misaki's hands around his throat, but Min couldn't understand why he was standing in a Samsung office, speaking with a man he disliked, doing something he despised. The job was nothing more than vanity, a celebration of everything he'd come to loathe. He was nothing more than a glorified salesman, shilling Western propaganda, convincing people like Woo-jin that their hair was too straight, their faces too big, their eyes too small. If he stayed, what did that make him?

But no more. He told Sun he was finished. He was quitting. While he packed his desk, Sun reminded him that Samsung was the official sponsor of his work visa, and when they revoked it, which they would, he'd have thirty days to leave the country. That was fine by him, Min said.

Halfway down the block Min heard someone calling his name. It was Woo-jin, hiding his monstrosity with a baseball cap. "You can't just leave. Are you crazy? We need you. We need your expertise."

"You never did," Min said. "Both of you are perfectly qualified to close the deal. Just get that hair cleaned up."

"But you were our insight into Americans. Without you we won't know what they're thinking. It'll be impossible to know what they want."

Min took out his phone to check the time. "People generally want the same things, Woo-jin. I think you'll find that to be the case wherever you go."

The two said their goodbyes and parted ways. Min would need to find another company to work for in Seoul—unless he decided to go home. Maybe it was time. What else was here for him? But if he left now, he'd never be able to forgive himself. He owed it to Yu-jin, to her memory. And even if the tape was nothing, he wanted to see it; he wanted to see the part of Yu-jin she'd hidden from him all this time.

He hoped Chaz's album release party would provide him with an opportunity to find out more. He planned on confronting Misaki about her involvement, even if it meant the end of whatever they were.

·⊪·

According to the address on the CD demo Chaz had slipped Min at the bar, the release party was being held in Mullae-dong, a sliver of neighborhood on the south side of the river. The taxi let Min off in a back alley, where he emerged to the aroma of steaming fish cakes. Scattered about the streets, university students sat on plastic stools and chairs taking in the cool evening, drinking beer from plastic cups and passing skewers of meat back and forth. Double-checking the address, Min stood in front of a decrepit two-story building that had once been an auto repair shop. The door was barred and locked, newspaper plastered on the windows.

He was about to call Misaki when he heard his name. Chaz was leaning over the roof of the building, hair in his face. He told Min to sit tight. He'd be right there. The people in the alleyway looked on, indifferent. Music had started up farther down the street, where a small crowd was growing.

Chaz led Min into the building. "Right up those stairs. Stick to the right and be careful. Still haven't gotten around to cleaning the old car parts out of the first floor."

The stairs led to a doorway that opened up to a large living area and kitchen. Hardwood floors and high ceilings—it was hard to imagine this existed inside the ugly facade. A few people Min recognized from the club mingled about. A massive canvas splashed with red paint adorned one wall; on another, a silent black-and-white film spilled from an overhead projector. Something to do with a samurai, from the looks of it.

"Help yourself to a beer in the fridge," Chaz said, slapping Min on the shoulder. "Gotta play host."

In search of Misaki, Min moved through whispering hallways, up couple-filled staircases, and past beer-bottle-covered tables, blinking green like sea glass. From somewhere, the rumor of more music, half-hearted apologies as partygoers pushed by, all black pants and leather jackets. On the roof garden Min found her, dressed in pale blue jeans and a cotton blouse, white wine in hand, studying the ivy growing up the concrete walls. A string of lightbulbs murmured overhead.

"I made it," Min said from behind her.

She turned. Under the lights and the dimmed stars, it struck Min how lonely he would have felt after Yu-jin's death if it had not been for Misaki. At times he'd felt helpless, even aimless in his search for answers. Except for when she'd helped him with the memorial, sat with him at the Buddhist temple, invited him to her subterranean bar of otherworldliness. He'd felt something with her, a togetherness, some conspiratorial language only *they* spoke. It's why he'd never brought himself to ask more questions regarding Yu-jin's death. He'd been afraid of what she might say.

"I wasn't sure if you'd come," she said, her wineglass trembling. Min couldn't help but marvel how someone so brash and effervescent could appear so unsure of herself. It was a moment of weakness he'd never witnessed before. "I'm sorry for leaving so early in the morning."

Min recalled her shuddering figure. Everything inside him resisted; he didn't want this to end, whatever lay between them. The words sprang from his mouth. "I spoke with So-ra. She told me everything."

Misaki studied him, then slowly finished the rest of her wine. The distance between them shrank as she moved closer. If Min was hoping this statement would reveal the truth behind what Misaki had known or done, he was disappointed. Her expression remained unchanged, eyes sad but hopeful. "I knew So-ra and Yu-jin were together," she finally said. "They thought they were smart about it, waiting until I went to bed or left for class. But it was obvious— anyone could look at them and see they were sleeping together."

"Anyone but me."

"I was going to tell you. But then I saw you were happy with Yu-jin, with both of them. I knew they were lying to you, even to themselves maybe. But the three of you seemed like good friends. It wasn't my place to say anything, even if I was interested in you. And then everything went so horribly wrong and it seemed even worse to expose Yu-jin in death."

"You talk about it like you had nothing to do with it."

Misaki toyed with the silver bangles on her wrist. "If this is about the classes . . . the recording . . . It's not a moment I'm proud of. He—"

"Why'd you tell Yu-jin's father? Were you jealous? Did you want to get back at her for the way she treated you?"

"How little you must think of me," she said.

All Min wanted was a simple admission of guilt. Exasperation flared in his voice. "Because of you, So-ra's half mad in some sanatorium. Because of you, the Minister discovered everything."

From inside, an acoustic set was being played, a woman's voice slurred with drink. Misaki's face was serene, her eyes still. "I didn't have a choice. The Minister confronted me, more than once, asking for information on Yu-jin or So-ra. He threatened me. If I didn't give him something, he was going to have me expelled from university and deported back to Japan. I suppose you're going to tell me I should have left."

Min had never considered Misaki would be targeted by Yu-jin's father. "No, of course not," he said, feeling something give way. "I didn't know. You should have—"

"What?" Misaki snapped. "Said something? You'd have thought I was crazy. No. I had to give him something, something he didn't already know. So I thought of a little thing, small and inconsequential. I could have told him the truth; I could have outed them, but I didn't. I protected them. I kept their secret . . . Film courses and a silly recording, that's all I gave him. I heard them talking about it. They said it was a class project—how was I supposed to know it was bad? I didn't think they'd be that reckless, showing themselves on tape."

Slowly, Min began to understand. He remembered what she'd

told him at the Buddhist temple after the funeral: "I wanted to make things right. I've been wondering what I could've done differently. And I can't help feeling guilty." She thought she was directly responsible for Yu-jin's death. She believed she'd led the Minister directly to a tape containing irrefutable proof of Yu-jin's relationship with So-ra.

Min moved to her. "Misaki."

She put up her hands, stopping him from coming any closer.

"Please," Min said, "I didn't realize he'd threatened you. You did the right thing . . . But the tape. It isn't what you think. So-ra told me. There's nothing salacious about it."

"I suppose you wanted us to sleep together before confronting me about all this," she said coolly. "How convenient."

Min stood still, his body numb.

"And now you're telling me I shouldn't feel guilty because of something So-ra told you? The girl who carried on with Yu-jin for a year and a half behind your back? Have you even seen the recording with your own eyes? And if the tape isn't the reason they were discovered, how'd Yu-jin's father find out? Do you hear yourself? It was me. I did this."

The lights overhead swam, the filament crackling in Min's ears. He pressed his fingers against his temples. "Let me make this right, Misaki. I'm sorry, I shouldn't have said those things. But you've got to trust me. You aren't responsible."

Misaki only shook her head as she walked back to the apartment. Pausing on the uneven wooden planks, she rocked back and forth before turning around to face him. "There isn't anything to make right."

Min watched her leave, speechless. The questions and doubts

snarled in his muddled mind. Even if Misaki doubted So-ra's word, Professor Lee had suggested the tape was harmless.

Misaki had given the Minister nothing of use. Why then had he continued to probe and scrutinize until he'd found the truth?

Leaving the party, Min decided to walk a bit before catching a ride home. He needed to cool off, reframe his thoughts. If Min could find the tape, he could at least convince Misaki that she wasn't responsible for Yu-jin's death. He could free her from her sense of guilt. It was the least he could do after the way he'd treated her.

The streets were empty. Min passed vintage clothing stores and coffee shops, all closed for the night. With no clubs or bars, the silence gathered weight, leaning down on the streetlights. He went in the direction of the river, thinking there'd be a better chance of a cab. After another block, Min noticed a man in a suit, talking on his phone, a block behind him. He couldn't be sure, but he didn't think he was one of the men who'd been following him since Yu-jin's memorial. It certainly wasn't Chipped Tooth. Min wouldn't forget his face for a long time.

To be safe, he stopped at a bodega and bought an instant ramen, waiting for the man to pass the window while the store attendant filled the Styrofoam bowl with hot water and set it to rest on the counter, a pair of disposable chopsticks across the top. The old woman stared at Min, the twenty-four-hour shifts stitched across her face. Her candy-coated nails plunked a slow death on the counter as she watched the steam pucker and warp the paper cover of the soup bowl.

The man walked slowly. He was in no rush. Min looked for anything that would tell him he worked for Yu-jin's father. There was nothing: black jacket, white shirt, black shoes, no cuff links, no jewelry, bland as cardboard. Then he saw it, the plastic earpiece curling into his shirt collar. There was no phone; the man had been pressing his hand against his ear. Min sank lower, out of sight, mouth dry, sweat in his eyes. The Minister clearly thought he might still lead them to the tape. Why else would they be following him? Knees aching, Min stayed crouched for another minute before standing up.

"Your noodles are overcooked," the old woman said.

By the time Min arrived at home, it was nearly daylight. He pushed the door open to find a thin envelope slipped under his door. After his shoes were off, Min poured himself a glass of water and sat at the small kitchen table. He tore open the envelope from the side and took out a scribbled note. It was from Detective Park. It read: Assume your cell is compromised, ask for a package from Kyung-tae at the convenience store downstairs.

TWENTY-SIX

YU-JIN

Oblivion awaited

Anger and suspicion fanned the flames of my paranoia. On the train ride home, I ran frantically between cars, looking back each time the door sucked closed behind me. Teeth clenched, stomach roiling, I considered my options. Thanks to Misaki, my father was convinced I was sabotaging his well-laid plans for me. My own mother had conspired against me, trying to extract every kernel of truth. And yet, despite my transgressions, I knew all could be forgiven as long as the true nature of my relationship with So-ra remained undiscovered.

I'd left the lake house earlier that morning, insisting on calling a cab for myself. My mother was all smiles and niceness, packing a bag with fruit and yogurt for me to take. Had that really been her in the kitchen with my father last night? Perhaps I'd inherited it from her, the ability to conceal and obscure with the flash of a smile. As I waited outside for the taxi, the bedroom curtains had moved ever so slightly, and I knew my father was watching.

The train gained speed, the straightaway track compelling it to Seoul, as if drawn by hulking magnets. I closed my eyes, imagining myself atop the train, wind tugging at my hair, my eyelids, tearing away the memories of last night, the look of disgust on my father's face. Had my mother predicted all of this? My demise, my failure. The inevitable disappointment of those who'd given me everything. But it wasn't too late. That's why she'd told me about the American soldier. I'd made a mistake, she was saying, but I could still redeem myself.

At Seoul station I went in the bathroom and switched jackets and put on a baseball cap in the stall. I had to assume I was being watched at all times. I stopped at a mobile store and bought a cheap prepaid cell phone. After entering Min's and So-ra's numbers, I messaged them, saying my old number wasn't good anymore. I kept my old phone active. My father would get suspicious if I disconnected the service. Keeping up appearances with everyone was essential. I was especially worried how So-ra would react if she learned about Misaki's betrayal and my father's espionage. Everything had to be kept quiet if I wanted any semblance of a future.

Two subways later I was in my apartment, thankful no one was home. At my bedroom door I stopped and listened. Did I expect to catch someone in the act, stealing the recording, ready to hand it over to my father?

But in the cool darkness of the room there was no one. Only my made bed, my textbooks lined up in rows upon my desk, the air conditioner clicking on and then off. Tossing my bag on the bed, I went to the closet, drew open the doors, and pushed aside my coats and dresses, the hangers clacking in plastic hollowness against one another. I plunged my hand down into the warm, soft toe of my leather boot. Relief flooded over me as my fingers wrapped around the memory stick. Dark spots blotted the brown leather, spreading out, flattening. Only when I put my hands to my face did I realize I was crying. They were tears of gratitude, I realized, putting the boots back and closing the closet door. The tape was safe, unseen. It would remain this way forever. I wouldn't hand it in to my professor; no one would see it. And when I was weak, beaten down by the normalcy, the mundanity of my life, I could return to this place, this unequivocal record of a life I'd had, however briefly. It would be my salvation, a light against the darkness.

I imagined a future, my future, filled with more grueling study sessions or tedious meetings, my every waking moment measured in business cards and mannered business functions, where men appraised you with beady eyes. Farther ahead, I saw myself married to a faceless man, swollen with child, forced to leave a job I'd never loved to raise a family. Even among Ewha's most ambitious students, it was a universally acknowledged truth that men expected women to retire from their professional lives and care for the children when the time came. There was no debate to be had, no feelings to consider. It was a matter of course. This fate that awaited me produced only dread, and yet I was determined to fulfill it. No matter how trivial and monotonous my existence became, at least I'd always have the tape, proof of a life lived.

I thought about Misaki. I had to give her credit, I hadn't thought her capable of exacting revenge on me. It must have been jealousy. All this time she'd played the laid-back, aloof girl, but when it came down to it, she hated what I had: So-ra, Min, a future. Realizing we never intended to be friends with her, that we'd used her as cover, she'd resorted to sabotage. And she still had other cards to play with only two months left in our time at Ewha. At any moment she could tell my father about my relationship with So-ra, but as more time passed, I grew convinced she was keeping the information to herself, holding it over my head as a threat. No doubt she'd expect me to panic, fall apart, combust like the weak woman she thought me to be. But I'd never give her the satisfaction. I'd go on as if nothing had happened. She wasn't going to ruin the last two months of college for me.

-||-

I returned all three calls from the offices that had offered me jobs only a few weeks ago. The only one with a position still open was with Chairman Song. The secretary replied icily that yes, the position was mine if I wanted it. I was to start the third Monday of June. "Wear something short and cute. The boss likes that," she said, before hanging up.

I went through the motions in all my other academic classes, earning high marks without much effort. How easy it was now, to go through the motions. At times, university had felt like a cool, refreshing breeze compared to the furnace that was high school. Many of my classmates were riddled with angst about their job prospects or future academic endeavors. Some girls, a great number of them, in fact, had already gone under the knife—plastic surgery—after their first failed round of interviews. More angular chins, dimpled cheeks, thinner thighs and calves, anything to gain an edge. Others were already steeped in books again, drilling themselves with index cards late into the night for medical or law school. I should have been happy. Comparatively, my future, my career, if I could bear to think of it as such, was decided.

Ewha was the one place I knew I was safe from my father's gaze. I doubted any women worked for him, and men stood out on campus. In my film class we were screening the final projects, all renditions of the classic films we'd studied. I was impressed, even awed by some of my cohorts' skill and originality. For students who'd never studied the mechanics of making a film, they were astounding. Professor Lee had barred us from going outside the university for cast members, so any male parts in the short recordings were also played by women. It made for some odd, even humorous moments. There was a remake of a scene from *The African Queen*, a student dumping *soju* into a river while another slept on a makeshift raft, a beard painted on her face, a grungy captain's hat shading her eyes, à la Humphrey Bogart. A larger group had found some Japanese samurai costumes and trudged out to the countryside, sitting among the waving grain in black and white, reenacting the opening scene of Kurosawa's *Ran*.

What had I made with So-ra? Not a rendition or interpretation; it was merely an expression, a gesture of everything I'd always wanted to say but never had the words to express. My dreams undreamt, my lives unlived, played out in black and white, spoken in a language I finally understood. This recording, this mold of my innermost heart, was for no one but myself.

Before my turn to share I was out the broad double doors, the classroom still dark, projector whirring. In the empty hall I walked swiftly, out into the sun-spilled quad, the recording still in my pocket. I couldn't show this to anyone. It spoke too many truths.

Later that evening, when So-ra heard that I'd decided against showing my film, she grew distraught. "But we put so much work into it," she said, pushing the refrigerator door closed, face still flushed from the gym. "You spent a week on the editing alone."

"It wasn't any good. You should have seen the ones we watched.

They were so polished and professional. It would have been embarrassing. Plus, it's not like I'm getting graded on it."

The kitchen fell into darkness as the sun dipped behind a skyscraper or a mountain peak, stretching long shadows even longer. So-ra moved around the kitchen island, tracing the granite corners with a fingertip. With a swift twist, she cracked her neck, then her lower back. "What's the real reason you didn't show it?" she said, her voice thick with resentment.

I resisted the urge to tell her about Misaki and my parents, all that they knew. I was so close to graduating. I couldn't afford more complications. "I already told you."

So-ra snickered.

I felt an old bitterness reawaken, hardening with each passing second. For all her strength, independence, and vision, perhaps So-ra was incapable of letting me make this decision. She had gone along with it, played my game until it was unbearable for her. The film represented something else to her. She wanted to be seen, witnessed; then it would all be valid.

"Why's it so hard for you to understand? I just don't want to show it. I don't like the idea of people seeing it, seeing us."

"It's nothing."

"It's something to me."

So-ra shook her head, chewing the corner of her mouth. "You're still worried, even though you have Min to protect you. Wasn't that his whole purpose? To show everyone how much you like men. To prove you'd never touch a woman."

"That isn't what this about."

"You think I'm like your parents, like Min, clueless? You don't think I see what you're doing?"

I wasn't in the mood for her disdain, her superiority in all things. She was always reminding me of her assured spot on the moral high ground. "I'm not *doing* anything. I'm just trying to make it through the end of the year."

So-ra scoffed. "Go then. No one's stopping you. Wrap everything in a nice little box so you can graduate and pretend this never happened."

As my face warmed, I told myself she was just lashing out. She didn't mean what she was saying. "Don't twist my words."

"Was this always the plan?" she went on, her voice looping and cruel. "Mess around for a few years before running off to a normal life and your big important job?"

I felt something slip open inside me, throat aching, simmering heat below. "You have no idea what it's been like for me."

She went to say something, but I cut her off, my voice rising and shrill. "You wouldn't survive in my family. You think you're so tough. But the truth is, you wouldn't last a second if you had to make the choices I do."

"Don't kid yourself, Yu-jin," So-ra sneered. "Everyone like us has it tough, we just don't all go around playing the victim."

"The victim!? What the hell is that supposed to mean?"

In the half-shadows of the kitchen, So-ra's face hardened, lips thin and bloodless. "Just admit it. You're ashamed of us. And worse, you're ashamed of yourself. You can't fool me, Yu-jin. I know who you are, who you'll always be," she said, snatching her gym bag from the stool and disappearing down the hall, the bedroom door slamming behind her.

Could I tell her it was neither? Shame—it was that, yes. I was ashamed of what I'd become, what I'd done to the people around me.

Throwing open the kitchen cabinets, I grabbed the plates we'd bought together for the apartment—back when everything was easier, when all we needed was each other—and dashed them on the tile floor, ceramic flecks exploding like shrapnel at my feet.

Silence engulfed me. I listened for So-ra's cries from her bedroom, but they never came.

···‖···

What followed was a time when I waited for my father to confront me, when I waited for Min to question the nature of our relationship, when I kept So-ra at bay. If she had made a dance company, she didn't tell me. If I was terrified at the prospect of a new job in a field that didn't hold my interest, I didn't tell her. We were engaged in a war of silence, neither side willing to surrender. I was angry with her, even disappointed. She'd led me to follow this feeling, this yearning for sovereignty over myself. And now she was punishing me. Why? Because my idea of truth, of self-determination, wasn't the same as hers.

Within our silence, doubt flowered. Did So-ra even believe in the things she purported to live by? When confronted with the harsh realities my parents spoke of, would she hold fast to her beliefs about living one's life the way it ought to be lived, no matter the cost? The sneaking suspicion she wouldn't, that she'd look back in retrospection on her strident views and realize how foolish and naïve they were, only grew.

As a result, I threw myself into my relationship with Min. If my father's men were watching, if we were seen together, so be it; our affection would only protect me from my father discovering the truth about me and So-ra. There were other reasons for my recommitment to Min. Truly, that relationship was the only facet of my life that brought me joy, distracted me from the realities of my future. Despite its transitory nature, I found my time with him a welcome reprieve, a chance to forget about everything ahead of me. I imagined it was the same for him. There'd been no illusions about where we started and where we would end. There was no talk of the future. And I was convinced we found this freeing, even exhilarating.

Was it possible he thought otherwise? Yes. And in that case what I was doing was more deception than anything else. But I was confident I wasn't tricking Min into thinking our relationship meant more than it did. Whether he knew what kind of person I was seemed an entirely different question, and one that I ignored whenever it pried into my consciousness, like slanting light through closed shades. I decided instead to focus on how, with Min, I could forget about everything else. That was his gift, I realized those last few days in May, when Seoul was beginning to steam with the first heat waves of summer, when the voices of my mother and father arguing in the kitchen began to fade. He helped me forget about who I was, who I was going to become.

On the last Friday of the month, he took me out to an Italian restaurant in Sinsa-dong. To celebrate my job, he said. When I told him it wasn't necessary—a restaurant, especially a Western one, was excessive and expensive—he insisted. What was the point of making all this money at Samsung if he couldn't spend it on anything?

Min showed me how to twirl the linguine in my spoon before eating it. He swirled the wine pretentiously, sticking his entire nose in before drinking, mentioning hints of vanilla, plums, thunderstorms, innocence. It took all my self-control not to spew wine out of my

nose. A few tables stared, annoyed by our laughter. We took no notice. With Min, it was easy to forget my obligations, my responsibilities, not just to my parents but to my country, my ever more
suffocating sense of the world around me. He was a stranger among
everything that was familiar to me. He moved freely within this
place that I'd been battling against. Sitting across from him, I
couldn't help but wonder if I was repeating the past, if I was doing
what my mother had done so many years before with the American
soldier. Was there something about us Kim women that drew us to
these fleeting relationships?

Settling in, I tried to adopt a casual tone. Lately, every conversation with So-ra had felt like an interrogation, a battle for information
and secrets. With Min, I had to remind myself, there were no such
battles. We withheld things from each other, but that was something
different. He spoke about his love of music. The way it could trans-
port you, breathe color into your life. It provided you with something you'd never known was missing. He told me his favorite
albums, about what live concerts he wished he could travel back in
time to attend: Springsteen at the Roxy, 1978; the Band at Winterland
Ballroom, 1976; anything at the Troubadour.

How badly I wished to share those same passionate thoughts
about *Tokyo Story*, *Lawrence of Arabia*, and *La Dolce Vita*, where the
essence of humanity seemed boiled down to the point where you
could hardly stand to watch or to look away. It was painfully mes-
merizing. What would he think if I said such a thing, so far outside
the version of myself he knew? I'd painted a picture. I had to stay in
my frame. But what would he say, what could he say, about me and
So-ra? Did it matter we hadn't touched each other in weeks? He
would be hurt, yes, but he would understand. He understood the

realities of being like that here, in Korea. He knew what people thought of you once that was known. It's all they saw, all they knew. Would he blame me for hiding such a thing? For trying to be something else by finding him, falling for him?

But it would only bring him pain, to find that this was even less than we both already knew it was. If it was love, it was love of companionship, of convenience. And what was it with So-ra? A love against all odds. A madness. I would never tell him. I'd rather die, I thought, almost laughing at the idea.

I remember feeling disembodied. Observing us, sitting at that table in the window. We looked happy, normal even. What a difference it was, to see what others saw, rather than the panicked confusion through which I viewed myself from within. Handsome, dashing even, Min was all energy and enthusiasm. We had a magnetism to us, that much was undeniable.

After dinner we caught a cab to my apartment, the closer of the two. We lay against each other in the backseat, neon glowing like effervescent plankton in the night sky. Close to Min, I felt the stress of the previous few weeks dry and crumble like sunbaked clay. Time made no difference with him. We patched it together, stretching seconds and minutes into infinity. He was carefree. I was carefree. He was happy. I was happy. It was the easiest thing in the world, and that counted for something, didn't it? What if that's what mattered—not the hard stuff, the struggle, the pain, the agony, but what was easy. Was there any shame in taking the easy way, not out but in? Into something real?

I roused him when we pulled up to my apartment. I paid the cabbie. Tipsy and full, we snaked our way down the sidewalk. I slid my hand down into his pocket and reached for him as we walked. He laughed and pushed my hand away.

"We're almost to your place. Can't you wait?"

The answer was no. Oblivion awaited, and I couldn't wait. I couldn't wait to have him on top of me, being with me, in a way So-ra never could be. I couldn't wait to forget everything with him. But then I noticed something and stopped. A black Mercedes sat idling outside my apartment building, my father's car.

TWENTY-SEVEN

MIN

A shade for every season

Min read Detective Park's note again: Assume your cell is compromised, ask for a package from Kyung-tae at the convenience store downstairs. No wonder he'd never called back. The Minister had Park spooked. Just to be safe, Min left his phone in the apartment before heading downstairs. Maybe that was how he was being tracked. Nothing seemed too far-fetched anymore.

Standing in the lobby of his building, Min peered through the convenience store's glass wall. He recognized the teenager working at the register; he'd sold Min the cigarettes a month or so ago, the ones Yu-jin liked to smoke. Before entering, Min loitered around his mailbox to make sure nobody was following him. Through the double-doored entryway, he watched the steady stream of headlights in the night. His feet tapped a nervous beat on the buffed granite floor.

Taking one more look around, Min ducked inside the store and grabbed a soda from the immaculately organized fridge, aglow in clinical white. When the place was free of other customers, Min approached the register. "Package from Kyung-tae," he said, voice shrinking.

The cashier looked up from his phone and studied his face. Seeming to reach a favorable conclusion, he groped for something under the counter and retrieved a bulky envelope. Min snatched it from him and went to leave.

"Don't you want your soda?" the kid called after him.

Min was already out the door. Instead of heading back up to his apartment, he decided to walk. Safer to keep moving, he thought. It was a warm night, and Min weaved between midnight revelers and boisterous businessmen clutching at one another as they stumbled down the sidewalk. After cutting down an alley, Min ensconced himself in a doorway and opened the envelope and reached inside. There was a prepaid phone still in its plastic casing. Another note read: Cell is preloaded with minutes. Call number below.

After discarding the bulky packaging, Min powered on the phone and punched in the number. "What the hell is going on?" he said when Park picked up after the first ring.

"Come to the parking garage on the western side of Seoul station. Take a cab. Make sure you aren't followed. I'll be two levels down. Look for a blue sedan. I can explain everything when you get here."

Before Min could ask any questions, the line went dead. Min shoved the note into his pocket. Emerging from the backstreet, Min hailed the first taxi he saw and gave the driver directions. While they drove, Min looked out the rear window, making sure they weren't being tailed. Headphones dangling from one ear, the cabbie talked in hushed tones. Min was relieved to find he was only comforting his daughter. It seemed she'd had a nightmare and woken up, calling for her father.

It was close to one A.M. when he arrived in front of the underground parking garage. An old man in the booth gave him a toothless grin as he walked by. Taking the elevator two floors down, Min emerged into a low-ceilinged space with sputtering lights. Among the shadowed columns sat Detective Park's car. As he approached, the driver's-side door opened and Park emerged. Dark jeans and an untucked button-down had replaced his usual suit.

"Pretty risky, leaving that note under my door," Min said, catching sight of Park's haggard face.

"I figured they'd already tossed your apartment."

"How'd you know?"

"They searched mine a few days ago. It was a risk worth taking."

"The Minister's men have been hounding me."

"We should be safe here. Only one way in and one way out. Safest place for us to meet. Get it in the car."

Min hesitated, suddenly fearful of Park's intentions. Had he thought this through?

The detective looked at him incredulously. "What, now you're getting cautious? Stop messing around. I've got some things to show you."

He was right, of course. Why would the thought even have crossed Min's mind? He had to get a handle on his paranoia. Sliding into the passenger seat, Min was hit by the sharp smell of musk and tobacco. How long had Park been waiting here?

"What did you find on Jawoldo?"

Min described the state he'd discovered So-ra in, her secret relationship with Yu-jin, the Minister's threat of disownment. Park stared intently in his side mirror and picked at his fraying cuticles while Min went on talking.

Park chewed on his lower lip, as if it might yield the answers to some conundrum. He seemed to be wrestling with something, making his way through a maze in the fog. "Yu-jin and So-ra . . . together," he murmured. "I never considered it, but it does explain some things . . . That's why the Minister's been all over this investigation. He doesn't want it to get out."

"Does this mean you'll close her case now?"

"Not exactly," Park said. He produced a brown binder from the backseat and pushed it into Min's hands. "Take this," he said. "Don't look at it until you get home."

"What is it?"

"Yu-jin's class project, and notes from when I first arrived on scene."

"The recording. You had it this entire time."

"I didn't mention finding it in my notes or log it into evidence. I had a feeling her father would be after it."

"But why are you giving these things to me?"

"I've been taken off the case. Well, forced into early retirement is a more accurate description. My superiors threatened to remove my commendations and go after my pension if I didn't stop. I guess they didn't appreciate me drawing things out. Seems I was asking too many questions. Or just asking the wrong people. But listen," Park said, shifting his weight toward Min. "I want you to have the recording. Maybe you'll understand it. I've watched the tape over twenty times, and I still can't make heads or tails of it. But for some reason the Minister's been after it since the day Yu-jin died. It's safer with you. Who knows how many men he's got on his payroll."

"What will you do now?"

Park sucked his teeth. "I'll figure something out. Maybe I'll go to Busan or Jeju. I can't remember the last time I took a vacation."

"I'm sorry about your job," Min said.

"It's all right," Park said. "It's been a long time coming."

"What about your notes? You can't just give them to me. You'll get in trouble."

Park laughed and dug a pack of cigarettes from his shirt pocket. "I'm retired, remember. They can't do anything to me. Plus, I want you to have them. Maybe they'll give you closure. I keep thinking about my best friend who took his life and all the questions I'm still haunted by. If someone had information, no matter how awful, I'd want to see it, to know it for myself."

Min didn't know what to say. He felt something like kinship with Detective Park. How would he ever repay him?

Cigarette lit, Park was already pushing his door open and getting out. "Best not to stick around too long. Can't be sure you weren't followed."

Standing with Park in the flickering fluorescent light, Min shook the detective's hand and thanked him. Park nodded, smoke in his eyes, big hand enveloping Min's. "One thing still bothers me about this case," he said in a near whisper. "Like you said from the very start, Yu-jin wasn't weak; she wasn't fragile. I can't see her taking her life just because she'd been outed."

"I've been wondering the same thing. I just can't believe she'd lose hope like that."

Park nodded in agreement. "Better get going."

"I can't thank you enough."

Park scoffed. "Not necessary. Sticking it to those unprincipled careerists is the best retirement present I could ask for. Now get out of here, and be careful."

⊣⊢

Back at his place, Min stared at the contents of the brown binder he'd dumped onto his kitchen table. A small USB drive sat atop several xeroxed documents that looked like a case report. After taking out his laptop, Min inserted the thumb drive and powered it up. There was a single FLV file titled Final Project. Min turned off the lights and moved to his bed.

The recording opened to a black-and-white shot tracking over a rice field. In the background, a lone figure worked the crop, wading thoughtfully through the ankle-deep water. The camera panned upwards to the sky. Stills of the city flashed by: Seoul City Wall in Naksan Park, crowded stalls in Gwangjang Market, Buddhist temples, a megachurch on Yeouido, blinking white facades of coffeehouses, nightclubs, massage parlors, twenty-four-hour arcades, and *hagwons*. Then darkness.

Was this an ode to the city, a love letter? Min recognized a few of the places. Some he'd visited with Yu-jin and So-ra, others only with Yu-jin. How these places related to *La Dolce Vita*, Min didn't know. So far nothing resonated with anything the film professor had said.

The next scene: a woman wearing a strapless black dress and white shawl walked down a narrow street at night, blond hair falling to her back. The camera followed as she moved cautiously between buildings, looking in wonder at apartment windows and shuttered storefronts, her way lit by a few dim streetlamps. There was a playful sensuality to the way she moved, gazing up at the imagined night sky. Only when she turned a corner and let out an audible gasp—her face visible—did Min realize it was Yu-jin. Yu-jin wearing a wig; Yu-jin in the dress.

"It's beautiful," she purred, the camera panning away to the Cheonggyecheon stream, meandering through the man-made canal lined with ferns and sedges. Judging from the lack of cars and pedestrians, Min guessed she'd filmed the scene sometime in the early morning.

The elegant black dress trailing behind her, Yu-jin stepped nimbly down the stairs. The camera followed, capturing her submersion into the water, twirling happily as she moved upstream, the murmur of water growing more audible. Ahead, a waterfall rushed down from an elevated platform that fed the stream. Shakily, the camera zoomed in on her heavily made-up face. Eyes smoky, lips full, almost pouting as she ran her hand under the water. Then she stared at the camera, as if to communicate some unsayable command to the audience. Almost imperceptibly, the camera came to rest on the scene, a close shot of Yu-jin. From a corner emerged a figure. Dressed in a smart dark suit with long hair pulled back into a ponytail, the person approached Yu-jin, who was now dancing under the waterfall, gesturing with open arms toward the figure.

It was shocking to see Yu-jin as the seductress. In this role, in black and white, under the thunderous water, she was something new to Min, filled with a deeper yearning. She'd always seemed like a girl to him. A beautiful girl, yes. But this—this self-realized woman—was someone he'd never known.

It was as if she'd been reborn, unshackled, free to express her every whim and desire. Gone was the veneer, the polish, and beneath—a character, a persona wholly inhabited, a being singularly concerned with the present, the good life. And even under the wig, behind the dress and the makeup, Min recognized a Yu-jin who had always been there, just out of sight, dying to be seen. Perhaps he'd ignored, even stifled her, but now he was reckoning with someone who'd always wanted something so simple, so inherent to life: the chance to exist, unencumbered by classification, free from conformity.

Slowly, the figure descended into the river to join Yu-jin, slogging through the chilled morning water until they were standing in front of each other. Only then did Min recognize So-ra. She was born anew, hair slicked, shoulders thrown back. The profiles of their faces weren't more than a few inches apart. So-ra appeared to be saying something to Yu-jin, her mouth moving rapidly. They stood like that for some time, the sound of tumbling water nearly deafening. Then it was morning; So-ra looked about frantically, still clutching Yu-jin's hands. Light danced off stone and water. The sound of cars and trucks off-screen. Bewildered and embarrassed, So-ra led Yu-jin from the water, the train of Yu-jin's dress floating behind her, like a drowned peacock. Then the screen cut to black.

Creative, artistically daring, this was a Yu-jin Min had never known. How many times had she wanted to broach the subject of film with him and resisted? How often had she forced their conversation up to the surface, like a diver gasping for breath? There was nothing obscene or salacious about the recording. If anything, it was a tribute to Yu-jin's burgeoning artistic passions. He saw then, in full, the tragedy of her life, and he knew he'd never be able to look back on their time together and not wonder, wonder what she'd been thinking, what she'd been dreaming.

Why was the Minister after the video? It was something to be proud of, to celebrate. Even if Min wasn't sure about the themes or the deeper message, he knew it was an achievement. It was an artistic leap of faith, irrational and necessary, and though he'd never seen *La Dolce Vita*, the images of Yu-jin's rendition clung to his consciousness. The confident elegance in the way she walked, the look of ecstasy when she ran her hand under the waterfall, So-ra's eyes hanging on her every move, her every breath—he could see it all so vividly.

Even after closing the laptop, Min found himself playing the recording over and over again in his head, watching Yu-jin walk down the alleyway, hair swaying back and forth, the shawl snow-white against the black dress. Something unspooled from the back of his mind; he finally understood. The project had been her rebellion against the titanic expectations, the norms that flattened her every wrinkle, every gorgeous imperfection. It was the purest declaration of her personhood in all its tangled glory. After her death, Min had finally glimpsed the real Yu-jin.

Turning his attention to the case file, Min scanned the first page of Park's notes.

Time: 10:35 AM. Room still dark, indicating that the subject closed the blinds. Room clean. Bed made. Air conditioner on. Noticeably cold. State of room displays premeditation. Subject was concerned about appearance. Textbooks and school notebooks on desk. Picture of family. Headphones on bedside table next to USB drive. Black sequined handbag on the bedside table. Contents include makeup case, small wallet, few packages of gum, two cell phones. Both turned off, one looks like a burner.

So far no note. Moving to closet. Subject in kneeling
position. Two belts looped together and hanging from
clothing rack. Subject's head tilted away from the closet,
weight forward. Unclear, but death seems to be from
partial hanging. Subject's face pale. No swelling or
engorgement, indicating a slow death. Pupils dilated.
Tongue protruding from the mouth. Tip discolored—
brown, almost black. Lips blue. No initial sign of blood or
foam. Subject wearing a white nightgown. Time of death
estimated between midnight and two AM. State of scene
displays a meticulous attention to detail and
premeditation. Lack of a note interesting. No obvious signs
of foul play. Door locked from the inside. Scene and subject
are typical. Cause of death, most likely asphyxiation.

Min read the notes through again and again, imagining Yu-jin on
her knees, dressed in her nightgown, shoulders slumped forward,
lips blue, face pale. A brown-and-black tongue—the image repulsed
him, and yet he couldn't get it out of his head. Verging on sickness,
he staggered to the bathroom, where he stood over the toilet, hands
to knees, waiting for something to come out. He saw Yu-jin's brown
eyes, dilated pupils expanding forever. He saw her slender shoulders,
stripped and bare in the flimsy nightgown, her knees red and bruised
against the hard floor. He felt her lifeless hair between his fingers. He
felt himself being pulled back from the scene, arms and legs flailing,
watching her pale white figure sink into darkness, the outline of her
body growing faint. She was a star among that darkness, burning
with cold, faint light.

He sobbed and heaved, hands gripping the toilet bowl. He begged for Yu-jin's forgiveness, for his transgressions with Misaki. Tears came, welling up from some inexhaustible source, pumping to the surface, where they fell, down, down, into the water below.

Detective Park's case notes had spared no detail, embellished nothing. The promising politician, the aspiring filmmaker, the sure bet, the flirt, a shade for every season. Min hoped she'd found peace being some version of herself; he hoped the recording had brought her happiness; he hoped So-ra had given her something he hadn't.

According to Park, Yu-jin's father was desperate to get his hands on the tape. He must have been convinced it showed his daughter in a poor light. How wrong he was. Min would bring the Minister what he'd been after all this time. He'd show him the gifted and creative woman he'd pressured and stifled. He'd show him what kind of daughter he might have killed.

TWENTY-EIGHT

YU-JIN

The only way out was in

The only way out was in. There were no do-overs, no second acts, I thought, sitting in the backseat of my father's car, his personal driver navigating the emptying streets. Why had he chosen this moment to summon me and not earlier? Perhaps he'd continued spying on me after the lake house, hoping I'd slip up. Or maybe he'd expected me to cut things off with Min immediately, commit myself to my family's plan. If so, he'd surely been disappointed. I'd continued seeing Min. Even if my father punished me, it was the lesser of two betrayals. And eventually, if I was contrite, apologetic, admitting my mistakes—the film class, Min, the botched interview follow-ups— he'd forgive me. He might forget this bump in the road, these brief diversions that had taken me into the wilderness. I was confident he'd see what I now saw: I was too big to fail. Too many resources— time, money, and love—had been invested in me. I couldn't turn away now.

Moments before on the sidewalk, I'd feigned sudden illness after seeing the black Mercedes, telling Min I felt sick and needed to lie down. How easily those lies came to me. We made plans for the next day: coffee and something touristy. Maybe Gyeongbokgung.

Before entering the building, I'd braced myself for my father's disappointment, even his rage, only to find that he hadn't come himself, which somehow alarmed me more.

In the car I tapped on the tinted window dividing me from the driver. "Where are we going?"

It descended with velvety ease: "Incheon," the driver said, eyeing me from under the brim of her hat. "The Minister is waiting for you there."

I leaned back and closed my eyes, shoulders tight, neck throbbing. Why not meet me in my building? Driving me all the way out to a city outside Seoul, where the risk of seeing anyone we knew was minimal—it spoke to my father's paranoia, a paranoia I'd inherited. Would this be the reckoning I'd been waiting for? I was ready to face him. I could make him understand. I was tired of the machinations and the lies. I was ready to give up my cinematic aspirations. I'd tell him I had every intention of ending my relationship with Min and pursuing a career in whatever he saw fit. I was going to end things with So-ra, too, but he didn't need to know that. There were certain parts of my life my father couldn't understand; So-ra was one of them.

The ocean lay placid and moon-dappled to my right when I opened my eyes. We were driving on a narrow strip of road, past leaning chain-link fences and crumbling facades. Ahead, the blazing of a thousand stadium lights, like some alien ship had nestled to Earth in search of close encounters. As we drew nearer, the structure took shape, a rectangular string of lights suspended against the black curtains of night.

"The Minister is waiting out there," the driver said, stopping the car, her stoic expression giving nothing away.

We were at the end of a peninsula, the edge of the world, where my father stood in the middle of an enormous driving range, surrounded by neglected golf balls and bright green turf. He paced back and forth like an actor rehearsing their lines, committing each word to memory before they stepped onstage.

I made my way through the outdoor club room, through tee boxes and sand traps. I suspected this was a place only inhabited by businessmen who came on weekends to escape their wives and families, to close deals and perform for each other, relieved to inhabit a sphere wholly their own. There was no reason I'd know this place. It was of no use to me. I'd never be invited. But here was my father, waiting for me to join him under the lights, hemmed in by an invisible net to catch stray balls, a slice, a shank.

I stopped a few steps in front of him. He regarded me icily, as if atop a high mountain peak, squinting down at a mere speck. Off the water the wind whistled.

Heart knocking at my ribs, I groped for the right words. His body seemed to tremble. I'd seen that same serenity on his face before, the calm before the storm. He kept flattening an eyebrow with his thick forefinger, again and again, as if he hoped to scrub it from existence.

"Father, I need to tell—"

"Don't. Don't, Yu-jin," he said, shaking his head. "You don't get to tell me anything. You've lost that privilege." He looked away from me. "When did lying get so easy for you? Where's the daughter who honored her parents with hard work and honesty?"

Even as I stood before him, eyes level, shoulders back, I could feel myself shrinking. I remembered the camping trips, the time I left my bicycle in the rain, cold and afraid, his reprimands like a slap in the face. I wanted to tell him I was still that person; I'd never stopped being her.

My father cleared his throat. He spoke in strained and even tones. "I want the truth, Yu-jin. I want to know about the film classes, and this boy you've been seeing."

There was a part of me that thought I could still win him over, show how much happiness this new path had brought me. So I told him then in a rush of words, about Min, my newfound passion for film. I told him I'd never been happier; I'd never felt more alive. The way Min treated me—he'd given me the space to be someone; he'd given me assurances I was enough. The films I'd studied, watched countless times in that darkened lecture hall, pen to paper, scribbling notes like I was back in *hagwon*, preparing for the CSAT. Except there was no test, no exam. Yet it had still mattered to me, more than anything I'd ever done. For the first time in my life, I'd been genuinely excited about something. And it wasn't for ambition or pride or reputation. It was pure uncalculated joy of discovery and understanding.

While I spoke, my father stood with his arms crossed, his creased forehead gleaming under the lights. "Your mother is helping me understand the boyfriend part, but these other things, Yu-jin. This isn't who you are," he affirmed, his voice cresting. "You didn't study all those hours in high school so you could waste your time pursuing the arts. When did you stop caring about making something of yourself, getting a good job? I personally recommended you for these positions. I put my reputation at stake!"

"But don't you see? None of that matters now. It was just a phase, and now I'm ready to refocus and get back to work. Everything's still on track. I'm gonna to take that job with the Saenuri Party. I'll go to law school. I'll do whatever is necessary. I'm still that person."

"You think it's that easy, Yu-jin!?" my father bellowed, his face disfigured in agony. "We can't just pretend like this didn't happen. There are consequences."

White-hot fury seethed in my chest. Who was he to lecture me about respect and honor? He'd spied on me, twisted my thoughts, pushed me to pursue things that only benefited him. So-ra was right. All he'd ever tried to do was re-create me in his image. Thumbs inside my fists, I squeezed until they seemed ready to pop from their sockets.

"What about the recording?" my father kept on, his voice raw.

"It doesn't matter!" I screamed, severing something invisible between us.

My father looked at me for the first time, eyes wide and still. In all my life I'd never raised my voice at him. He seemed unable to comprehend the woman before him. A glower flickered over his features, and he pointed a thick finger at me. "You will give me the recording, Yu-jin. This isn't up for debate. You have put this family in an untenable position. I'm the Minister of National Defense, for God's sake. Did that thought ever cross your mind? The tape could ruin everything. Not just for me and your mother, but for you. So if the tape is nothing, give it to me, and I'll have it destroyed."

I found myself shaking my head. It wasn't for anyone but me. It represented an alternate ending, a parallel existence, one I'd never know, but I still wanted the reminder, the spirit of it. It was a memento of what I could do, what I could be. In the course of my meticulously charted life, it was the only thing I'd ever done, ever made, that truly mattered to me. The hope, the future it represented—one I'd never pursue—but still, I couldn't extinguish it, abandon it to darkness.

"It's not yours to have."

"Tell me what went wrong, Yu-jin. Where did your mother and I fail you? We've given you every opportunity to succeed."

Something tugged at my insides, the bottom dropping out. The lights grew dim, my vision tunneling. I stared at my father's shoes, impeccably clean and shimmering in the moonlight. I remembered So-ra's feet, callused and bruised, torn and bleeding as she fled across the dance floor. I remembered the wind and the snow swirling around Min and me as we bore down city blocks, unrepentant. I remembered sitting at a desk, the CSAT exam booklet in front of me, watching the clock on the wall, waiting to begin, waiting for my life to start.

My father grabbed me by the elbow, pulling me upright. "Whether you give me the tape or not, we'll be returning to Gyeryong, as a family. I've made the necessary preparations to resign my post. I've already called Chairman Song and told him you won't be taking the job."

I yanked myself free, nearly stumbling backwards. "What are you talking about? What about everything we've planned?"

"Our plans," my father said, choking back an anguished cry. "You ruined them, Yu-jin! All of them. So-ra came to me. She told me everything. At first I didn't believe her. I didn't want to believe her. But she insisted you two were together, a couple."

I tried to say something, but my voice failed me.

"I can't condone this . . . this lifestyle. You will come home with us immediately after graduation, and if you choose to stay in Seoul, it will be on your own terms. There will be no financial support from me. I refuse to aid in your own destruction."

"That's not possible. She wouldn't . . . You're lying," I managed, the air suddenly thick and stifling. Clouds of insects swarmed the stadium lights. A ferry horn bellowed in the night. Had Misaki finally taken her revenge, or was this Hae-sook's doing? I remembered how she'd teased me and So-ra for holding hands. Perhaps word had finally gotten back to my father.

"I wish I was, Yu-jin. I think So-ra believed she was helping you. She kept saying you didn't have the strength to tell me yourself, that you weren't living your truth."

"Do you really think you can turn us against each other so easily? You've always hated her, but she was right. All the things you've pushed me to do, the grades, my major, the direction of my life. It was for you. Not me. You've never cared about what I wanted."

My father's hands dropped to his sides, his gaze wandering beyond where we stood. He suddenly seemed exhausted. "Come home, Yu-jin," he said. "We will always love you, and you'll always have a place to stay with me and your mother. You're our only child after all. We've only ever wanted the best for you. But the tape must be destroyed. If something like that got out, it would be catastrophic, for everyone, but especially for you. Think of the embarrassment it will cause, for all of us."

"You really don't believe me. You think the tape proves I was with So-ra? That I . . . That we . . ."

He held up his hands. "It's not to be discussed."

How far I'd fallen in his estimation. How little he thought of me. In his imagination, did he think me capable of such degradation, such base behavior? It didn't matter that I'd scored in the top 1 percent on the CSAT, that I was top of my class at Ewha, that I could have any job, any future I wanted. I was still capable of blasphemy, of bringing shame upon my family with some smutty recording. Whoever I became, whatever I did—I'd still be his daughter, a girl, a woman, forever destined to the inevitable slip, the fall that would illuminate the fissures of my soul, the blackness of my character, damning my family forever for the depths of shame. No matter where my education, my career took me, it would always lead back to him, to this.

I walked away—where I don't know. Anywhere away from him, toward the water, toward the sky. His presence, his voice repulsed me. As I pulled myself from his outstretched arms, I called him a liar and a fraud. I called him things I knew he was not. I wanted to hurt him. I wanted to leave a wound that would fester and scar, forever remind him of what he'd done to me, what he'd done to our family.

Knees trembling, ankles weak, I stumbled to the netting that surrounded us, and my mind went blank. I gasped for the air I did not want, stars swirling, the lights of Incheon blinking in and out.

So-ra would never, I thought. She would never.

TWENTY-NINE

MIN

It wasn't personal

The Minister's house was located in a wooded suburban community bordering Bukhansan National Park, where the Western-styled homes were dwarfed by the pale peaks of Baekundae, Insubong, and Mangnyeongdae. Among the lush front lawns, lengthy driveways, and shingled roofs, Min felt oddly at home. He stood outside a black-matte gate, looking up at a security camera. Slipping the memory stick from his pocket, he held it up to the camera, imagining some insidious character in a shadowy room zooming in on his granular face.

An electric buzz, and the gate clicked and retracted, its plastic wheels trundling across the cobblestone driveway. The front door of the Georgian colonial opened before he made it up the steps, and a man in a black suit greeted him. Min didn't recognize him as one of the men who'd followed him, but there was still something familiar about him—the way he stood, the snug fit of his jacket.

Shutting the door, he led Min down the austere hall. Above, the floorboards creaked, and Min wondered if Yu-jin's mother was home. Outside an engraved wooden door, the bodyguard stopped, holding up his hand like he was directing traffic. They stood in silence. Then he knocked twice.

"He'll see you now," the bodyguard said. "I'll be right outside."

Hand in his pocket, Min touched the flash drive, steeling himself. I'm here to prove Yu-jin's innocence to her father, to clear her name, to show him just how mistaken he was about his daughter.

Min was surprised to find the Minister in a gray running suit, contemplating something on his bookshelf. He was larger than Min remembered, the contours of his figure pressing out against his tight-fitting jacket. Even when dressed in something casual, Yu-jin's father held a certain presence in the room—a command of the space around him—like he was pulling everything toward his center, ever so gradually: a black hole.

With its venetian blinds, built-in teak bookshelves, partners desk, and double chesterfield chairs, the office made Min feel like he'd stumbled into the past. Even the yellowed lampshades gave off a se-pia glow that soaked the room in a haziness of time gone by. The shelves were crowded with old books, model cars, and assorted Americana: a miniature Mount Rushmore, a vintage glass Coke bottle.

"What do you think?" the Minister said, sitting down. "I imagine you're a bit more at home in here than out there," he continued with a smile. "I'm somewhat of a collector."

Min wondered why someone who'd expressed such disdain for American culture would fill his office with these trinkets. Did the Minister secretly admire America? Min could only add this to the list of things that didn't quite add up about Yu-jin's father. He'd welcomed

Min into his home, and yet the way he looked at him—it was the same way he'd regarded him at the funeral home, as if he were insignificant, almost bothersome. A dark undercurrent lingered. This was a man who would do whatever it took to obtain what he must.

"It's all very nice," Min managed to say. This wasn't how he'd imagined their conversation going. "I never had a study growing up. But this reminds me of some houses I've been to back home."

"The land of opportunity," the Minister said, almost nostalgically, rubbing his hands together. "I was just there a few months ago, in Arlington. Have you ever been to Arlington, Virginia?"

Min shook his head.

"Very green. Lots of trees and space. It's amazing just how large America is. It seems to be the single most defining element of your country. It inspires everything. The people, the cars, the foreign policy, the military—everything is big." The Minister held his arms apart. "It's the opposite here in Korea. Our country is comparatively small, our resources few. We live in smaller apartments, drive smaller cars; even physically, we are smaller, shorter, skinnier. But we do have our advantages. We've yet to buy completely into the delusion of the American dream. Not yet anyway. Life, liberty, and the pursuit of happiness." The Minister's voice was controlled and precise. "The pursuit of happiness. A foolish idea to place in the minds of the weak."

"I've already heard all this. I was at the memorial."

"So you *were* listening that day."

"I came to speak with you about your daughter. Whatever your opinion of America is, it doesn't matter to me. I'm not an ambassador for my country."

"Oh, but you are," the Minister said, getting up from the chair and resting an arm on one of the bookshelves. "You're a spokesperson for your country wherever you go. We all are. That's your American arrogance talking. To think you can carry your nationality without being forced to understand or defend the principles of your country." The Minister paused, suddenly appearing weary of the subject. "Forgive me," he continued, rubbing his eyes. "I have a vast appreciation for the West, or perhaps I should say respect. But something has been perverted in the process here in Korea, something has gone terribly wrong. Of course we will boast of our education system, our GDP, our internet speed, but I'm not sure any of it is good for us. Yes, it is better than the alternative—no one can argue that. Just take one look across the border . . ." The Minister trailed off, his eyes wandering over his cluttered office. "Korea is a bridge," he finally said. "Geographically, culturally, geopolitically—countries have crossed into us, over us, they've burned us down and built us back up. That does something to a place, to its identity. To be neither on one side nor the other—that is the difficult thing about being a bridge. You are neither here nor there. You are simply between."

Min remembered what Misaki had told him about *Han*: "It's a feeling of sorts. A kind of collective despair in response to being conquered and oppressed for long periods of time, over generations. To choose your own destiny—that's what an individual, a nation, craves most. *Han* is a result of that most basic desire being crushed."

Perhaps this was what the Minister was trying to explain to him. But why? How was all of this connected to Yu-jin's suicide? Did he think Western ideals were somehow to blame? That Min had corrupted her?

"I don't see what this has to do with me," Min said.

"I thought it might interest you. You're a man with cultural interests, given your position at Samsung. You're a bridge yourself. Between two worlds, not American and certainly not Korean. How many times have you been walked over? Left to consider your place in all this, one foot on each side. You see, I know who you are, Min-jun Ford. I know you've come to give me the evidence Detective Park left with you after his unfortunate resignation. Or at the very least, I hope that's why you're here."

"So you admit to having me followed."

"It wasn't personal. I thought you might lead us to the tape. I'm sorry about my men getting rough with you. That was never agreed upon."

"And So-ra. Did you have her committed to House of the Lotus Tree?"

The Minister stiffened, his eyes narrowing. "So-ra was unstable. She needed help. House of the Lotus Tree provided it."

"Then you admit to making her go there."

"Yes, at first she wasn't very willing, but I think she's found it quite healing. You saw her yourself. She's free to leave at any time."

"You really expect me to believe that?"

The Minister sat down in his chair. "I think you've got the wrong opinion of me. I can assure you, I never purposefully hurt anyone. Was I an overly concerned parent, did I check-in on Yu-jin one too many times, did I push too hard?" The Minister's voice wavered. Leaning forward, he cupped his hands around his nose and mouth and let out a ghostly breath. "Maybe I did. But it was out of love," he said, head bent in solemn grief.

Dusty light slanted through the wooden shades, stretching across the Minister's broad shoulders, heaving and terrible. Min could only watch in disbelief. The Minister removed a silk handkerchief from his pocket and ran it over his face before raising his eyes, red-rimmed and vacant. "I only ever wanted the best for her."

Min swallowed the ache in his throat, refusing to accept the Minister's pain and suffering. "What about the police? Why'd they arrive at the apartment before anyone had found Yu-jin's body? Were you spying on her, too?"

"She texted me," the Minister said softly, "telling me she was going to take her life. When I saw the message, I called the police immediately. As for your other question, I kept tabs on her, and I occasionally looked into her private correspondences, but it was only because I was worried about her. I did what any parent would do. I tried to save my child."

The yawning discrepancies between the portrait of Yu-jin's father Min had sculpted and the man now before him were impossible to ignore any longer. He was no killer, intent on destruction.

This was a man wracked with sorrow, broken by grief. Min was ashamed of himself. He'd been convinced the Minister was evil, capable of intentionally harming his own daughter. But she'd clearly meant something to him, and with her gone, he was left groping in the dark, searching for answers, forever shining his light back into the past.

Unprompted, the Minister continued. "Yu-jin was a confused girl. She didn't understand what she was doing."

"Even if you didn't kill her," Min's voice broke out, "you threatened to disown her, cut her out of the family if she didn't stop carrying on with So-ra. You pushed her to suicide. You didn't give her a choice. I spoke with So-ra. She told me everything."

Puzzlement soured the Minister's face, deep creases framing his lips. He spoke slowly and deliberately, "I was angry when I first discovered Yu-jin was lying to me. And I may have said some rash and hurtful things. I was heartbroken. But I would never close my door to her. Could a parent do such a thing? True, I asked her to return to Gyeryong, but that was for her own protection. All I asked was that she give me the recording she'd made. It was a danger to everyone. She couldn't comprehend the explosive nature of recording something like that. But she refused. Inexplicably. Even after I begged her."

"So you won't admit to playing a role in her death?"

"Even if what you say is true, do you really think my daughter would take her life if threatened with disownment? She was strong—even you know that," the Minister said. "I'm surprised. I assumed you thought more highly of her. I was hoping you knew something I didn't. I was hoping you could tell me why she did it."

"Me? How would I have more information than you?"

The Minister seemed at a loss. "I know my daughter. She cared a great deal about what her family thought. She wanted to make us proud. But Yu-jin would never have taken her life only because of shame."

"Maybe she cared more about your approval than you thought," Min said, growing agitated. He'd expected her father to capitulate when presented with all the facts. Instead he had more questions. Whatever the Minister had said to Yu-jin, he didn't believe it powerful enough to pull her down into hopelessness. He believed there was something more. Did he understand the power of his words, the pain they could inflict? He was still in denial. "You shamed her for what she did, for who she was. You used Misaki to get information on Yu-jin's relationship with So-ra and then used it against her."

The Minister let out a desolate laugh. "Misaki? Their roommate?

She didn't give me much. Not that I didn't press her. At least she told me about the classes and the recording. That's when I knew something else was going on."

Min's stomach turned. Misaki had been telling the truth. She'd only told the Minister about the tape and the film class, which she'd thought were harmless. He must have uncovered Yu-jin and So-ra's relationship some other way.

"You really think this tape is dangerous, that it threatens your legacy and reputation, that it will explain her death?" Min said. "That's why you've been after it this whole time. You think whatever's on it will vindicate you, make everything you've done worth it."

"I don't have the luxury of thinking only about myself," the Minister said. "I have to consider my country, my wife, not just my immediate family but everyone that has preceded me. I couldn't risk the tape getting out."

Min stood, aware that his knees and hands were shaking, adrenaline thrumming through his body like lightning. He took out the USB stick and placed on the desk. The Minister's eyes widened, staring at it like a child transfixed by a trinket. "It won't relieve your guilt. I know it didn't for me." Two paces and Min was at the door. "It's not explicit. It's art. It never would've threatened your public standing."

"That's not for you to decide." The Minister took the flash drive and weighed it in his palm. "Yes, I was concerned with my own political career, but I was also concerned for my daughter. Her life would have been unbearable. I was trying to protect her from herself."

"It was unbearable anyway," Min said, turning to leave.

The Minister was saying something else, but Min was already

striding down the hallway, bursting out the front door. Outside, a summer shower was passing through, rain on the wind.

All this time, he'd been consumed with the desire to know the *truth*, what *really* happened to Yu-jin, in the hope that it would bring him peace. So desperate to vindicate himself, he'd believed someone else could have killed her, even suspecting her own father. With each secret revealed, every layer peeled back, Min had discovered a Yu-jin unrecognizable to the one he'd known. This realization had once brought fear and insecurity, but with the Minister's voice still echoing in his ears, Min felt like he'd finally grasped the real Yu-jin, piece by piece. From the parts she'd secreted away—her budding artistic brilliance in her film class, the love she'd found with So-ra—he'd fashioned a memory of Yu-jin that felt whole and true. But even this had felt lacking, somehow incomplete, until now. Her family's refusal to ever truly understand her, their determination to force her into this small and suffocating life they'd constructed, no matter her dreams or desires—Min could imagine the narrowness of that existence. And even if he never discovered the exact thing that had pushed her into darkness, he felt her pain and loneliness, and the despair that must have filled her final moments.

THIRTY

YU-JIN

No tears, no fireworks

How do you say goodbye without saying goodbye? How do you thank someone, ask for their forgiveness, without uttering a word?

I wanted to know what Min saw, what he thought and felt. For too long, I'd kept him at a distance, on the periphery, ensuring he remained indistinct and undefinable. Yes, we'd shared early-morning coffee and long city walks, afternoon sex and midnight taxi rides, but I'd never been fully present, my mind drifting to So-ra, the future, the persistent fear that Min was much more than he was letting on, that I was so much less.

Why had he come here? What was he hoping to find? I wanted to know what had brought him to Seoul. But I couldn't risk it. There was my future to consider, my parents' expectations, our agreement that things would end amicably. No tears, no fireworks. We'd come this far, sailing on the placid surface of the world. It was unfair to change the rules of our game now.

We'd agreed to spend the day together, a date Min kept, despite dislocating his shoulder the day before.

We stopped for coffee in Insa-dong, where we watched tourists and locals, mingling like oil and vinegar. There were the baristas who made our coffee, studying us, the gears in their heads grinding so loud I could almost hear them: Are they a couple, does she only date Americans, what is he? Did Min see all this, too? Did he see their jealousy and disdain?

After coffee, I insisted on Gyeongbokgung, the royal palace, much to Min's chagrin.

"That tourist trap? What for?" he said. "You hate those kinds of places."

He was right, of course. He knew me well. In a way that saddened me. I took his hand, pulling him with me, down the sidewalks, early June air sticking to our skin, portending the muggy, insufferable heat to come. "Humor me."

In the storefronts, in the windows of passing buses and cars, I watched our reflections, warped together, all six-foot-two of him, muscular and lanky all at once, in his khakis and faded blue oxford shirt. He towered over most of the people we passed. Did things look different from up there?

Even walking with Min, I couldn't forget my father's attempts to pit me against So-ra, the only person I'd ever really trusted. At times our relationship had been arduous and convoluted; we'd had our differences. I'd asked a great deal of her: sacrifice, loyalty. But through it all—even when I let my fears get the best of me—I knew she'd always protect me. We'd made that unspoken oath when we'd let our hearts be known in that dorm room at Ewha.

Did my father really think me so easily manipulated? Through any means possible—Misaki, surveillance, reading my every communication, maybe even Hae-sook—he'd discovered my most prized secret, and now he was using it to ensure I remained faithful to the future he'd always imagined for me. Whatever he'd seen or read, whatever one of his men had reported back to him—I wouldn't allow it to be twisted and used against So-ra.

Still, I needed assurance. If only she'd picked up her phone a few hours before. If only I could hear her voice confirm what I already knew: she'd kept our secret. As for my father, as for now, contingency plans, ways to make amends to him, to rekindle his faith—that's what mattered most. It would require sacrifice of the highest order. He wanted the tape, the one thing he couldn't have. What he failed to grasp, what he failed to understand, was that it had ceased to be about the tape. All my life I'd acquiesced to my father's every wish, every command. This one thing was mine. He couldn't get everything he wanted. And yet I was resolved to fix things with him. There was still time to secure my future. I just needed more time to think. Giving him the tape was an impossibility, but perhaps there was another solution, something I wasn't seeing. After all, I was his only child, the thing he cherished most in this world. I'd always found a way to succeed. I'd have to regain my family's trust. Perhaps an extra summer course, volunteer work, a more ambitious career track. It wasn't too late to go into medicine, even finance. I could appeal to my mother. She'd been in my position once. She'd understand why I couldn't leave Seoul. If there were sides in all of this, she'd be on mine.

With Min's help, I slowly shook off the ugly memories of the previous night, delighting in the way my shoulder fit perfectly under his arm, the way he tucked my hair behind my ears. He was oblivious to it all: my father, So-ra, my potential departure from this beautiful city. With him, I could forget everything. There were other inevitabilities, like his departure back to America, the conclusion of our relationship, but we'd found common ground, understood why we needed to end. Unlike with So-ra there'd be no arguments, no hurt feelings. It's why I was so drawn to him. I never doubted where I stood in his estimation. And yet the nature of our relationship had never produced real intimacy. I'd thought it one of the best qualities about us, but now, again, I wondered, touring the grounds of the palace: What had brought him to Seoul? What had he hoped to find?

I'd known why I'd wanted to leave Gyeryong. Sure, Seoul hadn't been another country. I hadn't flown across the Pacific like Min, in search of something lost or forgotten. Still, we'd both gone somewhere in search of something. We'd both had an inkling, a terrible hunch refusing to wane, that the answers to our confusion, the explanation for our displacement, lay out there somewhere in the city, among the wailing sirens and endless bustle. Didn't we hope that if we listened close enough, if we looked hard enough, we'd find the clue we'd been looking for all along?

How desperately I wanted to ask him why he'd *really* come to Korea. Had he found what he was looking for? And would he miss me? Was any of this—pulling up his ancestral roots, finding a place that seemed so unwilling to accept him, anticipating the end of our relationship—difficult for him?

But I couldn't ask him any of those things as we toured the expansive courtyard of Gyeongbokgung, navigating our way through the crowds waiting for the changing of the royal guard, where men in brilliant-colored robes and fake beards marched to an ancient drumbeat. Despite being the main tourist attraction, it wasn't what I wanted Min to see as I led him deeper into the palace, down mildew-tinged hallways.

Eventually we arrived at a massive reflecting pool surrounding the royal banquet hall. The second story of the open-air building was supported by stone pillars. Here, away from the crowds, the drumbeats were only a rumor. The hall, with its dark blue shingles and upturned eaves, struck an arresting pose against the mountains in the distance, its liquid reflection something half formed and indistinct in the water below. Min observed the structure from all angles, studying it while I studied him. I wasn't here for the sights; I was here for him. What reaction was I hoping to elicit? What did I want to see him see?

"It's beautiful," was all he said. There must have been more he thought or felt, but I dared not ask.

After the palace, we went to lunch in Gahoe-dong, the cramped alleys reminding me of Rome in *La Dolce Vita*, where Marcello and Sylvia walked in black-and-white perfection. Min had never been to this part of the city and took an interest in the small shops and family-run restaurants. However briefly, I allowed myself to slip into a fantasy, a dream where I could bring him to my parents, a dream where they approved of him, of us. What was there to disapprove of? He was tall; he was handsome. A respected job, a college degree, and he was American—from that place we held in such jealous reverence. Such daydreaming, such an audacious imaginary outcome, was dangerous, and I quickly snapped myself from my musings. It was all impossible, of course. I could do no such thing. Our relationship was predicated on casual convenience. There was no room for dramatic acts. It wasn't who we were.

Over steaming soup we bantered, avoiding the same questions as always, like veteran captains guiding our ships into port. Night or day. We could do it with our eyes closed, hands on the wheel, engine thrumming through our fingertips. We knew where danger lurked, menacing and ugly beneath the surface. Smiling, laughing, making our plans for the summer months—it was easy to push off those lingering questions that looked to the future. By summer's end he would be gone; I would be working somewhere in Seoul.

"Only one final left," Min said, raising his glass of barley water. "Government, right?"

I nodded vigorously. I hadn't given the exam much thought. The film project had been all-consuming. I remembered the icy water around my ankles, the starless sky above, revealed in slivers between alleyways and towering high-rises. Would Min understand why I'd needed to make such a thing, take such a leap? Would he see what had compelled me?

"What is it?" he said, leaning forward on his elbows.

"Nothing," I said, catching myself.

He gave me a wink and went to the bathroom, but not before paying the bill. He was always doing those little things that somehow added up to some unexplainable goodness.

Wondering if So-ra had messaged me, I checked my phone. Only an email, from Professor Lee. For a moment I had the terrified thought that she'd somehow seen the recording, only to realize that was impossible. I laughed at my foolishness while I read.

Dear Yu-jin,

I'm emailing you because your mother stopped by my office a few days ago. She was lucky to catch me, as I was only there to check my mailbox. She asked if I was in possession

of the project you made, and when I said no, she remained
adamant that I provide it for her at my nearest convenience.
When I informed her professors were not at liberty to share
the work of their students without their consent, she became
quite distraught. I most certainly would have called campus
security had she not been an alumna of Ewha University.

I thought it best to contact you so that you can remedy
this situation. Your mother seems to be under some
misconceptions about the content of my class.

Thank you,
Professor Lee

The letters blurred and bled. The phone clattered to the floor.
Trying to collect myself, I groped around under the table, blood
rushing to my head. Retrieving my phone, I looked at the email one
more time before deleting it. Why had my mother gone to my professor? Was she no longer on my side?

I was under no illusions about my mother's loyalty to my father
and his aspirations for our family, but I'd always thought we'd shared
a bond, not just as mother and daughter, but as women. She must have
known what it was like to be denied opportunities, whittled down to
a single point. I knew she, more than anyone, understood my desire
not just to survive and succeed, but to live on my own terms.

But it seemed I'd underestimated the severity of my situation. If
she was against me, returning to Gyeryong was now a reality. With
both my parents involved, there'd be no convincing them otherwise.
There was nowhere to go. Nowhere to run.

"Is everything okay?" our waitress said.

"Yes," I managed, giving her a smile.

I shoved the phone into my bag and took a long drink of water. I imagined I was somewhere else, Rome, walking the streets. I imagined So-ra was with me. We had the city to ourselves, meandering down boulevards, lingering in courtyards, serenaded by bubbling fountains with moonlight catching long-forgotten coins tossed for good luck. My heart slowed; my breathing normalized. I blinked the tears from the corners of my eyes just as Min sat down.

If he had asked me then what was wrong, in that fleeting moment, I would have told him everything: So-ra, my father, the tape, this paralyzing fear that all we'd done was pass the time. But he didn't. Inexplicably, I found myself angry at him. How could he not discern in my voice, my eyes, that something was amiss? All he had to do was ask me what was wrong, and I would have given him everything. Instead he smiled, reaching into his pocket to reveal two dangling wires. "It's a splicer. So we can listen to music together. Let's walk around and try it out," he said with a smile. "I know you said no gifts. But you only graduate college once."

I took the gift in my palm. How could he know anything was wrong when I'd hidden everything from him? When I'd played my part to perfection?

⊣⊦

It took every ounce of focus and discipline to be present with Min. All those grueling hours at *hagwon*, the test-taking skills, my gift for narrowing my vision to a single beam of light—I used it all to hear the music, *really* hear it.

Hushed and muted, the city moved around us, hand in hand,

headphones on, the forked splicer dangling between us. Through what neighborhoods, through what time we moved . . . All that was certain, all that could be grasped, was in our ears. I don't know what Min saw. Did he notice the taxicab with the flat tire, the toothless beggar offering free fortunes, the businesswoman with a broken stiletto heel? The twilight air teasing and warm, the clamminess between our fingers. Somewhere near a park, I watched a child flying a kite, listless and easy in the breeze. Voice, strings, and bass like a mantra in our ears. What a comfort to know Min heard what I heard. At this very moment, crossing against the signal, laughing at honking cars, we were transported, together, born again into some fleeting moment of understanding requiring no affirmation, merely our presence. The world—vendors hawking food, motorbikes idling at traffic lights, infants swaddled on grandmothers' backs—spun out across our eyes, closed in unison to the unbearable beauty of it all.

Even when Min was on the far side of the ocean, we would have this—we could find each other, somewhere in this slipstream. Underground and hurtling toward home, we swung, arms extended from the center pole of our subway car. Not built for this place, Min was so tall his head nearly touched the ceiling. I leaned against him, felt his mass, rolling my head to the music, drumming on his thigh.

"This is you," he said with a gentle nudge.

The music stopped. The world came rushing back: harsh fluorescent light, the immutable earth outside our windows, gray slabs of train platform. The doors opening with a pleasant *ding!* "Good luck on the exam," he shouted over the platform announcements.

I turned and waved goodbye, hair caught in my mouth, the train flashing out of sight, Min a blur.

THIRTY-ONE

MIN

Did you find what you were looking for?

With the sultry late-August heat spelled by the storm, Min decided to forgo a cab and left the Minister's neighborhood on foot, navigating the tortuous residential roads in the direction of downtown. He walked with no distinct destination in mind, his only desire to keep moving. For the past three months he'd thought only of Yu-jin, the past. His conversation with the Minister had convinced him now that Yu-jin really had committed suicide, and he'd come to terms with never knowing her precise reasons. Only she knew the truth. And now, with no more memories to dissect, no mysteries to solve, Min felt listless. He'd searched in earnest for answers, at first frantic to redeem himself, then to try and understand the woman he'd never really known. Throughout their relationship they'd worked tirelessly to maintain their emotional distance, lest they see each other for what they both were: lost souls, desperate to belong.

If only they'd let each other in, perhaps Yu-jin would still be alive, Min thought. He saw now how tangible their relationship might have been. A deep and terrible sorrow welled up inside him. Throat tightening, Min choked back tears and kept moving. In the distance, beyond gray buildings and crisscrossing telephone lines, he thought he could make out a metro stop through the wispy drizzle. Hair clinging to his forehead, shirt heavy and damp, Min let his mind drift.

She's gone, he thought. It wasn't one person's fault. We all failed her. And even if what we had was superficial, that doesn't cheapen who we were, what we might have meant to each other. Min felt something loosen and break away. His efforts hadn't all been in vain. With Misaki and Detective Park's help, he'd finally recognized Yu-jin's depth and humanity, and even in death, she'd helped him admit his own reasons for coming to Seoul.

Everything he'd ever done, everywhere he'd gone, Min had only wanted one thing: acceptance. It was a desire Yu-jin must have known well. In Seoul, he'd hoped to find that elusive and tenuous sense that he'd finally come home. But Korea had provided no such epiphany. Even among people he'd thought his own, Min had been an outsider, a guest. So he'd grown pessimistic and callous, pursuing a job he cared little for, gravitating toward something easy and light with Yu-jin. It wasn't long before he'd abandoned any interest in exploring his lost culture, even neglecting to visit his great-grandfather's grave, the only place his mother had asked him to go. He'd thought himself a fool, a tired cliché.

With his search for answers at an end, he wondered if he'd been mistaken. Since arriving in Seoul, Min had expected to find validation in something external to himself. From the familiar smells wafting from street stalls to the harsh and luxurious tones of his ancestral language bellowed by construction workers and squealed by schoolchildren—he'd watched and listened with eager wonderment. And when he'd felt nothing, he'd kept looking, hoping something would bring him peace, make him feel whole.

Min found himself standing on the top step of the metro entrance. Hands in his pockets, he watched commuters emerge from the darkness and into the light, their eyes cast upwards. In the opposite direction, a teenager, rushing to catch their train, took the stairs two a time, backpack swinging, hair whirling. Overhead, an airplane cruised effortlessly. All of this—the city's perpetual bustle and tangled humanity—would endure, long after he left.

Now, with Yu-jin gone, he realized she'd been searching, too. Her academic achievements and promising career had offered no joy, no satisfaction, so she'd looked inward, panning the innermost channels of her heart for a glint, a shimmer, as she turned to film and art.

The recording was an affirmation of what she'd found, a deed done not for grades or accolades, but for herself. And however fleetingly, Yu-jin had found something real; she'd loved So-ra. But without unconditional love from her parents, without friends she could trust, she'd despaired, utterly alone, surrounded by everyone and no one.

Min finally saw his luck and good fortune, with a mother who loved and supported him, a father who was just worried about a son who'd always seemed a mystery, an obstinate riddle. It only seemed right then to do as Yu-jin had done, to cast a light inward and look unflinchingly at what was revealed. Min had thought coming to Seoul, living in Seoul, was a requirement for fitting in, feeling whole, but he knew now that was never the case. There was nothing Seoul could offer that he didn't already have, and he knew then that he could leave, that he would leave. And even in the future, when those questions and doubts of half belonging might wedge between his ribs like a knife, he would be okay. He would breathe. He would live. He would know how to grasp and hold them until he knew their truth.

Descending the stairs, Min found that a heaviness lifted from him as he thought about flying back to California, seeing that sunbaked coast emerge from the mist. He would be strong for Yu-jin. He would listen to that iron string within, no matter how faint, no matter how terrifying. But first he needed to find Misaki. He couldn't leave without speaking to her. Now that he'd spoken to the Minister, he knew she bore no responsibility for Yu-jin's death; she needed to know.

·‖·

When he finally got to the apartment, the door was ajar, and he burst inside, only to find men dressed in white overalls painting the walls. The furniture had been cleared out; the kitchen shelves were bare. He ran from room to room, calling Misaki's name. He was too late; he'd missed her. In her empty bedroom, he tried to imagine what it must have looked like, but all he could focus on were the simple writing desk and unadorned walls. Min felt an unbearable sorrow at the idea of never seeing Misaki again. She'd never know the truth about Yu-jin, about how much she meant to him. Out in the living room the painters gave him bewildered looks, their feet crinkling on the plastic-covered floor. Then Min saw it on the fridge. Gleaming neon pink against the cool stainless steel. A sticky note. Misaki was waiting for him at the Conrad hotel. She'd known he'd come looking for her.

Apologizing to the workers, Min made one last pass through the apartment. Everything was gone. Only Yu-jin's room remained locked—empty or full, he didn't know.

·⊪·

Night was falling, and in the Conrad's open-air lobby, a low murmur of greetings hummed from the mouths of deferential bellhops and concierges. From the sliding doors, the *vroooom* of sports cars echoed as guests came and went, valets scurrying about with frantic politeness. A piano was being played somewhere, the notes drifting lazily down to Min like sunlight through a jungle canopy.

In the elevator, Min told the attendant his desired floor, and they were whisked upwards with clean, metallic utility. This elevator's nothing like the one in Yu-jin's building, Min thought. No creaks or twangs. No cables protesting at every floor. Min remembered when he'd first banged on the apartment door, demanding answers from Misaki, delirious with grief. He could still see her, clear as ever, standing in the darkness, scared and alone. Or was it I who was scared and alone then? Min wondered. Yes, that was more like it. Misaki was just fine, always would be. She didn't need him for anything. She'd always been two steps ahead. Still, waiting in the hall outside her door, he hoped she'd at least listen to him, accept his apology.

Exhaling, he gave three solid knocks. A bolt lock on a chain slid from behind the door, another lock clicked, the door handle turned, and then Misaki was standing before him wrapped in a white towel, her glistening black hair clinging flat against her ears, Seoul's skyline burning like a metallic bonfire behind her.

"You came," she said.

"I got your note."

"I just need to finish drying off," she said, before disappearing into the bathroom.

The space was something out of a magazine; everything from the upholstery to the wallpaper was white, giving the room a sense of perpetual expansion, like if left alone the walls might stretch forever. Min took note of the four black suitcases stacked on top of one another by the bed.

At the window, he took in the view of the city he'd called home for nearly three years. Lights from tugboats and ferries dotted the Han, slick with moonlight. Nose to the glass, Min thought he could detect the vibrations of life below.

"You know," Misaki said, standing beside him in a cutoff sweatshirt and jeans, "I never knew the rooms got more expensive the higher you went in a hotel. It makes perfect sense. I just never gave it much thought."

She answered Min's question before he had a chance to ask it.

"My dad's paying for it. His way of saying thanks for coming home."

Afraid that if he didn't speak then, he never would, Min focused on a single speck of light in the distance and told Misaki he was sorry he'd blamed her for Yu-jin's death. He'd hurt one of the only people who'd tried to help him. He was sorry for everything: his suspicion, his blindness, his pride.

She made an indiscernible noise, and Min wanted to see her face but was afraid to look. After all the times he'd searched it for meaning, he was ashamed to see it now.

"We're all guilty of something," she said.

Words whispered from him. "You didn't do anything wrong.

After her father tried to intimidate you. You had every right to say something."

Misaki took Min's hands, forcing him to look at her. "When I told him about her classes, the recording, I never thought it would end up like this. I just wanted to get her in a little trouble. It was petty, a moment of weakness. I was angry at them for tricking me into living with them, and I couldn't stand knowing they were doing the same to you. I regret it now, of course. I led Yu-jin's father straight to their secret."

"That's the thing," Min said. "I've seen it with my own eyes. It was a project for her film class, nothing more. I swear. The Minister thought it was something compromising, but it wasn't. That's what I'm here to tell you. You can't keep blaming yourself for Yu-jin's suicide."

Misaki remained quiet, as if she suspected absolution didn't come so easily. "Then how'd Yu-jin's father find out?"

"I went to see him earlier this morning and gave him the record-ing. He had his men following me and Yu-jin. The detective on the case said the Minister could hack email accounts and read text mes-sages. That's how he must have found out."

Misaki shuddered. "I hated when he'd drop by the apartment. He gave me the creeps, always snooping around, asking questions about Yu-jin's whereabouts."

"I still don't understand why she didn't just give her father the tape. Did I make a mistake letting him have it? I wanted him to see how wrong he was about her. I thought it was okay, but maybe I missed something."

"You did what you thought was right," Misaki said. "That's all that matters."

They retreated from the window and sat on the couch together, their shadowed reflections playing back to them on the blank television screen, two ghosts side by side. "Did you love her?" she finally asked.

"It wasn't that kind of relationship. But I don't blame her for doing what she did. At first I was angry and hurt, but now all I can think about is how lost and terrified she must have been. She was desperate for a way out."

"I wish I could be as generous as you. There were times when I hated Yu-jin and So-ra for lying to you. I was jealous from the moment Yu-jin introduced you to me in the lobby of our building. There were even times I resented you for liking her. And the more you searched for answers . . . the more you tried to find things out, the angrier I got. It was so childish. But I wanted you to see . . . I wanted you to see . . ."

"I know," Min said, taking her hand in his. "I see that now. I see you."

It was an oddly intimate moment. Even though they'd slept together, caressed each other under the cover of darkness, somehow a kiss felt far riskier, more revealing of what they wanted. It was as if the Min and Misaki who had slept together belonged to a separate world, a place that had no bearing on the here and now. They weren't beholden to those versions of themselves, what they'd said and done, the mistakes they'd made.

"I'll be going home soon," Misaki said in a near whisper. "My family said I could stay for a year after graduation, but too much has happened here. Everywhere I look, I'm reminded of things I'd rather forget."

Min thought about the memories he was leaving behind. Yu-jin skiing down a mountainside, Misaki whirling in her overalls, So-ra speaking to him through the blue muslin house in the art gallery.

"I'm leaving, too," he said.

"What made you decide?"

"When I came to Seoul, I kept waiting for something to happen. Or maybe 'happen' is the wrong word," he said. "I kept waiting for a feeling, like when you click in a seat belt. But after all this time here, after Yu-jin's death, I realized Seoul can't give me that feeling, no place can. You have to find it within yourself."

"Where will you go?" she said.

"Back to Los Angeles. I've been away from home for too long. I should see my mom, maybe even my dad."

"What about your job at Samsung?"

Min relaxed into the plush cushions of the couch. "I quit."

Misaki said she was happy for him. There were plenty of other things he could do. "No reason to use your powers for evil," she told him with a wink, easily dispersing any tension and regret that remained. The uniform hotel decor lent them a sense of anonymity, and they laughed about things that had once brought them pain and confusion. They could be anyone. They could be anywhere.

"We'll both be going home then," Misaki said.

"I guess so."

"Are you ready?" she said. "Did you find everything you were looking for?"

Min told her then. About how maybe he wasn't meant to find anything. Maybe he didn't need some external truth to make sense of himself. He reminded Misaki about what she'd said the day of Yu-jin's memorial, when she spoke of *Han*. He always felt that undefinable sorrow, he told her. That inexplicable feeling that he was lacking, half of a whole. Coming to Korea, he was certain he'd find that missing piece. But now he wasn't sure such a thing existed.

Misaki smiled. "We can choose our own destiny."

Min leaned his head back and closed his eyes momentarily. There was so much to do—parents to call, a ticket to buy, an apartment to pack and clean—but for now, all he wanted was to sit next to Misaki in this luxurious hotel, high above the city, speaking in hushed tones like fugitives on the run.

Outside, the sun loosened its grip on the sky, streaking twilight with rusted claws. Darkness deepened, the faint beat of stars beguiling anyone who stopped to look up. Frenzied tourists on Mount Namsam, fishermen with backs bowed, slickers stiff with fish scales mooring their boats, students peering from the tiny windows of their *hagwons*. At night a different city awakened, one ruled by steaming food stalls and amber windows in high-rise apartment buildings, mammoth towers of boxed light.

Hours passed, a weight lifting from Min with each minute that took him further from the memory of the Minister, Samsung, even Yu-jin. He gave himself permission to let go. Finishing a bottle of wine Misaki had ordered to the room, the two found themselves relishing the ease with which they spoke, a contentment they'd never known. They folded into each other, bodies exhausted. Min focused on their breathing; they fit together, just how they'd walked in unison, how they'd ended up here, in this place together. All was quiet—the madness outside muted.

"Stay tonight," Misaki mumbled into his neck, hand caressing his stubble.

They moved to the bed, lay beside each other fully clothed, too weary to get under the sheets. The mini-fridge clicked on, humming a comforting tune. A strange pattern danced across the ceiling.

Min ran his hand through her hair. "What about you? Did you find what you were looking for?"

"Sometimes it's enough just to get away for a bit. It doesn't always matter if you find something or not, just the act of looking can change the way you see the world."

Min held Misaki close, tighter than he'd ever held anything in his life. They drifted off.

He awoke to a sky buffed gray. In the fog of his dreams the shower was running; steam crept from under the bathroom door, filling the room with hints of lavender. Starched sheets between his feet, Min stayed still, picturing Misaki, hair sopping, water circling the drain, eyes closed to drumming rain.

The room was silent and bright when he woke again. Someone was knocking on the door, a polite, gloved hand. "Room service."

Min told them to enter, looking around the room. There was no sign of Misaki. No bags. No steam. A bellhop entered wheeling a cart covered with a white tablecloth. "American breakfast, sir?" the boy said with a hopeful smile, lifting up a silver lid to reveal crispy bacon and eggs. "Miss Komatsu gave us strict instructions to serve you breakfast in bed. She took care of all your affairs and arranged a late checkout. She said you'd understand."

Min could only sit up and smile. He did understand. Goodbyes were too difficult, too unsavory, like a bitter fruit. Better to leave it this way. If there were no goodbyes, there was no end. Realizing the bellhop was waiting for a tip, Min fished a few bills from the pocket of his pants on the floor and sheepishly handed them to him. When had they undressed last night?

"Thank you, sir," the boy said. "And if you need any recommendations on sights to see, don't hesitate to ask. Seoul has plenty to offer tourists."

Min thanked the boy and wheeled the cart up to the edge of the bed. He tied the heavy cloth napkin around his neck. I don't need any recommendations, he thought, cutting the over-easy egg in half, the yolk spilling across the plate. I know exactly where I'm going.

THIRTY-TWO

YU-JIN

Nothing, just air

While transferring trains at Jongno 3, music still in my ears, the touch of Min's hand still around my waist, I got a call from So-ra, her voice stretched and thin. Could she see me? Not at the apartment, but somewhere more private, like the LP bar in Sinchon-dong?

She'd returned my call. Finally she'd be able to verify that she'd told my father nothing. His machinations and espionage would be laid bare.

"When?" I said breathlessly, feeling myself drawn in by So-ra's gravitational pull. Even though we'd argued bitterly, she'd still listen. I could tell her about my father's plan to take me away from Seoul. I could tell her about my mother's visit to my film professor, about Misaki. She would understand what all this meant. She'd hear what Min could not.

"Now," she said.

It was all I needed, agreeing to meet her, even while berating myself. I was all the things my father said, and more, but I needed to hear So-ra proclaim him false.

By the time I arrived, the bar was crammed with students celebrating the end of exams and a spattering of American expats. It occurred to me that Min never spent time with any of these people, his people. He'd alluded to the rugby games, but only if I questioned the source of a bruise blossoming on his thigh or forearm like a yellow marigold. So-ra and I were his only friends.

Joni Mitchell cut through the smoky air. Her sorrowful voice at odds with the celebrating patrons, but no one took notice. I scanned the room, eyes burning.

So-ra appeared through the jumbled mass, beckoning me to the far wall, where she'd snagged a table. I hesitated, thinking about the hurtful things we'd said to each other. How silly that all seemed now. With hair combed neat, resting just above her earlobes, a tight black turtleneck clinging to her, she looked beautiful and composed.

"Thanks for coming," she said, wrapping me in an iron embrace. She smelled good, like freshly cut cucumbers, like summer dawns. I was taken aback. I'd expected resentment and anger; we'd been near strangers the past two months.

We sat down. She'd taken the liberty of getting drinks.

"I'm glad you called," I said. "I know we've been ignoring each other since our fight. I don't remember half the things I said, but I'm sorry. I don't know what to do. I feel like I'm trapped in a room and there's no escape without hurting someone."

So-ra took a long drink of her beer and waved off my concerns. "Yu-jin," she said, "it's okay. It's me."

"Thanks," I said. "Really, I'm so relieved. I thought you'd be upset with me. Everything's gone terribly wrong, and I need to tell you about what my father did."

"What your father did," So-ra repeated, flattening her already flat shirt against her stomach, a stomach I knew well, hard like granite, smooth like a washboard.

"He's been spying on me, on us. And since I've been at Ewha, he's been reading my emails, my text messages. He even recruited Misaki to give him information about the film classes and my project. I think Hae-sook might have even told him something. She saw us that day. Remember? He knows about us, So-ra. He knows everything."

So-ra rubbed her palm with her thumb like it was a good-luck charm. "How did he take it?"

"Terribly, of course," I said, invigorated by the freedom of putting words to what had transpired between my father and me. "He's threatened to move the family back to Gyeryong. He's refusing to pay for anything beyond Ewha. Once I graduate, I'm on my own. Unless I leave the city."

"But you can't go back. That's ludicrous. You're an adult. You can do what you want with your life."

"I can't blame Misaki for tipping him off. We treated her terribly."

"We did what was necessary."

What was necessary—yes, we had. It had never seemed like a choice, my relationship with So-ra. It had happened, been a fact, a pit in my stomach, a beating heart. We'd seen it through. What other options had there been?

"But that isn't the worst of it. When my father confronted me, he said you were the one to confirm his suspicions about us. He said you went and told him yourself. He isn't just trying to control my future; he's trying to push us apart. He wants it be like when I was a kid, when I was dependent on him for everything."

"He was telling the truth," So-ra said, her voice barely audible in the noisy bar. "I went to him."

"You did what?"

"I told him about us."

I studied the wet rings on the tabletop from our beers, dark, perfectly symmetrical. They expanded and shrank, bled and faded until there was nothing to differentiate the old from the new. I couldn't meet So-ra's gaze, unable to accept what she'd said. I'd misheard her. If I didn't look at her, if I never saw her again, it couldn't come true. I waited for her to say something else, to wake me from this nightmare. When nothing came, I stood to leave. I couldn't be here; I had to get away.

"Yu-jin," she said, holding my wrist. "Sit down. Please."

I forced myself to look at her then, those soulful eyes and tender lips. "What did you do?"

So-ra's mouth moved, but I heard nothing. Splotches of light filled my vision, spreading out like a watercolor. Bar patrons pressed down around us. Ears popping, lungs aching, I looked at her as if from the bottom of the ocean, her face indiscernible through layered light. Here on the seafloor everything was hushed, while a tempest raged above, dim lightning flashing through the misty chop. If only I could stay here; if only I didn't need air.

"You can't keep running." So-ra's voice cut through the deluge. "This is who you are. I couldn't stand by and watch you live a life unfulfilled. I couldn't watch you throw away your life. You have the right to love who you love. To do anything less is suicide."

"You told my father. You."

"It's better this way. You won't have to live a lie. Don't you see? We're free. You're free. Your parents will accept you. They have no choice. You're all they have."

Was it possible for someone who'd known you completely to so wrongfully misinterpret your character, your very being? So-ra had seen parts of me I'd never known existed; she'd coaxed me to a sense of belonging. With her, I'd felt invincible. And now she'd done this—something for which I had no name. Was it betrayal? It seemed the only word, and yet was that what she'd done? It was impossible, yet it was.

My face felt frozen, a death mask. My father knew everything, all my intimacies. Nothing remained untouched. I imagined myself a box turtle flipped on its back, flailing helplessly, waiting for something to come along—a predator, a rogue wave—and annihilate me. Had she told him every detail, every happiness? I could never return home.

On the other side of the table, So-ra's excitement only grew as I sat down again, the warmth from her hands bleeding through my jeans. "I'm going to Zurich. I auditioned for a dance company based there. I was waiting for the right time to tell you. But I got accepted. I'm leaving at the end of the summer."

"Zurich. In Switzerland?" So she was leaving, too. Just like Min. Everyone had somewhere else to go.

"Yes, but they tour all over Europe. London. Paris. Milan."

Did So-ra hear herself? Could she not see the mistake she'd made, the wrong she'd committed? Now it all made sense, my father's urgency to move us back home, my mother questioning my film professor. So-ra had left nothing to their imagination. There was no way to escape this, no possible room for misinterpretation. When I tried to speak, my throat made a dry croaking noise. The walls pressed inward until it was only me, a spotlight glaring on me in the darkness.

"It wasn't your secret to tell. You had no right to do a thing like that," I managed.

"This is the only way, Yu-jin. Don't you see? Get away from all of this," So-ra was saying, her eyes shining with all the possibilities she'd imagined for us. "We can go anywhere, be anyone. Don't you want to get out of this country? Think of all the places you've seen in the films you love, the narrow cobblestone streets, the crooked houses and sun-filled plazas, the cafés, the markets. We could see all those things, go to all those places—together."

While I listened, something fractured inside me and fell away, down into the abyss below. So-ra wasn't hearing me. She couldn't understand what she'd done. I thought about all the things I could say. Tell her I was ruined. I was doomed. That my parents wouldn't see it like she did; they'd already pulled my name from the job with Chairman Song. They were ashamed to call me their daughter. The only future I'd ever have would be back in Gyeryong, forever under their watchful eye. I could have told her all of this—made her see what she'd always blissfully ignored. She'd hurt me, fatally, broken the only promise that had ever mattered. I would have said it all, made her feel it, made her understand the pain that seemed to bore a hole deeper and deeper into my core.

But I didn't. I couldn't. At least one of us could follow our dreams. She was happy. She'd given everything to dance, and this was the payoff, the reward. I wasn't going to ruin her moment, even if it was merely make-believe. I would never go with her to Europe. I'd never leave Korea. I'd never leave Seoul.

So instead of taking her by the shoulders and shaking her, forcing her to understand that she'd driven a knife through my heart, instead of telling her this was goodbye, forever, I captured a smile in the stale air of the bar and infused it into my lips and eyes. I found happiness somewhere within me and forced it into my voice. Forever the actress, the con artist.

To hide my devastation, I started up from the table and ordered us another round of drinks. I congratulated her on the dance company. She'd always been stronger than me, and now So-ra had willed her dreams to fruition. It wouldn't be long before she'd be on a plane, leaving Seoul behind, far from these familiar walls. She was already gone, lost in her imagined future.

We drank our beers and moved next to each other on a narrow bench along the wall. The bar emptied; the music played; I held her close, squeezed our hips together, buried my nose in her neck, considering what this world was and wasn't. She'd meant well, she was just trying to help, I repeated to myself, again and again, until I could believe nothing else.

Cigarettes were smoked; dreams of winters in Rome and summers in Paris shone out as if from a projector in a dark lecture hall. I let her make plans for a future I knew would never materialize.

So-ra had given me freedom. It was true. But now there was nothing, and I was left to cast out into the unknown for a foothold, an outcropping, anything to catch my fall, only to find nothing, just air. So-ra, the only person I'd ever really trusted. So-ra, the only one who'd made me feel possible, had obliterated me. Desperate to be alone, fearful that I might betray my desolation and loneliness, I made an excuse about needing a book from the library at Ewha.

"Then you'll be done," she said, pulling me into a side street and pressing her lips against mine. She swayed back and forth, around us, a cacophony of blaring taxi horns and chattering students. My head spun. "That's the first time you've let me do that in public."

I tried to smile, memorizing her face, her kiss, for the last time. What else could I have done?

She squeezed my hand. "I'll see you when you get home."

"Don't wait up," I called after her.

Without aim or motive, I made my way south, to the river. Block by block, the sky grew darker, stars winking their fire. The buggy summer air gave way to a cool breeze. Alone, I could breathe again. Uniform apartment buildings rose up around me. I took in the night air one gulp at a time, greedily.

Finding myself at a four-lane thoroughfare, I was startled by a jogger garbed in a reflective yellow vest. She *whooshed* in front of me, a flashlight affixed to her forehead, a torch in the night. She held me in her gaze as she ran by. Then she was gone, and I watched her bleached-blond ponytail bouncing into the night.

Where and for how long I walked, I could not say. What was important was that I keep moving, keep putting distance between myself and everything. If I stopped, if I paused and listened to the world, I thought I would surely die.

After time that I could not count, I was lost, which made me feel better. Across the street and down a tree-lined pathway, I came to a clearing overlooking three pristine athletic fields. They must have been made for when Korea hosted the World Cup. I wondered whether this was where Min played rugby. He'd never invited me to one of his games; I'd never asked to go.

My once white shoes, gleaming like the surface of the moon, were now smudged with mud. Kneeling, I wiped some, still moist, from the toe, smearing it like paint. Between my fingers, the substance was utterly foreign to me. Soil was as rare as gold in a city. I searched my memories for hints. Any sign, any prognostication that would explain how I'd gotten here, to this place, on the brink, left with only myself. My father's words rattled through my head: "Everything that comes to you is meant for you. You deserve everything—good or bad." I'd been one of the lucky ones. Loving and supportive parents, a stable household, a safe environment to grow up in. I had no trauma to blame, no acceptable explanation for why I was the way I was. I was privileged. I'd gone through life with the confidence and knowledge that if I slipped, if I fell from this tightrope, I'd be caught. Invisible hands were guiding me, holding me, protecting me—I knew this growing up. I never doubted it. And what had I done with this gift of security? Squandered it, taken it all for granted. So steeped in my own self-deception, consumed by self-discovery, always looking inward, I'd failed to notice my net had disappeared. No matter how rich an inner life I cultivated and pruned, it was worthless without the warmth of a community, a family. I was alone with myself. There were no hands left to guide me. It was better this way, I thought. Easier for everyone.

Like earthworms, like iron and blood, my fingers smelled like things I'd forgotten or perhaps never known. Then I was remembering the camping trips my father used to take me on, silent hours around a sparkling fire, shadows dancing off his smiling face. I remembered my first fish, the way the rod leapt and bent, the squeal of excitement that seemed to shoot from my throat. I remembered my father releasing the fish back into the clear water. "Always let your first one go," he'd said. "For good luck."

On a timer, the lights over the athletic fields shut off with a resounding *clack*—more darkness to disappear into. What better place to hide? If I looked hard enough, squinted my eyes nearly shut, letting my vision blur and crack, I could see Min out there, running back and forth, gasping, reaching out for something.

Taking out my second phone, I typed a message to him. He'd be asleep by now.

> I'm glad you got me the splicer. Is there anything better than walking around a city, knowing someone is hearing exactly what you're hearing? Seeing exactly what you're seeing?

And he had. It was true. I hoped he would understand somehow why this was the only way to make things right. I hoped he would remember the good things, the security we lent each other. We had given each other something; no one could take that away from us.

I typed out a message to my father. This one I would send later, alerting him before anyone else. I couldn't bear the thought of So-ra or Min finding me. This way their final memories of me wouldn't be tarnished or disfigured.

I stared at the message, a bright fuzzy box of light.

There were other arrangements to make, a room to clean, personal effects to get in order. I needed time say goodbye to the city, to Min and So-ra, without saying a word. I wanted them to know this wasn't their fault. I wanted them to know I'd tried to find something real in this world, and for that brief and brilliant moment I'd possessed it, even as it had slipped through my fingers.

THIRTY-THREE

MIN

A song he'd never learned

Min spent the morning running errands. From the hotel he went to the bank, where he closed his account after wiring the full balance to his American account. He called Korean Air on his way back to the apartment and booked a seat on a flight from Seoul to Los Angeles for that evening. Back at the apartment, Min cleaned feverishly, mopping the floors and scrubbing soap scum from the bathroom tiles. Once he'd finished clearing out the fridge and wiping down the stove, he set his attention to packing. Even after living in Seoul for nearly three years, Min had little to pack, as if he'd always expected to leave suddenly. After much struggle folding and refolding, stuffing and zipping, Min managed to fit everything into two rolling suitcases.

Sitting at the edge of the stripped mattress, he admired his work. A lemony fresh scent permeated the room; the floors glistened from the sun slanting through the window. There was something Min appreciated about manual work; it was tangible, quantifiable.

He checked the time. A little past noon. His mom was an early riser; she'd be up. The call went straight to voicemail. She was always letting the battery die. At the tone, Min told his mom he was coming home. The work at Samsung was wrapping up, and it felt like it was time to come back. He was taking a flight later that night. He told her not to worry about picking him up at the airport; he'd catch a cab.

Min remembered his mother's request for him to go see where his great-grandfather was buried. It was the only thing she'd asked him to do while in Seoul. He'd avoided visiting all this time, fearful he wouldn't know what to think or feel, but now, after everything, his insecurities seemed foolish. It wasn't just about finding kinship with his ancestors; it was about the act of remembrance.

-||-

Initially built in 1965 and then expanded in 1976, the National Cemetery housed veterans of the Korean and Vietnam Wars, and patriots of the 1919 independence movement. After putting it off again and again, he was finally here, visiting the burial site of his great-grandfather, his namesake, the man who'd risked everything for Korean independence from the Japanese.

At best, details were sketchy, but Min knew he'd fiercely advocated for his country's freedom, even flying to America in the hope of garnering their support in Korea's fight. The Americans declined, seeing no appreciable benefit. It wouldn't be until later, with the Red Scare spreading throughout the country like a virus, that America would answer the call in the name of democracy and freedom. By then, Min's great-grandfather had already fled, a political refugee, to China and then Hawaii. After the US installed a puppet government headed by Syngman Rhee in South Korea, signaling the end for any hope of reconciliation with the North, he vowed never to return. It was only after the Korean government offered an official apology and recognized him as a patriot that Min's mother agreed to send his remains back.

This was how one side of Min's family came to be in America, how they put down roots at the turn of the century, toiling as field hands on pineapple plantations in Hawaii. Soon after, with backs bowed and hands hardened, they made the final push to the mainland, Los Angeles, where they opened laundromats and nail salons, restaurants and flower shops. This was how they came to be, how they chipped out a life from the unforgiving rock of a country, one second, one child, one generation at a time. And when the Korean War broke out some thirty years later, it happened all over again: diplomats became dishwashers; professors became janitors and gardeners. Scattered to the wind, they were war refugees, scrambling to escape a thing they did not understand. They became pastors, gangsters, thespians, salesmen, playwrights, and barbacks. They became anything that might be called American.

These thoughts still felt like some imaginative exercise, where Min filled in the blanks, created realities from rumors. On his mother's side, the family history was rarely discussed. What they came from, who they were before—it was dust. Min's grandfather never spoke of anything before America; there was simply no reason, no time, no place for it.

The opposite was true of his father's family, who'd come across the Atlantic on the *Mayflower* and worked the hard New England soil, eventually going west, as if conquering one coast hadn't been enough. It was a lineage to be touted, turned into myth.

Intentionally or not, Min's Korean ancestry had been obscured, pushed to the side in the name of survival, even patriotism. Min knew of no such sacrifice, was never forced to consider himself the invader, the refugee, something wholly un-American. Those sentiments had been reserved for his grandfather and grandmother, *Not Japanese* pins adorning their lapels after the bombing of Pearl Harbor. More valuable than any sapphire or emerald, those brooches saved them from certain harm, from the camps in Utah and Arizona. And while his mother had never spoken of it, Min could imagine the cruelty of high schoolers, fingers at corners of their innocent eyes, mocking what they could not know. Watered-down, lessened somehow, Min had faced no such hardship. No one had denied him access to an education, a job, dignity. Unlike generations before him who'd fought and died, suffered unimaginable hardship for beliefs and ideologies like freedom and liberty, words that meant little to him, Min was beholden to nothing.

So he'd come to Korea, to Seoul, in search of where things had fallen apart, hoping to piece himself together. He'd craved an experience, a struggle that might forge him into something. He remembered what Misaki had told him in the gray dawn of their hotel room: "Just the act of looking can change the way you see the world."

Min followed the gravel path that cut a swath down the massive grass ocean punctuated by granite headstones in perfect lines, stretching as far as he could see. Some were accompanied by flowers, others by South Korean flags. A few families and lone individuals, like Min, mingled around graves in the distance. Ahead, where the ground rose in levels, like rice paddies dug into a mountainside, larger tablets stood in rows on either side of a metal cauldron filled with sand for joss sticks.

With no trees, no clouds, just the sun casting over the nearly four-hundred-acre stretch of land, Min was humbled by all those lives, the silence, only the occasional shift of gusting wind, whistling down granite-cut lanes.

Rechecking the identification number he'd scrawled on the back of his hand, Min walked with purpose up a small set of stairs set into the grassy hillside, counted three gravestones down, and came to his great-grandfather. There was no special marking on the grave, only his name and dates of birth and death. Min lit a joss stick. Smoke swirled. He remembered the instructions Misaki had given him before Yu-jin's memorial service. How long ago that all seemed now.

After burying the stick in the sand, he returned to the grave and knelt, trying to empty his mind. The soil was warm and soft beneath his knees. If only I could sink down a little further, Min thought. Down, down, down. Eyes closed, hands in the grass, each blade rough between his fingers, Min ceased to worry what people saw. This boy or man, shoulders wide, shirt dark with sweat, singing a song he could not remember. A song he'd never learned.

It mattered a great deal, this land that held the ashes of so many; his ancestors were with him. He was an iteration of their struggle, their success. And yet, simultaneously, it didn't matter; it was inessential to his life. He'd come, experienced a part of them. Now he could forget.

He had the power to let it go, all the memories he'd never remembered, all the weight he'd unwittingly carried since birth. Min inhaled the scented smoke, considered the ground beneath him, the spirits around him. They whispered sacrifice, desires petty and grand, forgiveness and love.

Could you find something you weren't looking for? Min

wondered as he stood, brushing grass from his knees. Could you lose something you never had?

∙⫯∙

Standing on the escalator at Dongjak metro station, his body weightless, Min thought about Yu-jin. "We can escape," she'd said to him, as if it was possible to leave everything behind. Maybe that's what they'd been for each other. Whatever it was she'd been running from—her predetermined life, the monumental expectations, her love for So-ra—Min would never know exactly, but he found solace in the belief he'd been something to her, however brief and fleeting, however minor. He'd been her escape and she his. They'd given each other something. And the overwhelming question that rose to the surface of his consciousness, the question he now gave permission to exist, wasn't so very important.

Waiting on the platform, Min toed the yellow line, watching the train approach, all lights and metal hurtling toward him. Eyes closed, he felt the inevitable hush that precedes all things, and then the wind whipping through his hair and warming his cheeks, the interlinked cars flying by, inches from his face.

∙⫯∙

That evening, dried sweat from the afternoon still on his brow, Min boarded his flight from Incheon to LAX. The only ticket available had been in first class, and Min settled into his palatial window seat next to a businessman typing furiously on his laptop. A flight attendant came through the cabin and offered Min a hot towel and a glass of champagne, which he gladly accepted while his neighbor ignored her, muttering to himself and hammering away on his keyboard. Out the small window, Min could see people waiting to board another flight inside the terminal, bright and glassy against the night. Some, flying for business, stood impatiently checking their phones; others lounged on benches, mothers and fathers corralling their children while zipping up backpacks and rescuing fallen stuffed animals.

He thought of his own parents and all they must have done for him when he was a child, all the things he couldn't remember. Slipping his phone from his pocket, Min composed an email to his father, saying he'd like to take a trip down to San Diego once he got settled. He finally felt like he had the right words to explain why he'd needed to quit his job and go to Seoul. Min didn't expect his father to understand everything, but he wanted them to talk. He wanted them to speak to each other as if for the first time, unadorned and openhearted.

The pilot's soothing voice came over the speaker and announced they were preparing for departure. A different flight attendant politely reminded Min's neighbor to shut off all his electronic devices. As they taxied to the runway, Min watched the marshallers on the ground, directing traffic with their orange cones aglow. Then the plane's mammoth frame turned slowly onto the runway, and from his seat, Min could see the runway lights glowing white, crossing the darkness, and he knew they led home.

ACKNOWLEDGMENTS

The author would like to express his immense gratitude to the following people:

Marta Pérez-Carbonell, Woody Skinner, Joey Lemon, Scott Armstrong, Kelly Farber, Jennifer Solomon, and Susannah Parker, for their encouragement and honesty while reading various drafts of the novel.

Blanche Boyd, David Greven, Richard Spilman, Margaret Dawe, Josh Barkan, Kenny Cook, Peter Behrens, John Gregory Brown, and Josh Rolnick, for their patience and wisdom in the classroom.

Jinhee Jacqy Chung, Ann Babe, Charlotte Cho, Monica Park, and Robert Joe, for their knowledge of all things Korea.

Lindsey Rose, Bethan Jones, and Debora Sun de la Cruz, for their vision and keen editorial work.

Catherine Cho, for her belief.

Mike McGroddy and Matt Cummings, for their enduring friendship.

Jennifer Wiley, for her strength and love.

ABOUT THE AUTHOR

A native of Nyack, New York, Soon Wiley attended Connecticut College and Wichita State University, where he received an MFA. His writing has been nominated for a Pushcart Prize and earned him fellowships in Wyoming and France. He resides in Connecticut with his wife and their two cats. *When We Fell Apart* is his debut novel.